THE
TRIPODS
ATTACK!

JOHN McNICHOL

THE
TRIPODS
ATTACK!

THE YOUNG CHESTERTON CHRONICLES
BOOK 1

Imagio
CATHOLIC FICTION
FROM SOPHIA INSTITUTE PRESS

Sophia Institute Press®
Box 5284, Manchester, NH 03108
1-800-888-9344
www.sophiainstitute.com

Library of Congress Cataloging-in-Publication Data

McNichol, John.
   The tripods attack! / by John McNichol.
      p. cm. — (The Young Chesterton chronicles ; bk. 1)
      Summary: In early twentieth-century London, orphaned sixteen-year-old Gilbert, pulled from his factory job to write a news story about meteors, finds himself facing invaders from Mars and also learning of a sinister conspiracy related to his own past.
      ISBN 978-1-933184-26-5 (pbk. : alk. paper)
      1. Chesterton, G. K. (Gilbert Keith), 1874-1936 — Child-hood and youth — Fiction. [1. Chesterton, G. K. (Gilbert Keith), 1874-1936 — Fiction. 2. Conduct of life — Fiction. 3. Extraterrestrial beings — Fiction. 4. Conspiracies — Fiction. 5. Orphans — Fiction. 6. Science fiction.] I. Title.
      PZ7.M4787955Tri 2008
      [Fic] — dc22

                                                                  2007048675

08 09 10 11 12   9 8 7 6 5 4 3 2 1

TO GOD, MY WIFE,
MY FAMILY AND MY FRIENDS,
FOR LOVING AND
BELIEVING IN ME ALWAYS

THE
TRIPODS
ATTACK!

Prologue

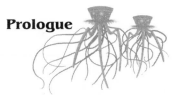

> "The modern city is ugly not because it is a city but because it is not enough of a city, because it is a jungle, because it is confused and anarchic, and surging with selfish and materialistic energies." — GKC

The night came as it always did during midsummer in London, with the darkness, falling in a black stain over the whole of the city, made even murkier by the clouds of billowing soot and ash that spewed from the factories every minute of every day. London had been called "The Smoke" for years, and this late July night did nothing to take away from the city's reputation as a hot, dirty place to live and die.

And it was in one of the dirtiest alleyways of the hottest sections of the city that the young woman had been walking for the better part of a half-hour. She made little effort to avoid the piles of garbage and waste that had collected in her path, and the clacking rhythm of her leather boots on the cracked pavement was occasionally broken by the squishy sound of something stepped in.

She wore a brown longcoat over her tailored dress, dark lady's gloves, and a shapely hat with a veil to keep the larger particles of soot off her face. She was dressed all out of place for this quarter of the city, where the adults, huddling in cramped rooms, snatched a few hours of sleep in between their twelve-hour factory shifts, while their children ran through the streets in rags. Yet she didn't appear in the least uncomfortable. Her walk was the patient, measured gait of a woman who had been taught to have her way in all things without ever needing to act like a man. Her china-blue eyes pierced even the thick lace of her veil.

You will not steal from me, was the message her walk and eyes sent out, *and it is in your best interests not to be the first to learn why.* And the cutpurses and street urchins accordingly stayed out of her path, awaiting easier prey.

Suddenly the young woman turned right and entered a rickety doorway. She didn't bother to check the address; she didn't need to. She mounted the stairs, her boot soles making small, purpose-driven *tap-tap-taps* where they landed. She passed first one floor, then two, ignoring the din of angry men, shrewish women, and hungry babies in the apartments. At the third floor of the slum, she strode to a door, knocked twice, then three times, opened the door, and entered the darkened room. She stopped after three steps and began taking off her hat and gloves, making a point of ignoring the large triple-barreled pistol that the room's occupant had pointed at her.

"Put the toy away," she said in a voice that was sweet but firm. The unshaven man in the black longcoat and gray bowler hat began to holster his weapon. She hadn't bothered to look at him.

"Sorry, love," he said, with no trace of apology in his voice. "The regulations an' all."

"I know them."

There were two battered wooden chairs in the center of the room. She sat down with a sigh, pushed aside her veil, and stared past the man at the gray stucco wall behind him.

He stared at her, his face mostly hidden in shadow. "Well?" he barked at last.

She reached into her coat and pulled out an envelope, which he snatched from her and tore open greedily, rifling though its contents like a child with a Christmas present.

"You'll find the fee is more than usual," she said, still preferring to stare at the wall. "But they are demanding absolute accuracy and all possible speed."

He looked in the envelope again and gave a low whistle. Slowly, he pulled a wad of bills from the envelope and then counted them with deft movements of thumb and forefinger. "For this price, love, I'd send me own mother to the prison hulks by the next o'clock. They must need this right badly."

When she didn't answer, he looked in the envelope again. He pulled out a scrap of paper and unfolded it, holding it up to the dim streetlight that filtered through the fog and the tenement window.

"Can you translate it?" she asked.

"Give us a minute."

He focused on the paper's odd markings, mumbling to himself. After a minute, he was seated on the floor, pulling out other papers, a pencil, two dice, and a small pocketbook. Dice were rolled, the pocketbook consulted, markings made on the new paper, and still more of his pockets were emptied, and dirtier, older papers were consulted. More markings made.

This sort of thing went on for about half an hour, until he slapped his hand on the floor and swept the paper under her face with a flourish.

" 'Ere you go, miss. A personal record for me, if I do say so meself."

She looked at the words he'd written in perfect, flowing calligraphic capital letters at the bottom of the page from her envelope. Save for a slight widening of the eyes and a barely visible swallow, she showed no emotion.

"Pretty piece o' flash your lot's given me, all for a few words, m'lady. Is that what you wanted?"

"No," she folded the paper and slipped it into the inner pocket of her coat. "But it is what we thought it would be. Good day to you."

She rose and began to leave. His voice stopped her at the door.

"Ah, miss?" he began awkwardly. "Miss, I was, ah, terrible sad to hear about wot happened to your man, miss. I heard he was a good chap, an' all."

Her expression did not change, although she did push a stray lock of her red hair back into place from where it had fallen. "I appreciate your sentiment, Jimmy. It's the kind of thing I've seen precious little of for the past few years." She turned to the door, paused, then looked back again. "Some free advice to you: spend that money swift as you can. Preferably someplace other than this sinkhole you choose to live in."

Jimmy smiled, revealing a gap where one of his corner teeth had been. "Yes, miss! Them's orders I can follow right quick! But don't you worry about me lodgings. I grew up here, an', please God, I'll die here too."

She gave him a sad smile in return and started down the stairs. As she walked out through the dark streets, she paused under a gaslamp and read the paper again.

Scrawled at the top was a series of symbols and designs that would have been incomprehensible to virtually everyone on Earth. But it was what Jimmy had written beneath them that she read over and over again, her breath coming faster each time:

THEYARECOMING

One

"All but the hard-hearted man must be torn with pity for this pathetic dilemma of the rich man, who has to keep the poor man just stout enough to do the work and just thin enough to have to do it." — GKC

The teenage boy looked at the punchcard-making machine in front of him and felt a sick, twisting knot at the bottom of his stomach. He sneaked a peek at the clock, but that only made him feel worse. He looked again behind him at the Overseer with the clipboard, a lean man who had been walking up and down the aisles of the rows of cardmakers with the look of a hungry vulture. "One more slipup, Chesterton!" the Overseer had said yesterday, looking down at the boy over the frames of his glasses. "One singular instance of being behind on your quota is all I'll need now to remove your presence from my cardroom permanently! How you ever obtained a position of trust with this company is one of life's subtle mysteries that I feel I'll never be privy to, but I know just how you'll lose this job if you don't shape up!"

With a mixture of fear and self-loathing, the boy looked down through his own round glasses at the little punchcard he'd printed out from his machine. The cardroom was chilly, even in summer, and he had to wear fingerless gloves to keep his hands warm while leaving his fingers free to do detailed work.

Not that having his fingers free was helping him much with details today. A position of trust, he thought. Position of trust, my foot! He was one of over two hundred young men and boys in the oversized room, dressed in old, ratty clothes, sitting at a desk with a small gaslamp and a clacking machine in front of him. The small buttons on the keyboard of his analytical engine stared at him reproachfully, as if scolding him for the mistakes he'd made with them on the punchcard. Position of trust? Please. They just needed a warm body who could add figures well enough to spit these card-things out, and it was rapidly looking as if he would fail at that, too, if he didn't shape up.

"Psst! Gilbert!"

He tried to ignore the whisper, and instead ran a hand through his wavy brown hair, trying to look deep in thought. Oliver, the eleven-year-old boy whispering to him from the desk on his right, was one of the more annoying human beings he had met since he'd arrived in London.

"Gilbert!"

Would this guy ever be quiet? "Oliver, I'm trying to work here." Sitting next to Oliver was a constant balancing act; your whispers had to be loud enough to shut him up, but quiet enough to escape the notice of the Overseer.

It seemed this time Gilbert hadn't been loud enough. "Whadja think of the comet lights last night, Gilbert? Whadja think of 'em, huh?"

"I didn't see any comet lights last night, Oliver. I was too busy trying to get some sleep."

"Ooo, Gilbert! You should've seen it! Smashing, Gilbert! Big, glowing green rocks, streakin' out've the sky, screamin' like banshees, an' lit up the whole night! I heard they hit in the countryside somewhere. Everyone in London's talking about 'em! I can't believe you missed it!"

"I can't believe you still have a job, with all the talking you do."

Oliver was quiet. Gilbert took what he knew would be a very few moments of silence to try to improve his work. He pushed his glasses up the bridge of his nose with his index finger and looked at the holes in his punchcard a second time. It was no use. The mistakes he'd made in this one were so obvious that even he could catch them without any serious effort.

What was wrong with him? He was going to destroy the best opportunity he'd probably ever have for a life in this miserable world, and all because he couldn't stop himself from daydreaming . . .

"Right, that's it. You're fired!"

Gilbert gulped at the sound of the Overseer's voice behind him, but then made a sigh of relief as he risked a second peek behind his workstation. There he saw the Overseer standing over Wiggins, another clacker on the floor who had been making more than his share of mistakes lately. Poor guy, thought Gilbert, as he watched Wiggins trying to explain himself to the Overseer. His head shook more and more emphatically, his dark, unkempt locks of hair whipping back and forth. Once again, and likely for the last time, Wiggins had been caught with too-few completed punchcards in his outgoing basket. Wiggins sat only three seats behind Gilbert, and had claimed to have a new wife and a baby on the way at home. The poor guy.

For just a moment, Gilbert allowed his thoughts to drift to the callousness of the Overseer, and how poor Wiggins might be saved from his plight.

Big mistake.

"All right, Chesterton. Let's see your quota, shall we?" Now Gilbert nearly jumped out of his seat. Having dispatched Wiggins, the Overseer had moved to Gilbert's station and scooped up the wire basket that held the punchcards Gilbert had been laboring over for the last half-hour. Gilbert looked up at his boss. Could the Overseer possibly miss the mistake Gilbert had made in that last card?

"See here, Chesterton. You've made a glaring error on card forty-three. We place that into the difference engine at the dyeing factory, and goodness only knows what vile color they'll be spewing out by dinnertime. Still, this is an example of — keep working, Chesterton! Your quota doesn't stop just because I'm inspecting you."

"Yes, sir." Gilbert went back to his punchcard-making, tapping out instructions on the keyboard that would make holes in the card that would be read by a pin-pricking, difference engine that would make . . . dyeing colors? Gilbert had wondered exactly why some factories would bother to purchase an expensive machine to mix colors and dye cloths when it could be done just as well by human beings who'd be happy to work cheap. His own job paid just enough to give him a cramped room and a few lumps of food each day.

Gilbert suddenly realized that the Overseer had stopped looking at his cards, and was instead looking intently at the back of Gilbert's head.

"Gilbert," he said quietly.

"Yessir?" Gilbert spoke while he continued working, with what he hoped was an efficient-sounding voice. Why did he call me that? Gilbert wondered to himself. He'd never heard the Overseer call someone by his first name before.

"Gilbert, I received a communication from head office today. It appears you've been summoned to the Office of the Undersecretary of Operations, for a ten o'clock appointment."

Gilbert paused and looked at his supervisor. Something had changed about the hard eyes behind the horn-rimmed glasses. Normally, they looked like a pair of glass orbs with pupils. The man wore what appeared to be the same immaculately tailored, dark-colored waistcoat to work every single day. His white collar had been starched stiff to imitate the fashion worn by members of the upper class that year. Philandron's attitude toward those who worked beneath him matched his collar and clothes: unyielding and pitiless when it discovered laziness or error.

But now, as Gilbert looked at the Overseer, the usual stiff exterior was suddenly gone, replaced by a countenance that was both pleading and gracious. Even the reflection that bounced off Philandron's bald head from the room's naked bulbs seemed a little less harsh.

"What for? Am I in trouble?"

The Overseer was suddenly gruff and grumbly again. "If you were in trouble, Gilbert, I would have fired you, as I did Wiggins over there." He jabbed his index finger at the now empty desk three rows behind. "For whatever reason, my own supervisor wants to see you. By ten o'clock."

Gilbert looked up at the wall clock that hung near the top of the ceiling, nearly fifty-feet high from the cardroom floor. Over six feet in diameter, it was a bright, polished white and brass thing that always looked out of place amid the cardroom's bleak cinderblocks.

The clock read a total of twenty-four minutes before ten o'clock in the morning.

"You have some time, Gilbert" — and once again, the Overseer's voice was soft in a way that Gilbert hadn't heard in the eight months he had worked for the company. "Allow me to say that, in your time here, we've all been adjusting to a lot of new routines. And, for this reason, I think the possibility exists that I was a little . . . hasty . . . at times . . . in the way I have treated you."

The patient, kindly tone in his voice fired a shot of mistrust through Gilbert's innards. Edward J. Philandron had never done anything to suggest he had an immortal soul, much less concern for the workers placed under him. But Gilbert tried hard to pretend to be eager to hear the Overseer's words, and to not see the unpleasant gestures that the other punchcard makers were making toward the back of Mr. Philandron's head.

"What I'm trying to say, Gilbert, is that although I've had to be hard on you during your time here, I only have wanted you and others to be a success here at Longton and Harburry. The truth is" — now Mr. Philandron's voice shifted from kindly to pleading to almost desperate — "the truth is, I've never been asked to see the Undersecretary of Operations, not in the nine years I've had this position. I doubt, in fact, the Undersecretary knows my face, or even my name, except as a group of letters next to a quota sheet each month.

"So you will remember this little talk we've had, won't you, Gilbert? You'll remember that I was kind to you, when you talk to the Undersecretary in" — he looked at the clock — "twelve minutes? I need what you Americans call a 'break,' a — touch from the wand of the fairy godmother of life; the kind of boon you apparently have been given. You *will* mention me, won't you? I can make life much easier for you, and for others you choose to name here." He began to speak louder. "You can look at me now, Gilbert! You have an appointment, do you understand? An appointment with your destiny! In ten minutes, Gilbert, ten minutes, you'll meet a man who could make or break your life as you know it — do you understand me? Make or break!"

"Y-yes, sir," Gilbert stammered, standing hesitantly. It was more than a little unsettling to see his boss practically groveling in front of him, even if part of Gilbert realized that it was the sort of thing workers around the world dreamed of. "I . . . can I go now to the appointment, Mr. Philandron? It's in nine minutes."

"But of course, my boy!" boomed the Overseer suddenly, convinced he'd made his point. As Philandron turned in what he tried to make a grand and dramatic gesture, the workers behind him suddenly scurried back to their workstations and began tapping obediently at their keyboards. "Off to your appointment!" roared Philandron, putting his arm around Gilbert and propelling him toward the exit of the cardroom. "To your destiny! Let me, in fact, escort you! You wouldn't want to lose your way, would you?"

"No sir," said Gilbert, smiling and trying to appear grateful. "To tell the truth, I don't know the way at all, sir."

When they reached the exit, the Overseer reached out with his free hand and pushed open the heavy oaken door with an ease that seemed almost magical. Philandron kept Gilbert's shoulders in a grip that was fatherly, protective, unbreakable, and as completely untrustworthy as sudden friendship from a schoolyard bully. As they walked along, Gilbert could dimly hear Philandron giving him pointers on how to behave in the presence of one's betters, how to make a good impression, and how to show loyalty to one's colleagues. It was the single longest group of words Gilbert had ever heard Mr. Philandron speak without the words "you're fired" being part of a single sentence.

Philandron propelled Gilbert down the long hallway that cardroom workers trudged through every day to reach their workstations. Right before the street exit, he steered Gilbert through another hallway to the left, which sloped upward. In a few minutes, the gray brick and grungy cracks of the hallway Gilbert had walked through twice a day for the last eight months gave way to whiter tile and windows.

The entire walk lasted almost exactly seven minutes, Philandron babbling instructions and advice the entire way. As they progressed down seemingly endless hallways and up countless flights of stairs, Gilbert saw grimy workstations give way to corridors lined with office doors, on which hung brass nameplates that declared the names of people with progressively longer titles.

Finally, long after Gilbert had stopped counting the number of twists, turns, and climbed stairwells, they arrived at a carpeted hallway that ended with a thick, shiny, dark wooden door. Gold-printed letters on the door's brass title plate proudly proclaimed for the entire world to know that the person within was

EDWARD EFFORTSON III
UNDERSECRETARY OF OPERATIONS
Thoroughfare and Solicitations Thoroughly Discouraged

Philandron stopped in mid-sentence, then straightened his back and pressed a small button set next to the brass plate. Gilbert shifted his weight nervously for a few seconds, and the door swung open.

"Remember, Gilbert," continued Philandron urgently, "most of us get only one real chance in our lives, one genuine, shining opportunity to alter the course of our destinies. Yours and mine are riding on how you perform in this office. This is *our* chance, Gilbert; don't squander it!"

The Overseer looked at Gilbert and patted both of the young man's shoulders with the open palms of his hands. He sighed once more, with the deep emotion of a father sending his son to fight in a foreign land, then turned and whisked himself down the hall back toward the cardroom. Gilbert couldn't be sure, but it looked as if the Overseer had tears under his eyes as he'd turned to go.

He followed Philandron with his gaze for several seconds until he heard a polite clearing-of-the-throat behind him.

⚜

Gilbert started and turned around. A plump woman stood in the doorway facing Gilbert, her hand on the doorknob inside the office. Dressed in a trim black and white frock with a frilly strip of material running down from her neck to the dark belt that held up her long skirt, she beamed at Gilbert with a satisfied look on her face that instantly put him at ease.

"An' would yew be Gilbert Chesterton?" she asked in a thick, East-ender's accent. It seemed out of place; more suited to the factory floor or the cardroom than the inside of a fancy office.

Gilbert looked at her quietly for a moment, for the world seemed to have stopped. Gilbert hadn't quite understood what it was about the woman that so mesmerized him, until he realized that she was *smiling* at him. He hadn't seen a single human being smile during all his months in the clacking room, and now it had the effect of a bucket of icewater being dumped on the head of a thirsty man in the desert. "Yes, yes I am. I think — I mean, Mr. Philandron told me . . ."

"Yes, young man. You have a ten o'clock appointment, an' you're nearly two minutes early. 'Ave a seat by his door, and Mr. Effortson will be with you as soon as he's finished with his other appointment." She floated in and out of the accent, as if she were trying to conquer it, with only partial success.

Gilbert entered the office, almost afraid to tread too heavily on the polished wooden floor with his filthy work shoes. He could see that the Undersecretary, whatever his actual duties, must be a very important person indeed. He had entered a kind of outer office, where the large woman — likely the secretary to the Undersecretary — had a desk of her own near one wall. On that wall could be seen a bizarre set of messenger pipes snaking out of over a dozen of small, circular ports cut into it. The tubes made a mad, twisting, knotted jumble of brass and steel until they arrived at the secretary's desk, where the pipes lined up in two sets of perfectly neat rows that resembled a church organ. Gilbert had seen similar setups in other offices; steam and pressurized air allowed message tubes to be fired, in a matter of minutes, from any point in the city to any office that had a connecting pipe.

The secretary's desk was just to the side of another dark wooden door with no nameplate of any kind on it. Presumably, this door led to the Undersecretary's private office. Outside that door, against the wall, was a polished wooden chair, and the large woman made a motion for him to sit in it. The chair felt very cold as Gilbert sat down, but he tried to look comfortable. He looked up at a small but ornate clock that hung on the spotless wall, and as it loudly ticked off the seconds, Gilbert realized just how shabby his clothes would seem to someone as important as the Undersecretary. He wasn't exactly sure what an Undersecretary was or what he did, but to hear Mr. Philandron talk about him, it seemed that to be an Undersecretary put you somewhere in importance between the President and God.

Gilbert quietly looked at his plain brown trousers, the black suspenders holding them up, the simple black shoes he'd tried so hard to shine for his first day on the job, and his completely ordinary gray shirt. His drab brown cap had been nervously crumpled into a near-unrecognizable lump of fabric. *This isn't a hat*, thought Gilbert. *Not anymore, anyway.* Miserably, he realized it was too large to hide in his back pocket, and too unsightly to hold in front of him during the interview. Had Philandron said anything about a hat? Was a hat necessary to advance in a company setting? He couldn't remember anything — not a thing at all of what Philandron had said.

Stop yourself, Gil.

Gilbert inhaled. Deep. Then he let it out again. He'd been five when he'd heard those words for the first time from his father. Ever since, he'd heard them almost every time he'd been about to let his emotions run away from him. Each time he'd felt like giving in to some form of despair, laziness, or panic, those three little words had nearly always pulled him through.

And they worked now. Yes, he was poorly dressed, but after all, he'd had no time to prepare. Since he'd been given no time to prepare, and since the Undersecretary likely knew his job, whatever the Undersecretary needed to see Gilbert about didn't require clothes that were top-notch-on-the-stick.

Either that, Gilbert reasoned, or the Undersecretary was a buffoon who couldn't get orders out to underlings like Philandron on time, and Gilbert could explain that lack of preparation time in preparing for this interview, which was why Gilbert didn't have time to find something appropriate to wear, even if this interview was going to quite possibly shake Gilbert's world into something completely unrecognizable and what if he messed up and had to return to the cardroom and Philandron thought that Gilbert had destroyed Philandron's chances for advancement and how long would Philandron give Gilbert before Philandron found a reason to sack Gilbert just like he'd done to Wiggins today and Gil would have no job, and get evicted from his little rented room, and have to take up thievery to survive and . . .

Stop yourself, Gil.

Inhale. Exhale. Better.

At least, Gilbert was better until the door of the Undersecretary's office opened right next to him.

Two

"Civilization has run on ahead of the soul of man, and is producing faster than he can think and give thanks." — GKC

When the door opened, Gilbert stood as his parents had taught him to do when someone important entered the room. With his back straight and hands at his sides, he was the picture of a relaxed yet respectful posture. He prepared himself to face the Undersecretary — undoubtedly the kind of authority figure he'd seen in the offices during his time with the firm: short, balding, with small, hard eyes, and with a way of walking that was angry when their subordinates were around and fearfully cautious when their own superiors were nearby.

But it wasn't the Undersecretary who'd opened the door to the Undersecretary's inner office. It was a young woman, one whom Gilbert was utterly unprepared to face.

She was tall, only perhaps an inch shorter than Gilbert himself. She had red hair, the brightest shade of red he'd ever seen in his sixteen years, swept up in a curled kind of bun. She wore a frilly, puffed white blouse that buttoned all the way up her neck. A dark, ruffle-edged skirt dropped from her slim waist to her ankles, and she wore small brown ladies' boots with a long, thin heel on the end. She carried a wine-red umbrella in one hand, along with a brown hat with a white ribbon wrapped neatly around it, ending in a pretty pair of ribbon tails.

Gilbert gaped at her dumbly.

"Excuse me," she said softly as she brushed past Gilbert out the door of the inner office. Her eyes met Gil's briefly as she spoke with a voice that was like liquid gold, making his heart jump into his throat and his throat turn into warm, unspeaking paste. By the time he found words, she was already out the main office door and away from him. He stood quiet and still on the threshold, trying to think of some way to bring her back and ask her the many questions that had suddenly sprung to his mind and heart.

"Hello." The voice came from inside the Undersecretary's office. It was not unkind, but it sounded full of an easy, happy life that had never known hunger or pain. Gilbert turned and saw that the voice belonged to a short man at least three times his age, whose eyes were nearly hidden behind large-lensed glasses. "And you are, young man?" The dwarfish man smiled at Gilbert, with perfect white teeth and the smallest hint of whiskers on his upper lip. He'd probably received a shave every morning from his personal manservant back at his estate.

"M-my name is Gilbert, Mister Undersecretary — *are* you the Undersecretary, sir?"

The small man laughed. It was not a sinister or unpleasant laugh, but something in it unnerved Gilbert anyway. "Miss Hodgeson," he bellowed happily, "would you please refresh my memory as to this charming young man's identity, and the reason he graces me with his presence?"

The secretary flipped open the appointment ledger, as thick as a handwritten Bible. "This is Mister Gilbert Keith Chesterson, sir."

"Chester*ton*," said Gilbert.

"Wot?" She looked at him with a single raised eyebrow. She wasn't used to being interrupted. "My name," said Gilbert, almost stammering. "You said Chester*son*; it's really Chester*ton*."

She sighed and continued in her toned-down but ultimately irrepressible accent. "I don't recawll making this entry, but it's in my handwrit'n', so I must have pu' it there. You're t'see him about that trip to London for the paper — about them big huge cans that fell from the sky the other night in Woking."

"Ah, yes!" said the Undersecretary, clapping his hands together. "Now I remember! Gilbert, Gilbert! From the cardroom, correct?" A light dawned on the little man's face.

"Come into my office, my young Gilbert. I have rather exciting news for you!" So far, so good, thought Gilbert. Maybe he'd have happy news for Mr. Philandron after all.

The office of the Undersecretary was completely unlike what he'd expected an important person's office to be like. There were no charts, ledgers, or invoices, no stacks of reports and balance sheets piled high atop desks. Instead, it looked more like a library. The wall to Gilbert's left as he walked in was hidden behind a high set of shelves with a very old-looking set of books stacked in them. There was almost no dust on the books either; they were either cared-for or read often. The other three visible walls were polished wood panel, and the desk was a solid-looking construct of shiny metal and wood that looked expensively handmade.

"Now, Gilbert! Our appointment lasts for only a half-hour, and here I've wasted nearly a minute of it already. Come, please sit down while I look at your file."

The small man looked at the pages in the folder like a wizened gnome reading an ancient book. "Eight months in the punchcard room, hm?" he said, looking at Gilbert over the lenses of his large glasses. "And you haven't been let go yet. You've got staying power, young Gilbert. Yes, you've got staying power . . . hm . . . your tests indicate that you're ideally suited for a few ventures . . . yes. Where did you go to school again, Gilbert?"

Gilbert was impressed. This fellow could read a card like a clacker, without having to get a printout of what it said first! He doubted even Philandron could have done half as well. "I was in high school in New York, Mr. Effortson, at a boarding school called St. Alban's. I'd just finished the first half of tenth grade when my parents died."

"Died? You're an orphan, then?"

"Yessir. My parents were killed back home in Minnesota. They were visiting friends in town while I was taking exams, and, well, they walked out of a bank when it was being robbed. The robbers pulled out their barkers when the police arrived . . ."

"Barkers?"

"Uh, those're guns. At least that's what I've heard them called out here in England." Gilbert waited. He felt it was a wise move to let the Undersecretary decide if he should continue his life story or not.

"Oh please, go on, young Gilbert. I love stories — even sad ones. If you don't mind telling it, that is. My own growing-up was somewhat sheltered until later in life, so I love to hear the stories of others. Please, do tell your life's tale."

Gilbert swallowed. "Well, there's not much to tell. The police saw the bad guys and started shooting. The robbers shot back, and my folks were caught in the crossfire. They didn't suffer much; the police told me they died almost instantly."

"But how did you come to be in England, my boy?" Mr. Effortson's eyes looked owl-like behind his wide glasses. "London is such a long way from either New York or Minnesota. How did you ever skip to this side of the pond?"

"Well, it's funny. I'm back in England all because of an accident. A punchcard accident, really, which makes it all the more odd when you consider what I do for a living."

"A punchcard accident, Gilbert? Do tell!"

"Well, at least, I think that was it, Mr. Effortson. Y'see, this all happened while I was taking my Christmas exams. I heard about it the day I finished my last one. Before the day was through, I was in a car bound for a ship that was supposed to take me to relatives over in Newfoundland, Canada."

"A ship? Water or air?"

"Water, sir. A new model of ship, in fact. A big one. Thousands of people aboard. Some called it a floating city, and the papers were all saying God Himself couldn't sink it. Newfoundland was its last stop before heading to England on its maiden voyage."

"I think I remember hearing about this, Gilbert! Wasn't it named the *Titular*, or the *Trident*, or something like that?"

"You know, I don't rightly remember myself, sir. I just remember a big white star at the top of my ticket, and that was all."

"Ah. I see. Well, no matter. What happened then?"

"It hit an iceberg and sank."

"Goodness me! How'd you escape?"

"Well, truth is, I didn't need to. See, when I went to the station, I handed in my ticket to the girl, she fed it into a card reader, and told me to go to a different dock. I couldn't understand all the markings on the ticket itself, and when you're trying to get on board a ship with everything you own, you don't always look at the ship's name. I ended up on the *Capsella*, bound for London. When I realized the mistake, we were already long out at sea. When we landed here, I had no money or friends, but it was still better than going to Davey Jones's Locker."

"How dreadful! I mean, for the rest. I recall this, lots of people dead, not enough lifeboats, or something like that. But what did you mean earlier about being *back* in England? This wasn't your first visit?"

"Well, Mr. Effortson, pretty much everyone in America is from somewhere else originally. When I was five, I asked my Ma where our people had come from. She told me that I had ties to England, but wouldn't say anything else about it. When I asked her to tell me more, she said she wouldn't give me any details until I was all grown up. Now I'm older, but she and my Pa are gone."

"My goodness. Quite a story you have, young man. Quite a story indeed. Well, Gilbert my lad, we have only nineteen minutes left in our meeting, and I haven't even told you why you've been called in to see me today. You *do* still wish to know that, correct?"

Gilbert nodded. The more they spoke, the more Gilbert liked the little man in front of him.

The Undersecretary flipped the file open in front of him again. "Ah, here we are!" He sat in his comfortable chair and gave a few soft chuckles to himself while he scanned the words on the file's last page.

Then Mr. Effortson's smile suddenly disappeared; his eyes darted back and forth in their lenses like a set of squirrel's feet in a circular cage. Gilbert sat for a very long minute, trying hard not to twiddle his thumbs or look nervous.

"Young Gilbert, it seems that you are a good writer. And according to your file, you have talents and aptitudes far in excess of what your current position demands." Effortson looked up. "How on earth did they put you in the cardroom, with Potentiality Test Scores like this?"

Gilbert looked puzzled. " 'Scuse me, sir?"

"Potentiality Test Scores, boy! Your scores say you should have been apprenticed in mechanical engineering, or at the very least, in journalism or legal work! Such a pity — we just filled a vacancy last week, too. Fellow named Bartleby got the scribner job. Well, no matter. Gilbert, we still have seven minutes left for this interview, before your future is decided." Effortson leaned forward and said in a lower voice, "Tell me, do you know what drives this world of ours forward?"

Gilbert paused, feeling that he was being tested. "I had a friend at school who said money made the world go 'round, sir."

"Your school chum, Gilbert, absorbed well the lessons of his parents. And his parents are soulless dunderheads. Have you any other thoughts?"

Gilbert waited. What would be the safe answer here? "My history teacher said it was Pioneer Spirit, being willing to go past the safe boundaries and stake out new territories."

"Your teacher, Gilbert, is also a dunderhead. But he at least possesses a soul, however much he misuses it. What, Gilbert, do *you* believe has moved us forward in this world?"

Gilbert thought for a moment. "Steam. Steam and difference engines, Mister Undersecretary. Those are what make all the machines run that do anything worthwhile today."

The Undersecretary smiled like a proud father. "Yes, Gilbert. You are correct. With the perfection of the difference engine, calculations that once took days or weeks instead took only hours, and then, minutes. Sums that needed to be checked and rechecked with fingers, pencils, paper, and ink could be entered *only once* into a machine of rods, gears, pistons, and buttons. Suddenly, as if by magic, the right answer would pop out every time! Steam, after all, is really only an application of water, which is itself the most limitless resource in our world. Once it was harnessed and merged with the power of the difference engines, immense calculations took only seconds. Rather frightful, when one considers how close Mr. Babbage came to losing his funding for the first difference engine back in the Thirties. If he'd never built the thing, where would we be today, eh? Still working out sums and differences with paper and ink, no doubt.

"Lastly" — here Effortson held up the punchcard he'd looked through earlier — "in the past twenty years, we've discovered that metal needles, when dropped through various holes in a card, can be made to imprint complex patterns upon a metal tray. The patterns on these cards can then be used to send signals to steam-powered, tirelessly working difference engines to design and carry out instructions limited only by our own imaginations. We can now use a difference engine to design machines that can shape the very earth, harnessing the power of steam to dig and move more dirt in a day than a dozen men with pick and shovel could move in a week. Once Britain reached this point, our technological victory over the rest of the world was virtually complete."

Gilbert nodded. He'd learned to do that when important people were talking to themselves about something important, whether Gilbert understood them or not.

"Truly, if we will be honest," said Effortson, who now stood and paced back and forth across the carpet, gesturing to a map on the wall, "at this point, how could the tribes in Tasmania compete with British troops? *Their* chief means of determining the outcome of a battle involved reading the entrails of dead chickens. We, on the other hand, feed the information on the numbers of men and the weapons involved, a description of the terrain, and a host of other factors into a difference engine, and out comes an impeccable battle plan each and every time. Only a pity that your American Colonies had already broken away by that point, wouldn't you say?"

Gilbert was quiet.

"Well, perhaps as an American, no, you don't think it's a pity. Tell me, how many countries are the Americas split into these days?"

"Five at last count, Mr. Effortson. I came from the United States of America, the USA. To the South you've got the Confederate states that broke away near fifty years ago, during the Civil War over the slavery thing, and farther to the West you've got the Texas Republic and the two Republics of Northern and Southern California."

"Ah, yes. Those five never seem to stop squabbling, do they? Especially those papists in the California Republics. Well, no matter. The point is this: our advances in technology have made us the unequaled power on the planet. We now belong precisely where we desire to go, and nowhere else. But . . ."

Mr. Effortson's face had shone while he spoke, looking at the map of the known corners of the world as if it had been his beloved childhood playground. But now his face suddenly went serious. "*But,* Gilbert, now and again our perfect, predictable world finds itself in a quandary. A single unplanned-for difficulty can throw a spanner in our engine-ordered steamworks and eventually topple such a civilization, just as a stray thread can unravel even the most carefully woven tapestry. And today we face, I think, just such a potentially serious setback on our own British shores. A flaw, Gilbert. A cipher. A dreaded, non-calculatable factor. Have you heard about the recent events in the town of Woking?"

"The guys at work were saying something about . . . shooting stars, or something like that, sir."

"There is more to it than that, young Gilbert. Much more to it than that, I fear. Now, listen." Effortson reached up and placed his right hand on Gilbert's shoulder, looking squarely into the young man's eyes. Gilbert could smell the scent of stale coffee on the older man's breath. "This firm owns interests in a number of the most profitable businesses in this town, due in no small part to our early involvement in the steam-engine industry. Do you understand that?"

Gilbert didn't, but nodded anyway.

"Good. Now, Gilbert, one of these businesses is the pre-eminent news-paper of the city — the *London Times*. Our difference engines have selected *you* for a task of great responsibility: you are going to be hired today as a reporter for the *London Times*. You will be sent off by train to cover the story that is unfolding in Woking, you will record what you observe there to the best of your ability, and you will return here to write an extended report. If something truly astounding happens, you will contact the *Times* offices through the use of telegraphic communication. Do I make myself clear?"

"Sir?" Gilbert's heart was pounding. He was going to be a journalist?

"Yes, Gilbert. Please hurry. You have only ninety seconds remaining in this interview."

"Sir, where do I go from here to complete this assignment?"

"My secretary will handle all these arrangements, Gilbert. Please ask her. Will there be anything else?"

Gilbert thought. "If I could make a suggestion regarding the punchcard room, sir?"

"Feel free, Gilbert," said the Undersecretary. "You have forty-five seconds remaining."

Gilbert talked fast. "Mr. Philandron can be a difficult man to work for when he feels the pressures of his job upon him. And he feels pressures often, sir. He fired a young man today, George Wiggins, who, from what I've seen, has always done his job well. He's also mentioned that he has a new wife and baby on the way, sir."

The wrinkles on Effortson's face softened with a sudden smile. "I shall do all in my power to rectify the situations you have illumined to me, Gilbert. Will that be all?"

"One more thing, sir. I know you said the machines are flawless, sir."

"As flawless as we make them, Gilbert, yes."

"Well, that's the thing, sir. You're sending me on this assignment based on some test you say I've taken."

"Yes, Gilbert. The Potentiality Test. It has read with 100-percent accuracy the ideal occupations that members of our staff should be placed in."

"Well, that's the thing, Mr. Effortson. You see, in all my time here, I never took a Potentiality Te—"

A bell went off somewhere in the office.

"Time, young Gilbert! Time! I have important letters to dictate. Please see Mrs. Hodgeson, as she will make all the travel arrangements. Mrs. Hodgeson? Please call personnel. Mr. Wiggins is to be rehired, and Philandron is to be placed elsewhere within the firm."

"But," started Gilbert, "I didn't mean . . ."

"Goodbye, young Gilbert!" said the Undersecretary, shaking Gilbert's hand enthusiastically. "Work hard, trust your instincts and all that. Good day!"

He swept back into his office and closed the door.

26

"Well, what should I do now?" Gilbert looked at Mrs. Hodgeson. She was a woman who looked as if life had handed her one too many plates of fish and chips, but she seemed cheerful about it.

"Take this, luv." She said, handing Gilbert a large yellow folder. "These're your tickets for the train to Woking. Don't lose that folder, now, and make sure y'keeps your return ticket, or you'll have yourself a very long walk back indeed, I'd say."

Gilbert opened the folder and looked at his tickets. They were real!

"Beg your pardon, Mrs. . . . Hodgeson. Before I go, I was wondering . . . could you tell me who the young lady was that had the appointment just before mine?"

"Really?" A knowing twinkle had appeared in the older woman's eye. "An' why would knowin' that be so important to you, Mister Gilbert?"

"She, ah, she looked familiar. I thought I knew her from somewhere."

Miss Hodgeson peered at Gilbert over the rims of her glasses. "Mister Gilbert, keep bein' a writer! You're too poor a liar to be successful in politics! Don't concern yourself with that lovely pile of red hair just yet. You've had the touch of an angel t'day, Mister Gilbert. Don't let no one take it away from you or dirty it up, understand?"

Gilbert swallowed. She was right. He had been touched by some angel of good fortune. This was his one shot, his one opportunity — maybe the only one he would get to make something of himself that he could be proud of.

He'd realized a long time ago that Canada wasn't going to be that opportunity. His would-be guardians in Newfoundland weren't even family, really, just friends of his parents he'd been taught to call "Aunt" and "Uncle." He knew nothing about his "cousins," either, since they'd been off traveling the one and only time he'd visited, five Christmases ago.

There's no contest, really, he thought. *I'm on my own, whether I succeed or fail.*

The bell from the message tube broke him out of his thoughts. "Ah," said Mrs. Hodgeson with a happy voice, "here 'tis. I always like using these things, Mister Gilbert. Just give your request in wonna these," she held up a metal cylinder, "then pop it in one of these here tubes." She opened up a slot in one of the twenty or so tubes lined up in their rows behind her desk. "And then *whoosh*! It's off into the ether! I 'aven't the faintest of ideas where these things end up at, or who they go to. All's I know is that whatever I need always comes back to me nice an' neat as you please. Like this 'ere did!" She handed Gilbert a brown folder. A small stack of what looked like clippings poked out of it at odd angles, shaken by its trip through the messenger tube.

"This is a bit of information for you," she said. "Put it in your folder — there's a good lad. The Undersecretary said you could use some o' this, maybe you won't, but who knows? Anyways, when you're on the train, make sure that you read this: it tells what some are thinkin' about them things that fell down in Woking, hey? Oh, and when you return, Mister Gilbert, you let me know what them things looked like when they was killed by the troopers. I'd love to hear it from someone who was actually there, hey?"

In a moment, Gilbert's brief flush of excitement was gone, replaced by another wave of anxiety. He looked at Mrs. Hodgeson and spoke in a voice that had suddenly gotten very small.

"Them *things*?"

Three

"An inconvenience is only an adventure wrongly considered; an adventure is an inconvenience rightly considered." — GKC

It was a normal London morning. Even in full sunlight, the air looked heavy and dirty. Gilbert trudged down the London street toward Fenchurch Station, trying to ignore the activity that flustered and blustered about him. He'd long ago learned to look at the ground and avoid eye contact with potential troublemakers, but he could never block out all the sounds of the filthy street culture. Even when he'd almost got the hang of ignoring the hungry cries of children and the angry screams of the newly pickpocketed, there were still the putrid smells of waste being spilled out of nearby windows onto the street and sidewalks, forcing him to breathe through his mouth.

Despite these attacks on his senses, Gilbert was already trying to put together in his head the first paragraphs of his story. But this wasn't easy: not only were there distractions all around him, but he knew very little about what had happened in Woking. He'd had no time to look at the clipped articles in his file, now tucked securely under his arm. That would come when he'd gotten on the train and begun the trip out to the countryside.

The company outfitter he'd reported to after the Undersecretary had prepared him well, giving him a small satchel to carry his folder full of articles and a used brown sport coat that at least covered his grimy shirt and suspenders. At Mrs. Hodgeson's suggestion, Gilbert had asked for and gotten a pair of eyeglasses especially designed for journalists and other company employees working in what she called "the field." The metal arms of the glasses, thin but strong, bent like a fishhook around his ears, and the round lenses had been rendered shatter-proof by some sort of engine-designed process. The outfitter, a large man with a thick, pointed mustache and a broad smile, had promised Gilbert that his head would come off his body before those specs fell off his face

Anxious to catch his train on time, Gilbert nimbly dodged and side-stepped his way through the busy street, pausing only once or twice to ask a friendly or official-looking face for directions. Finally he was forced to stop in spite of himself, to watch some street urchins play the oddest game he had ever seen.

About a half-dozen of them were gathered in an alleyway, just beneath a large picture of a horse's head that had been drawn with gray chalk. The children were perhaps between five and ten years old, dressed in little more than rags, and creeping forward silently in a rough semi-circle toward a large garbage can. The can, or dustbin, as the English insisted on calling them, was half-buried and pointing at an acute angle out of a pile of garbage. When the children reached a certain point, the lid suddenly flew open and a much larger boy jumped out of the can with a loud noise and began grabbing the squealing children.

By the game's second or third repetition, Gilbert saw an edge to the little performance that unnerved him. Perhaps it was the eerie, almost fearful silence with which the little ones approached the garbage can. Maybe it was the almost bloodthirsty look in the eyes of the larger boy when he erupted from the can and began snatching his "victims." Whatever the reason, Gilbert found himself shuddering. He tore himself away and quickly moved on.

Trying to shake the unsettled feeling that had gotten hold of him, Gilbert gazed up and tried to focus on a trio of silver Zeppelins traipsing across the sky. His job in the cardroom had been a nightmarish experience, but now he was free — free like those floating airships. As the reality of his new position sank in, Gilbert's anxiety was replaced by a sense of peace and gentle elation. Even when a carriage drove by carrying a portly man in a high-hat and splashed Gilbert's shoes with muddy water, Gilbert raised his hand to wave at him.

And it was just as his warm feeling of inner joy had reached its zenith that he felt a tap on his left shoulder and turned to face it. The punch slammed into his left cheekbone just below his eye, knocking him down as the world exploded into yellow light.

⚜

After the world had exploded, Gilbert felt for a brief moment as if he were floating in air, as if he'd jumped off a diving board into the pond like the one behind the house he grew up in. That had been a long time ago, back when he'd been a little boy at the family farm with his childhood friends. His father had watched over them like a slim, benevolent king; his mustache perfectly trimmed, the lenses of his glasses polished flawlessly. His mouth was set in that small smile that others always wondered about, and his hand looked occasionally for the pocket watch in his waistcoat. His mother in her brown dress and white apron, bringing out glasses of fizzy lemonade and a tray of cookies; dark-haired, smiling, kind and beautiful . . .

Then pain and sound returned, and the image of his mother's face sharpened and reformed as a young man with a thin nose, a pointed black beard, and a battered gray top hat.

" 'Ello, mate! Wakey wakey, sunshine!" the face said, the words echoing slowly.

Gilbert tried to speak through a mouth that seemed to be full of gum and cobwebs. "Huh . . . wha . . ." he stammered thickly. Behind the top hat, Gilbert spotted a familiar face hidden behind too-small glasses and a mop of shaggy, dark hair.

"Wig— Wiggins?" Gilbert wet his lips and swallowed as he recognized the face floating several feet from his own.

31

"Hey, Georgie," said Top Hat, his lips matching his words better as Gilbert came out of his stupor. "The little tosser remembers you, even after I knocked 'im one! What say to that, hey?"

"Eh, Georgie! 'E remembers you!" aped another voice, this one behind Wiggins. Top Hat had brought friends with him.

" 'E recognized Georgie! Usually it takes 'em a few more minutes to come to after Ed pops 'em one."

"Yeah, this bloke's a tough!"

"Or maybe Ed's not hittin' like he used to!"

"Shut yer mouth, Bill," growled the youth with the top hat, keeping his eyes on Gilbert.

"Sorry, Ed."

Gilbert made a groggy mental note: *Top Hat's name is Ed.*

"Eh, why'd ye hit him for, Ed?"

"Ed's got his reasons, right, Ed?"

"I knows he's got his reasons! I just wants to know what them reasons are!"

Wiggins, his own tousled dark hair looking a little more unkempt than earlier in the day, said nothing but smiled nervously, his eyes looking back and forth between Gilbert and the fellow with the gray top hat they called Ed.

Gilbert felt almost as dizzy from the voices flying around him as he was from the blow to his face. His cheek was singing Beethoven's Ninth Symphony, and his glasses and satchel were gone. "Wiggins," Gilbert stammered, "what — what's wrong?"

"What's wrong?" piped up Ed jovially, straightening his top hat. "Hold 'im, boys." Gilbert, who had been knocked down by the blow and was sitting uncomfortably in the alleyway, now felt himself dragged to his feet, and his arms pinned behind his back by several sets of hands. Wiggins moved back a step, all the while keeping his eye on Gilbert.

"I say, *Mistaah* Chesterton," began Ed, exaggerating his voice to sound like someone from the upper classes, "were you by chance aware of the misfortune that befell our mutual acquaintance, *Mistaah* Wiggins, today at your place of occupation?"

"What?" said Gilbert, becoming more upset with the whole situation as he came back to himself. Was he going to miss his train over this?

Ed dropped the act, leaning forward just enough that his hat stayed in place. "Sod you, you little sneak. You saw what happened to Wiggins at work today?"

Gilbert straightened up. "Yes, he got fired. I've got some good news about . . ."

"Yes, you're right." Ed paused and then resumed his act of being the polished, dapper gentleman in the middle of a monologue. "Our dear colleague, Mistaah Wiggins, was removed from his position today. And, we have it on the highest of cardroom authority, that right after dear Georgie here's dismissal, the Overseer began talking and smiling at *you*, Gilbert. And our sources furthermore state you were then taken up to the upper-management floors by the Overseer himself. Care to comment on that?"

A shot of scare went through Gilbert. Wiggins thought Gilbert had gotten him fired! "Wiggins," said Gilbert quickly, looking past Ed, "you've got to hear me out. You're not . . ."

"Whoops," said Ed, a look of mock surprise on his face, "I think he's dodgin' my question. You think he's dodging my question, Bill?"

"He's dodging your question, Ed," the smaller boy to his right answered dutifully. His eyes were fixed on Ed with a combination of fear and worship.

"I knew it!" Now Ed suddenly turned serious, his upper-class act replaced by something simpler and much more frightening. He leaned in again, close to Gilbert's face. "Why'd you leave work early today, Gilbert?" he growled. "An' don't try to give us any guff that you've been sacked, just like Georgie!" Gilbert could smell the acrid scent of onions and cheap wine on his breath. "You're not going to the East End Rookery, where card-workers live. You're headed to the train station. You did a tell-tale on Georgie, you little sneak. An' now you're gonna pay for it."

"Wiggins," said Gilbert, trying again to look past Ed at the tousle-haired boy, "I got you . . ."

"SACKED!" Ed roared with a scary smile, waving the knob-end of a silver-headed walking cane (obviously stolen from some upper-class citizen) in front of Gilbert's face. "Bounced! Fired! Shown the door! And right afterward, little Gilbert gets a little reward for being such a good boy, and blaming *Georgie* for *his* slip-ups, didn't he?"

Gilbert blinked. "You mean, you think *I* had him fired? Wiggins, let me finish what I'm . . ."

"Trying to wriggle out? Oh, no you don't." Ed waved his cane back and forth in time with his shaking head. "We've been trying to get Georgie here to join our little group for some time now, 'aven't we, Georgie? He's got a mind we could use, an' he knows the inside of the firm, too. Make life a lot easier for us if we hit the place, y'see. I've known how smart this lad is ever since we worked for that bloke on Baker Street. Now, though, thanks to you, Gilbert, he's 'at liberty' an' unemployed. Right then, Georgie here saw the light and joined up right quick, didn't he?"

"Ed," said Wiggins suddenly, "maybe we shouldn't . . . uh, maybe he didn't . . ."

The boy holding Gilbert was a bit younger and smaller than he, and when Wiggins spoke, he loosened his grip just long enough for Gilbert to jerk free. He quickly put twenty feet between himself and the gang, with Wiggins between them.

Gilbert whipped around and saw four more boys running toward him from the other direction. There would be no escape by running down the alley; it dead-ended a stone's throw away. The only path to freedom lay through Ed's gang, and then past Ed himself. Gilbert cut back and tried to run through them, but first one and then the rest laid hold of him. Although he was taller, they were much stockier and held him tightly. They dragged him, struggling, past Wiggins to face Ed.

"Y'see, Georgie?" Ed yelled at Wiggins, pointing his cane at Gilbert while yelling at Wiggins. "Y'see where being all nice to them ladder-jumpers gets you? You've gotta be a lot tougher than that if you wanna make it with the Gray Mare Boys! See?"

"Now, Gilbert," said Ed patiently, turning his attentions to Gilbert. "I'm a flexible person. Now I *was* just gonna show Georgie here how happy we were to have him aboard by grabbin' you, beating you into a little, bloody 'eap in the alley, and leaving you here with our mark carved on yer forehead. But now . . ." Ed stroked his black goatee a moment. "Now, little Gilbert, lookin' at you, I've decided that instead of trouncin' you all myself, I'll let Georgie Wiggins back there do the killin' blow after I've done givin' your insides a bit of a dance lesson. Wot'ja say to that, hey?"

"But Wiggins, you're not fi— OOF!"

Gilbert was cut off in mid-yell as Ed's fist pounded into his gut. His face was still screaming in pain where Ed had hit it a few minutes earlier, and now he felt as if someone had smashed his stomach with a steamhammer. Gilbert doubled over, coughing. If Ed's punks hadn't been holding him up, two on each arm, Gilbert would have fallen on the ground and curled up like a baby. But all he could do was groan and retch.

"Ed, let 'im go!" Wiggins yelled. "He didn't tell on me! An' even if he did, it's not worth killing him over!"

Ed paused, straightened his hat, and walked over to Wiggins with an air of menace. "Now, Georgie," he said, putting his arm around Wiggins's shoulder, "because you're new to the life o' the gang, and because you might've gone soft with the wife an' kid at home, I'll ignore that little outburst of yours *just* this once. You got one chance here to be in or out of the

Gray Mare Boys, Georgie Wiggins. Got it? Now, I'm going to go back there and soften up that overgrown broomstick. When I call for you, you come up an' finish the job. Got it?" He poked Wiggins in the chest for emphasis. They appeared to be about the same age — perhaps nineteen — but there was no doubt who would win in a fight between them. Wiggins gulped, looked at Gilbert, and looked back at the cold, hard eyes of Ed, leader of the Gray Mare Boys.

Before Wiggins could answer, Ed turned and stalked back to his prey. He paused in front of Gilbert, looked him up and down briefly, then brought his boot down as hard as he could on Gilbert's right foot. Gilbert, his lungs already empty of air, looked like a silent movie actor as his mouth quietly went through the motions of a tormented scream.

If Gilbert had been in any shape to notice, at that moment he would have seen Wiggins suddenly rush by him, Ed, and the five other smaller boys in a blur of fear.

"Wiggins!" roared Ed. "We won't forget this! We took you in when you was sacked!"

Wiggins stopped at the mouth of the alleyway and turned to face them all. "You never said nothing about killing no one, Ed Pearse!" yelled back Georgie Wiggins from the mouth of the alleyway. "An' I'm gonna get help now for Gilbert, so you better let 'im go!"

Wiggins ran out of sight. Two of the gang looked to Ed, silently asking permission to give chase.

"Leave off 'im," said Ed disgustedly. "He was a waste anyway, an' we'll give 'im 'is when we're done here. Meantime" — he turned back to Gilbert — "let's finish this little nob an' get back to business."

"What?" said Gilbert, able to draw a little breath. "But Wiggins isn't even here! You've got no reason to . . ."

"Sure I do, specs. An' here's the big reason why." He leaned in closer and lowered his voice.

"I'm going to mop this alley floor with your goggle-eyed, wavy-'aired 'ead for two reasons, little Gilbert. Because I want to, and" — he ticked off his reasons with his cane against the fingers of his left hand — "because I can."

Just then a voice sounded — "Hey!" — from the mouth of the alley. "Sod off!" yelled one of Ed's toadies, "we got business 'ere!" Ed ignored the voice, preferring to focus on Gilbert. "Now, me lad. Wot shall I start on with you? A cuff to the right cheek, to match your left? Or maybe I'll just 'ang all the in-between malarkey and give you a good, solid knee in the pills. Wot say you?"

Gilbert was about to protest his innocence one last futile time when he heard rapid footsteps pounding down the alley. A flash of tan-colored clothing caught his eye over Ed's right shoulder. Ed saw that Gilbert's attention had refocused from the terror in front of him to a curiosity behind him. Ed turned, just in time for a fist to catch him on the side of his face and send his top hat flying.

Justice, thought Gilbert. *This is what my teacher used to call poetic justice.*

Four

"There is a corollary to the conception of being too proud to fight. It is that the humble have to do most of the fighting." — GKC

Much later, when he looked back on the day he'd decided to make an example of Gilbert, Ed Pearse would come to terms with all the mistakes he'd made in handling the episode with little Gilbert Chesterton. It would be a management lesson worthy of the attentions of Messieurs Effortson, Philandron, and a host of others in their respective business cadres. But at this moment, Ed's mind had time only to register shock and surprise as his head reeled and fell earthward.

"All right, you lot, let him go!"

Gilbert squinted at his rescuer through his one unpuffed eye. The fellow wasn't any taller or very much older than he, although he was stockier. He wore a shirt and tie underneath a tidy brown jacket. Fierce dark eyes blazed out from beneath a shock of short, dark hair at the boys holding Gilbert's arms. "Any of you want what I just gave Ed here?" he bellowed. Silence met his challenge. "Right, then, I'll give you just two seconds to let go and clear off! One!" Gilbert felt the pincer-like hands melt away from his arms. His legs wobbled, and he promptly fell to the pavement again.

"Come on!" yelled the new boy, his voice bellowing over the sounds of the hasty retreat of the Gray Mare Boys. He grabbed Gilbert by the wrist, trying to bring him to his feet.

"Ow!" yelled Gilbert, pulling himself to a semi-standing position, "I can't run yet!"

"Did they bust up your leg?" asked the new boy.

"My foot," Gilbert gasped.

"Right. Here, hop to it. I don't think we have much time." He pulled Gilbert's left arm over his own shoulders, helping Gilbert hobble down the alley toward the sidewalk.

Meanwhile, Ed had picked himself up, blinked twice, and caught a glimpse of the fellow in the tan jacket leading Gilbert away toward the street.

Oh, no, thought Ed. *This will not do.* This will not do at all. He looked around as quickly as the pain would let him and saw that his henchmen had already disappeared.

Bunch of little gits, he thought to himself. *Now I'll have to beat those two up twice as bad, in public, build up a new gang, and beat up the old gang for running away. And Wiggins . . . oh, little Wiggins is dead. Dead as a doornail in a smithee's furnace, once I get my mitts on him.*

But, first things had to come first. First, he had to make an example of that cheeky little sod who'd just spoiled Ed's alley party.

"Wells!" roared Ed at the retreating pair. "I'm — get back here! I'm not finished with you yet!"

"Keep walking." mumbled the new boy, whom Gilbert presumed to be named Wells, into Gilbert's ear. Helping to shoulder Gilbert's weight, he hobbled the both of them out of the alley and made a quick left into a steady stream of people.

"Wells!" yelled Ed a second time, anger at being ignored blinding him to the pain on his cheekbone and head. He launched himself at the area where he'd seen them disappear, checking under his belt for the small knife he kept for personal protection and intimidation of his toadies. As he tore around the corner, deducing his quarry to be perhaps two dozen feet ahead of him, he suddenly tripped over someone's foot and went sprawling into the street for the second time.

"Ow!" he yelped as he hit the rough pavement. It had become a rare sunny day in London, and the streets were just starting to get crowded. Ed scrambled to his feet, planning to give whatever fool had tripped him a good, solid shot and then be on his way down to teach lessons to Wiggins, Wells, Gilbert, and the lads who had abandoned him in the alley.

But when he stood and saw the leg that had tripped him, he paused. It was a thick, sturdy leg, attached to a large man with a brown beard, wearing a dark cape and a fine silk top hat, and carrying a black walking cane with a white tip on its end. Even when he'd drawn himself to his full height, Ed found himself looking up into eyes that were calm but vaguely menacing.

Ed's bravado abandoned him, melting like fog in the face of the sun.

"Are you all right?" said the man without any expression of either pity or sarcasm. Ed looked at the man more closely and saw a chubby face covered by dark whiskers streaked with gray. *The old goat must be fifty or more*, Ed thought. *So what am I afraid of?*

"Edward?" said the older man, his face suddenly shifting from a blank stare to warm recognition.

"An' just 'ow do you know me?" replied Ed slowly, intentionally thickening his accent. "Oi've nevah seen yew before in my loife!" He had found more than once that when upper-class types were suddenly confronted with a loud voice in a cockney accent, they became intimidated and tended to give up their money more easily.

This man, not intimidated in the least, latched on to Ed's elbow with a firm grip and began talking to him like an old friend. "Edward, my son, I was just out for an afternoon stroll, but I should love to have you join me. Right this way. As a matter of fact . . ." he began walking back down the alleyway Ed had just come from. "In fact, dear boy, I'd love you to meet a dear friend of mine."

"Gotta go!" Ed mumbled, trying to shrug off the older man's arm. Yet with little apparent effort, the man was able to steer Ed in the opposite direction, back into the alley where all of these troubles had begun.

" 'Ere you, lay off!" Enough was enough. Ed pulled up his knife to show the bloke . . .

Nothing.

His knife was gone.

And there was something red on his hand.

With steadily increasing horror, Ed looked at the stump where his index finger had been a moment ago.

The man looked at Ed with an amused grin. Ed looked down to see the point of his own knife peeking out underneath his unlikely captor's dark sleeve, his severed finger lying by his right foot. " 'Ow?" started Ed quietly, shocked as much by the lack of pain as by the sight of his pointer on the dirty alley floor. " 'Ow did you . . ."

"My boy!" cried the older man, continuing to lead Ed down the alley as a man might lead a horse, pocketing the knife and ignoring his grisly handiwork. "This is your lucky day! After all, very few people are privileged enough to meet my good friend, especially when I am in the kind of rush in which I often find myself during these times."

" 'Ere, now, you took my knife," spoke Ed in voice made slow and stupid by shock, "an' me finger, too. Give 'em back an' clear off before I take your sod'n head off yer blinkin' shoulders."

"Young Edward," the older man said, his voice changing suddenly, "your knife is not important. Your finger is not important. *We* are not important, and *you* are not important. In fact, the only thing that is of real importance now is my friend, whom you are about to meet."

"Friend?" said Ed. He looked at the man more closely, then his eyes suddenly widened. "I remember you now," he said, "you're the friend of . . . you were only there that once, in the office on Baker Street, when Wiggins an' I were with the Irregulars. You're the doctor bloke, the doctor who . . ." Ed's sentence was cut off by a loud snapping sound. The older man had moved with startling speed to touch the back of Ed's neck with the white tip of his dark cane. A blue spark erupted from the cane and into Ed, making Ed jerk to the ground suddenly and flail about like a landed fish.

Once Ed had fallen, the man pushed a switch on his walking cane and a small sheath clicked into place over a bizarre-looking grouping of small metal protrusions and wires at the cane's white tip. He quickly walked to the mouth of the alley to ensure that there were still no witnesses. Then he turned back to Ed's body, now still. "Congratulations, Mister Pearse," said the older man, all trace of warmth gone from his voice, "you've just met my friend Nancy."

That was a bit of fun, he thought to himself. *And I'm still on schedule, no less.*

The older man turned on his heel and left the alley, leaving an unconscious Ed Pearse to be grabbed by the police and awaken in a jail cell with a crude bandage on his hand, few hazy memories of the last hour, and even fewer friends.

Five

"Moderate strength is shown in violence, supreme strength is shown in levity." — GKC

Gilbert and his rescuer limped and hobbled for the better part of a quarter-mile, coming near to the station, when Gilbert finally felt ready to try to walk again.

"Thanks," said Gilbert, as the boy eased him off his shoulder. "Thanks for helping me, back there."

"Eh, no trouble, friend," came the jaunty reply. The boy held out his hand: "Herb Wells."

Gilbert took it. "Gilber— *Gil* Chesterton."

"Good to meet you, Gil. A bit of help unlooked for never hurt anyone," Herb continued in an accent that was smoother and more cultured than Ed's clipped street cockney. "A scraggle-haired fellow told me someone was getting killed in the alley, so I ran to check it out. Besides, anyone who runs afoul of old Ed Pearse and the Gray Mare Boys is a friend of mine. He's made life miserable for more people in this part of town than you could shake a stick at. That fool's name is like a rash all up and down the crime files we've got over at the paper."

Gilbert raised a set of mental eyebrows. The paper? Was this guy a journalist too? Were they going to be on the train together, covering the same story? He hoped so. It would help to have a friend on this job, especially since he'd already been beaten up a bit on the way there.

"D'you think he'll make trouble once I get back from my trip?" Gilbert asked, hoping his voice didn't betray his fear.

"I wouldn't worry about him," Herb answered, his voice as casual as someone discussing football scores. "I've covered his antics in the paper. That's how he knew me, and the main reason he doesn't like me. If he's picked you out for his latest victim, it usually means he's down on his luck or needs you as an example to put his latest batch of grovellers in line. He gets mad when you fight back, but he's like any bully: once you teach him a lesson, you've taken care of him, and all his followers too. If you're going somewhere by train, he'll have forgotten about you by the time you return."

"By train!" yelped Gilbert. "My folder! He knocked it out of my hands! It had my ticket in there — the punchcard to print out my ticket, anyway. I can't go back to the firm and ask for another; I'll look like a fool! What am I going to do, Herb?"

"Oh, you mean *this*?" said Gilbert's new friend, reaching into the back of his pants under his jacket and pulling out the folder that had become so vitally important to Gilbert in the last few minutes.

Gilbert took the folder from Herb and quickly shuffled through it, checking off each item in his head as he found it intact. Ticket to Woking, *check*. Return ticket to London, *check*. And batch of clippings, oh yes, *check*. He gave a sigh of relief as his eyes rolled back into his head and his lips pursed in a kind of whistle. "That's the second time today you've saved my life, Herb."

"Once again, no trouble. What'd you do to Eddie Pearse to get him so steamed up, anyway?"

"He wanted to impress one of his new recruits, a fellow who thinks I got him fired from his job. The sad part is, he lost it on his own, but I pulled a few strings and got it back for him later."

"Must be a lousy job, Gil, if he's letting the Gray Mare Boys beat you up for getting it *back* for him."

"Well, it *is* a lousy job." Gilbert agreed. "I should know. It was *my* job, up until an hour ago. The worst of it is, if I don't make the most of this opportunity I've gotten today, it might become my job again."

"Opportunity? To do what?"

"Today, Herb, I was promoted to journalist! I'm working for the paper, like you, as a matter of fact!"

Herb smiled. "I don't know if it's such an honor, Gil. I've been working for my outfit, the *Telegraph*, for nearly a year now, and they've yet even to give me credit for my work. I think they're just sending me out to Woking because all the real reporters are busy, and the *Telly* doesn't want to look like they've been left behind."

"Just what *is* going on over there in Woking, Herb? Do you know?"

"Some meteors, I think. I guess they were remarkably well-preserved. The first one fell the other night, and another last night. There's some talk, too, but it's all rot."

They'd reached the doors of Fenchurch Station now, but Gilbert stopped. "What kind of talk?" he asked, pushing his glasses up on his nose again.

"Don't think I can tell you all that just yet, chum. I've got a story to write, and it wouldn't look right if I let out all I knew without confirming it first."

"You mean," said Gilbert, smiling, "that you think you've got some insider information, and you don't want to let it out so you'll look all the more brilliant when your copy hits the stands."

Herb suddenly looked serious. "Gil, just remember this, okay? Like most people, I think of myself as a good fellow. Maybe even a fairly decent one. But when it comes to getting a story, or getting any job done that needs to get done, I'm not always going to be a *really* nice fellow. At times, I might not even be what some would call a really *good* fellow, at all."

Gilbert paused. "Well, Herb, who isn't like that, really?" he said finally, trying to laugh. But Herb just pulled open the door to the station without further comment, and they took their place in one of the hundreds of lines that snaked this way and that everywhere in the largest train station in the city of London. It dawned then on Gilbert that he'd never been there before.

"Where do we go? Do you know, Herb?" For some reason, Gilbert suddenly recalled the time when he was five and got separated from his parents at a fair.

"Watch and learn, my friend."

Herb approached a long line of people, motioning quietly for Gilbert to stay close to him. The line was moving quickly, and the four or five people in front of them soon had gone on their way.

"Where to, dear?" said the ticket girl to Herb. She was young and pretty — only a little older than the two of them, Gilbert guessed. With quick green eyes and dark hair piled high in a thick bun. Gilbert felt a nudge at his ribs, and Herb turned his head back at him. "Watch," he mouthed silently. A smile broke over Herb's face as he looked at the young woman.

"They tell me Woking. I've got the card right here — but," he took his punchcard out of his coat's breast pocket and placed it on the ticket counter, just under the cage that separated them. "But I have a question about this, miss. You see, I need to know something, right here." The girl leaned forward to see the area of the ticket that Herb was pointing out to her.

Herb waited until their faces were only a few inches apart, grinned, and said softly, "I just need to know . . . what's your name?"

The girl blinked. She looked at Herb for two very long seconds, and smiled. "I can't flirt with the gents who get on the train, sir."

"You're not flirting, m'lady," countered Herb. "I am! Do you like coffee? A friend of mine owns a little shop 'round the corner. He gives me a sweet deal when I come in, but only if I bring a pretty girl like you in with me."

"I can't accept proposals while I'm on duty, sir." But she was still smiling.

"I'm not proposing — just wondering when you usually get off work, so's I can ask you to join me for a cup of coffee when I get back from Woking."

"An' wot if I told you I had me a male friend who's in the Dead Rabbits?"

Gilbert paused and swallowed. The Dead Rabbits were a gang of New York cutthroats that were known clear across the Atlantic for their brutality.

If the girl was telling the truth, there were very few stupider things Herb could do at this point than continue his pursuit. Trying to get a haircut from a guillotine, or juggling canisters of nitroglycerin might qualify, but just barely.

Herb didn't seem to be thinking about this at all. He was too busy looking into her eyes. "The Rabbits are an ocean away," he said lightly, "but we're right here."

Oh, cripes, thought Gilbert to himself, looking away from the scene at the increasingly agitated line of people behind them. *If those people behind don't lynch us, the ticket girl's boyfriend'll cut our throats.*

"You ain't afraid of a Rabbit?" she said, returning his gaze.

"I just gave a beating to Ed Pearse and his whole gang, my dear."

"Ed Pearse? 'Oo's that?" she asked, her eyes widening.

"Only the most dangerous criminal mastermind in London, the head of the Gray Mare Boys. Ask my friend, Gil, here," Herb said, pointing to Gilbert. "He'll tell you."

"Well, they're not exactly a gang," began Gilbert. "And I wouldn't exactly call Ed a criminal mastermi—"

"I've got to catch the train," said Herb, quickly, making sure he had eye contact with the girl again. "I'm covering the story of the happenings in Woking."

"Woking? You're going *there*?" she took a deep, almost horrified breath.

"Yes, and I may never come back alive. But . . . if I *do* make it back, could I see you again?"

She hesitated for barely a second. "I get off work at nine. I do like coffee."

"Right, m'lady, I'll be back then. Is my ticket all right?"

"Oh, yes . . . here, let me get it sent through . . . give me your friend's, too." She fed both their punchcard tickets through the machine to her right, and more holes were punched in the card. After a short reading of the holes, the pins told the printing machine to write with another set of ink-dipped pins in clear, neat stippled letters the destination and arrival time of the tickets. She slipped them back to Herb with a smile and a twinkle in her eye, and leaned over conspiratorially to say something to him that Gilbert couldn't make out.

"How'd you do that?" asked Gilbert when they turned away and got far enough out of earshot. "If I tried that, she'd look at me like I was pond scum."

"Confidence, Gil old boy," said Herb with the air of someone who'd had the same lesson repeated to him many times before. "Confidence is the life-blood of all leadership. You've got to go out there and advance on life's mysteries."

"And making advances to *that* little mystery might get your liver on a spike. Is a girl worth it, Herb?"

Herb was about to say something in return when they both walked out through the double doors and onto the platform.

"Is anything?" he answered, half to himself.

Six

"I have little doubt that when St. George had killed
the dragon he was heartily afraid of the princess."
— GKC

The man with the dark cloak strolled down the London street toward Fenchurch train station. There was nothing about him to suggest he had electrocuted young Ed into an unconscious stupor in a filthy alley just a quarter-hour before. He tapped the heavy end of his cane into the palm of his hand at the thought of it, and smiled.

When he entered the station, he did not join the back of the line, but moved through it with such confidence and speed that almost no one challenged him. Only near the front did he encounter resistance, when a very large bear of a man in the blue and black uniform of a stationmaster blocked his path. "An' where might you be goin', hey? Back o' the loine, loike everyone else!" Red veins stood out on the man's nose, matching the red epaulets on his shoulders. His black-brimmed pillbox of a hat bobbed as he made his loud orders known to the man in front of him and to any potential line-rushers in the near vicinity. His right hand pointed at the cloaked man at first, then stabbed the air behind him at the back of the line, exposing a clenched hand with calluses on both fingers and knuckles.

This was not the sort of station official who carried a pocket watch and dispensed kindly assistance, but one of the brutish elements of the lower classes who were often hired by railroads to serve as private security guards. They were cheaper and more bluntly effective than any policeman could be, and if there was one thing they liked better than having their orders obeyed, it was beating people up for not obeying them.

Seemingly oblivious to the danger, the cloaked man calmly looked up at his assailant, quickly raising his cane with both hands parallel to the ground in a protective stance.

"Archibald is my brother," he said, speaking to the burly man in a voice just loud enough for him to hear.

The result was immediate. The stationmaster's face changed from coarse and officious to the face of a man who had lived a very different sort of life. He stopped, looked around, and leaned in to speak in a quiet voice. "Right, guv. Special Branch, then? They told me to expect you at this time, but I had to be sure. This way. 'Ere, Sam!" The burly guard yelled, shifting back into his rough, station-tough mode of speaking, "I've gotta take this 'ere bigwig up the line! Watch these blokes 'til I get back!"

"Right, Bill!" answered another, similarly large and uniformed man at the head of the line. No one else seemed likely to break ranks.

The dark-cloaked man followed his new guide through the whirling mass of humanity.

"We don't get many fellows from the Special Branch here," he said pleasantly. "Wot brings you here?"

"Questions like that, my large friend, tend to get agents into trouble. We both have our jobs. My job is to get on the train and travel to a destination. Your job is to assist me. Now do your job, so that I can complete mine."

"Certainly, gov. It's rare these days anyone is troubled on the trains. Keep up, now, and I'll lead you through safely."

They walked a few more steps in silence. The cloaked man looked his guide up and down, as if sizing him up.

"You must accompany me on my journey once we reach the train," he said crisply, not bothering to check for understanding. "Prior to our departure, you will change your uniform to that of a laborer. Stay close to me until you are dismissed, but *do not speak to me* unless you are spoken to."

"Yes, sir," said the cloaked man's guide, his friendliness now tinged with uncertainty. He knew nothing about the Special Branch, only that he was to obey to the letter any order given by one of its members. "I used to be a steam monkey once, y'know, and I can be on the train an' wearing a red outfit inside o' five minutes, if that'll be to yer liking."

"My liking of anything has nothing to do with it. You will be either efficient or otherwise, and accept rewards or consequences. Clear?"

The big man so seldom had reason to feel fear that he didn't know how to hide it. But he tried. "Clear as Archibald is my brother, gov."

They were silent again as they neared the door to the train. *Archibald is my brother*, the cloaked man thought to himself. *The password that opens doors throughout the world.* In virtually every major city in the country, and many foreign ones, too, were well-placed individuals who responded to the phrase just as this brute had: with handshakes, opened doors, and the way smoothed for them.

We are everywhere, he thought to himself again. *Everywhere. Yet only a few of us know it. Most of the people in this world are sheep that will live out their lives not knowing or understanding the nature of the world around them, any more than worms understand the nature of the house of a king above their heads.*

And, one day, he thought with a sense of iron will, *I will live inside that house.*

⁂

Herb and Gilbert watched the train slowly drag its giant metal carcass down the tracks toward their platform: a long, lumbering dragon made of steel and smoke. Fully three stories tall and designed by the latest analytical engines, it was capable of transporting more than 1300 people like a bullet of steam. The engine alone weighed nearly twenty tons and looked it: nearly forty feet high from iron wheel to steel-roofed cab, it sported three tall, soot-belching smokestacks, and a toothy, ten-foot triangular cattle-catcher in front that dared anything of this earth to stand in its way. Set atop the huge iron-plated engine was the engineer's cabin, its wood and brass trimmings a carryover from a quainter age — or made to look that way.

And in the engineer's cab of the locomotive, Edgar Alberecht sat back on his padded chair and adjusted his blue overalls for the seventh or eighth time in the previous few minutes. The acrid smell of engine smoke had long since ceased to sting his nostrils, but he'd never gotten quite used to the searing heat that made him squint and wince whenever he opened the furnace. And although he'd never admit it to a fellow engineer, the new locomotives intimidated him. Sure, there were so many automated safeguards that an actual derailing was a very rare occurrence. And the engineer's cabin was almost as plush and comfortably appointed as the first-class cars behind it.

But still there was something about being so high in the open air that gave Edgar a sense that the whole train risked toppling over with every lever he threw, like a fat man losing his balance on a high wire. And Edgar had never gotten used to a cabin that felt more like a fancy-pants drawing room than a place where dirty men burned coal and drove the most massive vehicles known to man. Edgar's sense of disquiet made every trip a little more stressful than the last, much to the detriment of his mental well-being.

The human mind is a very tricky thing. In Edgar's case, a combination of poor example and bad experiences had taught him that such stresses could be calmed only by alcohol. Even the relief that came with every pull into a station did not ease his wish for drink. As the train slowed on its rails and came within a hundred, now seventy-five yards of the passenger platform, Edgar's breathing quickened, his throat feeling much more parched than it actually was. "Needs a daff," he muttered to himself. He sneaked a small flask from inside his coat and, ducking under the high window, took a quick gulp.

The train came to a stop, and the door to the car in front of Gilbert and Herb opened. A tide of people began to surge out of the train, the first wave sporting expensive waistcoats and traveling dresses and followed by servants lugging trunks; then another group attired neatly but modestly, in clothes chosen for comfort rather than style; and finally, held back until the porters' signal, a motley, slightly soiled collection of patched and cobbled poor, ambling out from the cheap seats. When the last of the passengers had stepped off, a porter alit from the car. Although he was not much older than the two boys, he looked older with his blue uniform and official railway headgear.

As they moved toward the porter, they could see something else distinctive about him. He was unmistakably Asian — perhaps Chinese — with thin dark hair, slanted eyes, and a complexion darker than any Englishman's. The sight made Gilbert stop for a moment and look a second time. Gilbert had seen many people of Oriental descent in New York, but none since he'd involuntarily moved to England.

"Fen-church station!" the porter called into the car, his body sideways. "Please 'scuse us!" said Gilbert as he indexed his body sideways and hopped into the car, holding the satchel bag that contained his precious file. Next came Herb at a pace that suggested he wasn't concerned about getting a good seat. Neither did he excuse himself or return the porter's smiling greeting.

Once inside, Gilbert turned to his left and started for the nearest set of hard wooden benches that were crammed together on the first floor of the train. But Herb grabbed his arm and gestured with his head in the other direction, toward a winding stairway. "Follow me, mate," he said with a grin. "Our place is up there."

As he followed Herb up the stairs, Gilbert realized that the train was organized according to class, not from car to car, but from level to level, like a luxury ship. On the *Capsella*, he and the other steerage passengers had slept eight to a room in the boat's bowels, heads against gurgling pipes, while the wealthy enjoyed accommodations that might have made a prince envious. Here, poorer passengers crowded each other on the first story of the train, while riders on the second-class middle level enjoyed more elbow room, upholstered seats, and some distance from the grime and soot of the rails. And first class? One more flight of stairs opened to a spacious upper level furnished with wide (and widely spaced) plush velour chairs, red-curtained windows, and velvet walls. Rich dark furniture, trimmings of wood and brass — a passenger up here could recline, write letters, or enjoy a drink just as if he were nestled in his London club.

"Amazing," breathed Gilbert as he brushed past Herb with his mouth open, chose one of the many empty seats, and sank down in it. The memory of his stiff workbench in the clacker room made it feel soft as eiderdown. Then, lowering his voice, he added, "But Herb, won't we get tossed off when they check our tickets? I don't think *mine* was first class, at least."

"Posh, eh?" Herb remarked nonchalantly, seeming at first to ignore Gilbert's concern. "The makers of this train wanted to make such a big splash, I hear they even had the engineer's cab done over in puffed-velvet walls." Herb moved through the car appreciatively, but careful not to appear *too* impressed, and took a place next to Gilbert. Or rather, across from him: for the high-backed seats mostly faced each other, as in a stagecoach.

Finally he acknowledged Gilbert's look of worry and smiled again. "Not a problem, my friend. Remember that lovely young thing at the ticket window? I charmed her into moving us up to first class." He made a wide gesture with his hand. "That's where we belong, you know. The best view, far above the rabble, grand comfort and style — well worth climbing a few stairs, don't you think?"

Gilbert didn't answer. He was too busy soaking up the finery; not sure if indeed he was where he *belonged*, but determined to enjoy it while it lasted.

A few comfortable minutes later, as Herb and Gilbert were relaxing and reliving the morning's excitement, a man strode in from the stairwell: a middle-aged gentleman dressed in a dark cloak and trousers, holding a white-tipped walking stick. *Merchant of some kind,* Gilbert thought, having seen his type come through the factory on occasion. Although the car wasn't crowded even by the spacious standards of first class, the man took a seat directly behind Gilbert.

Then a distant voice yelled out for all to be aboard. The train hissed, belched steam and smoke, and began grinding its metal wheels into motion once more.

Gilbert looked out the high window with a surge of excitement that all human beings feel when their train starts to move, and was just giving a deep, contented sigh when, from the corner of his eye, he caught a fierce look on Herb's face.

"Herb, is something wrong?"

"What?"

"You look like you're trying to burn a hole in that porter with your eyes. Did he do something to you?"

"That porter . . ." Herb began, his jaw twitching slightly.

"What's the matter, Herb?"

"I'm not used to seeing . . . *others* doing our jobs, that's all."

Gilbert looked back to where the porter had let them on the train. "You mean the Chinaman? What's the matter with him?"

Herb sighed, swallowed, and began to talk in a curious way that Gilbert had never encountered before.

"He's a Chinaman, yes. But he's in a smaller job than we are, and we've nothing to fear from people who want to take those jobs anyway, do we?" Herb continued, his voice gaining confidence, as if he were successfully rationalizing something. "I mean, now that I think of it, you and I, Gil, we're from a race that's done everything that's worthwhile for the last ten centuries, and the other races out there just try to snatch up our leftovers. Besides, most of them are so small and weak compared with us. It makes me wonder why they'd pick him for a job like a porter, anyway. What, with heavy bags to carry and the occasional angry yob to toss off the train."

Gilbert looked very carefully at his new friend. After being rescued from a savage beating or worse, Gilbert had thought there was no power on earth that could make him think ill of Herbert George Wells. But now, he wasn't so sure.

"I don't know," Gilbert said carefully, "I met quite a few Chinamen back in America. There are third- and fourth-generation families there from when the railroad went through the USA. They dressed a little different, but they worked as hard as anyone in town. The only folks who gave 'em trouble were the ignorant ones, like the school bullies. If I'd happened to have yellow skin and slanted eyes, Herb, would you've walked on by and let Ed Pearse tear me open a new breathing hole?"

Herb looked sideways. "Gil, I helped you because you looked like a decent chap, and because Ed is a rotter. Besides," he continued, his voice getting brisk, "you've got to realize the world doesn't work the way we'd like it to. You went to school. Well, remember the classroom? The schoolyard? Since you've started working as a punchcard clacker, what was real life more like?"

Gilbert thought about his most beloved teacher, Mrs. Hargrove, who'd taught him in kindergarten and made sure that everyone was treated like "a child of God." Bullies were never tolerated in her room, but the schoolyard was a different story. There, a husky ten-year-old named Luther had terrorized him whenever the teacher wasn't looking. Luther would never be punished for anything, the other students whispered, since Mrs. Hargrove needed the job and the bully's father was president of the school board. Gilbert had gotten off comparatively easy, only being pushed down a few times and having his ball taken from him. But other children had been given bloody noses, or made to choose between eating dirt and getting more severe beatings.

And Gilbert remembered Overseer Philandron, how he'd fired and terrorized the other workers there at will.

"Okay," said Gilbert, "real life is more like the schoolyard. There are more bullies in real life, and fewer teachers to keep them from hurting the little guys once you get out of school. So what?"

"Gilbert," said Herb, speaking slowly, as if trying to explain quantum physics to a simpleton, "the sooner you figure this out, the better off you'll be. The whole *world* is a schoolyard, Gil. We don't mind the other kids playing with us, but we've got every right to take what we want if we're bigger, stronger, or faster."

"You make us sound like a bunch of lions, or tigers."

"Well, Lord Darwin has proven we're a bunch of apes. You don't think it's horrible when apes take things from each other, do you?"

"No, but I do think it's bad when people do it. That's what makes us so different from them."

"Come again?" Herb looked at Gilbert quizzically.

"Apes, Herb," said Gilbert slowly, as if trying to wrap his own mind around his words for the first time, "apes don't really care if they do terrible things to each other. But us humans, we get upset when we hear about humans doing such things to other humans. That's how we're different from them. Animals just do what they do. When they're hungry, they kill something, and they ain't above putting their own offspring on the menu. We do what we *ought* to do. And when we don't, we know there's something wrong."

"Ah!" said Herb triumphantly, suddenly animated with the possibility of a debate, "but you see, Gil, that's where it all falls down, doesn't it? You only *think* it's wrong because you've been *taught* it's wrong — by your mother, or a teacher, or some meddling priest. You could've been taught otherwise, now, couldn't you?"

Gilbert thought for a moment. "Yes," said Gilbert, after a pause, "I suppose I could have been taught differently. But it doesn't always work like that, Herb. Negroes in my country were *taught* that they were supposed to be slaves. But no matter how much they were taught that, Herb, no matter how much they were told that European Science said it was the natural order, slaves still tried to escape to the free states or to Canada. No matter what they were taught, they still knew *inside* that slavery was wrong."

"Well . . . they're still inferior!" huffed Herb, his face beginning to take on a reddish tinge. "I mean, Gil, for pity sakes, we've got steam technology, ships that cross the Pacific, we can cause the world itself to shake if it suits our purposes. What have the Chinese done since they built the Great Wall?"

"Gunpowder," said Gilbert. "They had it before us, since you brought up the subject of the earth shaking."

"Besides that."

"Macaroni? I heard they invented it."

"Besides *that!*"

Gilbert racked his brain. "How about fireworks and ice cream? And since we're both reporters, how about paper? Or were you planning to file your story on wax tablets?"

"Fine, then. They had all these things first, but *we* actually applied them, shaped them, and put them to good use."

"Only if you define 'good use' as making gobs and gobs of money off it."

"And why not?"

"Because, Herb, a few seconds ago, you were saying that the greatest race was defined as the greatest innovators. Now you're backtracking and saying the greatest race is really defined as the greatest entrepreneurs?"

"Do I have to pick one?"

"No, but if you do choose one, you'll need to stick to it. I don't like debating someone who keeps moving the target because I stand my ground."

Herb stared at Gilbert for several seconds. Then he chuckled nervously and looked around himself, as if to make sure no one had seen he was beaten. "You *are* a fun one, Gil! You argue with genuine passion, but you don't seem to get upset with me when I disagree with you. I hope you're not a papist — no? Good. I'd hate to think you argued so well because of a bunch of training in Jesuitry."

Gilbert smiled. Although he couldn't exactly relax, Herb's comment had at least diffused the tension. He found himself enjoying Herb's company again. But what was Jesuitry?

"Not a problem, Herb. I don't have trouble with someone disagreeing with me. I'm only upset when someone's opinions make innocent people die. And from what I know of you so far, you're at least interested in protecting innocents like me more than letting predators like Ed eat us for supper. That makes you all right in my book."

They heard the train whistle, felt it rumble to a start and lurch forward. Herb said, "I'll eat an innocent rabbit, but that's about as far as I'll go. But, despite how charming your conversation, Gil, don't ever forget that in the great game of life, the English always win, and the rest of the world ends up the —" Herb stopped in mid-sentence. Something had caught his eye, grabbed it, and wouldn't let go.

Gilbert turned and felt his own jaw drop. The porter whom they'd been indirectly talking about for the past few minutes had suddenly appeared in the aisle. Had he overheard their conversation? The slight smile on his face suggested that he had.

"You . . ." started Herb.

"I've got my ticket, right here," said Gilbert quickly, fumbling for his ticket in the folder. He found it and snapped it between his thumb and forefinger in front of the porter in an attempt to look efficient.

"Thank you, sir," said the porter, punching the ticket with a small hand tool and returning it to Gilbert. "And yours, sir?" he said next, looking at Herb.

"But how did you . . . I didn't hear you behind me . . . oh, bother. Here's my ticket. Now go away, please." Herb pulled his own ticket out and tried to do the same as Gilbert, only with more success.

"Thank you, sir," the porter replied. He pronounced each word distinctively, looking Herb in the eye. "Are you gentlemen well? Have you any more questions for me?"

"Yes!" said Gilbert; "No!" said Herb, both simultaneously.

"How," Gilbert continued, "were you able to sneak up on us like that? I didn't hear or see you until you spoke!"

"I heard your conversation, and did not wish to intrude, sirs. As for your comments, sir," the porter said, turning to face Herb, "if I may make a suggestion that could broaden your mind?"

"Why are you still talking to me?"

"Sir, strike me."

Herb blinked. "What?"

"Strike. Me." The porter, still smiling, pronounced each word more distinctively than before, as if Herb hadn't heard him.

"*Hit* you?" Herb said quietly.

"Yes."

Herb rose, pulled back . . .

"Herb, don't!"

. . . and threw a hard, fast punch at the porter. Gilbert hadn't seen the blow that felled Ed earlier, but now he realized why the street hoodlum had gone down so quickly. Reflecting on it later, Gilbert realized that Herb had thrown quite possibly the most perfect punch he'd ever seen up close.

The porter stood in place, watching Herb's fist with the kind of dispassionate look one might give the approach of a harmless winged insect. Just before it connected, the porter suddenly reached out and slapped Herb's hand to the side.

Slapped? Herb blinked. Gilbert blinked. The porter stood with the same, relaxed smile on his face. If the porter had blinked, no one had noticed.

"What did you do?" Herb asked.

"Try again," the porter said. "Watch, and you might see." Herb aimed another hard punch, right at the porter's face. The porter moved his body slightly, reached up with his hand, and deflected Herb's fist with no more visible effort than that involved in smacking a paper ball aside.

"How'd you do that?" Gilbert asked.

The porter looked at Gilbert innocently. "I was hired for this job because I can defend myself and others if need be. If disturbances happen, I am to stop them. I must go now, and take more tickets. Have a pleasant trip." The porter spoke the *l* sound in *pleasant* distinctively, as if it were something he'd practiced many times.

As the porter walked away, Gilbert saw something slip out of his blue uniform pocket and brush against the side of the seats. It was a silver crucifix, attached to the end of a long string or loop of wooden beads.

Gilbert turned to Herb, who was slumped in his chair with a sulky expression on his face. Gilbert slid back into the seat across from Gilbert and looked at him, suppressing a smile. "About us being the master race, Herb, and everyone else being inferior . . ." he began quietly.

"Oh, do be quiet," Herb said morosely. "I'm tired, and I'm going to sleep."

"Right!" said Gilbert happily. He'd engaged in enough family debates around the supper table to know that he'd been the winner in their little verbal bout. Even if Herb wasn't willing to change his worldview, he'd have a hard time arguing that a religious Asian was so inferior to a rationalist Englishman when that Asian had managed to out-stealth and out-fight an Englishman, all without leaving a mark on either of them.

As they pulled out of the station, Edgar looked warily at the analytical engine next to the train's steam boiler. It had been installed a few weeks before to assist him and the other engineers in the task of driving the new breed of iron horses. The size of a nightstand, it sat like a squat, block-shaped spider in the midst of a web of brass pipes, cords, and small pistons. Edgar disliked trusting any aspect of his job to a machine, but the new feature allowed something that Edgar would never have dreamed possible in a decade of train helming. "This switch," the Master Engineer had told him, pointing to a lever smaller than Edgar's thumb, set below a dial with several stylishly drawn letters on the upper half of its dial, "is the automated direction system." Edgar had looked at the contraption as if it had fallen from the sky, walked about on three legs, and begun speaking to him in Mandarin Chinese.

"Look, it's very simple, Ed," continued the Master Engineer, his dirty overalls looking out of place in the ornate cabin. Whoever had designed this place certainly hadn't worked on a train for any space of time! "When you've got a bit of time that you're going to be on a straightaway, turn this here dial to 'A.' The train'll keep going, and the engine'll drive the engine, pull the levers, and make the steam run where it should, eh?"

Edgar looked puzzled and unconvinced at the same time. "So, 'ow does this little box know when we're rounding a turn? 'Ow does it know how much to drop the pressure, or shovel the coal in?"

"Ed, it doesn't, see? It can't drive the train *all* the way itself, or else we'd both be out've our jobs, wouldn't we? But if ye just set this little thing to 'A' on its dial when you've got a straightaway coming up for a while, it's like . . . it's like givin' the reins of a coach horse team to one've your young'uns when there's an easy patch of road to drive on, see?"

"But why use the thing, anyway? I don't trust a young'un to drive a coach when there's a few hundred along for the ride, do I? An' why'd they take out most of the controls? Practically all that's left is the throttle an' the coal shovel, an' they're not even marked!"

"The company says to do it, and that's why I do it, see? But have it your way. If it's not your cup o' tea, then drive the train yourself the rest of your days. Which, we both know, won't be long. The boxes are going in, an' you an' me will be out've jobs before too many more winters." The Master Engineer had thrown his meaty hands in the air and walked off with a frustrated air. In the end, it had taken one of the porters, that young Chinaman in fact, to show Ed how the thing worked in a way Ed could actually grasp.

Edgar felt the small tickle at the back of his throat as he thought of the Master Engineer's parting words. It was the calling for a drink that had become more pronounced with every stop he'd brought the train into. He drummed his sooty fingers on the sill of his compartment, dropping ash on the now-dull red padding and wishing for the ten-thousandth time that he could nerve himself to carry a larger flask of hard liquor hidden in his overalls. He knew that drinking more would likely hamper his skill at driving the train. But so long as he took only a small nip at a time, there was no danger to him or his passengers.

At least, so far as Edgar thought.

Seven

"I never could see anything wrong in sensationalism;
and I am sure our society is suffering more from
secrecy than from flamboyant revelations." — GKC

The train sped on through fields of gray grass and sickly trees. Herb had fallen asleep, and Gilbert looked out the window and began to wonder if there were any bright flowers in the whole of England. The air was a little better in the country than in the city, but as Gilbert could see, the factory smokestacks had left their mark here, too, scarring and blackening huge swaths of once-green forests and fertile fields. Trees that had once stood so proudly were now little more than blackened twigs. It was nearly summer; shouldn't things have bloomed by now?

The dreary countryside made Gilbert think about the fields that had surrounded his family's country home in Minnesota. *This summer,* he thought glumly, *I would have been swimming and getting ready for my last year of high school.*

He knew the arguments against complaining. He'd learned a trade, and any money he made from now until the end of his life would be his own. Still, he also knew that the quality of his new life would depend on how he performed his duties.

"You'll be paid for your skills, Gilbert," his father had said a couple of years ago, during a carriage ride. "Too many fellows in university forget that. They spend years getting degrees in languages, poetry, philosophy, or other some such, and then cry back to their parents if they can't make a living in this world. Knowledge for its own sake is well and good, but only after life's responsibilities are taken care of."

Now that he'd had a taste of the kind of life he'd be leading without an education, the thought of pursuing higher learning jumped into Gilbert's head rather forcefully. *University may not be an option for me,* he thought. *But perhaps if I could pull this newspaper assignment off, I'll be able to get and keep a position that I wouldn't need a degree to prosper in.*

But to prosper, I'll need a good story. And a good story starts with good research. He pulled the folder full of paper out of his satchel. Miraculously, even after his beating by Ed and the Gray Mare Boys, its contents were intact.

It would be a few hours before he arrived at the Woking station; a little reading now could save him a lot of embarrassment later when he tried to file his story. There were several articles in the folder, all printed and clipped within the past ten days. He pulled out the first one and began to read.

It was fascinating.

A large meteorite had streaked through the sky the night before and left an enormous crater just outside the small town of Woking. Gilbert noted the time of the meteor's impact. He would have been just drifting off to sleep after his twelve-hour shift in the clacking room when the meteorite had lit up the night sky with a green aura that had been seen as far as London. Gilbert still marveled that little Oliver had had enough energy to catch a glimpse of the thing, much less be carousing in a pub at the time.

The Woking locals had learned the meteor was actually a giant cylinder, seemingly buried in the mounds of earth at the center of the enormous crater it had dug out with its impact. The cylinder's cap was about thirty yards across, but they could only guess at its height, or how deep it had been buried. At the time the story had been filed, the cylinder was still so hot that no one could approach closer than ten paces.

Gilbert looked out the window, trying to imagine whether a giant crater would improve the look of the dry countryside. He flipped through several more articles and found it odd that none of them had to do with the Woking meteorite. A museum had been dedicated to the Babbage engines; a group of Luddites had rioted at a factory that had dared to install an assembly line; sightings of some mysterious airship, shaped like half a soccer ball and allegedly floating through the air of the Sierra mountains back in the Republic of Southern California. There was even a piece on some mad inventor, claiming that he had made an artificial humanoid out of metal, powered by steam and instructed by miniature Babbage engines and punchcards.

"Twaddle," his dad would have called it. It all amounted to a waste of time and energy. Even if you could use punchcards to make something like a mechanical man, what would be the purpose?

Gilbert looked over to the deeply breathing form of his new friend and decided he was feeling a little sleepy himself. But there was only one more article to go through. Gilbert forced his eyes open long enough to read it.

He was glad he did, since the last article was the oddest of all. It seemed some astronomer outside the city had noticed vast clouds of brightly colored gas blasting up from the planet Mars a few weeks ago. Furthermore, identical flashes from the same location on Mars were observed each subsequent day for the next ten days. After this, the eruptions ended completely.

Volcanic eruptions on Mars? Sightings of ball-shaped airships? What did that have to do with a meteorite buried in Woking? *Curiouser and curiouser*, thought Gilbert. Far from giving him relevant information, the head office had given him a jumble of tales related only by their oddball natures.

"Interesting reading?" said a voice over his shoulder. Gilbert turned and saw that the voice belonged to a short, almost plump man who stood behind him. The small man wore a pair of horn-rimmed glasses resting on a round, pinkish face that was very nearly perfectly clean-shaven. He was not smiling, but his eyes didn't frown, either. He had on a wide, black-brimmed hat and wore a black coat and trousers with a white collar.

"Um, yes," said Gilbert. He felt a little uncomfortable in the presence of a priest, having been raised in a home that couldn't exactly be called religious. At his school, the Catholic religion had been viewed as something like an exotic cult — something to be studied and looked at oddly, but never taken seriously as truth. Gilbert was just thinking about asking whether it was true that Catholics worshiped the Devil's wife when the priest spoke again.

"May I join you? I love train rides, but the things are dreadfully boring when one has to stare out a windowpane by oneself for hours on end."

"Well," started Gilbert. Inside, his discomfort struggled against years of training in etiquette and civility. Then Gilbert remembered Herb's disparaging comment about priests. It would give the guy a huge shock, he thought, to wake up sitting beside a cleric of the religion most hated by the world's rationalists. "Sure," Gilbert said with a sly smile, "have a seat. My name's Gilbert. Now that you mention it, the company would be nice. Especially since my friend's fallen asleep."

"A good thing to get, where we're going," said the priest as he sat down, keeping his voice to a whisper for Herb's sake. "Sleep is a luxury that not all can afford these days."

"What do you mean?" asked Gilbert. Sleep was free, after all, and you could do it most anywhere.

"Sleeping is something done to renew oneself. But for the many who work long days in the factories, sleep is only an escape, a way to pretend for a few fleeting hours that there isn't an Overseer at your heels. Would you agree?"

Gilbert looked at the little man again. He was no more than five feet tall, with a florid, moon-shaped face that was at least sixty years old. Gilbert instinctively knew he was bald beneath the wide-brimmed black hat.

"You know, Father, come to think of it, you're right. I've been working in a factory room myself for the last eight months. Most of the time, sleep was something I just did between shifts, right after and before eating. I'm surprised you know much about that."

"Indeed!" said the little priest. "And why is that?"

"Where I'm from, priests are known much more for grabbing money out of the parishioners' purses than for their fourteen-hour work days."

"Really? And where was this where-I'm-from, exactly?"

"Minnesota," said Gilbert. "There, if you were a papist, you were treated suspiciously, at least in our town."

"Such a pity," said the priest. "Those who know the least about the Church seem to be the ones who fault it the most. I've had my share of eighteen-, twenty-, and seventy-two-hour days in service to the Holy Father."

"No kidding? How do you know about life in a factory?"

"The same way you do, young man. Although I suspect you know less than you think, having worked at a punchcard machine instead of an engine or on an assembly line."

Gilbert started. " 'Scuse me?" he said. How had this guy figured out what Gilbert did — or used to do — for a living?

"I can tell your profession," the priest said, wiping his nose discreetly with a handkerchief, "from the machine oil that's soiled your fingers, but not your face or clothes. Only clackers have that kind of oil pattern on them. Much of my work in the last few years has been with workers that the industrial revolution has chewed up in its gears and spit back into the slums."

"Amputees?"

"Yes," said the priest quickly. "I've learned more than many care to learn about what life has become for workers in the bowels of a factory. At least once a week in my parish, a man loses a hand or a foot in the maw of a piston, a shredder, or punchpress. I minister to their needs as best I can, as I've been asked to by my . . . *order*, within the Church."

"So, you teach them a few Hail Marys and send them on their way?"

"No," replied the priest, "unless they'd benefit from that. I first try to find them relief, and work they can do even in their crippled states. Then I minister to their spiritual needs as I might. But when a man has lost his job because a machine has just eaten his right hand, the last thing he wants is to hear how his pain is part of God's great plan. No matter how true that may be."

"I should say," mumbled Herb. He'd been listening to the conversation for some time, while pretending to be asleep. "Religion doesn't do much more than keep poor blokes like that quiet so the mucky-mucks on top can keep their high places. Much like the high place you've got now over the rabble and the mids here on the train."

"Young man, there are those who misuse religion, true. But blaming religion itself is quite the wrongheaded approach. Do we blame steam power when a child is scalded by her mother's tea? True religion makes man a noble creature, and gives people like me the strength to do our jobs when people like the amputees lose theirs. And, in all fairness, I had a ticket for the lows, as you call them. I was offered this seat by a friend who is a porter here, and felt it would be . . . *right* to take the seat, this time."

Herb looked at the priest for a moment and realized he would not get anywhere in an argument. "I should think," he said, rising quickly, "that a train like this deserves a once-over before we commit ourselves to sleeping or talking our journey away. What say you, Gilbert?"

Gilbert looked at the priest. Although the little man's mouth was straight, his eyes danced cheerfully. "I'll be here later, young Gilbert. By the by, my name is Father Brown." Gilbert shook the priest's hand gravely, but Herb had already begun walking away. "And mind who your friends are, Gilbert. They can lead you places you'd not expect. Or you could do the same."

Gilbert smiled oddly, and followed Herb through to the next car.

Edgar had emptied his flask only a quarter-hour ago, but it seemed an eternity to him, and he'd begun sweating as the train neared the long stretch of track. As soon as they'd rounded the little hill he'd come to know so well, Edgar turned the small dial on the analytical engine that was attached to his steam boiler and steerage apparatus. With well-practiced surety, Edgar stood up and launched himself at the exit door of the engine car. Although he was normally suspicious of the analytical engine, Edgar was more than willing to suspend his doubts if the machine was willing to watch the train for five minutes while he quaffed a quick drink and filled his flask.

Unfortunately, on this occasion, he was so focused on the pleasures he thought awaited him in the club car that he didn't notice a stray loop dangling from his blue overalls. Nor did he notice as it caught on a punchcard that protruded from the dark box that housed the analytical engine. The card was partially yanked from the box and torn, its fragments blowing away into the gasps of wind that tore between the engine car and the passenger portion of the train. Edgar exited the car, and behind him the analytical engine dutifully opened and closed valves, pushed and pulled levers, and propelled the train down the long stretch of track toward its destination.

Eight

"The Bible tells us to love our neighbors, and also to love our enemies; probably because they are generally the same people." — GKC

Stupid old sods. And those useless old goats from the Church of Rome are the worst of the lot."

Gilbert was taken aback a little at Herb's forcefulness. "You mean priests? What's so bad about them? That guy back there seemed decent enough."

"Look, Gil," said Herb, turning around in the aisle suddenly, "don't ever let yourself be fooled. Religion's got just one purpose in this world. It keeps all the unwashed masses in line. It's only those who see through it that end up making a difference at all. Got it?"

Gilbert sidestepped a grunting, portly man moving intently in the opposite direction. "So, Herb, you're saying that religion is just a big conspiracy? That priest didn't look like he had that kind of agenda on his mind."

They reached the end of the car. Herb pulled the door open firmly, and they passed into what appeared to be the dining car. Gilbert could hear milling conversation over the sounds of clinking glasses. Clouds of smoke stung his eyes, and the small windows admitted little sunlight. Instead, everything in the car was overlit by a crimson gas lamp overhead. Two slender men stumbled out of the car past the boys, roughly shoving Gilbert and Herb out of the way as they staggered down the aisle. The men were obviously drunk, their arms draped around each other's shoulders, singing a song to which only they seemed to know the lyrics and tune. One wore a dark bowler hat, and between the verses he squeezed out the words, "They are coming, they are coming, they are comingggggggggg . . ." in a voice slurred by drink and high spirits.

"Here," said Herb after the men had passed, "let's take a seat. There, that's better. Comfy, eh?" Gilbert actually found the hard wooden barstools pretty *un*comfortable, but he wasn't going to let Herb know it. "*That* little fellow back there," continued Herb once they were seated, "was from the Church of Rome. And that lot all come in exactly two varieties. First, you've got your useful idiots. They're nice enough usually, because they actually *believe* the lies they're telling. Next, you've got the kind that knows it's all a lot of bosh, but stick with it because it beats being a blacksmith, a writer, or doing some other kind of real work."

"Herb, you're being unfair. Father Brown doesn't look like he's a liar. And he doesn't seem like an idiot, either. He picked up right away that I was a clacker, just by looking at me. Not everyone can do that, you know."

"Doesn't take any real load of talent to figure out what a man does for a living, Gil. You're not built like a blacksmith or a steam monkey."

"So, Herb, if I've got you right," said Gilbert, only half-playfully, "you're a member of the master race who couldn't lay a single punch on a Chinaman half your size. And you're also smarter than the priest two cars down, even though he told me what my job was *more* specifically and in less than *half* the time you did."

"Have you got a point, Gil?"

"Yep. You've just proven you're a worse fighter than someone from an 'inferior' race, and you're only half as quick and clever as someone you call a useful idiot."

Herb stared, and a dark and angry look passed over his face. For a moment a shot of scare went through Gilbert. The look disappeared, and Herb smiled, nodding his head slowly.

"*Touché*, my friend," he said. "You score another point. That means I buy you a drink. Barkeep!"

Before Gil could protest, Herb had verbally yanked the bartender over to their seats. Herb barked something in cockney English that Gil couldn't make out over the din of the many conversations in the bar car. Within seconds, there was a clear glass of fizzy, brown liquid in front of each of them.

"A little taste of home, for the Yanks, eh, Gil?" said Herb, downing most of the glass in one gulp. Gilbert sipped the drink, and tasted a hint of vanilla mixed with what tasted like his mother's sugar coffee, only colder and with so many fizzy bubbles in it that he couldn't drink it as quickly as Herb did.

"This is good!" said Gilbert, surprised.

"Vanilla cola," said Herb. "They'd probably serve me liquor if I asked, but why make trouble? This is your first time drinking it? I thought you Yanks had this stuff coming out of your taps at home."

"I've heard of it," said Gilbert, "but I've had it only a few times. And never with vanilla in it! Thanks, Herb. How much do I owe you?"

"Skip it," said Herb. "They overcharge you dreadfully for everything on the train, but I can always claim it as an expense later. You can buy next time. You *do* have an expense card, don't you?"

"Oh, of course, of course," said Gilbert, trying to look confident. After a few seconds, he looked around nervously. Then at his drink. Then at his feet.

Herb paused while a large man in blue overalls who smelled of coal moved past them, plunked down in his seat, and ordered something in a dialect neither boy could understand. "You've no idea what I'm talking about, do you," said Herb. It was a statement, not a question.

"Nope," said Gilbert without missing a beat. "I've barely got any idea how to write and file a story, let alone how to keep an expense account."

"Okay, Gil, let's see that folder of yours your boss gave you."

Gilbert slid the folder out of his satchel and handed it to Herb, who immediately began rifling through it. "No," Herb said, walking through several pieces of paper with his fingers, "No, no, no, not that one either . . . ah, here it is!" He pulled out a punchcard and held it under Gilbert's nose.

The card looked like any of the thousands that Gilbert had worked with during his time in the clacker room. It was about the size of a man's hand, three inches wide and five inches long. There were a series of holes across its surface in neat rows, each circle varying in size from a sixteenth to a quarter of an inch. Seen with the naked eye, the card was a jumble of fifteen to twenty rows of holes in an insignificant paper card. Placed into an analytical engine, the machine would drop a series of pins into the holes. The pattern of pins touching a metal plate beneath the card would send a series of coded instructions to the rest of the machine.

Punchcards were now used in virtually every industry and profession in the British Empire, directing engines in tasks as mundane as weaving clothes or as complex as searching criminal archives. There was talk in Parliament of increasing funding for research into a kind of super-engine, one that could store and display information on every resident of the Empire, each citizen being given a number that would be theirs for life, and all information being at her Majesty's beck and call for the rest of the Empire's days.

Gilbert could read the information on the card and knew it was useful, but it was useless to him until he learned exactly what an expense account was.

"See," continued Herb, "they don't mark it as an expense account, so's that if anyone nicks your folder, they won't know what they've got or how to use it. Now this row, up here," Herb's fingers traced the third row, crosswise across the card's face, "when you give this to a hotel clerk, he runs your card through the miniature engine at his desk. It clacks out how much money your employer's given you for food, rooms, tea, and the like. Each time you use it, they punch another hole in it, to show the change in your *balance* — how much money you have in the bank now. When your card goes through their engine, it punches your card for the amount and clacks out a bill for your company's bank to pay, out of the money your employer has set aside for you. Looking at this, I'd say you've got . . ." Herb looked at the line of dots, and his brow furled. He looked closer, and his eyes widened.

"What?" asked Gilbert. "Is something wrong?"

"Can you read these, Gil? There must be a mistake. It's got too many small dots here."

Gilbert's interest peaked. On a clacker card, the smallest dots were usually reserved for zeroes. On the row that Herb said covered his expense account, there were three small dots next to a number of larger ones.

The average servant in imperial Britain received an average annual salary of five pounds a year.

The standard dowry from a well-to-do family to a young man who married one of its daughters was an annual pension of one hundred pounds.

A Member of Parliament could expect to receive the princely sum of perhaps two hundred pounds a year as compensation from her Majesty for the service that he rendered to the queen's loyal subjects.

If Gilbert was reading the card correctly, he'd been granted an expense account of at least one thousand pounds.

Nine

"Modern broad-mindedness benefits the rich; and
benefits nobody else." — GKC

W hat d'you mean you don't want to let the barman check it? Are you
mad?" Herb's eyes had gone an interesting shade of gray and black
when Gilbert had told him the news of his sudden good fortune. "At least
find out if you've got the money we think you do! And if you do, skip town!
You're a rich man, Gil! Buy a house in the West End of London, and a factory in the East end to go with it! Act quickly, before someone realizes
what's happened!"

"No," said Gilbert, inhaling deeply, silently repeating his father's admo-
nitions to stop himself when he felt his emotions about to carry him away.
"No, I'm trying to stay calm here. It wouldn't matter, anyway."

"What in blazes are you —" began Herb loudly. At a sign from Gilbert,
he brought his voice to a quick and almost angry whisper, leaning close to
Gilbert to make up with nearness what he'd lose in volume. He needn't
have bothered; the only person who'd showed the slightest interest was the
blue-overalled man, but he quickly directed his attention back to the second small glass of clear liquid that he was about to gulp down.

"What in blazes are you saying, Gil? Don't you realize that you're sitting
on a gold mine? A thousand pounds! That's a fortune! If it's even a tenth of
that, you can go back to America in pure flash style!"

"Herb," began Gilbert, trying to keep his own voice even, "I know you
may not believe this, but I'm just as excited as you are right now. But I don't
need the barman to check this card to be certain. I'm a clacker, remember? I

can read this card like it was a page of the dictionary. And the holepunch code for one thousand pounds is clearly stated here." He used his fingertip to trace an invisible line beneath a row of holes that were slightly less intelligible to Herb than Chinese picture writing.

"And if it *is* a thousand pounds in my pocket, the last thing I want to do is let a trainful of people know I've got that kind of money on me. As soon as the barkeep ran the numbers on this punchcard, the word'd be out faster'n a jackrabbit with a bellyful o'coffee. I'm surprised you didn't think of that, you being so streetwise and all."

Herb started to speak again, but Gilbert held up his hand and closed his eyes firmly.

"No, Herb, I'm gonna sit on this until we get to Woking, do my job, and then get back to London. Some poor guy in the clacker room added too many zeroes on my card, and I don't intend to get him in trouble. Even," he added to himself grimly, "if the fellow who did it was that annoying twerp Oliver."

Herb looked at the spectacled eyes of the skinny teenager in front of him with a mix of admiration and disbelief. "You really are a special thing, aren't you, Gil? In my job, you tend to see the worst of people. Truth is, I'd been getting pretty cynical about the whole human race. I like to think of myself as pretty cool-headed, but one look at all that flash and I was ready to . . . well, who knows what? But seeing you sit on a fortune like that, being honest just because you may get someone in trouble that you don't even know, well, there's hope for us yet, I'd say. There's just one thing I think you're lacking."

"What's that?"

"I think, Gil, that you've just about got yourself a perfect life at this moment. I mean, sure, it's tough being an orphan and all, but right now, you've got a good job, a pile of money, and a chap like me for a chum. All you need now is the perfect lady friend and your life'd be smashing."

Gilbert smiled bashfully. "That's nice, Herb, but I guess you haven't looked too closely at me. I'm so skinny, if I wear a tie and turn sideways I look like a zipper. And I'm so tall that girls stare me straight in the throat. I've gotta put in twelve-hour days to make ends meet, and even though I'm technically a journalist now, I still dress like a poor clacker. Pretty women don't exactly line up to meet guys like me, you know?"

"Ah, Gil," Herb said, tousling his friend's hair. "Now I see why the hand of fate reached out and pushed me in your direction. You need the warm embrace and acceptance of a young lady's heart. Listen: looks don't always matter, Gil. A handsome appearance can get your foot in the door, but it won't get you into the parlor room. There's lots of pretty boys out there who'll never have a chance at the kind of girl we all long for, because they don't have what it takes."

"And just what *does* it take?" Gilbert was only half-joking. Even before his family had been lost, Gilbert went on, he had always found girls a mystery. What to say, when to say it, how to keep them from laughing at you when you were trying to have a serious conversation about man's place in the universe.

"You're not serious," Herb replied. "You really tried to interest a girl by talking to her about philosophy?"

"Well, it's something I liked, so why not?"

"Gil, Gil. Most girls don't care what kind of thinker you are. They probably don't even care so much about how you look, or even if you're rich. Remember that little sweet I was chatting up back at the station? The one with the gangster friend?"

Gilbert nodded.

"When she mentioned her beau, I knew just the sort she was talking about." Herb continued. "The bloke looks like something you'd scrape off your shoe in a garbage dump. But he's got the one thing that most women in the world want. More than anything, women are attracted to men who have one thing, and aren't afraid to use it."

"What's that?" Gilbert asked, serious now.

"The whole thing isn't their fault, really. Gil, the one thing women want more than anything is a man with *power*."

"Power? As in windmills turning and steam in factories?"

"No, Gil. I mean the ability to make things happen. Maybe people do what you say because you can beat them up, or because you're a smooth talker, or because you're all flash with tin in your pocket. Whatever it is, women want you only if you can make things happen. Period."

"So, if you have power, the women come to you?"

"Naw, Gil! That's what comes next: you learn how to charm 'em. Look," said Herb, leaning in and acting as if he were sharing a precious secret that only a privileged few in the world were allowed to know or possess, "the easiest thing to do is go up to one you like, and act like you've known 'em from someplace before. Now, if you were to see a young lass . . ." Herb paused for a second, then continued talking in a much softer voice while looking past Gilbert, ". . . with hair so red it makes you think of a Welsh sunset, and skin white as a newborn dove. A woman who sports the poise and grace of a royal family member out for an afternoon tea with a head of state."

Gilbert paused after Herb's speech drifted to a stop. "You've narrowed it down quite a bit, don't you think?" When Herb didn't answer, Gilbert turned around and saw the new object of Herb's devotion.

It was easy to see why Herb had gotten so distracted. The girl was quite beautiful. She was seated facing them at a small booth, talking to the man in the dark cloak who had sat near them earlier in the train car. Something about her seemed quite familiar, and then suddenly Gilbert had it.

"I know her," Gilbert said in quiet disbelief.

Herb didn't seem the least curious about how that could be. "I'm going to introduce myself," he said, with a voice that told Gilbert he'd have had a better chance at stopping Odysseus from listening to the sirens than keeping Herb from approaching her.

"Herb, do you really think that's a smart thing to do?" he asked nonetheless.

"Do I care?" answered Herb absently, still staring at the red-haired girl. "And by the by, while we're here, call me George. It's my middle name, and it sounds more dashing."

Gilbert watched sullenly as Herb/George drifted away from the table, oblivious to everything except the face of the red-haired girl in the booth. Herb seemed smooth. He walked past both the girl and the fellow in the hat whom she was talking to, appearing not to notice either of them at first. Then he stopped briefly, giving the girl a second look as if he'd seen her before.

Growing up, Gilbert had often watched the older, popular boys, trying hard to pick up their cues, to see exactly what it was that made their company desirable. He himself seemed to have few desirable qualities. He was bad at sports, seldom had a funny quip or insult up his sleeve, and felt awkward and ungainly around strangers. Not many people in the political jungles of the schoolyard much valued his talents for reading, writing, and debating, and he'd had to muddle through the social challenges of teen life as best he could.

Herb, though, seemed like the kind of person who'd had no trouble socially with anyone since the day he was born. He approached the girl's table and soon was smiling and chatting up its occupants as if he'd known them for years, although it seemed — Gilbert couldn't see their faces too well — that the cloaked fellow resented his presence, and the redhead looked as if she was forcing herself to be polite. Herb kept trying to be invited to join them, without success.

Gilbert sipped his cola slowly, listening to the steady thrumming of the rails beneath him. The car itself had grown quiet. All the men had stopped drinking or talking, and were trying hard not to look at the redhead's table. The few women in the club car were staring silently into their glasses.

Herb's flirting with the redhead had put her companion in a dark mood, and that mood seemed to infect everyone else in the car. Indeed, the only person besides Herb who seemed completely unaffected was the man in blue overalls, greedily gulping down a small glass of something.

Gilbert looked again at Herb, who was blithely chatting about how badly Americans made tea. Finally, the dark-whiskered man traveling with her looked up and spoke.

"Look, young fellow," the older man said, "I'm having a conversation here with my traveling companion, a conversation that is quite urgent and necessarily private. So if you'd like to make conversation with either of us, it would be much more welcome on the return trip." The words were polite, but they had an edge to them. They reminded Gilbert of the times his mother had said she wasn't going to get angry, but everyone in earshot knew she was a hair's breadth from inflicting major punishments on anyone within range.

Time seemed to stand still for Gilbert as his friend and the whiskered man stared at each other. The silence was broken by the blue-overalled man getting up slowly from his barstool. The large engineer had gone very pale, wheezing deeply, flexing his left arm and opening and closing his left hand repeatedly. Had Gilbert turned to look, he would have also seen that the engineer had finished no fewer than four small glasses of liquor.

Herb had paused at the whiskered man's words. But a second later, he regained his confidence. "Right, squire, no problem," he said, louder than he needed to. "I understand. A little conversation with your *friend*" — he winked — "and you don't want some yob bothering you. I'll take my leave forthwith, now, but in the future, if you should wish to entertain the notion of accompanying me to . . ."

Herb never finished his sentence. The train suddenly entered a tunnel, and all felt a slight disorientation as the lights dimmed. Even so, Gilbert could see clearly the silhouette of Edgar Alberecht the engineer as he fell slowly to one knee, gasped for breath, and then slumped sideways to the floor.

Alarmed and confused, Gilbert rose from his chair and tried to feel his way to the prone body of the engineer. By the time he reached the body on the floor, the lights had returned and a small crowd of four or five people had gathered.

Gilbert nudged past a couple of onlookers who seemed too scared to do more than stare, knelt on the carpet, and turned the fallen man over onto his back. The engineer's eyes were closed, his skin pale and slick with sweat, and his breathing came in short, shallow sucks of air.

"Here now, what's happenin' here?" barked a stern voice behind them. Gilbert looked over his shoulder and saw the barkeep who'd served him his cola. He was standing over Gilbert with an accusatory expression on his face.

"Nothing! He . . . was walking away from the bar, and he dropped to the floor. I think he's had a heart attack." Gilbert had seen a neighbor like this once years ago, who'd dropped at his plow while Gilbert's family was over for a visit. Gilbert's mother had given some kind of aid to the fellow, and maybe saved his life. Now, what was it?

"Blimey! If Ed's down there, then 'oo's gonna drive the train when we reach the 'ill?"

"What hill? What're you on about?" Herb asked, stepping up behind Gilbert. "The land's flat as a mirror out here."

"Thass *Ed*!" repeated the barkeep with rising urgency, pointing at the body on the floor. "The *engineer*! I served 'im a few to get 'im through the trip. But if 'e's on the floor, there's no one to take the 'elm of the train! Once we're in Surrey, we'll hit a hill curve where we join with another track, and no one's hand to steer or slow us down!"

There was a short, awkward pause. People hung their heads or looked at each other quietly.

Gilbert looked at the prone body of the engineer and took a deep, slow breath. His father had once told him, during a long walk on the dirt road into town, that the lives of most people are mostly determined in two ways: through the little decisions that add up over time, and by the large single choices that can change things forever in an instant. But then there were other choices, nexus points in the map of life that didn't seem crucial at the time, their importance only visible in hindsight. Too many men, he'd said, lay awake at nights regretting the times when they'd had a chance to act, but didn't, because they were afraid. They didn't learn until later how great would be the consequences of their cowardice.

Gilbert's father was unwilling at the time to speak of any such choices he'd made in his own life. "Someday," he'd said, "someday when you're old enough. But not before."

That was then. Right now, Gilbert's fears said the best thing to do would be to run and brace himself for the impact when the driverless train jumped the rails.

But an insistent little thought inside him said life wouldn't be worth living if he could have saved someone and didn't.

Gilbert looked around, but no one else was offering to help. He tried cupping his hands on the man's chest as he'd seen his mother do years ago to their neighbor. He pressed down rhythmically, once a second.

"Is there a doctor anywhere?" Gilbert said while trying to convince the man's heart to beat again. In between thrusts, he looked plaintively at the faces in the club-car booths, none of which seemed inclined to help him. "Please, this man's had a heart attack or something! Please . . . somebody!"

"I can help him," said a soft voice near Gilbert. He turned and saw the girl with the red hair kneeling down next to him. She deftly moved Gilbert aside and began pressing the man's chest more vigorously than Gilbert had, whispering numbers under her breath as she did so.

"You're . . . you're . . ." sputtered Gilbert, trying to speak around the very large thing his tongue had become. He could smell the scent of lilacs on her.

"A doctor? Not quite. But I can help here. Give me your jacket, please."

"You're a nurse, then?" Gilbert said, removing his jacket while still kneeling. He looked closely at her face for the first time. She didn't seem any older than he, really.

"I am educated in the healing profession, enough to know how to care for this man. Now, I'm going to bunch this up under his head, like this." She twisted Gilbert's cheap work jacket until it looked like a giant homemade cigar, and slid it under the man's neck. "That should keep his airway clear, so he'll avoid choking or anything equally unpleasant. Here, hold him steady." She took Gilbert's hands — causing his heart to do a happy little flip-flop — and placed them on each side of the man's head.

She pressed the engineer's chest with folded hands several more times and then quickly felt his wrist. "I've lost his pulse," she said, an edge of desperation creeping into her voice. Just then, a pair of black shoes attached to a dark pair of pants appeared quietly behind her. A white-tipped walking stick nudged the heel of her brown ladies' boot. She looked over her shoulder, grabbed the stick away from its owner and began to fiddle with it.

"What're you going to do with that?" Gilbert asked.

"Move your hands away! Get clear of his body!" she ordered suddenly. Gilbert jerked his hands back, and the small ring of people around them followed, moving back a step or two.

"Look! Out the window!" said a deep voice with excitement and authority. All eyes swiveled to the small window that had just opened in the darkened club car. All eyes but Gilbert's. His attentions were still riveted to Red Hair and her every action.

Gilbert's eyes soon goggled almost through the lenses of his glasses. The white-tipped head of the cane slid back at her touch, revealing several small metal rods and nodes. What looked like little blue threads danced and crackled between two of the tiny metal filaments, and Gilbert almost leapt backward in surprise. Outside of a storm, Gilbert had never seen raw electricity in action before!

"Whoa!" he said, leaning back and bringing up his hands. The red-haired girl pulled open the top buttons of the engineer's shirt, held the rod up to her face, tested it by making the rod's tip spark several times, and touched the tip to the engineer's chest.

At the rod's touch, the engineer's body jerked upward suddenly, as if it had been kicked from beneath the floor. At this, Gilbert *did* leap backward. What the blazes was going on?

She checked the engineer's pulse again, this time by holding two fingers to his neck. She closed her eyes and sighed with relief.

"Is he going to be all right?" Gilbert asked her while she checked and prodded various parts of the engineer's body.

"I believe he shall. His pulse has returned. But I fear he will not be conscious enough to drive a train before we jump the rails."

There was a pause while she checked several other points on the unconscious man's body. "I know you," Gilbert said to her suddenly.

"We may have met," she replied. "We live in a shrinking world. But this gentleman, here, needs more attention."

The fallen man suddenly inhaled deeply, his eyelids fluttering as he regained consciousness. The man undoubtedly needed attention, but Gilbert couldn't shake the feeling that the girl was more interested in distracting him.

"It was in the office," Gilbert said quietly. "I saw you, right before I went to see the Undersecretary and got this assignment. You were coming out of the office after I'd been told to go up there from the clacking room. Did you have anything to do with my promotion, Miss?"

"I can't say that I know what you're talking about," she said without looking at Gilbert, holding the back of her hand to the engineer's head, then putting the back of her hand on his forehead, and then holding his wrist and counting silently under her breath.

"What, what . . ." the man muttered, his voice sounding as if he were trying to speak through a foot of cotton batting, "Whahuppin?"

"You've had an attack of some kind, but you're quite safe now," the girl said. Gilbert noticed that when she talked, her head would bob slightly, and her bright, red hair and deep blue eyes would catch the light in a way that Gilbert would never quite forget. Then she stood and smoothed out her skirt. Gilbert stood, too, and noticed that the man who'd passed the walking stick to her was no longer behind her.

"Where's your friend?" asked Gilbert.

"What friend?" she asked as her face swung to look at him, suddenly blank as an unpunched card.

"The one who passed you the Franklin rod from under his coat."

"Pardon me?" she said, her eyes a pair of bright blue question marks.

"Miss," he said, "I may be fairly new in your town, but I'm not such a hayseed that I let myself get distracted when someone says to look out the window. For some reason, that fella didn't want anyone to see you revive the engineer, so he called everyone's attention to the window before you zapped him."

"I really have to say that I think this man has been quite lucky, and come out of an attack of the heart of some kind. Perhaps the pressure you applied earlier . . ."

Gilbert felt hot, but it was more the frustration than anything else now. "Pressure my foot! 'Scuse me, but back home in America, they call those electrical things Franklin rods, after Ben Franklin, the guy who first harnessed the stuff. Here in England, they call them something different — Shocking Nancys, or something like that."

She looked at Gilbert with a mixture of fear and surprise, and then some admiration. "You have a wonderful imagination, Mister . . ."

"Chesterton," said Gilbert. "But my friends call me Gil."

They both paused for a moment, and Gilbert was suddenly struck by the notion that he had met her somewhere, even before he saw her rushing out of Mister Effortson's office. Then the engineer sounded a groan from the floor, breaking the spell.

"Lie still a second, mister," said Gilbert, going down beside him on one knee. "You'll be all right, but you're going to have a heck of a chest ache for a while, and you might feel quite a bit thirsty, too. It's lucky for you that Miss . . . just what was your name, miss?" asked Gilbert, looking up suddenly.

She was gone. The door to the club car was sliding shut behind her. Gilbert stared at it with an open mouth.

How'd she do that?

"This is all well and good," said the barman, happy enough to see one of his regular customers alive once more, "but we still need to know: *'Oo's gonna drive the bloomin' train?*"

"Isn't there something you could do?" Gilbert asked. "Don't you have some emergency procedure to follow?"

"Not since they started with them black boxes in the engine car. They was s'posed to fix everything, but," the barman looked at the window, "we look like we're just goin' faster!"

Something the barman said tickled the back of Gilbert's mind. Black boxes? Gilbert brought his mouth close to the engineer's ear.

"Excuse me, mister." He spoke in a near-whisper, not wanting to upset the man into another attack. "Excuse me, but . . . could you drive the train?"

"The engine . . ." he responded, still muttering thickly. "The automated engine . . ."

"Automated?" said Gilbert slowly, trying to draw out more information. The engineer was still speaking in bits and snatches, his words punctuated by gasps for air.

"The . . . black box . . . [wheeze] punchcard can't drive [wheeze] around the curve . . ."

"Punchcard box?" Gilbert said, a tinge of fear creeping in his voice.

"Aw, no!" it was the barman again. "Ed's put the train on the automated driver again! It's not meant to drive the thing for more than a few minutes at a time! When we hit the curve at the hills, we'll . . ."

"I know, I know," jumped in Herb, "we'll jump the rails. Gil, can you help out here? He said something about a punchcard."

"I can take a look at it, but I can't promise anything, Herb. I've never even heard of a . . ."

"Right, let's move!" Herb ran for the exit door before Gilbert had finished his sentence. "C'mon, Gil! Move! Time's of the essence!"

"But Herb . . ."

"Gil, don't argue! My . . . I mean, hundreds of lives are at stake here!"

"Herb, I . . ."

"Will you come *on*! What's keeping you?"

"*HERB!*"

"*WHAT?*"

Gilbert pointed at the opposite end of the car.

"The engine car is *that* way, Herb."

Herb paused for less than a second, and ran through the crowd of clubgoers. "Then why didn't you run instead of arguing with me?" barked Herb. "C'mon, Gil, hop to it!"

Ten

"It is not bigotry to be certain we are right; but it is bigotry to be unable to imagine how we might possibly have gone wrong." — GKC

Herb and Gilbert raced through the train, the afternoon sun stinging their eyes and the wind boxing their ears each time they passed from one car to the next. Herb barreled past anyone unlucky enough to be in their path, while Gilbert followed, offering hurried apologies. He also struggled to maintain his equilibrium, running headlong at three stories above the ground. *Who had the crazy idea of calling this thing a train?* Gilbert thought to himself. *It's more like an ocean liner on wheels.*

Gilbert was just saying "excuse me" to the fourth or fifth person when he ran smack into Herb's suddenly stationary shoulder blades. He looked up to see the porter who had slapped Herb's best punches aside standing in front of them with a smile on his face, but the slightest hint of fear in his eyes.

"Can I help you again, sirs?" he asked, struggling to keep his balance as the train gave a slight lurch.

"Yes, we've got a big problem!" Herb piped up. "The engineer just had a heart attack in the club car and the train is speeding up and we're going to jump the tracks and die if my friend here can't take a look in the engine car!" Then he seemed to regain a measure of calm (or pride), and added in a voice one octave lower, "So be a good chap, would you, and let us pass?"

But Herb had said the words "jump the tracks" loud enough for every passenger in the car to hear him. A frantic buzzing and tittering began as women fainted, men caught the fainting women, girls began crying, and one boy began bouncing and squealing excitedly in his seat.

"Better calm down the passengers, Chinaman," said Herb, now wearing a smirk. "We'll slip by in the confusion, and my friend here can save the day. Unless you or someone else knows how to run this tub?"

"The porters aren't trained to drive or stop the train, sir. The black box is supposed to control and protect —" The train gave another lurch, bringing a fresh wave of cries from the passengers. "You can fix this?" he asked, looking at Gilbert.

"I think so," Gilbert said, struggling as a bump beneath the tracks caused another lurch and another wave of shrieks. "I can try at least."

"Go, then. I will calm the passengers."

The porter's hand darted down to the beads at his waist as he began speaking in a loud voice. Gilbert and Herb ran to the door while steadying themselves by holding on to the seats at their sides.

When they tramped through a set of car doors for the fourth time, Gilbert smelled the harsh scent of coal, felt a glow of warmth, and saw the dull glow of sunlight on the dirty, velvet-lined walls. An iron furnace against the far wall glowed orange and red behind a grating that looked like a set of clenched black teeth. An automated, steam-driven shovel whirred and hissed as it periodically fed pieces of coal into the furnace, its top opening briefly and bathing the room in hot red light just before snapping and locking itself shut again. To their left, a half-moon-shaped speedometer sat on an ornate brass pole that came up to their waist. Between the pole and the furnace was a very comfortable-looking chair with levers and minute gears to allow the driver to adjust his position. The chair sat near a set of levers, a panel of switches, and a squat black box from which a number of thin metal pipes sprouted, running into several irregular points in the wall and even into the cooler base portion of the furnace itself.

"This must be the place!" yelled Herb.

"Yes," Gilbert yelled back over the roars of the engine and the wind, "but where's this automated engine driver they were talking about?"

"Could this be it?" said Herb, kneeling next to the small black box made of thick wood.

"Yes, I think you're . . . oh, no," said Gilbert, his voice dropping from a shout to a whisper. There was a small slot in its almost featureless dark face where a piece of torn paper stuck out at the boys like a ragged tongue.

"Is that bad?" asked Herb.

"Yep!" said Gilbert, his eyes widening. "If I can't get a punchcard in there, then there's no way we could slow this thing down, even if the engineer were fit as a fiddle. We've gotta get this card out, or else we can't get any new instructions to the train."

"What can we do, Gil?"

Gilbert looked and quickly found the dial that shut off power to most of the functions on the analytical engine. The box was larger than most of the analytical engines he'd worked on as a clacker, but there were enough similarities to make Gilbert think he could operate it. "There. Okay, Herb, now that the power's off, I'm going to look for a kit on this thing. You try to pry that paper outta there."

"A kit?"

"No time to explain! Just trust me, Herb, all right?"

Gilbert went down on both knees and began tugging around the corners of the analytical engine in front of him, while Herb tried fruitlessly to grip the remains of the card with his blunt fingernails. After a few seconds, Gilbert began running his fingers excitedly in straight lines over the featureless side of the box that was closest to the train engine's furnace. Gilbert nodded to himself, then stood back and pushed the end of the black box closest to the floor with the fingertips of both his hands. A small drawer popped out with a springing sound from the black box's insides. Gilbert could hear the click and whirrs of gears and rods of the engine's innards as it tried to follow the instructions on its last, damaged punchcard.

Gilbert whooped triumphantly, pulling a drawer from the black box's lower end. Inside was a smaller, gray box, from which metal rattling noises came when Gilbert opened it.

"How'd you find *that*?" yelled Herb over a loud gust of wind.

"It's a toolbox, Herb. For clackers like me. They hide it inside so folks like you won't go mucking around with it. Here, hold it for a second."

Carefully, Gilbert pulled the lid on the black cover to reveal more of the analytical engine's insides. Herb looked over Gilbert's shoulder at the most complicated array of metal rods, pistons, switches, and whatnots he'd ever seen in one place in his life. How the devil did Gil make sense of something like that?

"Okay, Herb. Gimme the box."

Herb handed it over. "What are you going to do, Gil?"

"Hang on!"

Gilbert carefully pulled out a hand-held hole-puncher and a blank card.

"Herb, did you get the card out?"

"No, it's jammed in too tight. I could shred it or maybe burn it . . ."

"No! I need it to know what instructions were printed on it. Wait, hold these."

Gilbert hastily handed the card and hole-puncher to Herb, and ducked down to peer into the automated pilot engine.

"Gil, I don't want to pressure you, but I think . . ."

"Just a second!"

At that moment, Gilbert called on everything he had learned from his months in the cardroom. *Don't let fear run you*, his father had once told him. *Fear is great when you're running from a bear or a cougar, but that's because it kills your mind. When you need your mind, tell your fear to wait in line 'til after you're safe.*

It made sense now.

"Gil!"

"Almost!"

Gilbert looked inside. Good thing they were near an open furnace! There was just enough light to recognize the rods, levers, gears, and valves of the kind of machine he'd learned to work with when Philandron had been his Overseer and nemesis. The opening was just large enough for Gilbert to reach into with his fingers. He began moving parts around inside the analytical engine, talking his actions out to himself while he thought them through. Now . . . the last time Oliver had gotten one of the cards stuck in the machine, he'd popped it open, disconnected one rod here, re-connected it *there*, and . . .

"Gil! Whatever you did, the card's coming out!"

"Yes!" Gilbert whooped for joy. "Give it to me, Herb! Quick!"

"Gil . . ."

Gilbert saw the card held in Herb's hand. It had been nearly completely shredded from its halfway point onward, both from being caught and torn on the engineer's coveralls and from a pin that must have snagged it on the way out of the machine's jaws. There would be no repairing the card. A new one would have to be made.

Gilbert turned and looked at the approaching curve. The hill — built up by steam-driven earthmoving machines — wasn't huge, but had been made big enough to create a banked turn that brought the train around sharply. And, if the barman was right, just past the turn, the track would give way to a switching-junction where several tracks intersected. It was only a few miles away, and ordinarily the train would have begun decelerating to almost crawling speed before reaching it. If it reached the hill at anything near its current velocity, the train would surely derail in a spectacular mess.

Gilbert inhaled, knowing that even at his best, the quickest he'd ever made a card from scratch was in seven minutes.

I can't do it, he thought. *I'm the only person who can save us, and I can't do it, can't do it, can't do it!*

I . . .

Can't . . .

Stop yourself, Gil.

Inhale. Exhale. Fear won't help here. Fear kills your mind. Action cures fear.
Perhaps a second had passed since he'd asked for the card.

"Herb, give it here, I said!"

Herb gave the punchcard with no argument.

Gilbert took another deep breath. On his first day of work in the cardroom, Philandron had shown him the five steps to viable punchcard construction.

The First Step: Know your card's purpose. Here, it was to slow or stop the train. Along one side of the shredded card were a series of punched holes that grew progressively smaller as they moved down the card's side.

Gilbert stared at the analytical engine. A series of cables and tubes grew out of the left and right sides of the black box and intertwined with a number of features in the engine compartment. Gilbert quickly followed the lines of cable and metal tubing that grew to the left, looked out the window . . . Yes!

"Herb, these dots match to those cables going to the furnace, and outside to the wheels. I copy these little dots here onto the fresh card from the toolbox, and we'll slow down at an incremental rate of . . ."

"Gil, remember what I said earlier? About not wanting to pressure you?"

"Sure!"

"I take it back! Look! The hills are coming!"

Gilbert looked and gulped. The face of a green and brown hill loomed at them, along with the curves in the track. In the distance behind the hill they could see a large black water tower.

"Gil, I'm going to start throwing levers here, and see what happens."

"No, Herb! I thought of that, but most of them have been taken out to make way for the analytical engine. What's left isn't even marked. We could end up going even faster, or blow something up! Just give me thirty more seconds."

"Fine. One Piccadilly. Two Piccadilly . . ."

"*Quietly*, Herb!"

Herb was quiet. Gilbert focused.

Step Two: Always have the tools needed. Gilbert took a blank punchcard from the toolbox along with a small ruler, pencil stub, and an adjustable hole-puncher. All he needed. Breathe. Okay, now for . . .

Step Three: Have all necessary information for the task. "Current speed — Herb, what's our current speed?"

"Ah . . ." Herb looked at the ornate brass speedometer. A small red metal arrow had a number of little flares about it that made it look like a shot of flame from a dragon's mouth. "About fifty miles an hour! We're getting closer to the curves in the rails, Gil! That tower's disappeared from view behind the mountain!"

Fifty miles an hour! Back in America, trains that could do only half that speed were spoken about in hushed whispers. "Fifty miles an hour. Got it, Herb!"

While making his calculations, part of Gilbert wanted to wonder why someone would build a water tower so far away from a sizable town. No time for that now, though. He filed the thought away for later.

Step Four: Work quickly, correctly, and confidently. Gilbert scribbled down several calculations on the fresh card. He held the blank and the shredded one against each other to the light, and made several small but deliberate pinpricks with the sharpened pencil point on the blank card's face. Still mumbling to himself, Gilbert adjusted the head of the holepuncher with a small dial on the side of the tool. He checked the head of the puncher quickly with his ruler, and popped a hole in the card at the site of one of his pencil marks.

"Fifteen Piccadilly, Gil!"

"Way ahead of you, Herb!" Gilbert punched nearly a dozen more holes, following the pencil line he'd drawn along the blank card's side. After each punch, he made a slight adjustment to the hole-puncher, making each hole slightly smaller than the last. After the twelfth one, Gilbert prepared to slide the card into the engine's slot.

Step Five: Check your work.

No time for Step Five.

Remembering Father Brown, Gilbert said a quick prayer to anyone who could hear him.

Please let this work. He slid the card in and . . .

The card wouldn't go in. Something was blocking the slot!

"Herb! What did you do to the slot? It's still jammed!"

"I didn't do anything! *You're* the expert on these things, remember? Twenty Piccadilly!"

"I . . ." Gilbert tried to coax the card in twice more, and was just about to mash it against the machine in frustration when his pinky finger brushed a small, nearly invisible dial.

"I am the biggest fool in the universe," Gilbert said, turning the box's dial from the "Unpowered" setting to "Powered." Small gears and machine parts began whirring, and the punchard was pulled through the entry slot by hungry metal teeth on the machine's entry gears.

"Gil . . . is it going to work?"

The train answered Herb by jerking suddenly, although not violently, to a slower speed. The massive train's slowdown was accompanied by the sound of steam escaping to the air and out of the turbines, and the high-pitched squeal of brakes upon metal.

"Gilbert!" yelled Herb. "Gil, you've done it! You've saved the lot of us! Look at the speed!"

Gilbert looked at the dial, as the flame-shaped red arrow began to move slowly from fifty to forty-five, and then forty.

Herb looked quietly at Gilbert for a few very long seconds while the steel wheels of the train continued to groan in protest at their sudden order to slow down. Outside, the flat ground punctuated by the occasional tree gave way on the left side to one of the artificial hills that preceded the switching-junction. Both boys saw the view tilt slightly with the incline, and they held their breath as the powerful engine shuddered and squealed, but stayed planted on the tracks. Soon gravity was doing its work to slow the train further. They were saved.

"Gil, you're a hero!" whooped Herb. "What a story this'll make! You could get a medal! And *I* . . . I could get a knighthood for my journalism when I print this!"

Gilbert sat back, suddenly exhausted.

"Print this? No thanks, Herb. I don't want any word of this to go out in the papers, if it's all the same to you."

"Are you mad?" Herb's eyes suddenly switched from excitement to puzzlement. "This is the second time in an hour that lady luck has dropped a sixteen-ton gold brick of good fortune in front of you, and you're just going to walk away from it? Think, man! Do you know what some would give for the chance I . . . the chance that *we* have here?"

Gilbert flushed red, the stress of the second most insane day of his life finally taking its toll. The train lurched slightly as it rounded the curve of the hill, but Gilbert was giving most of his attention to the changed friend in front of him. "Herb," he said, the barest hint of an edge creeping into his voice, "now *you* listen to *me* for a change! I don't care what you, I, we, or any *other* pronouns have to say about it! My part in this stays quiet, and we're *done* with it, y'see? No more craziness, no more coincidences, no more weird happenings, no more strange red-headed girls shocking people, and no more train drivers dropping on the floor in front of me!"

Herb started to speak, but Gilbert cut him off. "No! No more, Herb! No more! Today my whole life got turned upside down for the second or third time, and I'm *tired* of it, Herb! *No more!* I just want to live a very quiet life for the next little while. Maybe I'll just be asked to cover . . . I don't know, dog shows, or book tours, or exotic zoo animals, or something just as quiet for the next ten years. After we get back and I return this thousand-pound punchcard, I'm going to put every bit of craziness as far away from me as possible! Starting with this! Starting right now!"

Herb didn't respond. Gilbert found the clacker kit he'd used to save the train, and dropped the tools inside it. He snapped its lid shut, stuffed it back into the automated engine driver, and slammed the lid on the black box's compartment. He looked at the large black box with a triumphant feeling, as if, by shutting it, he'd also managed to shut down all the upsetting things that had happened today. *Finally,* thought Gilbert, *I am captain of my fate; I am master of my soul.* He'd just finished the thought when he felt the train slow to a crawl, a slow crawl, and then the slight *bump* and hiss of steam as the train finally stopped all movement and was still on the track.

The train still growled and vibrated from parts unseen, as if angered at its unplanned halting on the track. Gilbert could hear a dim cheering in the background, cheering from the passenger cars behind that quickly rose in pitch until it sounded almost like shrieks.

And it looks as if I am *a hero,* Gilbert thought. He stood up with a satisfied air, and had just turned the handle of the door to the car when he looked at Herb and saw that the expression on his friend's face had changed from one of pleading to one of mute horror.

Herb's eyes were looking over Gilbert's shoulder at something outside the train and farther down the tracks. His eyes were wide with fear, his mouth open and breathing quickly. Herb looked as if he wanted to run, hide, or escape, but fascination held him rooted to where he crouched, holding on to a brass rail.

Although miffed to realize that he hadn't been the one to silence Herb, Gilbert was more than a little interested in seeing what *had* done the miraculous deed. He turned around just in time to see an enormous, pincer-like black pole drop out of the sky and slam into the tracks in front of the halted train. The tracks twisted and broke like a set of licorice whips, while the thick, wooden railway ties snapped like toothpicks.

And then he saw —

Saw —

Saw . . .

Saw a . . . no, that couldn't be . . .

It was the water tower that Gilbert had seen earlier, when he had been struggling to master his panic attack. But water towers . . . no, this couldn't be a water tower!

It was indeed a tower, but unlike anything that Gilbert had ever seen, heard of, or read about. Not even in the penny-dreadfuls that some of his school chums would sneak into class. The black, three-legged mechanical monstrosity that had planted its foot directly in front of the train looked as if it belonged in someone's nightmares, not in the English countryside.

It was at least a hundred feet tall. Its pincer-like legs ended not in a point, but with a flat disc on the ground, attached by a kind of ball-and-socket joint. The legs themselves had many more joints, sockets, and bending-places, reaching all the way up its "body," which looked like a metal hatbox perhaps twenty feet in diameter. The body had large, green, bubble-shaped windows protruding from its surface seemingly at random. And most horribly, hanging from its undercarriage was a mass of writhing black tentacles. They were huge but moved quickly, darting back and forth like eyes looking for something.

"That's . . . that's . . ." a dim part of Gilbert's brain realized that his face probably looked exactly like Herb's had when Gilbert had looked at him a few moment's ago. "That's . . . impossible!" Gilbert finally spit out the word as the tripod's leg nearest them raised itself from the ground, then reared back on a segmented joint like a boy about to punt a football.

"Gil," gasped Herb, trying to snap out of his dreamlike funk as the gigantic leg swung silently at them like a wrecking ball. "Gil, brace yourself . . . I think we're going to . . ."

They crashed.

Eleven

"The modern world is a crowd of very rapid racing cars all brought to a standstill and stuck in a block of traffic." — GKC

While Herb and Gilbert were racing from car to car, Chang the porter had been looking forward to taking a short break from his duties and going to confession with the good Father Brown. But Herb's alarming statement had thrown the car into a chaos that took him and the other porters several minutes to calm, seating the passengers as a precautionary measure. Chang had managed to reach Father Brown's seat and begin his confession when the sound of screeching brakes raised a cheer from travelers and crew alike.

And he was saying his Act of Contrition when the train came to a halt, eliciting more cheers. But then the cheers stopped abruptly, replaced with screams of terror. Instinct made Chang grab a little girl who had rushed to look out a window, and dive for cover — an act that likely saved both their lives when the three-story-high car tipped over and crashed to the ground. Passengers bounced and flew out of their seats like rag dolls, some thrown into the aisle, some against windows. The engine had been lifted and twisted from the blow of the giant tripod's leg, its bulk slamming into the dirt and plowing sideways, digging a deep, furrowing scar in the earth.

It continued like that for nearly a dozen feet, taking the first three passenger cars with it, before it finally lay still, only a few dozen feet from a patch of woods that hadn't yet met the hungry maw of London's industrial enterprises. Its ornamental roof was gone, and steaming water and hot coals bled out its side. Meanwhile the fourth car of the ten on the train remained tilted at an angle, causing the stunned passengers within to begin a gingerly, almost comical series of careful movements toward the exits in an effort to escape without tipping the car further.

Later, some called it a miracle that the tripod's initial assault hadn't caused a single fatality. (Few would ever know that only the intervention of a teenage American clacker-turned-journalist had prevented the train from flying off the tracks on its own.) But there were many wounded and injured. In shielding the little girl with his body, Chang had knocked his head and gone briefly unconscious, but he soon awoke, aching and dazed. Father Brown (who, by virtue of cleverness or luck, was unhurt) was waving his hand over him and finishing the words of absolution.

They both struggled to their feet and began tending to other passengers in the car, all in various states of injury and distress. It was clear to both men that the train had derailed, for reasons yet unknown, but both felt that if they kept their calm and their wits, they would be able to help stabilize the situation. And they continued feeling that way, right up to the moment a black tentacle ripped off the roof of the car and began pulling people out of their seats and into the air.

⚜

Gilbert looked back and forth slowly. He eyes had been open for some time, but he'd been too stunned to realize he was both alive and awake. He blinked, twitched his head, and decided he must be dreaming. Gilbert occasionally had dreams in which he'd be changed into one of several animals. If he'd had a particularly awful day in the clacker room, he'd be a mouse trying to escape the claws of a cat with the features of Mr. Philandron. If he'd had a (very rare) good day, he'd dream he was an eagle, soaring high above homes and cities that looked like the toy villages he'd made in the sand pile behind his childhood home.

But now he was apparently having a very different dream. He was his normal size, but he was lying on his side on something soft, there was grit in his eyes and nose, there was a snake hissing somewhere in the room with him, and he was covered in shards of broken glass. He had a bad headache. There was also a giant black milking stool standing over him, with a thousand tentacles writhing beneath the stool's seat like a Medusa.

Gilbert began to sit up. Pins and needles jabbed throughout his body as a hand yanked him back down again.

"Don't get up," hissed a voice. It took Gilbert a second or two to recognize it as Herb's. "The thing is grabbing people," Herb continued, "but it's leaving the injured alone. If we move, it'll snatch us."

"What d'you mean?" Gilbert whispered back. "What *is* that thing?"

"Keep watching. Or just listen. Whatever you do, *stay down*."

Gilbert stayed prone, lying flat on the floor with his arms and legs splayed out in a star pattern and his head turned to the side, watching the thing above him as best he could with peripheral vision.

The monster was standing over the disabled train. Its dull black body bobbed from side to side slightly, like a person staring at an anthill from a few different perspectives. Gilbert heard people inside the train talking and moving about. Didn't they see what was watching them from above?

Suddenly, two thicker tentacles sprouted from the tripod's body. Gilbert dared to turn his head just enough to see glowing green lenses on the tentacles' tips, as they snaked down to the train and peered in the windows of the derailed train cars.

Gilbert's eyes widened in horror as a half-dozen of the thing's other tentacles speared themselves into the roof of one car, tearing it off with no more effort than Gilbert would have used to peel the wrapper off a piece of candy. They flung the twisted roof at least fifty feet, spinning it through the air over a distant copse of trees. It landed out of sight with a resounding thud. The passengers inside began to yell and scream in panicked voices.

Disregarding Herb's advice, Gilbert inched along on his back to the ragged edge where the roof of the engine car had been torn and blasted away by the crash . . . or *was* it a crash? Gilbert was slowly becoming more aware of his surroundings. What he'd thought was a soft floor was really the wall of the engine car. What he'd thought was a hissing snake was a ruptured steam pipe from the engine, blasting clouds of heated vapor into the air and blurring the sight of the black tower above him. The wrought-iron coal-burner had been well made, for it was still intact. A good thing, too! Gilbert was having a bad enough day without having to share his personal space with a bunch of angry hot coals.

Raising himself as slowly as he could, he peered between two twisted pieces of metal and watched with horrified fascination as the tentacles hovered over first this person, then that one, as if searching for the best specimens. Then, as if on cue, the tentacles shot out and snatched five men at once. One went easily, plucked like a daisy from a field. He was apparently so surprised that he didn't scream until he was dropped into a large steel basket or pen attached to the mechanical creature's side. Another man tried in vain to pry the tentacle off his body and escape, but Gilbert couldn't see that he budged it an inch. Two men tried to hang on to the train's seats, but were pulled off without any trouble. The last man had run out of the car and started across the field, but he, too, was grabbed by a tentacle that stretched to a seemingly impossible length, and placed into the basket with the rest of its catch.

Then the tripod seemed to hesitate for a moment. The two thicker tentacles with mechanical eyes on them poked into the giant basket and paused, as if to examine what it had gathered. Gilbert heard the sound of a gunshot — one of the men must have been armed — and the "eye" tentacle seemed to flinch. Instantly one of the other tentacles flashed and struck down into the basket like a hungry cobra. There were no more shots, and the basket was silent.

After that strike, the smaller tentacles that milled about the tripod's underbelly were retracted with lightning speed into the body of the mechanical beast, and the thing began to move.

It would have been very difficult for Gilbert at that moment to describe to someone exactly how the things moved themselves. With only three legs, it employed a kind of controlled wobbling: leaning backward slightly on two legs, lifting up the third, then quickly snapping the leg forward like a spider. Then it would lean forward and move each of its back legs the same way. It all happened far more quickly than it takes to describe, and within a minute, the three-legged machine had passed beyond the trees and Gilbert's sight. *It moves,* Gilbert thought, *faster than anything I've ever seen. Faster than the train we just stopped, faster than a steamship. Faster than anything man has built.*

Finally it seemed safe to move and speak. "Gil?" said Herb. "Are you all right?" Herb was sitting up now, pulling his knees close to his chest as if trying to warm himself.

"I'm all right, Herb," said Gilbert, not wanting to rise, "but what in the world was that thing?"

"I don't know. I don't know, Gil."

Gilbert sat up slowly, never taking his eyes from where the dark tower had disappeared behind the trees, trying to wrap his mind around what he'd just seen. Herb kept looking at his knees.

"Herb," prodded Gilbert, "what do you think it is?"

Herb ignored the question. "Let's get going," he said, rising slowly. "We'll want to get as far away as we can before it comes back."

Herb yanked on the door, then gave it a good kick with his heel. After it flung open, he and Gilbert carefully climbed down the bent and twisted ladder that ran down the outside of the wrecked engine. Somehow, they'd escaped with only minor injuries. Had the heavy frame of the engine absorbed most of the shock? No time to figure that out now! "First, Gil, let's get some of these people mobile. If fighting's an option, then we can use all the help we can get. If it's not, well, more people around us means more chance we could get ourselves lost in the shuffle if we're attacked again."

"That's cold, Herb."

"Maybe, but it's also realistic. If we want to live, that is."

Gilbert was too tired to argue. He rose stiffly and followed Herb toward the train and the struggling, bewildered passengers.

Several of the porters, including Chang, were helping people off the train. The injured had been laid out in rows in the shade of the trees. Gilbert could see little Father Brown comforting a middle-aged woman who couldn't stop crying.

Better, thought Gilbert, to leave the priest to his work. He strained his eyes, but saw no sign of the red-haired girl, for whose safety he felt himself surprisingly concerned. Up on a hill nearby, though, he saw her strange companion, dressed in his dark cloak and black top hat. He stood motionless at the top of the hill, with the sun at his back, surveying the damage but making nary a move to help anyone.

Twelve

"A thing may be too sad to be believed or too wicked to be believed or too good to be believed; but it cannot be too absurd to be believed in this planet of frogs and elephants, of crocodiles and cuttlefish." — GKC

Father Brown had seen many odd things in his life and had had more adventures than his round face and placid demeanor would suggest. But nothing could have prepared him for the sight of a walking tower the size of a cathedral, with tentacles that could tear the roof off a train like a tissue and snatch up its occupants like insects, striding off into the countryside faster than any train in Christendom.

But Father Brown knew he was needed, and that meant he had to master his shock. After calming a screaming woman to a point where she could be left alone for a few minutes, the old priest began seeing to the crowds who had (willingly or otherwise) exited the train.

"Father Brown!"

It was Chang the porter. Ever since he had helped rescue the young man years ago from the life of a street ruffian, Father Brown could pick Chang's accent out of a congregation of milling voices.

"Chang," said Father Brown in his practical voice, "whatever was that thing?"

"I'm sure I don't know, Father. I think, from the Kaiser? Remember those little automatons we saw in the store window? They make those in Prussia."

Father Brown frowned skeptically. "That was no toy automaton, Chang. And the Kaiser has no such weapons that I know of."

"Then, Father . . . what else could it be?"

"Well, I . . . oh, bother! Rather than worrying about that, let's get back to helping these people."

"Yes, Father, although we need not worry so much. It is good we were moving slowly along the track. Now the worst injuries we have are of the broken-limb variety. What of your meeting tomorrow morning?"

"Yes. I'd forgotten," said the little priest, pausing to help a lady exit some of the wreckage. "But I don't know that I've the gumption to walk the next ten miles or so to Woking, or to tramp the rest of the way back to London."

"We should be able to make everyone safe fairly quickly, Father, with or without you. We've enough able-bodied folk here, I think, to help others. And there are accommodations along the way. I was just bandaging the arm of a red-haired woman when I saw you, and when I was done, she began to organize a few other men to assist."

"It's good she got to them, then. It seems the idea of running off to Woking unencumbered by the injured has struck a number of our fellow passengers."

Father Brown was right: a long, snaky line of able-bodied passengers, some carrying children, others walking in a daze, had formed alongside the now-broken railway tracks and was headed toward Woking. A little slower but just as resolute were those injured and the healthy who were helping them.

"Why not leave on foot, Father? There's an inn only a few miles from this switching-junction. You could get there much faster than Woking, and warn the people there about those . . . mechanical beasts."

"Jolly good, Chang. You're a resourceful man, and you'll make an excellent priest someday, if you ever decide to continue pursuing that vocation. As for traveling to the inn, I'll do just that." He peered down the road. "What was the name of the place?"

"The Sign of the Broken Sword, Father. An easy name to remember. It's a little way off the main road, for it caters mainly to woodland hikers and walking tours. But you're in a bit of luck. This trail looks like it will lead you in the right direction." They embraced warmly. "When you see your family, Father, tell them that I send my best."

"As always, Chang."

Father John Paul Brown, age sixty-one, picked his way cautiously down the hill that had been carved and shaped by engineers to hold the rail tracks over a decade ago. He had experienced more challenging climbs both up and down mountains of many sizes, but he'd never been wearing sensible black dress shoes at the time. He'd almost wobbled his way to flat ground when he heard the loud voice at his back.

"Excuse me, sir?" Father Brown turned and looked at the origin of the voice. It was a man perhaps his own age, dressed similarly in black. But there the similarities ended. Where Father Brown's clothing was the traditional black shirt, wide-brimmed hat, and white collar of a cleric of the Church of Rome, the man addressing him wore the dark cloak, top hat, jacket, and trousers of a traveling gentleman.

"Can I help you?" asked Father Brown slowly. He did most things slowly unless someone's physical, mental, or spiritual health was at stake.

"Yes, my good man, I'm certain you can! I couldn't help but overhear how you were planning to seek out a nearby inn rather than carry on directly to Woking. May I journey with you? Accommodations along the main road are certain to be too . . . crowded for my tastes."

"By all means." The priest used the same tone he had answered with earlier. It was a tone of voice that set good men at ease, and led dishonest men to think they had found an easy target.

"Excellent, excellent!" the gentleman replied with friendly enthusiasm. They set out side by side, the man limping slightly with his stick, and had not gone but a few paces when they spotted something ahead.

"By Jove!" said the bearded man. "Do you see this? Two young men seem to have managed to extricate themselves from the wreck!" The older man strutted with his walking stick to where both Gilbert and Herb were sitting in the grass.

"May I help you, boys? I'm a Doctor." Somehow he managed to pronounce the word with a capital *D*.

Herb was looking up the hill at the roofless train with a thoughtful expression on his face. "We're fine, but I'm still trying to accept what just happened. Do you know what that thing was?"

"No, good lad," said the older man. He spoke gravely, but there was a small tic in his left eye. "But I am certain that whoever may be the pilots of that strange machine, they cannot mean us well. We must flee this place immediately, find shelter, and alert the authorities as to both the accident and the nature of this threat. I am given to understand that there is an inn within walking distance of this place. The good *padre* and I are making for it."

For a moment, Herb seemed to be in conflict; as if his sense of decency was dueling with a burning dislike for Father Brown and what he represented. The moment passed quickly, but not before Herb's brief, intense look of distaste registered in Gilbert's memory.

" 'Ere!" said a nearby voice. "Did you lot say you was going to an inn?"

Herb, Gilbert, the priest, and the Doctor all looked behind them and saw a very large man who had stumbled down the hill. His rough red shirt and dark pants were the typical outfit of a laborer, but his face had the clean-shaven look of a man of slightly higher station. The Doctor's face remained completely blank, and there was an awkward pause for a few seconds.

"Let's be going, then," Herb said sullenly.

The little priest regarded Herb, his countenance not changing an iota, and then Gilbert. "Well," he said, "it would seem that we've got to begin our little walking tour, if we're to have any hope of helping those poor souls back at the train." Without another word, Father Brown strode off to what seemed an impenetrable forest wall, slowing in his pace just enough to sneeze and blow his nose loudly before he crossed the tree line. But as the Father walked toward a very large tree, the path to the inn seemed suddenly obvious to the other four men, winding around the tree's thick trunk and into the woods.

"Well, come on!" said Gilbert, straightening his glasses and suddenly launching himself in pursuit. Herb followed quickly, the Doctor followed behind Herb, and the workman behind them all.

Thirteen

"None of the modern machines, none of the modern paraphernalia . . . have any power except over the people who choose to use them." — GKC

Gilbert guessed that the trek through the woods had lasted nearly an hour. He'd asked both the Doctor and the priest for the o'clock, but Father Brown said he had never bothered to carry a watch with him, and the Doctor didn't answer, giving the impression that walking through a forest path was taking all the energy and attention he could muster. The workman gave Gilbert a smile. "Be five o'clock or thereabouts. If I were at work, I'd still not be off for another three hours. Yet here I am instead, havin' me an adventure!"

"I'd hardly call being thrown from a train an adventure," said Herb. "More like a bloody inconvenience."

"Perhaps so," said Father Brown. "But perhaps an inconvenience is only an adventure wrongly considered."

"There, see," said the workman, "another chap what agrees with me!"

"Yes, another useful idiot," Herb mumbled under his breath.

The workman took no notice. "Gettin' some clean air and a good walk, fer me it's almost worth being on a train when it tipped up and over!" He began singing, a simple tune that matched his marching cadence:

Hi-ho! Down we go!
Steam above and the filth be-low!
Hi-ho! To an' fro,
Steam above an' the filth below!

"What kind of work do you do?" Gilbert asked politely, ignoring the pained look on Herb's face.

"Steam monkey!" the man said proudly. "Been workin' years wi' the lads, makin' sure that all the dirties you put in yer sink and down the loo don't come back to bite us. Steam moves the dirties, an' we move the steam!"

"Does anyone know how much further it is to the inn?" Gilbert said to no one in particular. No one answered. Finally Father Brown said offhandedly, "We have perhaps a quarter-mile to walk. Are you tiring, Gilbert?"

"Not *so* much," replied Gilbert, mostly truthfully, "but I'm looking forward to the inn. I've never stayed at one, you know."

"When you've seen one, you've seen 'em all," said Herb.

"Then I'm looking forward to seeing them all!" answered back Gilbert cheerfully, "and also finding a phone to get my story out to the *Times*. I don't think it's an exaggeration to say that nothing like this has happened before."

"You can say that about anything when it's new," Herb said. "We've managed to invent a whole chock of clever things in just the last ten years. Some of them, I'm sure, will be able to destroy that thing, and then life will go back to normal."

"Do you really think we'll be able to stop that machine so easily?" said Gilbert. "I saw a guy shoot at the thing's arm, and it killed him like a rattler taking out a gopher. What do we have that could stand up to it?"

"Have you ever seen a Maxim gun?" Herb's voice brightened with enthusiasm. "A Maxim can fire ten bullets *every second* without reloading or overheating. As long as you keep feeding it belts of ammunition, that's hundreds of bullets every minute. Anything that gets in the way of one of those is going to be shredded like so much wood in a sawmill. The Germans have been experimenting with a huge cannon that can fire lightning bolts; the Tesla gun they've called it. It can fire so much electrical energy, they had to invent a whole new measurement of energy for it — the *gigawatt*. And there's that inventor who says he's made a mechanical man . . . no more having to send humans to clear out lands for the colonies! Isn't that a marvel?"

"But what if the Maxim or the jig-a-what doesn't work, Herb? What then?"

"Don't be a defeatist, Gil. It doesn't suit you. You may not be British, but at least try to keep a stiff upper lip! After all, we *are* the masters of this world. Man rules the world, and the British rule men."

"But what if something's come that can rule *us*?"

"Gil, the Kaiser's giant tinpot might be able to wreck a train and capture a few hostages, but there's no way it could stand up to the British Army."

Gilbert stopped and looked at Herb. "You really don't understand what I'm saying, do you?"

Herb looked back at Gilbert. Father Brown had stopped walking and turned to face the boys, waiting for them to catch up. The Doctor and the workman had stopped too, and were watching Gilbert closely. The Doctor's hand gripped his walking stick rather tightly.

"I mean," said Gilbert, searching for the right words, "what if that thing isn't from here, Herb? Not just from outside England, but outside *Earth*? What if the thing is from so far away that we've got no idea *what* it means to do, or *how* it'll do it?"

Herb glanced around at the faces watching him. "Then we'll fight it, kill it, and send it back where it came from in little dripping portable segments. Look, Gil, I'm tired. Can we talk about this later?" Herb started walking again. Gilbert paused and almost said something else, but changed his mind and followed. The Doctor moved quickly until his pace was even with Gilbert's, and the workman maintained a steady six paces behind the Doctor. Father Brown waited until the four of them had caught up with him, and continued in what they all presumed to be the direction of the inn.

"Might I inquire, young man," said the Doctor to Gilbert, swinging his walking stick with every step he took, "where you came upon the notion that the pilot of that machine we saw was not a denizen of our humble Earth, but in fact traveled here from somewhere else?"

"I can't say I know, exactly," Gilbert said thoughtfully. "I guess it was this stack of articles I read on the train before it crashed. A lot of crazy stuff has been happening the last few weeks. Everything from the giant tin cans hitting the town of Woking to a whole bunch of volcanic explosions erupting from Mars a few weeks ago."

"Ah, the volcanic eruptions. Yes, young Gilbert. A most interesting phenomenon, true. And you think these, ah, *events,* are related somehow?"

"I think so. It could be that, well, maybe . . . well, it sounds too fantastic, perhaps, but . . ."

"Go on, Gilbert," said the Doctor. "Please continue. I find this fascinating."

"Well, one of the articles said there have been sightings of a gigantic airship, a kind of giant football with a set of ship's propellers on it. Reading about impossible things flying made me think about all the flap back in my home country about that young inventor who disappeared ten years ago."

"Inventor?"

"Yes, a fella by the name of Edison. He and a few others had some harebrained scheme to travel, not just through air, but space as well. He was swearing up and down that he had discovered the secret to flying through space, using something called *ether,* that'd let us all travel millions of miles if it were only harnessed properly. They were talking about going to the moon, then to *Mars.*"

"And, Gilbert, to your knowledge, did they succeed in this bold and intrepid venture?"

"No one knows, Doctor. He just up and vanished a few weeks before they said they were gonna make a public show of their flying contraption. Poof," said Gilbert, flicking open his hand quietly, "and no one's seen them since. But he was talking about going to Mars. And a few years later, these eruptions happen. And a few weeks after that, that overgrown milking stool knocks over a train."

The Doctor looked at Gilbert intently, not saying a word. Gilbert was just starting to feel uncomfortable with the way the Doctor's eyes seemed to penetrate him, as if weighing some important question, when they turned a bend and finally the older man spoke again.

"Indeed. Well, it would appear that we have reached our destination!"

It would seem they had. Gilbert looked up and saw in the dimming sunset a cheery, sleepy cottage that could only have been the Sign of the Broken Sword. There was something oddly comforting about the place, Gilbert thought. The timbers sagged just slightly, but not enough to look shabby or dilapidated. The path to it was well worn, and there were trim flowers in little boxes at the windowsills. There was a very old shingleboard sign moving lazily in the breeze, its lettering worn in places and difficult to read at their distance. They could barely make out the graphic of a yellow and blue sword hilt to one side of the lettering.

"Hot baths tonight," said the workman happily. "Lads, our adventure's near its end, but it's been a good walk, I'd say."

The sheer hominess of the place made Gilbert realize how tired he was, and long for peace and rest. But there was a small problem that Gilbert could not quite get rid of. The last eight months of clackerhood had bred in Gilbert an instinct for analysis, and he would study and pick apart both things and thoughts until he was satisfied that he understood them. At that moment, despite the inn's inviting appearance, Gilbert felt a sense of disquiet that, try as he might, he could neither satisfy by analysis nor simply ignore. Was it the way the air had suddenly grown very still, and the birds very silent?

But if Gilbert did have a reason to feel uneasy, it hadn't affected Herb or the rest of the company. "At last!" said Herb as they drew near. The other members of the party, surely no less tired or hungry, perked up with thoughts of food, fire, and a comfortable chair.

They were still perhaps fifty paces from the inn's yellow front door when Gilbert felt the slightest vibration in the ground at his feet, as if someone had dropped something heavy behind him. Then there was another one — stronger. The leaves of a nearby oak quivered. Gilbert froze, then turned . . .

The black tower was behind them! It seemed far off — more than the distance of a football field away — but it was there, visible above even the tallest trees. And it was coming right for them.

For a moment, Gilbert stood transfixed. Finally he was able to yell, "It's coming!" But as he turned back, he saw that the Doctor and the workman had already begun running for the inn ahead of Gilbert (without saying a word to *him*). Gilbert ran quickly to catch up, his satchel making rhythmic *chuff-chuff, chuff-chuff* noises against his body as he ran.

Herb had turned to Gilbert with an annoyed expression on his face, but it changed to a white mask of fear once he saw the tripod striding toward them. In the few moments since Gil had yelled his warning, the thing had wobbled at least twenty more yards in their direction and showed no sign of stopping or slowing down. It crashed through the forest, heedless of even the thickest trees, knocking them aside with its legs and tentacles like a man on a stroll through tall grass.

"Make for the inn!" yelled Herb, as the Doctor ran past him. Father Brown stood still a moment longer, watching the tower intently, and did not move until Gilbert caught up to him. The five of them ran for the door of the inn with every ounce of energy they could muster on a day that had already sapped so much of their adrenaline and endurance.

Come on, thought Gilbert. *Come on, faster!* He pumped his legs like he used to on the St. Albans cross-country team. He looked back to see that the little priest was huffing, his face red from the exertion of propelling his rotund body, but he moved with surprising speed. Gilbert fastened his eyes forward again on the inn and kept running.

He could see the inn was closer now; maybe a quarter-minute of running over the rough track and through the scattered trees. But how close was the tripod?

Gilbert did the one thing that his coach had said was the mortal sin of any runner: he looked back to see how close his opponent was.

It was closer — much closer! He turned back with an extra jolt to his legs. Forty yards to the door! Inconceivably, the thing had quickened its own pace. It whipped back and forth in its teetering motion, lifting one leg and then the other, shifting in different directions to allow its three legs to lift and drop, the huge metal disc-shaped feet driving craven fear into Gilbert each time they pounded the dirt, like fists of angry gods. Only twenty yards, fifteen — unbelievable! Impossible that something so like a drunken man could move so quickly without toppling! Ten . . . the Doctor had arrived at the door; Gilbert heard the workman yelp something behind him. No, won't look back again . . . then Herb at the door in front of him, then . . . Gilbert's heart sank in his chest even as he quickened his pace — the door was locked. They were banging and pulling on the handle, the door, but nothing was opening! What was going on! Five yards, two, one.

"What's wrong?" Gilbert gasped as he reached the doorway.

"The bleedin' door's bolted!" yelped Herb, banging on the door and doorframe and yelling for anyone home to open up, open *up!*

Gilbert slammed into the door with every ounce of weight and momentum his body could give it. And since he was so skinny, it did no good whatsoever. A more rational part of his brain told him that slamming into a solid wood door was no good for his body either, and that he'd be hurting something awful once things calmed down. *Assuming I'm still alive in the next few hours.*

He heard another slam behind him, much louder than before. One of the tripod's huge metal feet crushed a copse of trees no more than a stone's throw from where the four of them were now cowering in the doorway.

Then the thing paused, its two thicker tentacles extending out and sweeping in all directions. Once again, Gilbert thought of a dog looking for a scent. He heard the priest mumbling a prayer in front of him. Gilbert put his hands over his eyes — perhaps it wouldn't hurt, being snatched alive by one of these things. Perhaps they really didn't mean any harm, after all. Perhaps . . .

One of the thing's rubbery tentacles struck out like an angry rattlesnake, and Gilbert heard a scream of pure terror as it reached its target.

Fourteen

"War is not 'the best way of settling differences'; it is the only way of preventing their being settled for you." — GKC

Gilbert looked between his fingers to see who among them had been grabbed by the black tower's snaking arm. He saw in a blink that the screaming man's voice belonged to no one in his little group. Herb and the Doctor were both at the door behind Gilbert, and Father Brown was still standing in front of him. The priest was a head shorter than Gilbert, and Gilbert saw every detail of the tripod's capture of its prize.

It was the workman. His yelp had not been a warning, or just a cry of fear. He must have fallen behind and been caught! He'd somehow gotten one arm free from the tripod's grip and was trying to use a smooth, dark rod of some kind against the black, ropy arm that gripped him tightly, carrying him toward its catching-basket.

"Listen," said Gilbert, cutting off another angry spit from Herb, "what's he saying?"

"Archibald is my brother!" roared the man, stabbing at the tentacle that had fastened itself around his chest and lower torso. They could see blue and white sparks fly where the rod hit the creature's arm, but it had no other visible effect.

"Archibald is my brother!" the man shrieked one last time, while another tentacle flipped open the basket lid, waited while the man was dropped into it like a plucked apple, and then slammed the lid back down again.

"Quick!" said the Doctor. Gilbert turned and saw that he'd somehow gotten the door open. "Get in! Get in, quickly!"

None of them needed the encouragement. Doctor, priest, and both boys charged through the doorway into the inn's foyer. It was dim inside; there were no lights or lamps, and the low sun of late afternoon cast only a diminishing beam through a few small windows.

The priest shut and fastened the door behind them. Gilbert slumped against the door and its illusion of safety, but the others shuffled off deeper into the house. "Come along, lad!" Father Brown said gently but firmly. "You know how strong that thing's arms are. If it can tear open a metal train car, it can tear open a wooden door! We've got to get into a cellar, or someplace equally difficult to access."

Gilbert numbly held the priest's offered hand, and they passed into what seemed to be the inn's common room, with a fireplace, a few couches, and a circular table with chairs arranged around it. He could hear more whispering over the sounds of feet in front of him. Herb and the Doctor were arguing over something. "No more," the Doctor suddenly said emphatically, "no more. You'll just have to trust me. Here, sit. Sit. Sit." With each "sit" from the Doctor, he firmly placed another person in one of the chairs that surrounded the table. Herb sat first, more from the Doctor's giving him a good shove with his cane than anything else, then the priest, and then Gilbert himself. Sitting down for the first time in hours after such a series of shocks, Gilbert suddenly felt very, very tired. Had the tentacled tripod suddenly appeared, he would have chosen to be captured rather than run anymore. *I am completely out of steam*, he thought to himself. *I will wait here until the tripod gets me, or until I get a good rest, whichever comes first.*

"And now, gentlemen," spoke the Doctor in a voice that reminded Gilbert both of a magician and a teacher calling pupils to attention, "hold your seats tightly." With that, Gilbert saw the reflection of light from the table shift, as if someone had spun the table violently to the right. At the same moment, the beams in the roof of the inn groaned, and then snapped, as the arms of the tripod ripped off the roof and cast it away as a child might do to an orange peel. The twilight of the setting sun streamed into the room. Gilbert looked up, unable to will himself to move and save his life.

It was then the table dropped through the floor, taking Gilbert, his friends, and all the chairs with it.

⁂

When the pit of his stomach had settled from the initial drop, Gilbert relaxed his grip on the arms of his chair and looked around. Then he risked letting one hand go to his face so he could rub his eyes under his glasses, and looked around again. He wasn't seeing things! The table, the floor around it, the chairs on the floor, and the people in the chairs were all descending, as if in some giant elevator shaft. The sky above, with its silhouette of waving, probing tentacles, appeared in a dim circle that was rapidly shrinking as the floor moved deeper and deeper into the earth.

"Follow me quickly when we stop moving," the Doctor said, just loud enough to be heard over the machinery of the elevator winch, "it won't take long for that thing to deduce where we've gone."

He was right. Gilbert could already see the shiny black ropes of the tripod probing the edge of the pit. The floor came to a sudden halt, bouncing its passengers slightly. That noise seemed to alert the tentacles, and Gilbert saw three of them shoot down toward them like evil black streams of water.

"Now!" yelled the Doctor, launching himself from his sitting position. He fled to a depression in the wall of the narrow chamber they'd landed in, and disappeared into it. The other three followed quickly. Gilbert was the last to go through, and as he did so, the Doctor slammed a metal door behind Gilbert and fastened it with three heavy beams.

"There," said the Doctor, panting slightly but pleased with himself. "It won't be getting through that any time soon. I believe we're too deep underground even for its tentacles to reach."

"Good enough," said Herb, "but where are we?"

Gilbert looked around. They were standing in a large, round hall, perhaps a hundred feet in diameter. There were about fifty chairs arranged in three concentric circles around the center of the hall, facing inward. Across from them were a half-dozen metal locker cabinets. They were gray, square in shape, and each large enough to hold three grown men.

"This," said the Doctor, "appears to be a meeting hall. But tonight it shall be where we shall rest and replenish ourselves before we continue our journey. Come, there are supplies in the lockers."

"How do you know that?" said Herb suspiciously.

"Why, young Herbert," said the Doctor, his face suddenly a mask of happiness, "whatever else are lockers for, but to hold supplies? Come and join us. *If* you are hungry, that is."

"I'm hungry, but before I follow you, I want some answers." Herb's voice was tired, but resolute. Gilbert knew Herb well enough to know that he wouldn't budge from his position. Better to try to bend a rock!

"Herbert, please," said the Doctor, his own voice suddenly sounding very weary as the mask of cheerfulness dropped. "I understand that you have many fair questions. Believe me when I say that I can and will answer all of them, but only after a civilized repast, and perhaps a short slumber to revive us from our trials. Would that be satisfactory?"

Herb closed his eyes and sighed. "Fine," he said, "but don't think I'm going to forget just because you're feeding me. I want to know not only how you know about this place, but also why you weren't up front with us about it beforehand. Understand?"

"But of course, dear Herbert! Of course! And there's enough for our friend Gilbert and the good *padre* as well! Come, please!" He strode to the lockers, clacking his walking stick on the hard stone floor.

Gilbert scanned the room, trying to place the source of a small humming noise that he alone seemed to have noticed since their arrival. He looked at the walls, and then followed the shadows up to the ceiling.

"Doctor?" he said. "What's that up there?"

"Up where, dear boy?" The Doctor paused from opening one of the lockers.

"Up *there*. I was wondering where the light was coming from!" he exclaimed with a mixture of surprise and wonder. Gilbert pointed upward to a thing neither he, Herb, or Father Brown had ever seen in their lives. It was a glowing orb, shining with a light that illuminated the entire cavern.

"That, Gilbert, is an application of one of your own countrymen's inventions. That is an *electric light*."

"*Electric* light?" yelped Gilbert. "But electric light's a myth! Edison said he discovered it, but then he disappeared! And none of his assistants were able to produce it!"

The Doctor smirked and turned back toward the locker. "Not until properly motivated, no," he said to himself softly, his voice muffled further by the walls of the locker. Then, in a louder voice, "All in good time, Gilbert. All your questions shall be addressed. First, let us eat."

The Doctor produced several tins of food, each one with a small key attached to the top that, when twisted, opened the tin and revealed the food within. At the smell of sardines, cold ham, and corned beef, Gilbert's mouth began watering like mad. He had been living for weeks on bread, cheese, and water, with the very occasional cup of milk thrown in. After a diet like that, meat was a welcome treat indeed!

They ate their cold meal in relative silence, sitting in a semicircle and speaking little. Most of the conversation was provided by the Doctor, who questioned Gilbert and Herb about their lives. Herb was guarded at first, and Gilbert spoke only a few words between bites. But after a half-hour, the Doctor's questions and compliments began to win them over. He displayed a remarkable knack for knowing just what to say to set Herb and Gilbert at ease. Had there not been a three-legged monster tramping about a hundred feet above their heads, the scene might have resembled a jolly picnic.

As they ate, Gilbert noted that the priest said very little, although he smiled and led the group in saying Grace before they ate. (Although he'd been raised with very little religion, Gilbert had bowed his head while the priest made the Sign of the Cross and thanked God for their deliverance thus far and for the food before them, and asked for the grace to accept His will, whatever it might be. The Doctor had looked straight ahead with a wan smile on his face, while Herb had folded his arms and stared at the floor.) But after that, it was nigh impossible for even the Doctor to get Father Brown to speak more than two or three words at a time about anything. Herb, who seemed to have formed a total and complete disdain for the priest, made no attempt to draw him out.

At the same moment that an unexpected joke of Herb's sent the whole party into peals of unrestrained laughter, they heard suddenly a distant thud-thud-thudding above them, and instantly fell silent, reminded of exactly why they were huddling a hundred feet underground in the first place. "Now," said the Doctor, after a moment, "it would seem that rest is in order. In another cabinet, if I am not mistaken, we have . . ." He got up and rummaged in another of the lockers, and produced several pillows and thick, wool blankets. "We are as safe here as, perhaps, we could be anywhere in England. And if we hope to continue to Woking tomorrow, or anywhere else, for that matter, we will need our rest. I'll be able to answer your questions after that, Herbert, I hope to your satisfaction."

"Starting with what your name is, Doctor. We've heard your title many times since we started, but never your name."

"All in good time, Herbert. All in good time."

He tossed a pillow and a rolled-up blanket to each of them, unrolled his own, and doffed his cloak, jacket, and vest. "It might be," noted the Doctor, "a good idea to sleep in our shoes, in case flight is called for."

"Where would we fly *to*?" grumbled Herb, almost to himself but just loud enough to be heard by the group and ignored by the Doctor.

Gilbert readied himself for sleep, unpacking his bedroll, placing his satchel near him for comfort, and then removing and folding his glasses. Once under the cover, he lay for a time, staring upward at the light. He was almost certain it had dimmed somehow since he'd first noticed it. He stayed like that for several minutes, even after Herb and the Doctor had begun the heavy, regular breathing of the sleeper.

"Are you having trouble, Gilbert?" whispered Father Brown.

"Trouble's not the word for it. I don't know how they can sleep after a day like this. This morning, I got up before it was light and went to work. I was a little person doing a little job. Now, I'm still a little person, but part of a very, very big mess, who's got to stay alive and write a story about it afterward. There's all this craziness above us with that machine stomping around. It's driven by who-knows-who, and wrecking everything for who-knows-why, and here I am, safe and sound, under a glowing ball that everyone knows shouldn't be here, trying to do something as normal as sleeping. Suddenly I'm in an unreal world, a kind of . . ." he paused, lost for words.

"Fairyland," said the priest. It was less a questioning, helping word than one that Father Brown knew for certain was the correct one.

"Fairyland?" asked Gilbert quizzically. "What're you talking about? This is a dangerous world I'm in, not something out of a fairy tale!"

"That's where you're wrong, Gilbert. Not about the world, but about Fairyland and fairy tales. The stories of Fairyland were written long ago, when men still lived in caves or mud huts and feared the night. Back then, they needed something to explain the curdling of the milk, getting lost on a clear day, the disappearance of someone for years at a time, or just the sense of wonder at how big and unpredictable — and dangerous — the world and universe truly is. In short, Fairyland is any world we stumble into that doesn't follow our rules. And that describes the world outside quite accurately, don't you think?"

"Do you seriously believe in fairy tales, Father? With you being a priest, and in this scientific day and age?"

"It is always dangerous to enter Fairyland, Gilbert, but it isn't necessarily *wrong*. I am free to believe or disbelieve in fairies, but I always will believe in what inspired them. And I believe that science won't ever tame the world. Not fully, anyway. If that thing above us truly does come from some place other than Earth, it proves that our science can't do or know everything, despite how earnestly it insists it can."

The priest turned onto his back, and folded his hands on his chest. "Now, as to the business of this day and age, I'm not really certain what challenge awaits us if we reach Woking. But whatever it is, I feel we can meet it better with some sleep. Now do try to get some rest yourself, young Gilbert." The priest yawned as he said these last words, turning over to sleep. Within a few minutes, Gilbert could hear by his breath that the priest was asleep, too, or doing an excellent job of pretending.

But sleep remained as elusive as ever for Gilbert, and he lay awake for a long while, thinking of Father Brown's words. Without a clock, he had no real way of knowing how much time had passed. Was it hours? He had almost decided to get up and roam about the hall some more, when he heard the thunder above him.

That was odd, he thought. Thunder? There hadn't been a cloud in the sky when they were running from the giant tripod. But who knew what could happen with the weather in Merrie Olde England?

The thunderclap sounded again, followed by several more. What kind of a storm was brewing above that could be heard a hundred feet underground?

"Gil," a voice whispered behind him. Herb had awakened and was looking around with very large eyes at the ceiling.

"What is it, Herb?"

"It sounds like thunder. But it's not. It's too loud, too near, and too steady. There's only a single clap and a small echo, and it's done. Those are artillery shells. Whatever that tripod thing is, it's gotten the army upset enough to bring out the big guns."

"Artillery shells? Can they really be firing that many?"

"If they're worried enough, Gil, they'll be pulling out more than that. Anyway, even with one of those analytical engines driving them, those guns aren't terribly accurate. Just the shock of firing them throws off their aim half the time. So they have to fire a whole bunch at once, in the hope of some of them hitting something. Although it still seems a bit much for one black tower, I'd think."

"Are you sure there's only one, Herb?"

Herb paused. "Well, that's all we've seen."

"Yes, but what if there's a whole army of the things? What if there's a dozen of them ready to level London?"

"Well, it can pluck things apart well enough, Gil, but I doubt that even several of them would pose *that* great a threat. Not if their best weapon is that bunch of giant arms growing out've their bellies. Strong as they are, they won't stop *artillery* shells."

The guns kept firing above them. A volley of ten or fifteen loud blasts would report within a second or two of each other, and then pause for a minute or two before they started up again.

"How can they possibly sleep through this?" mumbled Herb, looking at the bodies of the two older men.

"My guess is they're both ex-military. My Pa said when you're in the service, you get to the point where you can sleep through just about anything."

"Maybe," Herb grumbled. "Which branch of the service was he in? I'd like to know how you learn to sleep through something like *this*."

"You know," Gilbert replied, "I never found that out. He always said he'd tell me when I was older, but —"

"Listen!" hissed Herb suddenly. "It's stopped." They waited as a few very long minutes passed without a sound from above.

"They must have destroyed the thing," Herb said happily. "We can go back to sleep and wake up in the morning to a normal countryside again."

"Do you think so, Herb?"

"I know so." Herb's face became rigid. "If the guns haven't wiped out that thing and any others, assuming there are any, the army would call out everything it had to deal with them. And nothing, nothing, Gilbert, can stand up to a British-made, fully loaded, fully trained-and-motivated army in her Majesty's service!"

"What if something *could*, Herb? What then?"

Herb paused and looked at Gilbert as if he were phenomenally stupid even to ask such a question. "Gil, that's like asking what we would use to kill an enemy soldier if you shot him in the head and *that* didn't work. It would work, and that's that. Now let's get some sleep."

Herb slid under his covers again and turned away from Gilbert to face the wall. Gilbert tried to do the same, but something just didn't sit well with him. His analytical clacker's mind had found something wrong with Herb's explanation of what was happening up top, and he wouldn't be satisfied until he figured out just what it was.

The guns had been firing regularly until very recently. They had stopped suddenly, which meant that they'd either hit their targets or been prevented somehow from firing. Why was it so hard to believe that they'd been victorious, that the black tower had been vanquished, and that the British Army had prevailed on its own soil as it had literally everywhere else in the world up to that point?

After all, if all the guns . . .

That was it.

The guns *hadn't* all stopped at once.

They had stopped *gradually*.

First, the thunderclaps of the mortar shells had stopped farther off in the distance, and gradually the one right above them had silenced itself. If a large number of shooters were trying to hit a target, they would all stop at once when the target had been hit. And if the shooters stopped shooting far away, and gradually the shooters closer to Gilbert and his position had ceased firing . . .

The guns hadn't silenced themselves. Something had silenced *them*, a few at a time. Was a tripod *that* powerful?

Gilbert wrinkled his forehead and wondered for a few more minutes. His musing was distracted by a large, pale moth that had begun circling the dimmed light above them, but after a moment, he pulled himself back on track. If the black tower-thing had somehow quieted or destroyed the guns above them, what would keep them from finding some way down here very soon?

Gilbert's eye was drawn up to the moth again as it bounced repeatedly off the miraculous lamp above. Then something caused him to squint and re-focus his vision.

A dark mist or smoke had begun slowly enveloping the light. When the moth flew through one of its opaque arcs, it suddenly dropped straight down to the floor and landed with a small *tick* sound about a foot from Gilbert's head. He looked at the creature, and his eyes widened.

It was dissolving.

Before Gilbert's eyes, the moth's wings and legs were shriveling up and falling off its body. Although it had been white, a dark stain was enveloping every portion of what was left of the insect's body. After thirty seconds, there was nothing left to see except for a few tiny wisps of fine, dark ash on the floor.

Gilbert swallowed, and for a few seconds, he became more afraid than he had ever been in his life. The gray smoke was getting darker, and was drifting down from the ceiling toward him and his companions.

Fifteen

"The simplification of anything is always sensational."
— GKC

So, Gilbert, you say that this was once a moth?"

The Doctor was poking at the blackish spot of dust with the pointed end of an instrument from his bag. He moved in close to examine it with a bleary eye; just a moment before, he had been wakened by a frantic Gilbert shaking his shoulder.

"That's right," Gilbert said. "I couldn't sleep. First, because of the guns going off above us and later, because of the way they stopped. A few guns stopped firing far off from us at the start, then they stopped right above us, then they stopped altogether."

"And so you think, Gilbert, that they did not stop shooting voluntarily?" The priest had spoken this time.

"No, I don't just *think* that," answered Gilbert. "I *know* from when my dad took me hunting. When the bird gets shot, *everyone* stops shooting. If the army guns had taken down the tower, they all would've stopped at once. Whatever the army was shooting at, it took their guns out a few at a time. And I think they did it with *that*," he pointed to the black gas that was now little more than a half-dozen feet above them, "and now *that* is drifting down the elevator shaft toward *us*, so it can do *that*." He pointed at the decomposed moth remains on the floor and then to himself.

"Perhaps," said the Doctor, his eyes darting about quickly between their faces and the dark mist above, "it would be advisable to relocate ourselves before these foul fumes reach us. This gas appears to be lighter than air, fortunately, but it is billowing down toward us as it fills the top of the room and the shaft. Now, if you would all kindly follow me . . ."

"I think it's a lot of nonsense," interrupted Herb, crossing his arms, "and besides, I was told I'd get some answers once we woke up. Well, I'm awake now, and I don't seem any closer to getting answers than before. Just who are you, Doctor? I'd like a proper name to go with what we keep calling you. And how do you know which inns have deep holes in the ground, and giant dumbwaiters that end in underground meeting halls lit by lights that supposedly don't exist. Not to mention holes stocked with food and armed-to-the-teeth like bunkers!"

"Armed?" said Gilbert. "Herb, what're you talking about?"

"I'm talking about this!" Herb strode to one of the lockers, produced a key from his pocket and popped it into the lock. A twist and a jiggle of the handle, and Herb had flung the locker door open. There were several rifles standing on end in the first locker, of a kind Gilbert had never seen any hunter use, and in the next one, there were several boxes of ammunition and a number of oddly shaped belts that, on closer inspection, were made completely of bullets — easily the biggest bullets he'd ever seen!

"Where did you get that key from, boy?" breathed the Doctor, his voice betraying the smallest hint of wonder as his hand quietly searched his right jacket pocket.

"That's a trick I learned from a young lady I met on a story," said Herb, "a sharp little pickpocket in the rookery who called herself Aldonza the Nimble. When all of us were stampeding into the room from the lift, I bumped into you several times. It occurred to me that a man who knows where to find impossible holes in the floors of deserted inns might have something very interesting in his pockets indeed. The lock seemed just the size for this little key, and it appears that my gamble paid off, with dividends!"

"Indeed," said the Doctor, looking at Herb with narrowed eyes.

"Now, what is this place, Doctor?" Herb asked. "You knew exactly where to go when we started for the inn. And that chap who got grabbed by the tripod? He had a cane almost exactly like yours, the one you passed to the little redhead so she could fire a lightning bolt into the engineer. And not only could you find your way to the big elevator shaft in the dark with mechanical octopus legs ripping the roof apart, but, once down here, you knew just which locker to go to for food. And you flinched when I gambled and said there were weapons in this locker, as if you were hoping no one would go near it! Just *what in blazes is going on?*

The Doctor glanced up nervously at the dark mist above, swirling ever closer to their heads. "Please, Herbert, if you would follow me, I can give a full explanation as we make our way . . ."

"Herb, maybe he's right," said Gilbert. "You didn't see what that gas could do."

"Yes, Herbert," said Father Brown this time, "you are putting yourself and us at risk with this gambit."

"No," said Herb quietly, moving to a point between the doorway and the open locker, ignoring both Gilbert and Father Brown while fixing his gaze on the Doctor. "No, Doctor. You said that before. You owe us an explanation for all that's been going on, and I want it *now.* You put us off earlier, saying that you'd tell us the truth when we woke up. Well, we're awake now. If you don't tell us now, you'll put us off until the next crisis, and then use *that* as your excuse next time. Based on how fast the smoke's drifting down, we've got a few minutes before it touches us. You can at least give us a few sentences before we go."

The Doctor looked at Gilbert's tall, skinny frame, and then at Herb's slightly shorter but much stockier build, and the resolute expressions on the faces of both boys. Father Brown was looking at the Doctor with an inscrutable expression. The Doctor looked up again at the smoke, and sighed.

"Dash it all," he muttered under his breath, looking at his shoes for a moment, and then bringing his eyes up again to meet theirs. "You win, lads," the Doctor said, talking like someone who'd been beaten in a sporting event. "Three sentences. I can give you boys three sentences about our situation, and I'll tell you the rest as we move on. Have we an arrangement?" he said, extending his hand in the manner of a gentleman.

"Deal!" said Gilbert, reaching for the Doctor's hand and shaking it even as Herb opened his mouth to argue the point some more. "Now, Doc, tell us what you know."

"Our adversaries," began the Doctor, "are a race of mollusk-like creatures from the planet Mars, and until recently our worlds have shared a treaty of nonaggression and mutual benefit."

The Doctor paused to enjoy the effect of these words on his companions.

"They have met significant resistance on Mars for the last few years from other creatures that live there, and have decided to move on to our world in the hopes that it will be easier to poach due to our comparatively inferior technology. Furthermore, they see human beings as little more than we see cows or other lower animals, and plan to treat us accordingly once they have established themselves on Earth as the new dominant species."

There was silence. Herb looked as if he'd eaten something that didn't agree with him.

"Do you see why I was not eager to reveal this to you?" said the Doctor, his voice rising. "Now do as I say, quickly!"

The Doctor flung open several of the other lockers and called the others around him. He hastily loaded three small backpacks and passed them around. By this time, the black smoke had moved to within perhaps two feet of their heads. Gilbert, who was the tallest, had begun instinctively to walk stooped over in an effort to avoid inhaling any of the noxious fumes. He was about to drop the satchel he'd been given by the outfitters, but he hesitated. He'd grown oddly attached to the now slightly battered shoulder bag. While the Doctor was distracted with helping Herb and the priest mount their packs, Gilbert quickly and almost silently upended the backpack he'd been hastily given and spilled its contents into his satchel, watching small packets of food, bandages, and at least one small box of matches slide quietly into their new home. He slipped the strap over his shoulder and fell into line behind Herb, Father Brown, and the Doctor.

Next they stepped to the locker filled with weapons. Inside, Gilbert could see rifles, muskets, and other standard-issue weapons for many, if not all, soldiers in the British army. There were stacks of small, fuse-lit bombs that looked more like clay apples than anything else that had been in use for decades. And there were stacks upon stacks of brown cardboard and paper boxes, containing what Gilbert presumed to be ammunition.

But through the dim electric ceiling light that shone in from the room behind them, Gilbert could also see other peculiar devices that had to have been designed with the help of analytical engines. There looked to be something like a Maxim machine gun, but a bit larger and mounted on a huge tripod. There was also a truly odd-looking contraption: a large tube, seemingly made of a single, enormous gun barrel that was at least six feet long and a handspan in diameter, but with a normal-sized trigger and handle.

"That, dear boy, is a piece of work from your own shores." The Doctor had noticed Gilbert eying the weapon as he sealed the door behind them. "A truly impressive tool of destruction known as a *bazooka*, developed in the Texas Republic."

"Bazooka?" snorted Herb. "It sounds like a German beer-hall dance. How do you carry the thing?"

"*You* don't," said the Doctor flatly. "It takes a two-man team to load and fire it, and none here have the requisite experience. Being an American, Gilbert, perhaps you would be better suited to these." The Doctor took out what appeared to be a pair of revolvers and a belt with holsters on either side. Seeing them, Gilbert would have drooled mentally if it were possible. Those were Colt .45s! The kind used by almost every cowboy hero in the nickel novels he'd read and dreamed about as a child.

"You mean I get to *use* these?" said Gilbert, strapping on the belt and cradling the pistols like saints' relics.

"Hopefully not, my lad. Now, er, Father, I'd venture to suggest that, if you see anything you can use, please feel free to pick it up. I can't guess at anything in your background that would suggest a suitable weapon for you."

"My chief, and most powerful weapon," said the priest, holding his rosary between his thumb and forefinger of his right hand, "uses no bullets. Still, if we are forced to defend our lives, a pistol and a few of those little bombs might also be of some use. I'll examine these whilst you outfit the young men."

Father Brown began puttering among the firearms while the Doctor selected a very oddly shaped pistol, one with no fewer than eight barrels. If you were unlucky enough to have one pointed at you, you'd think you were staring at a gunmetal honeycomb.

"It's a lovely invention, really," the Doctor said, showing the eight-barreled pistol to Herb. "They call it the Pepperbox pistol, since it fires bullets like pepper from a shaker. As close as one can get to carrying a Maxim gun in your pocket." He smiled at it in admiration.

"These are well and good, Doctor," said Herb, reaching for the weapon, "but are they really going to protect us from those machines out there?"

The Doctor brushed Herb's eager hands away from the Pepperbox pistol, putting it in his own pocket and handing Herb a more conventional, breech-loading rifle instead. "These toys we carry, in all likelihood, will not. We'd need the firepower of an ironclad battleship to defeat one of those Martian war machines. Still, we could put a good-size dent in one of their smaller craft, if we had to. But on our journey," he concluded grimly, "we're more likely to use these weapons on . . . our own kind."

"What? You mean we'll be shooting *people?*" Gilbert's voice was tinged with fear.

The Doctor's face did not change. "We're likely to encounter mobs of panicked refugees on the road and may need to protect ourselves from them, sad to say." He pulled something bulky from the back wall of the locker. "I say, *padre,* could you help me with this?" The Doctor held up what looked like a large tank of water or compressed air. It had several round gauges on it, and a hose that, for the moment, trailed on the floor.

"Mobs," Herb mumbled as he examined his rifle and ammunition. "If those machines did come from another world, it's no wonder they picked Earth as a target. Next to them, we're like a group of ants scurrying around."

"It's not quite as bad as all that," grunted the Doctor as Father Brown helped lift the tank onto his back while the Doctor finished buckling the tank's straps across his shoulders and chest. "It would be more accurate to suggest that we're as chimpanzees or cows to them. *There,*" he said after tightening the hose and turning a few knobs under the gauges. There was a hissing sound from the tank and from the hose's large nozzle, and then silence. "Now, if you will first return my key, Herbert, shall we go?"

After a moment or two, Herb reluctantly slapped the key into the Doctor's open palm. The Doctor strode to another one of the lockers, inserted the key and swung the door open. As the space widened, Gilbert saw it was not another locker, but an entryway to a tunnel that disappeared into the wall.

"I cannot tell you this passage is completely safe," said the Doctor matter-of-factly, "but it would seem that any other route of escape has been cut off by the black smoke. Our Martian nemeses are as clever as they are relentless."

"I wouldn't say they were so clever, myself," Father Brown said.

"Clever enough to steal a planet, Father."

"But a thief isn't clever, Doctor. To become clever enough to steal a great deal of money, one must be foolish enough to want it in the first place. Imagine, then, how foolish one has to be to try to steal an entire planet."

"Or an empire," quipped the Doctor. "But we've waited here enough. Off we go!" He walked through the entryway at a good pace, pausing only long enough to reach out, grab, and light an oil lamp that none but the priest had seen earlier.

"You each should have smaller versions of this light in your packs."

"How is it you know so much about the equipment, Doctor?" interrupted Father Brown. "Have you used it before?"

"This lair was once a meeting space to a group of anarchists. I managed to infiltrate them long ago, and have maintained ties with them since. The equipment was provided to the anarchists by a larger and more powerful organization that had found the anarchists very useful for eliminating opponents to the organization's agendas. These packs in particular were designed for the anarchist leaders in the event a quick escape was called for."

"What's an anarchist?" asked Gilbert as they entered the darkness.

"A person who hates all existing governments, believing them to be thieves of freedom," said Father Brown. "Sadly, in practice, most anarchists resort to violence against those who disagree."

"But doesn't *that* take away someone *else's* freedom?" asked Gilbert, adjusting his glasses in the darkness with his thumb and index finger.

"No one said anarchists were consistent, Gilbert. Only dangerous."

"At least we benefit from their inconsistency," grumbled Herb. "We get to feel a little better about walking in the dark before something reaches out and eats us."

"Don't speak of such things!" said the Doctor, his voice uncharacteristically earnest.

Sixteen

"When you break the big laws, you do not get freedom; you do not even get anarchy. You get the small
laws." — GKC

When they had begun their slow journey through the narrow, dark
stone passage, Gilbert felt like an explorer in King Solomon's mines,
or perhaps an archaeologist skulking in an Egyptian pharaoh's tomb. His
romantic imagination seemed unperturbed by the many recent threats to
his life. Then the Doctor's large lantern, which had been passed around the
party at regular intervals, finally came to him.

After five minutes of holding the lantern, he began to feel awkward.
Another five minutes and the lantern became quite heavy, his arm aching
with its weight. He tried to carry it slack against his leg, but the glass was
hot, and Gilbert was afraid that oil might slosh out and set his leg on fire.
So for the next hour, Gilbert switched the burden from one sore arm to the
other. Full of that pride specific to young men who feel they have something to prove, under no circumstances did Gilbert intend to ask for help.

"How much farther does this tunnel go on for, Doctor?" Gilbert asked,
trying hard to hide his fatigue. "How far until we reach the surface?"

"I truly wish I could answer that question," said the Doctor, his own voice
sounding tired. "In truth, I would not have guessed it even to be this far."

"I should think that to one as well traveled as yourself, Doctor, this
would seem an easy jaunt to take," said Father Brown, unique among the
group in that he showed no signs of exhaustion.

"What precisely do you mean, *padre*? Just how would *you* know where
I've traveled to?"

147

"Oh, it's really not that difficult. I once caught a thief by listening very closely to a set of footsteps in a crowd. The thief had a talent for changing the way he walked, fitting it to the company he was chattering with. In doing so, he could blend in seamlessly with either the well-to-do or the servants, as his needs demanded.

"In your case, Doctor," continued Father Brown, "when you were playing the role of the well-to-do physician, your steps were measured and precise, like one who has been taught to distinguish himself from a common country doctor. But when you become tired, and more focused on the business at hand, rather than playing a role, you walked with a more plodding, loping gait, much like the men I traveled with in my younger days as a missionary, men who blazed trails through forests and jungles."

The Doctor made no reply, but Gilbert noticed that he began to walk more stiffly, suddenly conscious of every step.

"So, Doctor," began Herb, breaking the awkward silence, "you said that there were a number of other races on Mars that the mollusks were fighting. What are they?"

The Doctor sighed. "Not that you'll completely believe me, but Mars once had a substantial amount of water on its surface — millions of years ago. So much water, in fact, that it isolated several continents on the surface of the planet. And where continents are isolated, life often develops quite differently. On one continent, there developed a race of tall, almost insect-like creatures called the *Sorn*. Then there's an interesting species possessing four arms and tusks, with whom a Confederate soldier fellow named Carter from Gilbert's country once fell in."

"I'm not from the Confederate States, Doctor. I'm from the USA. It's farther north than the CSA, and there's no slavery."

"Yes, I'm certain the distinction is important to you and your fellow Americans, Gilbert. Where was I?"

"Horns and tusks," said Herb.

"Ah, yes. Another fellow, a . . . colleague of mine, named Ransom, he took up with a hirsute, feline race called the *Hross,* or some such, before we lost contact with him."

"Lost contact? When?"

"When he went to Venus," said the Doctor, as matter-of-factly as if he'd said they'd lost touch after graduating from school.

Herb was quiet for a few minutes after that, unsure whether the Doctor was serious or only playing a game with him.

"So, how did you hear about all this, Doctor?" asked Gilbert finally, if only, he thought to himself, to continue passing the time.

"For the last twenty years," answered the Doctor, "I have been employed by a special branch of Her Majesty's realm. One that operates in secret, but works primarily to secure the best interests of the British Empire."

"Wot?" asked Herb.

"The Doctor is a spy," Father Brown said. "He operates in the shadows, with most of us in the regular world unaware of his activities."

"Correct, Father. My group, the Special Branch, does operate in secret, since many people would consider what we do to be . . . unacceptable."

"In what way, 'unacceptable'?" asked Gilbert, trying to keep his voice sounding light.

"Unacceptable from a legal, moral, or scientific standpoint," came the Doctor's terse reply.

Here Herb chimed in again, intrigued. "I could see a spy breaking legal and moral rules," he said. "But what d'you mean *scientifically unacceptable?*"

"*Legally,* the Special Branch has no authority to interfere in the affairs of other nations. *Morally,* most ethical fundamentalists would call assassinating a president reprehensible. *Scientifically,* many would say our ability to predict future events with such accuracy is impossible without assistance from the netherworld. Consider the Americas, where young Gilbert was raised. If President Lincoln had not been assassinated at the beginning of the American

Civil War some forty years ago, some scholars believe the United States of America and the Confederate States of America would still be one country today, as likely would the two Californian republics and Texas."

Gilbert chuckled. "What, are you trying to say that the British government had President Lincoln killed?"

"No, Gilbert. The British government didn't do it. The Special Branch did. The Special Branch decided that it was in Britain's best interests for America to be a second-rate power, and the way to ensure that was to keep her divided. Thus, Britain would have no competition in her drive toward Empire. The Special Branch serves the interests of the British government, but we don't take orders from it."

"Then who *does* give you your marching orders?" said Gilbert, suddenly serious.

The Doctor ignored him. "Furthermore, Gilbert, using its own, specialized analytical engines, the Special Branch calculated that casualties from a protracted war between the North and the South would number over a half-million dead. Quite wasteful. Far better, the Branch decided, to have Lincoln killed by a deranged actor before the war had even properly begun.

"And our engines were perfectly correct, as usual. Without Lincoln's iron resolve, the Northern states didn't have the will to fight. Vice President Andrew Jackson was elevated to presidential office as soon as Lincoln died, and he proved to be a much more *reasonable* man, supporting freedom of choice for slave states and allowing them to break away from the North without any fuss. As you know, the republics of Texas, Northern California, and Southern California soon became independent countries as well," he added with a satisfied flourish.

"So, just like that, you decided the fate of a whole country? That's just plain wrong, and sick!"

"And who are you, Gilbert, to make such a judgment?" replied the Doctor, his strides becoming longer and more energetic. "We are living in a new and exciting age, one in which the old, outdated rules of right and wrong do not apply. Indeed, 'right' and 'wrong' have always been petty notions useful only for keeping the rabble in line. We as a race have grown far, far beyond such impractical notions! We now know that this world is for the strong, for those willing to fight for their existence. There is no good or evil in our world, Gilbert. There is only power, and those who are willing enough to use it."

"That is odd," Father Brown said quietly. "I heard a German philosopher use much the same language. He went on incessantly about how he was beyond good and evil, and how Christianity's weakness needed to be stamped out before a person could claim the power due to all superior beings."

"He sounds like he would have done well for the Special Branch," the Doctor said with admiration. "Where is he today?"

"Mister Nee-chee, for that was his name, took ill," Father Brown answered. "He became weak and bedridden. His sister, moved by Christian charity, began to care for him. And then a curious thing happened. He stopped saying the weak needed to be weeded out. He also stopped blathering about Christianity being all rot."

"What's your point, Father?" grumbled Herb.

"My point, Herbert, is that the ones who say, 'Blessed are the strong' do so only while *they* are the strong. Once they find themselves laid low, they realize their claims of superiority were a house of cards built on dry sand in a windstorm. Right and wrong will always be, Doctor. Just like gravity and the stars. Even the meanest dictator wants justice, at least when it comes to how he himself is treated. He could not desire it if it did not exist, if it were not part of what we are. And it is part of what we are only because we were made by the very author of both rightness and the stars."

Neither the Doctor nor Herb had anything to say against that, and both used the deepening ditch on the right side of their path as a convenient excuse to divert their attentions from the little priest. After twenty or more feet of walking, it had deepened to the point where the bottom could not be seen by lamplight. Herb and the Doctor compensated by walking closer to the jagged rock wall on their left, as far from the little chasm as they could get without appearing too concerned.

Gilbert, oblivious to their actions, had followed the priest's words with great interest. But there was something else he wanted to ask the Doctor about, and he feared he might not get another chance. "So then, Doctor . . . that red-headed girl you were sitting with on the train. Is she part of the Special Branch, too?"

The Doctor gave Gilbert a sidelong glance, the lantern creating a large, grotesque shadow of his head on the passage wall, and then fixed his vision forward again. "The young lady of whom you speak has been . . . something of a quarry of mine for some time now. The whole affair is frightfully complicated, and I would rather not divulge its particulars at this time."

Gilbert was trying to think of a reply when his foot kicked a loose stone to the right of his footpath, causing him to stumble. For a moment, he seemed to lose his balance as he struggled to keep hold of the heavy lantern, wobbling in place like a bowling pin that had been glanced by a bowling ball but refused to fall over.

The Doctor only stood, watching Gilbert's flailing. By the time Herb and Father Brown had reached out to him, poor Gilbert had completely fallen off the right side of the path. As he splayed out on the dirt ground, Gilbert instinctively stuck his hands and feet outward to try to slow his slide. But the dirt slide became more and more like a dirt *wall* as he accelerated down it, tumbling headlong. For a moment, he was in a sickening freefall, utterly disoriented in the total darkness. Then he heard the glass of his lantern break somewhere near him, and a split-second later, he landed hard on his head and shoulder. Loose sand and pebbles trailed down on top of him, and then all was still.

Seventeen

"He is a (sane) man who can have tragedy in his heart and comedy in his head." — GKC

Gilbert could hear someone calling his name. His head was ringing, and his mouth was full of sand. He opened his eyes, but it made no difference; it was just as dark with them open or closed.

"Gilbert?" The voice again. It sounded familiar, but very far away. Gilbert felt very tired, and wished the voice would be quiet so he could sleep. But the throbbing pains in his head, shoulder, and leg wouldn't let him sleep either. *Might as well answer the voice,* he thought; *at least I can tell it to be quiet.* He felt around and heard gravel scrape beneath his hands and feet. The sound of it seemed to rouse him from his daze. He stood up as his stunned state faded, ignoring the pain in his leg. He could feel the strap of his satchel across his shoulder and the weight of the pack as he pulled himself up. Lucky him! He'd landed on a fairly flat piece of ground. But he was alone.

"Down here!" shouted Gilbert.

"I *know* you're down there!" It was Herb's voice. "But are you all right?"

"Nothing seems broken," Gilbert said, bending arms, legs, and even giving his back and neck a careful bend or two as he'd seen a cowboy do back in the States. He touched his glasses, and found they were still secure on his face — and true to the outfitter's word, unbroken!

"Are you bleeding, Gil?"

"I wouldn't know. It's so dark down here, I can't see my hand in front of my face. Could you lower me a piece of rope or something? Or another lantern? I dropped mine on the way down here, and I don't think it followed me."

"Do remain but a moment, young Gilbert!" It was the Doctor's voice. "We'll see if we can procure something from among our provisions that might assist you!"

Why can't he just say he's looking for rope? Gilbert thought to himself sullenly. *Everyone in this whole crazy country wants to use ten-dollar words where two bits would do just fine.* He heard the sound of rummaging above him. Silence. Then more metallic tinkling, more shuffling, and muffled voices that ranged from muttering to outright argument. The only voice Gilbert could actually make out through the whole experience was Herb's. The older men's voices were too similar to distinguish at this distance, especially at a whisper.

Right after one of the older men had muttered something, Gilbert heard Herb bark the word *no* with a finality that seemed to stop any chance of debate. More mutters from what sounded now like the Doctor. "It's bloody-well not strong enough!" Herb's voice bellowed down to Gilbert, "You'll kill him with that!"

"Hey, guys?" Gilbert called upward, trying to keep the creeping fear out of his voice. "I'm not getting any younger down here."

The voices stopped arguing, and there was a pause. Gilbert didn't like that.

"Gil? Look up, Gil. Can you see me at all?"

Gilbert looked up and could barely see the smudged outline of Herb's head against the light of the older boy's lamp. "I can see you, Herb. What's the bad news?"

"Gil, we've upended everything in the supply packs that Father Brown and I were carrying. They've got some odd stuff here — gear that I don't even recognize, much less could use. But there's not a scrap of rope to be found in the whole mess of it."

"Well, could you try making a chain of your shirts or something? I'm not very particular, you know."

"Wait a minute, Gil. Just hang on, all right?"

"I don't have a lot of other options, Herb."

"Right."

They tried lowering a line made of their jackets and other articles of clothing, but it was no use. Gilbert guessed he was at least forty feet down, judging by the light of the lamp above. Even with their socks and undershirts added, the line was only a little more than half long enough to reach him.

The line was slowly pulled up. Herb's light and head disappeared. More pauses. More mutterings.

"Gilbert?" Father Brown's voice this time.

"Yes, Father?"

"Can you feel the wall in front of you?"

"Yes. And the floor beneath me, too. Why?"

"Don't try to wander about yet! For all you know, you might be standing on a ledge over a chasm. Another slip could mean your death, so please keep in one place as much as possible!"

"Like I told Herb, Father, my list of options is knee-high to a grasshopper!" Then Gilbert stood still and listened. "I . . . I don't hear any echoes, so that argues against me standing on a high ledge of some kind."

"Good, Gilbert. Now please listen carefully. The lantern you were carrying has indeed been damaged beyond repair. We have two lanterns left, and I am going to try to drop one down to you. Can you try to catch it?"

"Sure, I guess."

"I've padded the lamp inside my pack, Gilbert. Hopefully you can grab it safely, and it will be preserved in case you miss it and it falls onto the ground. I shall let it go on three!"

It seemed to take a year for the priest to count to three, and Gilbert thought back to a time with his father — specifically, one of the exactly three times he had gone outside to play ball with him in the dirt field be-hind their home.

The field was dust in high summer and thick mud during the rainy sea-sons. It had once been full of grass and fertile soil like much of their land, but had been worn down by their home's previous owners long ago from uncountable walks to and from the barn behind the house. Usually, Gilbert and his father (he didn't much like being called "Pa" as so many other fa-thers in the area were, but learned to live with it when little Gilbert kept calling him that) took a few walks every week down to the barn and around their land. Sometimes they had brought along a round ball to kick back and forth.

Pa hadn't been much for sports; it was still a joke in some of the stores in town how Edward Chesterton had called a soccer game a "football match" when they'd just moved into the area. But one day, Edward Chesterton had decided that since the other boys had been learning for years how to throw a baseball, it was time his son learned too.

"Just keep your eye on the ball, son." Apparently, Edward had learned how to throw and catch from somewhere, at least. "Eye on the ball, move your hands, and they'll catch the thing on their own."

Unfortunately, Gilbert was a quick study only when it came to book learning. He'd been a truly awful player in September of his fourth-grade year, and despite a lot of practice with Pa, only Billy "Fat-Body" Peabody, four feet tall and 150 pounds, was a poorer fielder and hitter than Gilbert by year's end. But Gilbert was saved from the absolute bottom of the sports barrel by virtue of his ability to run and steal bases well enough on the rare occasions he reached base, and Pa hadn't seemed to mind. Once, after the hundredth-or-so dropped ball, he ruffled Gilbert's hair and said, "When things really matter, son, you'll step up and do what you need to do."

"You mean when there's a championship on the line?"

"Something like that, son. Something like that."

There was no championship on the line, but Gilbert was hoping he could step up and make a decent catch *right now*.

Eye on the pack, he told himself as he saw it fall. Eye on the tiny pack and the heavy, fragile lamp filled with oil inside it. As it falls at about thirty feet per second.

When things really matter, son.

Step up.

Really matter . . .

Hands out.

Step up.

Eye on the pack.

And do what . . .

Falling to him, twenty feet away, fifteen . . .

Do what you need to.

So many times, he'd gotten scared. So many times he'd failed, because . . .

Because then it didn't matter.

Now, it mattered.

Eye on the pack, and the hands will do the . . .

POP!

≈≈✿≈≈

"Gil! What's happened?" Herb's voice made it sound as if he was trying to keep a stiff upper lip but failing miserably at it.

Gilbert swallowed and looked at the perfectly caught pack that rested in his hands.

"I caught it!" he shouted to the top of his little canyon, his eyes wide with surprise and delight. "I caught it, Herb! I caught it!" he shouted louder, resisting the urge to do a little dance. Gilbert slowly brought the pack to his chest and went into a crouch on the floor before gently setting it down. His victory was bittersweet, he thought; for the first time in his life, he'd made a decent catch and literally *no one* had seen it! If Luther and the rest of his gang could have seen him just now!

"That's good, Gil, but check the lamp inside. Does it still work?"

Gilbert opened the backpack and gingerly pulled the lamp out by the base.

The lamp glass did have hairline cracks in several places, but at least there didn't seem to be an oil leak or anything. When he tried to light it with the matches at the bottom of the satchel, the lamp shone bright enough to see around him. Huzzah!

"Gilbert, I can see the glow from here. I take it the lamp is intact?"

"Yes, Father, it is. But there's not much to see, really." And there wasn't. Gilbert was in a space the size of a medium-size room, minus the ceiling, of course, with each of the stone "walls" about ten feet long.

"Gilbert," said Father Brown, "tell me about the floor down there. Does it slope in any particular direction?"

Gilbert felt with his feet. "Yes, yes it does. Down to my left, when I'm facing you."

"As I thought. Gilbert, now listen carefully. I want you to take the lamp and follow the slope where you are, all the way to the wall. Tell me what you see."

Gilbert looked. "There's some kind of a hole in the wall, Father Brown. It's got a trickle of water running through it."

"How big is the hole?" Herb's voice, sounding a tad hopeful.

"The hole is about three feet wide. Enough for me to squeeze through, Herb. There's a . . ." Gilbert sniffed cautiously, feeling the slight wind stroke his hair like a gentle hand. "There's also a bit of a breeze coming through it."

"Excellent, Gilbert!" said Father Brown. "Excellent! You have a passage, possibly, to the surface!"

"Does that mean you're gonna come join me down here? It's already getting lonely!"

"I wish we could, Gilbert. But following you down there would prove problematic at best. Were we to try to join you, I'd be virtually assured to break at least one limb in the process, and then we'd all be prisoners here."

"Speak for yourself," mumbled the Doctor.

"I heard that!" yelled Gilbert. "Father, you're saying I've got to find my own way out?"

"Use the lamp, Gilbert, and follow the stream of air. We can't help you now any more than that. Will you be all right?"

"If I said no, *padre*, would you jump down here to help me?" Gilbert said despondently. They were going to cut him loose!

"Yes," the priest said simply.

Gilbert paused, feeling slightly ashamed. The old priest would risk injury, perhaps death, simply to give comfort to a fearful teenager! For a year, Gilbert had been so starved for kindness that now he almost wanted to weep. Part of Gilbert wanted to accept Father Brown's offer. But the rational part of his brain knew that the priest would likely be injured in the descent. Getting out on his own would be difficult enough; getting out with a crippled Father Brown behind him would be impossible. And for what purpose? Because he was afraid of the dark, like a child?

He pulled himself together. "Father, I'll be all right. I'm a little . . . well, a little worried about walking in the dark down here, but I'll make it all right."

"Gilbert, there is one more thing I can do for you. Can you still see upward?"

Gilbert looked up. By the lamplight he could see both the priest's white moon face and the dark halo of a hat that surrounded it. "I can see you, Father."

"I'm going to throw something down to you. It gave me courage when I needed it years ago in the jungles of darkest Africa."

"Toss away. I could use all the courage you can give me."

Gilbert saw something flutter down from the priest's hand. It drifted and circled in the air without any hurry, landing at Gilbert's feet.

Gilbert picked it up. It was a small card, with writing on one side and an illustration on the other. The picture was of a winged man with a spear in one hand and a set of small scales in the other, looking triumphantly down at a horned man. The horned head of the second man was held to the ground by the winged man's sandaled foot.

"Do you see the print on the card? Say the words now and again, young Gilbert, when you need strength. When I needed courage in Africa, I found it very comforting to know there were things much bigger than myself watching and working in the background of our world." Father Brown snuffled again. His flu was acting up worse in the cold and damp of the cave.

"Thank you, Father," said Gilbert in a voice he hoped sounded brave.

"Good luck, Gil." It was Herb's voice. "The Doctor says he knows the way out. If you want to try waiting, I can come back for you once we find it."

"That's okay, Herb. I'll be all right."

Gilbert lied, of course. Just as he knew that Herb was lying about coming back for him. Maybe Herb and the priest would try, but if the black tower had friends walking around the English countryside, they'd be too busy trying to stay alive to mount any kind of rescue operation.

Gilbert saw the light at the top of the pit begin to dim, and he swallowed hard. Then suddenly he heard the shuffling of footsteps and saw a bright light. The priest peered over the edge once more. "Gilbert, lad," he said quietly, just loud enough for Gilbert to hear.

"Yes, Father?"

"Gilbert, it's quite rare that I act on impulse, much less speak on it. But I wanted you to know that I have an overwhelming sense that you're going to be looked after while you're here. I would stay with you if you asked, but your best chance of survival" — it was as if the priest had read his mind earlier — "is by yourself. And I truly feel that if you remain here and act, you'll be destined for great things."

Gilbert felt a warm rush of pride and confidence. He had been as starved for praise as he was for kindness.

"Gilbert," Father continued, "I have a piece of chalk in my pocket. I will make an arrow every twenty feet or so to show you the way we have been proceeding. In fact . . ." Gilbert heard a slight rustle, followed by a snap and the sound of something dropping down to him from above. "I've broken the chalk in half. You can use it to mark your own trail in case this place becomes a labyrinth at some point."

"Thank you, Father. Good luck to you!"

"God's speed, Gilbert. Don't waste too much time, now. That lamp will run out eventually. Even if you escape your little cell quickly, you may find you have need of the light."

"Yes, Father. Thank you for all you've done. I'll be all right."

"Go with God, Gilbert. Don't forget what I've given you."

Gilbert heard the Doctor's echoing voice call out to Father Brown, as the light from the priest's lamp faded and disappeared. Within a minute, the sounds of voices and footsteps above were gone as well.

Gilbert was alone, and he didn't feel all right at all.

Eighteen

"I decline to show any respect for those who . . . close all the doors of the cosmic prison on us with a clang of eternal iron, tell us that our emancipation is a dream and our dungeon a necessity; and then calmly turn round and tell us they have a freer thought and a more liberal theology." — GKC

Gilbert looked around the pit that had become his prison. It was wedge-shaped, and its walls were smooth, having been cut out from the rock over a thousand millennia. The wider part of the pit was at the top, perhaps thirty or forty feet wide before it narrowed down to where Gilbert stood, a smaller space, perhaps eight by ten feet. Gilbert's "cell" also had a small trickle of water that sloped downward, as Father Brown had thought. The trickle ended at a hole three or four feet in diameter.

I'm probably the first human being ever to see the inside of this pit, Gilbert thought. Gilbert's suspicions were at least partly confirmed when he began to explore with his lamp. There were no other footprints and (thankfully!) no skeletons of other unfortunate travelers down there with him.

Well, he thought, *time to look at getting out.* He thrust the flickering light of his lamp into the hole in the wall and . . .

It was a dead end. Just more rock in the space beyond. His heart sank.

Wait, no — it wasn't a dead end! The back of the hole curved downward, making it look as if it ended, but really it extended down like a chute. Gilbert stretched his head as far as he could into the opening. The hole was easily wide enough for his shoulders to fit through, but that curve would be tricky. The hole went forward for perhaps five feet before it curved downward, and then curved *again*, with the little tunnel bending to point back toward Gilbert's cell. It would be a tight squeeze.

I could be stuck in there, Gilbert thought to himself. *Skinny as I am, I could still get stuck in one of those tight bends and never get out.* Sweat beaded on his forehead. He swallowed nervously at the thought of starving to death bent over, facing downward, pinched by rock in a claustrophobic's nightmare.

And even if he didn't get stuck, what if he just kept traveling in a series of small tunnels, like a human worm that could never quite turn?

"Maybe they'll come back," Gilbert said to himself aloud. "Maybe if I just stay here and don't move, if I'm just patient, they'll come back."

Gilbert paused. This sounded better the more he talked about it.

"They'll come back with a better rope, and they'll pull me out, and lead the way out of here. After all," he began to talk louder, finding that the louder he spoke, the less fearful he was about the future. "After all, they might've only been an hour from the surface. A quick stop at a local shop — a good shop always, always carries rope, right? Right."

Gilbert paused. Had he just answered his own question?

"Nothing wrong with talking to yourself, Pa used to say." His voice was tinged with a bit of nervousness now. "Nothing wrong at all, so long as you don't start hearing answers."

He chuckled, but the sound fell flat to his ears, and only stressed how alone he was and how soundless everything was around him.

He caught motion with the corner of his eye and turned his head abruptly: it was a large bug, very much like a millipede, crawling in the corner. Then he heard a flutter above him, and saw a moth flapping around the light given by his lamp, about two feet above his head.

The bugs, he thought, *they're attracted to the light.* If he stayed here, there might be tons of insects in his pit before long. Gilbert's imagination suddenly manufactured an unpleasant picture of being overwhelmed by a pool of arthropods and crunching exoskeletons.

Then again, maybe the lamp wouldn't burn long enough for that. How long — an hour, maybe two? Maybe a day, or a week? Even if he could keep walking, even if the tunnel was one he *could* walk in, there'd be no chance of rescue or escape without light. No chance at all.

He'd heard about two children in some Missouri town who'd managed to walk through five miles of underground caves before coming out alive at another end after two days of total darkness. But after that, another person had been stuck inside the same cave and died of thirst within a week. Survival in caves — the whole thing seemed the luck of the draw, and Gilbert didn't like his odds.

"I could try, you know," he said to no one, hardly even himself. "I could try to go through the hole, see how far it goes. If I don't like it, I could always come back."

Come back? Maybe not. He had a mental picture of trying to struggle his way out of the tunnel, going backward up through the tunnel's weird U-shape. No, this place he was in now was better. If he had to starve to death, wouldn't it be better to starve in a place in which you can at least move around freely? There's no reason to believe that you'd die quicker cramped up than you would walking free.

"Free?" Gilbert yelled suddenly. "Free, in a tiny cave, a thousand feet underground?"

Free enough, said the maddening little mind-monkey in his head. *Free enough at least to hope that someone will come back for you. Free enough you can die hoping, instead of swallowed up by a stone mouth that will take a million years to digest you.*

"I don't know," Gilbert moaned as he set his lamp down and sat with his back to the wall. "I don't know." For a minute he held his face in his hands. He felt tears under his eyes, but for some reason they wouldn't come. He wished he had a watch. He had a sudden and overpowering want to know what time it was.

"I wish I was back in the cardroom!" Gilbert yelled. "At least there I could look at a clock! At least there I knew when my shift ended, and where the door was, and where it led to!" He'd thought the cardroom was a prison, but at least there was space, and air, and light . . .

More moths had collected around the lamplight. Their shadows flapped around him, making odd shapes that looked dark and terrible.

"Stop yourself, Gilbert," he said to himself. But this time, his father's advice rang hollow.

What good was keeping his head? Was this why people went mad, he wondered to himself? Could madness make *sense*? Or didn't the two contradict each other? What good was rationality and sanity when death stared you in the face? At least one could live with madness. Rationality gave no comfort to the empty stomach, the hurting heart, or the aching spirit. And rationality told him that his best bet for rescue, or more likely, a slightly less painful death, would be to stay put. He had a little food, he had the trickle of water.

"Stay put," he said aloud. "Stay put, and at least starve where you can move around."

He felt satisfied, and relaxed for a few short seconds. "But," he said, standing suddenly, "the problem with staying put is that *I'm still going to starve!* I can't eat bugs for the next twenty years! I'm never going to be rescued! If I stay put, I'll die down here! *I'm going to die!*"

Gilbert turned slowly, as if fighting a heavy weight, back to the space in the wall.

Earlier, Father Brown had called it Gilbert's chance for freedom. He'd said that God would be with him. *But if there really is a God,* Gilbert thought, *he has a sick sense of humor.* Did God delight in forcing him to choose between two kinds of agonizing deaths?

Gilbert found himself breathing quickly. *Mustn't panic,* he thought; *panic kills the mind. Panic keeps the mind from working, only makes it good for running and fighting. And here I can't run and can't fight and I need to make my mind focus but I can't because I'm gonna starve in this dark hole down here.*

He sat down on the hard, pebble-dusted ground, and felt the pistols tug at his side in their holsters as they poked the earth.

Gilbert looked down at his right hand and at the gun beside it. His hand moved gently over its wooden grip, and slowly tightened on it. With a will not entirely his own, he slid the Colt out and looked at it in the lantern light.

He remembered pirate stories in which exiled buccaneers were sent to a lonely desert island. Their survival kit included one loaf of bread, a jug of water, and a pistol . . . with one bullet in the chamber.

At the time, Gilbert had thought the bullet was just to help fight off wild animals. But now, a hundred or more feet underground, with hope of rescue dwindling like an icicle on an August afternoon, Gilbert realized just *why* the gun had only one bullet.

His hand carefully off the trigger, Gilbert slowly examined the barrel from many angles.

I'm going to die anyway, he thought. *It'd be quick. It'd be quick, and then my troubles would be over. I'd see whatever's on the other side, and I'd be out of this hole forever. No long process of starving to death. No pain, and I'd be free!*

"I'm going to die anyway!" he said aloud, and not to himself.

Gilbert had swallowed again, the idea of suicide taking a stronger hold on his mind. *So much easier,* he thought. *No pain. A flash, and it'd all be done.* He was just turning the barrel around for a closer look down to the bottom when two thoughts stabbed through his head with rapid-fire speed.

The first was a memory, a wounded man he'd seen at the general store when he'd been seven or eight. A dark scar had been torn in his face, making his mouth on the right side look like a grotesque jack-o-lantern's smile. Gilbert's mother had been in a different room in the store, leaving her son to stare at the man's deformity with impolite innocence.

The wounded man had made his purchases quietly and left, making eye contact with no one but the shopkeeper. A trio of older men in the store, sitting in their work clothes and playing checkers on a barrel board that had been in place since about the War of 1812, had chuckled when the scarred man had left.

"Fool up 'n' tried killin' hisself with a bullet through his brains," old Hatfield had said in a voice made near unrecognizable from years of smoking. "Ayuh," said McFinty, moving checkers with an index finger cut off from a farming accident at the first knuckle, "but it looks like he done *missed*! What kind've fool tries t'be a suicide, but misses his own blamed *head?*"

Gilbert inhaled. What if he fired and *missed?* What if his nerve faltered at the last moment, and he turned the gun just enough that he was wounded in the same way? Starving was bad enough; starving and being in massive pain from a botched suicide attempt was even worse!

What if his nerve . . .

"Throwing your life away is a coward's way out, Gilbert."

It was his father's voice that he remembered. Gilbert had gone to him and asked what a suicide was.

"Dying to save others is the way of the hero, Gilbert, and dying for the truth is the way of the martyr. There's no other good reason to let your life go."

"What about the story you told me? The one about the Greek hero, Horatius? He knew he was gonna die if he got on the bridge, but he did it anyway. Isn't he just a crazy man killing himself?"

"Horatius destroyed the bridge he stood on to save his whole city from invaders, son. And he did it only because every other defender of the city ran away. Dying to save another is the only kind of dying worthwhile, Gilbert. A martyr cares for something outside him so much, he'll give his life to save it. But a suicide is so sick of everything outside him that he never wants to see it again. Dying to get away from your own pain or trouble is the surest mark of a coward there is in this world."

"But why die to save a bunch of cowards? Isn't it suicide to die for someone who isn't worth it?"

"They may not always be cowards, Gil. Especially if they see a hero in action. Martyrs can make cowards into heroes."

"I don't wanna be a hero," Gilbert had said after some thought. Pa had smiled and placed his hand on his son's head, and they kept walking home.

Gilbert was about to put the pistol back in the holster when his hand brushed the gun belt. He looked down and saw one of the bullets sitting without any intended trouble, nestled safely in the small loop of leather next to a number of its brothers.

"No, I won't kill myself," he spoke aloud again. *But it might be good to see if the gun is loaded. Just in case . . . just in case I meet someone . . . something that might cause me harm. Something that might need a bullet, something like (my head . . . NO!) . . . well, something. Just to check if it's loaded, just in case . . .*

As his hand started working at the bullet, his eye fell on the scrap of paper the priest had thrown down to him before they'd left.

Finish getting the bullet first, he thought, *then see if your gun is loaded (shoot), then you can be sure (bullet) you'll be safe from (starving) anything that might attack you here in (your head) this hole (in your head) . . .*

Gilbert stopped, realizing he'd been working at the bullet while staring at the paper on the ground.

Finish the bullet, first! The thought was insistent, intrusive. He pushed it away, angry at his own thought for its aggression.

Why not look at the paper first? Another thought entered his mind out of nowhere, gentler and relaxed. *You have nothing but time, and plenty of it.*

"I think I'm cracking," Gilbert said, silencing the argument in his head. "But if I'm cracking, I'll at least listen to the nicer voice."

Gilbert picked up the small paper rectangle and looked at the illustration. He flipped it over and saw the gothic lettering on the back. English writing.

Read, he thought, *because a mind that's reading can't panic or crack. It's too busy doing something to panic. So read until it passes. Then think.*

What he said made sense. He read to himself:

St. Michael the Archangel,
Defend us in battle.
Be our defense against the wickedness
and snares of the Devil.
May God rebuke him, we humbly pray,
And do thou, O Prince of the heavenly hosts,
By the power of God,
Thrust into hell Satan, and all the evil spirits
Who prowl about the world seeking the ruin of souls.
Amen.

Gilbert inhaled and then read it aloud. And then he read it again, almost shouting. He didn't know yet if he believed in God, angels, or the Devil, but the act of reading, of recognizing patterns on a printed page, helped Gilbert hold on to *something* that made sense, in the middle of a day that made less sense than any day of Gilbert's life. He read it again. And again. He didn't know how many times. After a hundred, the walls of his stone cell stopped looking as if they were closing in on him. Then he read more, until the storm in his head finally passed. Then he repeated it from memory, in a firm and pronounced voice, until he was able to think like a person again instead of a trapped animal. Then he then read again, silently, slowly, contemplating every word.

And then he looked upward.

Funny thing, he thought to himself. *Lots of folks today say they don't believe in God or angels. But a day ago, I didn't believe in giant tripods, either.*

His mind was trying to make a deal with his soul, and part of him wanted out. But he couldn't shut down the logical part of his brain.

People see evidence of things all the time, and ignore it. If I'd just seen the tripod in the forest, and no one else did, I might go on living as if I'd never seen it. I might still say I didn't believe in fairies, even if I happened upon a bunch of 'em dancing in a ring in the woods. 'Cause the minute you believe, you have to change the way you live.

And God? Could there, his calming brain wondered, could there be something to all that the priest and the churches talked about, no matter what others said?

Gilbert lobbed the thought around in his head for a while. And after a time, he felt a peace that hadn't been there since before he'd been enrolled at St. Alban's school nearly three years ago.

Once he was relaxed enough, he stood, carefully put the portrait of St. Michael in his pocket, and then lay on his back again, staring upward while thinking about his next move. His body felt sore all over, especially his joints and his back and his temples. He stared at the distant roof of the cave in the flickering lamplight, trying hard to keep his eyes focused on the rock patterns above. Considering the kind of day he had been through, it was a very small miracle that he fell asleep on the floor.

⚜

"We're a bunch of rotters," Herb growled. They had been walking for what seemed like an hour since leaving Gilbert in the small chasm.

"Don't be so hard on yourself, Herbert," said the Doctor, almost absentmindedly. "There is no shame in being among the fit and able."

"What does that mean?"

"It means, Herbert," said Father Brown, "that he believes you have more of a right to live than Gilbert does, since you aren't injured and are therefore more fit."

Herb looked at the Doctor in front of him, and the priest behind him. "Did you mean that?"

"I did," the Doctor said curtly. "We have no responsibility to those who cannot do for themselves. In this case, we have enough lanterns to spare, so we lost nothing by leaving one for Gilbert. It also may have kept him from screaming in fear and despair as we left, which might have hurt our own morale, or awakened some dormant, outmoded moral codes that you were taught as a child, and caused you to attempt some irrational rescue."

"You mean you just plan on leaving him there, Doctor? Leaving him there to starve to death?"

"I didn't plan on anything other than surviving, Herbert. Gilbert decided his fate when he allowed himself the luxury of carelessness once too often, and fell from the ranks of the fit."

Herb turned to the priest. "And I suppose you told Gilbert what you did just to keep him quiet, so's we could get away?"

"Herbert," said Father Brown without breaking stride, "I told Gilbert the truth. His best chance of survival involved following his nose toward the clean air."

"Don't let him fool you, Herbert," interjected the Doctor with surprising passion. "The priest is a man, a biologic unit, the same as you or I. Religion is the first refuge of a weakling, and there's no religion that houses more weaklings than the Church of Rome."

Herb sensed that the Doctor was trying to goad Father Brown into some kind of action, but he couldn't guess exactly what.

"What d'you say to that, Father Brown?"

"I say the Doctor is *right*, Herbert. I need religion because I'm weak. So does every member of our Church, from the pew-warmer to the Pope. The difference between the Doctor and me is that I realize how weak I am. From Adam to Napoleon, mistaking pride for wisdom and arrogance for strength has been the downfall of more men than any other character defect."

The Doctor seemed as if he was about to reply when he stopped walking suddenly. "Wait," he said, pointing his weapon at the ceiling. "Do you hear something?"

"What?" whispered Herb.

"Listen," the Doctor whispered back. "Quickly, extinguish the lamps, stand back here, and be quiet."

The three of them doused their lights immediately, then flattened themselves against the rock wall of the tunnel. There was a high-pitched hum in the air that Herb couldn't quite place; he'd never heard anything quite like that before.

The hum grew louder. It sounded something like steam escaping a valve, but not as shrill. Herb sneaked a look at the Doctor. The older man's face had hardly changed expression, even when the giant tripod was chasing them, but now it was ghost-white with beads of sweat collecting along his forehead. Herb looked back at the little priest, who either had no idea that something threatening was approaching, or was very good at covering his fear.

The tunnel ahead of them broke into a T-shape. A light appeared from the left branch of the T and got brighter as the mechanical sound increased.

And then Herb could hear a new sound. When he was five years old, a mouse had sneaked into the walls of his nursery, and he'd spent the longest night of his life listening in terror to the chittering sound of the rodent's claws. Now he heard a clickering-clackering similar to that sound — but many times louder and faster than any mouse could make — and it was Herb's turn to become white with fear. He could taste something coppery at the back of his mouth as he tried to wet his lips.

Then the humming and chittering thing sped past the opening to their tunnel. Herb saw it for only an instant, but what he saw was burned into his brain for the remainder of his life. It looked like a metal crab with a dozen twisting silver tentacles, being ridden or piloted by a pulsing blob like a giant gray brain. Its great yellow eyes reflected the light shining up from its craft.

And then it was gone, and the sounds it made echoed back into the cave, grew distant, and disappeared.

When Herb was able to move again, he shook his head and leaned down to speak to the Doctor. "What," he stammered, "what was . . ."

"Shh," said the Doctor quickly. "Be silent, unless you wish to make us its next meal."

Herb waited for a very long five minutes, sitting as still as he believed possible. For the first minute, he was sure that the sound of his breath and his thundering heart would give him away.

"The immediate danger has most likely passed," the Doctor whispered finally. "But we must continue to be on guard. Their vehicles are loud enough to warn us of their approach, but at times those creatures are able to move with a silence so absolute it defies logic."

"How d'you know so much about 'em?" Herb's whisper was quiet, but a kind of fearful rage could be heard at its edges.

"Later, Herbert."

They waited several minutes more. When they had heard nothing else, the Doctor began to speak quietly.

"I saw them for the first time when I was at the British Martian colony on Sirtis Major, three years ago. They attacked in force when we got too close to one of their canals. A horrible fight, hundreds of British soldiers dead, and scores of those mollusks, too, looking like deflated balloons as they lay in the field."

"You're lying," Herb gasped.

"I am not. And we must be moving again. If they haven't heard us after this conversation, we've nothing to fear for a while. That was likely a scout: it somehow found the tunnel and decided to do some exploring."

"That makes sense," Father Brown said aloud, more to himself than the others. "I would imagine water is quite a precious resource on Mars, and they are likely trying to map every possible source of it."

"You're quite right, Father," said the Doctor, walking again with the priest behind him and Herb obediently bringing up the rear. "For a Catholic priest, you're surprisingly well-versed in practical logistics."

"I served in the military for a time, Doctor. Granted, my role was that of chaplain rather than soldier. But I managed to absorb quite a bit, and develop skills and knowledge that routinely surprise those ignorant of the Church and the versatility of her servants."

The Doctor gave the priest a dark glare. If Father Brown was actively trying to ignore it, he gave no sign.

"Doctor, you mentioned British lads who died fighting the Martians," Herb said as the Doctor stared. "Is it true, then? We've made it to *Mars*?"

"My dear boy," began the Doctor, almost casual again, "for the past ten years, Mars has been explored by the British, Americans from the United States, the Germans, and the Belgians. That fellow Gilbert mentioned, the inventor chap, Edison, managed to get there first, and from there, it was only a matter of time. Our spaceships now travel to and from the inner planets quite regularly, powered by a hydrogen-boiling mechanism that no one but Edison himself fully understands to this day. That impractical fellow managed to pilot his prototype spacecraft all the way to the red planet and back. Within a few months, he and a few of his assistants were on Mars and claiming the place as American territory.

"They were not the only ones, of course. A dotty professor named Cavor began selling his anti-gravitational rocks to the Belgians, and our own dear Weston from the Special Branch found his way there with Cavor's lunatic contraptions. If only he hadn't dragged that narrow-minded fool Ransom along!"

Herb and the priest followed in silence, listening to the sound of the rocks beneath their feet.

"This is all quite interesting," said Father Brown at length, "but I can't help but wonder about something."

"You are curious as to why you haven't heard about any of this before, Father?"

"Oh, no no no. I have heard about it before. And so has young Gilbert, although he may not fully realize it. No, I was thinking on a completely different track. Why on earth did you bother forming colonies on Mars? Whatever could be there to interest you? I can't imagine anything there you want that we don't have in greater abundance right here at home."

"We had our reasons, Father. For one, the various Martian races possess technological advances that we hoped to obtain in trade."

"Well, Father Brown may not want to know," interjected Herb, "but I do: if we've been traveling into space for a decade, how did you keep the whole world from finding out about it?"

"National governments," said the Doctor, "have cooperated to hide the reality of space travel by leaking stories about it to the 'yellow' journals, publishers of the nickel novels, and other disreputable media outlets."

"And if," said Herb, beginning to understand, "a real journalist for a real newspaper like the *Times* were to hear about it, he'd be too afraid to try to publish it, for fear of being laughed at as a loony."

"Precisely. So much more effective than trying to hide the truth completely. The Special Branch has been doing business like that for over a century now."

"Perhaps," said Herb slowly, "but I have one more question. One that has been gnawing at me for a long time."

"Go on, Herbert."

"Why are you telling us this, Doctor? An organization like your Special Branch thrives on secrecy; in fact, it's wholly incapable of operating without it."

"Herbert," the priest spoke up, interrupting the Doctor before he had a chance to speak. "I'm really quite surprised you haven't figured this out, really. It's because he intends to kill us at the first opportunity. Or perhaps recruit you at any rate into his services, as our attackers have captured his other colleague. Am I correct, Docto— ugh!"

Faster than either Herb or Father Brown would have thought possible, the Doctor had spun around and struck the little priest on the side of the head with the barrel of his weapon. Father Brown fell to the ground on his side, stunned for the moment. Herb stared with his mouth open. Despite the carnage he'd already seen today, Herb was surprised by the sudden and unexpected use of violence.

"Why'd you hit him for?" Herb barked angrily, his distaste for the priest's profession forgotten in a blaze of anger at the Doctor's behavior.

"Herbert," said the Doctor quietly, "in this world, one must be either the wielder of the hammer, or the metal shaped upon the anvil. It is occasionally necessary to remind others not only of their place in the world, but also the consequences for straying too far above their station."

The Doctor stood, staring at Father Brown with a look that could have curdled milk. When the priest had recovered enough to sit up dazedly, the Doctor spoke as if nothing had happened.

"Yes, Father Brown. For once, a priest of the Church of Rome is utterly correct. All except the part about recruiting Herb into our ranks; that hasn't been decided yet."

Herb helped the little priest to his feet with one hand, all the while staring at the Doctor while his left hand gripped the barrel of his rifle tightly. "So you *do* plan to kill us?" Herb asked.

"Not necessarily, Herbert," drawled the Doctor. "But if you prove a threat to me, I will *remove* you with all available speed."

Father Brown saw a look creep into the younger man's eyes that the priest had seen too many times. It was the look of a young man who had just been dared to try something dangerous, like knock a stick off the shoulder of a bully or play chicken with an approaching train.

"Take care, Herbert," said the priest.

"For once I agree with the *padre*, Herbert," said the Doctor. "If you shoot me, that mollusk and its machine are bound to return. Would you like to know what they do to their captives? I hope you are not squeamish. Even were you to avoid capture somehow, would you like to gamble on the odds of ever leaving this underground labyrinth without my guidance?" He smiled tightly.

"But," the Doctor continued, "killing you is not part of my current list of things to do. I generally prefer a more subtle means of eliminating my opponents, such as what happened with that little, unassuming rock under Gilbert's foot a while back."

"You!" roared Herb. "Are you saying you made Gil fall? You . . ." Here Herb brought up the muzzle of his musket rifle, pointing the barrel of his weapon to within a few inches of the Doctor's cool and utterly unruffled face. Herb then used several words that Father Brown had heard a number of Catholic sailors go to confession over. After insulting the Doctor, Herb went on to describe the Doctor's parents and most of the Doctor's ancestors going back several generations. When Herb was finished, he was red in the face, breathing hard and sweating profusely. It was only the threat of the creature's return that held Herb at bay.

The Doctor suddenly looked more than a little ridiculous, with his curled whiskers, top hat, lethal weapon in hand and canister of who-knew-what strapped to his back. But ridiculous as he might appear, Herb had to admit he held all the cards.

"I'm in check for now, mate," said Herb sullenly, lowering the musket.

"A wise decision, young man. And for the record, I did not cause Gilbert's plunge into the stony abyss."

Herb looked quizzically at the Doctor. "Then why'd you say you did?"

"I said nothing of the sort. I only said that, if I could, I *would* choose to eliminate my opponents in a manner *like* Gilbert's fall. I purposely led you in that direction to test your reaction. Thankfully, you are capable of controlling your emotions to a point. If you'd failed, you would have proven yourself likely to be the sort who'd panic in the face of a threat and bring the aliens down upon us, and thus would necessitate your *removal*."

"Of course," Herb said, "if I'd failed, you'd be dead with a bullet in your brains. And that mollusk would hear and come after you."

"Herbert, one of my few faults is the love of an occasional gamble — when I have time, opportunity, and acceptable levels of risk. Believe me when I say that preventing you from ever pulling that trigger would have been child's play for a man of my talents, training, and breeding. But as it was, you managed to hold your emotions in check. And I was granted the pleasure of sparing your life. Now, if you'll be so kind to walk in *front* of me for the rest of this little journey, whilst I direct you? That way, I'll not have to be looking over my shoulder all the time. I've no worry about the good *padre* trying to put a bullet in my back, so he can keep bringing up the rear."

"Which way, then?" mumbled Herb.

"Forward, then left. Back the way our spongy friend came from. Keep your ears open, and don't stop moving. Pausing too long with these monsters around can prove fatal. Right? For-ward, march!"

Herb began to tread over crunching dirt, his musket in his right hand, and his lantern in his left.

"So," he said quietly, "was it *you lot* who were responsible for all that's happened to Gil the past day or so? All the weirdness, the crazy happenings that got him pulled out here?"

"I'm afraid I don't know what you're talking about precisely, Herbert. Do tell me. It may be another member of the Branch, and if they've gotten sloppy, I'll need to include them in my report."

Herb shrugged and, seeing no reason to keep it secret, told the Doctor and the priest about the clerical error at Gilbert's office that had him suddenly promoted to journalist and provided with an expense account worth five times more than a member of Parliament made in a year, bribes included.

"It could be the work of the Branch," mused the Doctor when Herb had finished, "but again, it may not. There's more than one organization vying for influence in this great ball of dirt and water we call the Earth, and they're nearly all looking for fresh blood to take the place of old warhorses, bunglers, traitors, and corpses. Perhaps Gilbert was being primed by a recruiter, perhaps not. I wasn't entirely displeased that he rejected the backpack I gave him in favor of his satchel; it showed initiative on his part, and more than a little cunning to keep me from noticing it until we were well on our way through the tunnels. Incidentally, you were correct, *padre*, about the chap who was captured by that tripod. He was an associate of mine within the Special Branch. For the best, really, that the mollusks took him. He was a bit too shoddy in his own sphere of operation, and I might have had to eliminate him myself. Perhaps young Mister . . . what did you say Gilbert's last name was?"

"I didn't. It's Chesterton."

"What?" snapped the Doctor, stopping suddenly.

Herb was annoyed. "Didn't you say to keep moving, Doctor?" When the Doctor neither moved nor replied, Herb repeated, "*Chesterton.* Gil's last name is Chesterton. Is there some policy against that in the Special Branch, or something?"

"Chesterton," the Doctor muttered to himself, walking again but at a slower pace, staring vaguely into space as he moved. "By Jove, it just might be. Chesterton. Who would have thought? All this time. He is the right age, after all, and now that I think of it, he does have the looks of old Edward and Marie Chesterton!" Slowing to a stop, he began to chuckle. And then laugh.

"What's so funny?" said Herb. The Doctor's laughter unnerved him.

"My dear boy," said the Doctor, his laughter suddenly taking on an aspect that was both gleeful and rueful at the same time, "if your friend is indeed who I think he might be, I just might begin to believe that there is a

God in the universe. And not only that He exists, but that He has a sense of humor besides. Chesterton. Who would have believed it?"

"Look, Doctor, we're trapped underground, monsters from Mars are chasing us, and we've no idea if we're going to live, starve, or be something's dinner. D'you mind telling me just what you find so amusing about our situation?"

"It's there!" Father Brown interrupted with a whisper.

"Wot?" snapped Herb, his blood running cold. He heard the noise and saw the light down the tunnel only a few dozen yards away behind them.

The mollusk was returning.

Nineteen

"The center of every man's existence is a dream. Death, disease, insanity are merely material accidents, like a toothache or a twisted ankle. That these brutal forces always besiege and often capture the citadel does not prove that they are the citadel."
— GKC

Gilbert was dreaming about his parents.

In truth, dreaming wasn't the best word. Gilbert was in that state between sleep and dreams, when memories long hidden and forgotten return unbidden. His mind turned to his childhood home in Minnesota. It had been fairly large — about two dozen rooms all together — and located "in the middle of nowhere's attic," as his father had often put it. Indeed, the home was something of a landmark on its empty patch of Minnesota prairie.

Then Gilbert was inside the house, five years old, and skipping through the long hallway that connected his bedroom to the large family room where his parents often sat up at night, talking with each other.

"This was a good choice, Edward," Ma had said. Gilbert had listened in on many conversations that had started with this comment.

"Yes," Pa's voice sounded through Gilbert's memory like a soft bass drum. It could get surprisingly deep, considering how skinny his Pa was. "You can look in any direction and see company coming from miles away. Even at night, if the moon's up."

"Miles away," Ma echoed. Gilbert was wearing pajamas that came with warm cotton feet attached, and they slipped on the polished wood floor as he came to a sudden stop. He peered around the wall at the silhouettes of his parents against the small windows of the living room. "Them winders ye got, they look like gun ports," one of their neighbors, a farmer's wife named Demaris Wilson, had remarked once. With the clarity his half-sleeping memory afforded, Gilbert heard her voice behind him now.

"This place sure gots a lot of odd nooks and crannies in it, too," Demaris had continued, half-jokingly. "Y'all could hold off the whole blamed C.S.A. Army from this place, if'n you had enough guns and people to shoot 'em."

Demaris and her husband had emigrated from the Confederate States a year before, and she often tried to bring politics and the war into her conversations. Gilbert's mother had just smiled.

Demaris Wilson faded away. The memory-dream resumed.

"And what if there was no moonlight? What then?" Ma was seldom upset unless Gilbert was in danger somehow. But on this night, there was an edge in her voice that Gilbert didn't like. Another part of his memory reminded his dreaming consciousness that she alone among all the farming wives had locked her doors and windows every night.

"Then," said Pa, "we'd listen close until we heard their footsteps. I'd take my rifle and you'd take your stilettos, and we'd put holes in the whole bloody lot of them." Gilbert started. Something had changed in his father's voice. There was a lilt to his speech now, a way of sounding words that Gilbert had never heard before. At the age of five, all his memories had been of living on the Minnesota prairie. He didn't know what an accent *was*, let alone recognize the British manner of speaking into which his Pa had just slipped.

"How long can we keep this up, Edward?" Now his mother, too! Gilbert's brow furrowed. This was wrong, somehow. In his child's mind, there was a *right* way for the world to work. Eating chicken at night and sneaking scraps to the dog was the *right* way of the world. Pa hitching up the team to try plowing a field that never seemed to yield as much as the other farmers' fields was the *right* way of the world. Ma kissing a cut better before she washed and bandaged it was the *right* way of the world. Pa dropping a possum between the eyes with his special hunting rifle at a longer range than any of the other prairie fathers could, or Ma spinning a pair of razor-sharp knives in her hands before slicing, gutting, and skinning the kill for use in a delicious possum meatloaf in half the time it took other wives — these were the *right* ways of the world.

Well, right for *his* parents, anyway.

But having your parents speak in new and strange voices late at night when they thought you were asleep, speaking of putting holes in people with guns, was *not* the right way of the world.

"Do you think it will get better? Do you think we'll ever be able to stop looking over our shoulders?" Ma's voice was strong, but tired.

"No, love. Never," Pa had said. Although he might put truth softly to spare a sensitive soul, his father never lied to anyone. "One day they'll find us, and we'll need to be ready. If we beat them soundly, they'll learn it's better to leave well enough alone."

Gilbert's mother closed her eyes and pursed her lips, as if to keep something inside. "Soundly or not, you know as well as I that they'll never give up."

His father seemed to consider that for a moment. "Marie, I know that they'll always keep an eye out for us. But my great hope is that the world will go through interesting times, and they'll have bigger fish to fry than us. Or little Gilbert."

Ma gasped. "Would they ever try it, Edward? Would that horrible man ever press our little boy into the service?"

"Yes, if only to spite us for trying to leave the life. And to spite you, for rejecting him after he was *selected* for you." Pa had used the word *selected* as if it tasted like soap in his mouth.

"What if *he* comes himself, Edward? You know how he can be; *he* wouldn't try to hide himself by clouds at night; *he'd* come straight at us at high noon, just because he knows that *he* could, and disappear after he lets you take the first shot at him."

Pa looked out the window at the darkness, and Gilbert could see the ghostly face of his father's reflection. Pa was too preoccupied to notice Gilbert's own reflection, watching him. Gilbert saw Pa's eyes narrow with a steely resolve; it was an expression that he'd never seen on his Pa's face before. Gilbert couldn't be certain, but his Pa seemed to have become exactly still. The only thing moving on his father's body at all was his index finger, flexing slowly in the small loop of his teacup.

"If he threatened us, Marie," Pa said, breaking the silent moment, "then we would *remove* him, with all available speed. You remember what they taught us."

Pa, who's this he *person you keep talking about?*

Gilbert could think the words in his mind, but they couldn't or wouldn't be formed into words that he could speak and be heard by.

Ma, why do you lock the windows at night? What are you afraid of?

Pa, Ma, why did your voices change when you thought no one was listening? What is this "life" you're tying to escape?

And what are stilettos?

Gilbert felt a tremor under his feet and looked down. He was still in his pajamas, but now a set of adult clothes had somehow grown over him. They were too big, and very uncomfortable.

A part of his mind knew that he had slipped into the world of full-blown dreams. There would be no hope of waking himself until the drama was fully played out.

Gilbert whimpered. All he wanted to do was crawl back into bed and wake up in the morning to the smell of his mother's flapjacks and home-butchered sausages. But as he turned toward the stairs that led up to his room, he saw they had somehow gotten very, very far away. Too great a distance for a little boy like him ever to cross.

Another tremor shook the floor, this one hard enough to make him wobble and nearly lose his balance. He turned to his parents for help, but yelped in surprise as a deep, zig-zagging fissure opened up between them and Gilbert. Their half of the home suddenly dropped away, faster than the ground did when a balloon took off into the sky.

Within a second, Gilbert could no longer see the faces of his parents. They hadn't seemed to notice their son's half of the house suddenly flying upward and away from them. Gilbert looked up and struggled to move in the clothes and shoes that were far too large for him to fill. The stars loomed bright above him — not delicate and sparkly, but cold, immovable, and unpitying. A chill wind cut his face like a knife, and Gilbert huddled himself into an unseeing ball, cowering on what was now a broken section of the wooden floor floating in space. He risked peeking out with one eye to see if the nightmare was over, but each time he looked, he saw more and more of the giant, yellow cylinders from Mars hurtling toward Earth.

Gilbert swallowed and hid his eyes again. *This is a dream,* he thought to himself. *This is all a dream, and I will wake up in my bed in the farmhouse with Ma and Pa in the living room.* But even as he said it, he knew he would never awaken in that house again.

He buried his head in his knees, whimpering and tearing up, fearful of moving and falling off the platform into the uncaring nothingness that surrounded him.

Then a hand touched his shoulder. There was another person with him on the platform.

It was a young man, not much older than Gilbert. He had wavy brown hair, and wore a shirt and trousers. His face was neither old nor young; with eyes that managed to be soft with a focus that still held Gilbert's gaze. Oddly enough, Gilbert couldn't quite pin down the color of the clothes. They seemed white, but always had a different undertone to them. The shirt would now be a bluish white, and if Gilbert looked again, even without blinking, it changed to a yellowish, and now a reddish white. The trousers had the same odd hues, shifting without seeming to really shift, more like the faces of a jewel would reflect different colors if you moved, no matter how long you kept your eyes on it. Beside the man, propped up on the disconnected strip of wooden floor, Gilbert could see a sword and a pair of weighing scales.

Then the man spoke — or did he? Gilbert seemed to hear him without using his ears. *Trust,* he said. *You can trust, if you wish.*

I want to go home, said Gilbert without opening his mouth.

We all do. You can, but not yet, answered the man in the same way. He looked away from Gilbert into the stars.

What is like them, in the whole of the universe?

Gilbert couldn't speak. Like almost every boy in history, he'd dreamed of what it would be like to visit the stars, to fly in space like a bird among the planets and heavens. But now, with the never-ending cosmos in front of him, all he felt was sick with fear. Each time he tried to fix his gaze on a star or a planet, he could see farther, and farther than that. And farther beyond *that.* The harder he tried to fasten his mind on some fixed point, the more immense the distance became, and his fear grew. He tore his eyes away and looked back at his new companion.

They are never-ending. What is like them? Who is like their Maker? said the young man again.

Now Gilbert's attention was drawn to something else. The infinite expanse of stars had been replaced by a kind of black whirlpool in space; a hole as wide as a planet, a solar system, or even a galaxy. Pulling him toward it. And the more Gilbert looked, the larger it became.

Gilbert clutched at the floor for something, anything to hold on to, anything to keep him from sliding into the nothingness. He realized that his tiny raft of split wood could never protect him from the swirling void around him; he still wanted to clutch it as a child on a sinking ship would clutch a doll for comfort.

Consumed with his own terror, Gilbert had forgotten the other passenger on his dream raft. He felt a touch at his hand, and looked into the young man's face.

Trust, he said again, as the raft began to tilt and Gilbert felt himself start to slide on the polished wood. The black hole was drawing him in, and would surely destroy him.

SomebodysomebodysomebodyOhGodsomebodyhelpme! Gilbert shrieked without words. There was no sound in this drama now, only maddening, crushing silence.

Then the boy smiled and reached out. He grasped the hole with his hand and crumpled it like a piece of newspaper. All was still.

Gilbert blinked. The boy hadn't moved, hadn't grown to gigantic size.

Who are you? was all Gilbert could say.

Who is like Him, the boy replied, taking Gilbert's arm and shaking it.

What?

Gilbert opened his eyes. He was staring at the ceiling and the dancing light from his lamp. He sat up abruptly, suddenly free of aches and pains as if he'd been sleeping on a down cushion rather than a cave floor. How long had he slept, anyway?

Gilbert stood, and as he moved, he was glad for the sound of gravel beneath his feet. After a dream of such unimaginable terror, even the solid ground of his underground prison seemed comforting.

Thirsty, Gilbert drank from the small trickle of water that crept along the floor. It wasn't easy — the water came out in such a small dribble that he had to dip his fingers in it and lick the drops off a few at a time. He spit out the grains of sand that collected in his mouth.

"What a funny dream I've had," Gilbert said aloud, looking at the floor. It was a few moments before he could look at the hole in the wall again, but when he did, it seemed to have changed. Before, it had looked like a giant mouth ready to chew him up; the trickle of water a string of hungry drool.

Now it just looked like a hole in a rock. A crude little doorway he needed to get busy shimmying through.

He took a deep breath, grabbed the lantern, and poked his head through the opening.

It went downward. Gilbert was puzzled; if the hole slanted down, away from his cell, how did the water trickle through it up to him? He was answered by a drop of water that splatted on the back of his neck. Of course! The water dripped down from above, and went in two separate directions. The tunnel wasn't shaped so much like an *S* after all, but more like an arrowhead. If he left his cell, he'd move down about a foot and have to bend his body at an angle of about ninety degrees to continue onward. Besides his worry about being caught in the tunnel, he'd have to decide how he would bring the satchel and lantern along with him through the cramped space.

Clutching the lantern carefully, he pulled his head and shoulders out of the hole and stood again in his cell. *Can't be too bulky,* he thought to himself. The satchel would have to stay behind if he kept everything he'd brought with him — even if he hooked it to his ankle and dragged it behind him, it was too big right now to fit through every part of the narrow passage. He carefully packed just the most necessary items into his satchel, put the strap over his head, and made sure it fit securely yet comfortably. Then he checked the lantern for leaks as carefully as he could and, after taking a deep breath and orienting himself, turned it off.

Gilbert breathed again. The darkness was absolute, but no longer crushing; it seemed paltry in comparison to the void he'd escaped in his dream. He felt his way to the space in the wall, put one leg up and into it, and then the other, wriggling into the arrowhead-shaped passage feet first. When his feet reached the bend in the rock, Gilbert twisted himself until he lay on his stomach. It would have been impossible to follow the angle of the tunnel by bending over backward.

It was still difficult. The tunnel wasn't much bigger than Gilbert to begin with. He had to move the satchel around to keep it from binding. Finally he was able to bend and twist himself into the upside-down *V* shape he needed to, and once past the bent roof of the tunnel, he found there was more room than he'd thought.

He squirmed through the tight space, curved down and backward, for what seemed like an hour. Once his head had moved a foot or so past the tunnel's apex, his feet suddenly kicked free! There was open air beneath him!

I could be free, he thought. *Or maybe,* said another voice inside him, *I'm a hundred feet above the ground, about to fall to my death.*

Then a voice in Gilbert's head: *Trust.*

Did he just think that?

"I need help," he said aloud.

He felt water, which had been matting his hair, now dripping down into his eyes. Of course! The trickle still came out both ways! He listened carefully, his legs still dangling down beneath him.

There! He definitely heard the sound of droplets hitting rock. The water seemed to take almost no time at all to hit the floor. But sounds inside a cave could prove deceiving, couldn't they? Could it be so far to the ground that he was hearing an echo or something similar?

He pushed his way out, his eyes open, taking care to hold on to the edge of the tunnel with his hands as he emerged.

He felt his calves, knees, thighs, and midsection slide over the last hump of rock at the tunnel's edge.

He took a deep breath, slid farther out of the cramped space and . . .

Trust.

. . . jumped blindly, his arms stretching out to his sides as if to keep his balance in midair.

Less than a half-second later, he hit the floor. The drop couldn't have been more than eight feet.

Gilbert blinked. Then he laughed. Then paused to breathe. Then he laughed more, and louder. "That was too easy!" he almost crowed. "Too easy! And here's me, all upset! All over a coupla feet of tunnel! This is going to be a joke of a trip from here on in! You hear me? A joke!"

He laughed. He was so nearly crazed with relief and the absurdity of his situation that he did a little victory dance, as he'd seen cowboy drifters perform in the hoedowns back home. He laughed and twirled like a top, right up to the point that his satchel smacked into an unseen wall beside him. The crack of his lantern's glass breaking inside sounded like a cannon shot, stopping Gilbert cold.

Twenty

"Alone of all creeds, Christianity has added courage to the virtues of the Creator. For the only courage worth calling courage must necessarily mean
that the soul passes a breaking point and does not
break." — GKC

The sounds of the returning creature grew louder. Around a curve of the long tunnel, the wall began to glow with a sickly green light.

"Can we run?" Herb said quickly. "We can double back along the tunnel where we came."

"No," said the Doctor, "their machines can track us. And we can't outrun it. Therefore," he brought up the long barrel of his own weapon, the black hose attaching it to the tank on the Doctor's back glistening dully in the lantern light, "we fight! Herbert! On my right! Father Brown on my left! When the creature comes into sight, let loose *on the machine only*. Don't try to hit the creature itself. Your weapons cannot harm it!

"But," he continued as he removed the long, nozzle-shaped pistol from the holster on his side, "don't stop shooting. You will provide a necessary distraction until I've finished it off."

"And how do you plan to do that?" grumbled Herb. "By pushing us into it, and running off while it eats us?"

The Doctor didn't answer, but continued preparing his weapon. Herb watched as the Doctor began turning knobs on the tank he carried on his back, to which his weapon was connected by a long hose. Then he turned a smaller knob near the trigger of the weapon, setting off a hissing noise. Finally, he pulled a small trigger near the stock, causing two small hammers near the open muzzle to click together. A spark shot out, and then a small, steady flame appeared.

"That's it?" yelled Herb. "You're going to try to kill that thing with a glorified cigarette lighter?"

"You just keep that monster busy with your bullets, and mind not to hit me as I stand in front of you," the Doctor said grimly, putting a set of dark goggles over his eyes.

Herb mumbled something unprintable under his breath as he knelt down with his rifle, while Father Brown calmly removed his pistol, standing sideways and extending his arm to its full length, while bending his elbow just slightly. The humming sound grew louder, and as the machine rounded the corner, Herb could at last see its pilot clearly.

It truly was a creature, not a person at all. True, the Doctor had described it as a mollusk, but Herb, of course, had never seen an intelligent being shaped like anything other than a human. The best even Herb's fertile imagination had been able to conjure up was a human-like creature, with small tentacles for fingers and webbing between the toes. Indeed, since Herb was at the stage of male development where virtually all roads of life led to pretty girls, while tramping through the tunnels he had even entertained the idea of winning the heart of a beautiful Martian princess, perhaps rescuing her from her black-hearted evil Martian captors.

Seeing the pilot of the machine in front of him turned all of Herb's romantic daydreams into so much steam and ashes. It was difficult to look closely at any one detail of the thing; for some reason, the air around it seemed to shift and change, keeping his eye from seeing any one specific point on the creature or its machine clearly. But what Herb *could* see repulsed yet fascinated him, the way spoiled milk demands to be smelled before it is thrown away. It looked to be all brain and arms, with no real body, but three angry, unblinking yellow eyes that Herb saw often in his dreams afterward. The machine's clicking came from the snapping, writhing motion of a collection of tentacles that emerged from under the eyes, where Herb thought its mouth and body should be. The thing was plugging and unplugging its whiplike arms in and out of a number of sockets in front of it, which apparently controlled the balancing of its craft in the air.

Herb blinked. The thing's machine was doing the *impossible*! It was hovering several inches *in the air*, with nothing supporting it beneath! How on earth could anything . . .

"Fire!" yelled the Doctor over the din of the machine's engine. Herb's rifle went off with a deafening *boom*, filling the stone corridor with a blazing flash and the acrid smell of burning powder. The priest's small pistol blasted a half-dozen times until the chambers were empty, its bullets sparking and pinging as they struck the machine. At the same time, a spray of rocks and sand flew up over the creature. Herb blinked. He had aimed poorly — the bullet had struck the cave floor a few feet in front of the machine — but it had a good effect. Temporarily blinded or distracted by the hail of pebbles, creature and machine swerved and slowed. This gave Father Brown time to reload and bring his pistol up a second time, and he let loose another volley of bullets.

Herb saw one of the priest's bullets strike the side of the craft, causing a momentary flicker of light in the air around the creature. It seemed to Herb that the sight of the monster . . . *changed* somehow, the air rippling and distorting the sight of the creature and its craft in the form of concentric waves fanning out from where the bullet had hit. A small blue bulb of viscous liquid on the side of the craft glowed brightly as the air shimmered around the alien, and when it was finished, Herb could see no damage at all to the craft. How, Herb thought, does anything take a bullet head-on like that and avoid even a scratch?

"Hold still, you little devil," the Doctor grumbled to himself as he stepped up and aimed his weapon. To Herb, it sounded like the voice one would use when stalking a fly with a rolled-up newspaper.

Then the monster's movement ceased for just a moment, as it seemed to take note of the Doctor for the first time. In that space of silence, the Doctor said casually, "Avoid looking at the blast, gentlemen," and then pulled the trigger.

Herb would later try to recount how the Doctor's weapon had fired. He first heard a kind of sloshing sound, starting at the tank on the Doctor's back and running through the flexible tube that attached the tank to the Doctor's odd, cylinder-shaped gun.

Herb was confused. How would water help them? And why was there a tiny flame coming out of the tube? Wouldn't water just put the flame out?

Suddenly the cavern was lit up as if by a thousand lanterns. Herb was wrong; the liquid wasn't water, but some kind of burning oil. As it sprayed from the Doctor's gun, the small flame at the tip of the gun's barrel ignited it, making a liquid fire that charged out and engulfed the alien and his ship in an inferno. The close corridor became so hot and bright that both Herb and Father Brown had to squint their eyes nearly shut. Herb turned his head and hid his face in the crook of his arm.

"*Ulla! Ulla!*" The creature's voice climbed to a high-pitched shriek, piercing the corridor and filling all three men's ears with a sense of sick dread. As the liquid flame splashed against its target, the blue bulb glowed even more intensely, expanded slightly, then exploded into a million tiny fragments with the sound of a cork popping out of a bottle of champagne.

Herb saw all this happen in less than a second. The air had flickered around the creature when the bulb had shattered. Now Herb could see the fiery monster even more clearly, the deep wrinkles in its gray, blob-like body and its writhing tentacles standing out even more horribly than before as the fire melted and twisted them like wax in a furnace. Herb stood frozen in place, the horror in front of him leaving him speechless and unable to move.

Father Brown didn't pause, but continued firing. A line of tiny explosions drilled into the mollusk's ship by the priest's bullets moved up and led toward the center of the craft. The last two bullets struck into the alien pilot, splattering into the bulbous, burning flesh with dull squishing sounds. The last bullet by the priest was the most important — it slammed into one of the creature's eyes.

"*Ulla!*" the creature shrieked, in a guttural voice that was half-machine, half-beast. The wound to its eye brought a stop to the hovering craft. It unplugged its tentacles and began to claw and slap at the flames engulfing its body; a beaked mouth emerged from a cavity near its eyes, and from it emanated an even louder rhythmic sounding of "*Ulla! Ulla!*" that echoed through the cavern. While the mollusk writhed in agony, its craft still stayed perfectly still, hovering in the air with no visible means of support.

The Doctor poured his weapon's liquid flame onto the alien for several very long seconds. Its oozing flesh crackled, blistered, and melted, its tentacles slapping the walls of the cavern madly until, one by one, they became useless. Its craft crashed to the ground and became a pyre, giving off a nauseating smell that made Herb retch.

The Doctor continued to pour flame upon the creature. His face was slick with sweat, and grimy with soot and dirt. His top hat, although dusty, remained inexplicably in place. His eyes were completely hidden behind the black lenses of the goggles, but his teeth, bared slightly and gritted, were visible through the thick whiskers. In the searing flamelight, Father Brown stood his ground, his pistol once again extended, firing round after round into the raging mass of flame. His eyes widened as he stared at the shrieking creature, and the corner of his mouth began to twitch slightly.

Finally, after the longest ten seconds of Herb's life, the Doctor released the trigger and fire stopped erupting from his gun. The alien and its craft were a bright heap of dancing flame, but the fire was the only thing that moved in it.

The Doctor raised his goggles and surveyed his deadly handiwork. "Right," he said crisply. "Ready to move on?"

⁂

His earlier joy now subdued by his return to darkness, Gilbert breathed slowly several times while he thought out his next move. He knelt and took a match from the little matchbox in his satchel. He lit it, and dropped it into the oil lamp while he shook its base slightly. There must have been a few drops of oil somewhere in the thing's reservoir or whatever held its fuel, because the cavern suddenly lit up again and shone with the dull yellow glow of the lamp through its partially broken glass shell. At least there would be a little light left for him on this adventure!

I'll have to get a move on, Gilbert thought. *There's no telling when this'll run out now.* He pulled himself to his feet, faintly surprised at how calmly he was taking the latest setback, and took in his surroundings. The walls of the stone corridor were bumpy and rocky; if they had been carved out by man, it had been done with fairly crude tools. The floor, however, was smooth, with only a fine layer of pebbles and grit, perhaps a half-inch deep in spots. He sealed up his satchel once more, not for the first time marveling at how ingeniously the large bag closed. (It was amazing, simply amazing what they were able to come up with these days using analytical engines!) Instead of cumbersome buckles, there was a seam that one simply pinched together, sealing the main compartment tightly. Gilbert noticed a small bit of lettering near the top corner of the seam. "Water resistant," he read aloud solemnly. "Well, that'll be good, if I have to resist any water that jumps me in a dark alley!" He laughed. His gentle, slightly childish sense of humor wasn't always appreciated in school, especially by the popular girls and carnivorous bullies, but when he was trapped in a dark cave all alone, it was something of a comfort.

"And there's no bullies here," he said jauntily, slinging the strap of the satchel over his shoulder and scooping up the lamp by its wire handle. "Got that? I can be a loony bird if I want, and there's NO BULLIES HERE!" He paused again, listening to the final *here* as it echoed down the tunnel.

Well, thought Gilbert, *the cavern must go on for quite a ways if my voice could echo so far. Still, that means I've got all kinds of places to find a spring of water, or even an exit!*

An exit . . .

Which way now to go? He paused. He shuffled his feet slightly on the gravelly floor, put down the satchel and lantern and held out his arms slightly with his eyes closed, like a tightrope artist trying to keep his balance. He turned in a circle, slowly, his head cocked as if trying to listen to a very soft voice over several others.

The corridor floor definitely tilted slightly up toward the . . . which direction was it? There was no sun to tell by. Where the tunnel tilted downward, though, there was a soft but definite breeze that caressed his chin, as if beckoning him downward.

Hadn't Father Brown said something about fresh air leading to freedom? Plus, the floor looked a lot like a dry riverbed. If water had flowed downhill from here, perhaps he could find its source and get a drink. He could always return to this spot later, if he struck a dead end.

That settled it! Better to walk down the slope toward hope of air and drink, than up to a complete unknown. He took up his gear and started walking, now with a bounce in his step. A part of him tried hard to whisper that he really shouldn't feel so confident. He was who-knew-how-many feet underground, had no idea where he was going, or if he would ever get out alive, and no assurances anyone would even find his body if he died.

But as he continued onward, Gilbert dashed such thoughts, preferring instead to think about the strange dream he'd had. He wondered about the accents his parents had slipped into when they thought no one was listening. Odd how he'd remembered it, yet never thought of it before. And who was the person that they were afraid would come and seek them out? Oddest of all by far, who was the young man who had rescued him from the black hole? Was he a long-lost cousin or something?

All he knew was, ever since his dream, Gilbert had found an unusual sense of assurance. Cold reason told him he had very little to swagger about, but he couldn't shake the sense of confidence and trust that whatever it was he'd dreamed of would somehow get him through this trial.

And then the lamp went out.

In total darkness once more, Gilbert found his cheerful attitude evaporating as quickly as the heat from the now-cooling lamp base. But his resolve was too hard to be overcome now. He'd come this far — it was going to take more than a little fear of the dark to beat him this time!

Time to think, Gilbert. He shook the lamp gently, then vigorously, hoping to splash some stray oil onto the wick. Nothing. Wasn't it supposed to dim or something before going out?

Time to think some more.

Other animals live in darkness. How do they get around? He sniffed the air — nothing but the smell of very, very old dirt. Then Gilbert tried to sit still and listen; perhaps he could *hear* something useful. But that proved tougher than he'd thought. He kept thinking he could hear *something* other than himself, but he wasn't sure what, or even if it was his own imagination.

First, the sound of his breathing got in the way. Once he thought he'd managed to ignore his breathing, his heartbeat was too loud. Finally, after nearly an hour of sitting and trying to listen, he found the trick of listening to the world outside himself between heartbeats. And what he heard made his throat suddenly feel very parched and dry, and made his tongue ache for the small trickle of water back in his stone cell.

What he heard between his heartbeats, and very far off, was the steady murmur of flowing water.

"Wherever it is, it's not getting any closer to me on its own!" Abandoning the lamp, he stood and began walking down the passage in what he believed to be the direction of the sound, taking baby steps while holding his hands to his front and sides. He felt along the walls with his fingertips and gingerly with his toes to make sure he didn't smack into a wall, or trip over another rock — or plunge into a subterranean chasm.

Five minutes into this exercise, Gilbert had an unpleasant thought: What if the corridor branched off at some point? He was feeling along the right side of the wall; but if the corridor branched off, he'd automatically take the right branch without knowing the other passageway even existed. He could continue going on this way for hours, and could quite possibly go in circles and not know it until it was too late.

"Too late," Gilbert muttered. "Too late, if I'm . . ."

He stopped again. The sound of his voice had given him an idea. He turned to the wall and touched it, making certain it was about six inches away. "Hello," he said in a normal tone, his voice sounding flat against his ears. He turned slowly, listening to his own voice change in tone as he turned from the wall and faced the empty stone corridor. "Hello," he repeated again and again, "Hello, hello, hello . . ."

Bats called out to rock walls with their high-pitched squeaks, and the echo told them how close they were to walls, prey, or other bats in the dark.

Gilbert realized that *his* echo sounded slightly different with each slight turn of his body. *With no other distractions,* Gilbert thought, *I could use my voice to find an opening, or another branch in the cave. I'll avoid going in circles, maybe even find a way out before long. At the worst, I'll still be calling out enough for someone to hear me — maybe even Herb and the rest of them!*

Gradually, he moved forward. It was slow going at first: Gilbert would take a few steps, call out, note any differences, and then take a few more steps. After a little while, he had a routine set in place that was almost enjoyable. *So long as I don't get a sore throat,* he thought, *I could do this for a long time.*

But the rumbling in his stomach told him he wouldn't live off his ideas forever. After a while, the constant calling also made him wish for a drink of water. He wondered how far it was to the water, or whether he was getting closer to the surface. After a while, he realized the tunnel was sloping downward at a more severe angle. *That's how you find water, right?* he said, trying to reassure himself. *By going downhill?* But the surface had to be *up*. Still, he thought, once he found the source of water, he could always back-track and go upward again.

After a time, Gilbert heard a dull noise in the distance. At first, his heart leaped — he thought it might be a factory or a crowd of people talking!

But as he continued to listen, he realized that the noise wasn't rhythmic enough to be machinery, and too flowing without single voices raised to be a crowd . . .

Flowing! An underground river! A few more minutes of walking, and he was sure. It sounded every bit as full and vibrant as the creek did in springtime back home in Minnesota. But with no light, Gilbert hadn't a clue as to how far down it was, or how deep, or whether the water was even good to drink, or if there were river rats swimming in it, eager to chew morsels of his flesh down to his bones . . .

Stop it, Gilbert, he thought firmly. *Worrying isn't going to get you out any sooner.* Squirming through the opening in his cell had taught Gilbert that the only cure for fear was action, and action came only through decision.

I can wait here for someone to pull me out, which won't happen, or I can jump into the water. No, that was too dangerous. The water sounded still too far off to jump into. If the water was too shallow and the jump too far, he might break a leg, or worse. He dropped to his hands and knees and felt along the ground for the edge of the river. With his sharpened hearing, he could tell that it was only ten, maybe twenty feet away at most. But the ground didn't feel moist, so he couldn't be at a riverbank yet.

Suddenly, the rocky floor dropped away under his probing fingertips. His ears had been right! He was on a cliff of some kind! Feeling over the edge, he could tell that the cliff went from one wall of his tunnel to the other, and dropped straight down to where he heard the water running.

Where only hours before, Gilbert would have been paralyzed by worry, now he immediately had an idea and acted on it. He felt along the edge of the tunnel until he found a rock about as big as his hand. He returned to the edge, dropped the rock, and counted to himself as it fell. "One one-thou—" He was cut off in mid-count by the sound of a splash. *Good,* he thought, *and I never thought I'd use the stuff they taught me in physics class!* When dropped, Gilbert had recalled from class, an object falls at ten yards the first second. Math was never his strongest subject, but even Gilbert could figure that half a second meant about five yards, or fifteen feet.

"I bet I could jump fifteen feet and hit the ground and not feel it. Not much, anyway."

Still, first he slid his hands across the edge of the tunnel to see if . . . no, there was no chance of climbing down. The cliff wall moved inward, away from and under the edge. It was jump or wait for something to happen.

Gilbert could smell the water flowing beneath him. There was a cool freshness in the air that made him realize how dank, stale, and old the air was in this underground labyrinth.

Trust. Gilbert made sure his satchel was fastened snugly, and jumped. As he fell, he involuntarily stuck his hands out and made little flapping circles.

He hit the water feet first, keeping his knees bent. He had been ready to tuck and roll if he hit the riverbed suddenly, but he never touched bottom. The slow descent under the water was long, cool, and almost as refreshing as a jump into a Minnesota pond.

Gilbert held his breath, letting the air in his lungs lift him slowly to the surface.

Gilbert waited. Then waited some more.

Where was the surface?

He pumped his arms, trying to swim upward. Fifteen seconds. He still had water all around him!

Don't panic, he thought. *Just swim up . . .*

Which way was up?

How much time had passed? His clothes and shoes were now water-logged and heavy. His satchel dragged alongside him like a millstone. He began to flail like a fish on a hook, even though his rational mind knew it would only burn up his air faster.

More time. Seconds? How many? Can't count. Panic. No, *don't* panic! Gilbert's chest was screaming. He remembered the time his friend Japheth Gunderson almost drowned in a swollen spring river, how he'd said his lungs felt like they were burning. It wasn't like that for him. He just wanted to breathe, but couldn't. There was nothing to liken this to — only wanting desperately to breathe.

Trust! he thought frantically, pushing his arms and legs in any and every direction as the panic began to take over. I'll trus—

Then he felt something like a gentle finger or feather; it stroked him gently across his face without any hurry, from his left to his right.

What the —

Of course! A bubble! Hitting the water had made a pile of bubbles, and they had nowhere to go but up to the surface!

He could feel several of the little tickles and taps from them even now, all floating from his left to his right. He stopped trying to go up and turned to his right, swimming to follow where the direction the bubbles had traveled, even though his own senses told him to go elsewhere.

Then a very odd thing happened to Gilbert. Although he had thought he was *already* swimming up to the surface just a few seconds before, following the bubble's touch changed Gilbert's sense of direction. What had seemed sideways at first was really upward toward air and life.

His right hand broke the surface a split second before his face did. Gilbert opened his mouth, sucking in gulps of clean new air. Then he sank a few inches and accidentally breathed a mouthful of water. He gagged, kicked water, and bobbed back up to the surface, coughing and spluttering.

He paddled enough to tread water, floating gently with the current. He had no way of knowing how far off the other bank was — if there indeed was a bank — or where the river was taking him. But he thought it best to save his strength for a bit rather than trying to swim cross-current. Eventually, even an underground stream has to come out somewhere, doesn't it?

As he bobbed along, he forced himself not to think about what was waiting for him up top. Maybe the tripod had already been defeated. Maybe it had gotten tired of terrorizing Earth and moved on to Venus or something.

Any way the river flows, he thought. *Just so long as I keep my head above water, I'll be fine. Keep focused, Gil. That's what Herb would tell you now.*

After a few minutes, the stream dipped, then dipped again. Invisible rocks bumped his legs here and there as the river seemed to grow narrower and faster. And then . . .

Light! First, the rock walls around him became dimly discernible shadows rather than the shapeless blackness that had surrounded him for hours. Then he thought he caught a reflection on the water ahead. And then he looked up, and his heart leaped as he saw a grated metal ceiling, and through it, unmistakably, the sun.

Glad I'm a journalist, he thought ruefully. *I sure would've made a lousy coal miner.*

Gilbert looked around gratefully at the tunnel walls and the dancing sunlight. (He reckoned it must have been about noon outside. Fortunate for him it wasn't midnight!) The slimy walls were man-made, stout red brick, with a watermark several feet above the current level of the stream.

Now he knew where he was. Several decades ago, the British government had used analytical engines to plan, design, and construct a sewer system that would run underneath the city of London. For centuries before, people dumped human waste into the streets and let it dribble through the gutters toward the Thames River. But the underground sewer system allowed for indoor plumbing facilities inside every building in the city. The cost had been enormous, but the project had been undertaken with the promise of eliminating both plague and the city's infamous stink.

That had been in the 1850s, half a century ago. The system had worked so well in London that soon neighboring districts had clamored for sewers of their own. Over the course of four decades, systems were developed that drained water from surrounding lakes and reservoirs, pumped it under cities and even mid-size towns, collected what the Brits liked to call "the dirties," and pumped the wastewater out again into runoff rivers or treatment plants where the water would be filtered, cleaned out, boiled, or otherwise made ready for human use again. It was one of the great achievements of the age.

As the network of sewers expanded, smaller cities and towns began linking theirs to larger ones. And now Gilbert was using one of them to get a free ride to Woking!

The lights began to dim as he saw the tunnel widen. To his dismay, he saw that the tunnel branched off ahead into three new, different tunnels.

"Time to make a choice, Gil," he spoke over the nearly silent stream, still dog-paddling forward. More staying afloat now than actually trying to swim, he was beginning to feel a little tired. But the current was strong enough that he could let it carry him where it would.

Still, it would be nice to rest. His muscles were cold and tight, and the surge of adrenaline he'd gotten from jumping into the river was long gone. He looked around for a ledge on the walls, or maybe a ladder that would lead upward to a grating. But there was nothing visible that would help him. He had just started paddling in a circle to look behind him when he felt the tips of his feet touch the sewer-river bottom. After another few yards, he could walk, although with a little difficulty — the current kept pushing him toward the three doorways in front of him. *Either the water is even lower than usual,* he thought, *or I'm in a part of the sewers that is shallower than the rest. Maybe they did this on purpose, so that workers could get in here if they needed to.*

Another ten yards forward and Gilbert found himself faced with the choice of three directions. Bracing himself against the current, he sniffed the air coming out of all three passages, and noticed that the middle one still smelled fresh as the rest of the river he had been in. The waft of human waste and stink came from the doors on both his left and his right.

The middle way, then. His history teacher at St. Alban's had said something about this — how, in medieval times, the *via media*, or "middle way," was valued, since going to one extreme led you into pride or some other vice . . .

"*Via media*," he mumbled, and strode through the middle door. The water level was tapering off now, and he could almost walk normally. It was still fairly hard going, though — the water was up to his waist — but another few minutes of walking and sloshing, and it was down halfway to his knees.

I'm moving upward, Gilbert noted happily. *I'm going to get out of here! No more worrying about starving to death underground!* How it would feel to finally break the surface of the ground, to breathe fresh air and drink fresh water again! He imagined all kinds of earthly delights, from hot meals to warm baths to sleeping till noon in his own bed again.

Such was Gilbert's optimism that he was already rethinking his future as a journalist, fantasizing about being a ranch hand out in the Western Territories, or even the Texas or the Californian Republics. *See the world*, he thought. To be out in the sun, all day, every day. No more adventures! No more grimy London; no more caves or sewers. And, maybe, after he'd tired of his youthful wanderings, there'd be the chance of settling down with the red-headed girl, and raise a family in his old house . . .

That brought a bit of a pause to his steps. He didn't even know the girl's name. He had known her . . . well, known *about* her, anyway, for only a day. And yet she was so often in his thoughts! It was hardly his fault, though — she kept popping up. She'd been there at the office, and on the train, and . . .

Gilbert stopped. His clacker's mind couldn't release a thought that demanded to be examined and solved, and sometimes that meant he needed to stop moving in order to focus fully.

The girl had been at the office, right before he had gotten the journalist job.

And she'd been on the train, right before they'd crashed into the tripod. And . . .

"She'd been talking to the Doctor!" he shouted to no one in particular, the pieces suddenly rearranging themselves in his head. The Doctor had even given her that electric rod to resuscitate the engineer, a rod that had been carried and used by the guy the tripod had grabbed on their way to the inn.

Could she be connected somehow? To the Doctor, Gilbert's new job, and the tripods, all at once?

"If it looks like a duck . . ." he mumbled, beginning to walk again down the tunnel. There were too many coincidences, too many pieces with things in common. Pieces of a puzzle that looked similar must fit together in some way. But how? Did he need other pieces to make these ones fit? Did Red Hair work *with* the Doctor, *for* the Doctor, or could she be part of a group that was *opposed* to the Doctor, and all he stood for? Or would it be better not to even ask the questions, and take his thousand pounds and become an anonymous wanderer in the American West?

He'd just decided once and for all to end his career as a journalist in favor of Anonymous Wanderer life when he heard the humming and clicking sound. A sickly pale-green glow accompanied the sound, now just around a bend a dozen yards away.

Gilbert felt cold prickles at the back of his neck. He couldn't name his fear precisely, but the growing dread in his stomach told him something terrible was coming. And it knew Gilbert was near.

Twenty-One

"It has been often said, very truly, that religion is the thing that makes the ordinary man feel extraordinary; it is an equally important truth that religion is the thing that makes the extraordinary man feel ordinary." — GKC

Gilbert turned back down the corridor with a start, sploshing through the ankle-deep water. Just a dozen yards back, he had passed a small alcove in the wall, and now he ran back and flattened himself into it. Whether it was primal instinct or recent experience, he didn't know, but something told him to be afraid and hide for his life. The alcove was actually a bathroom ("water closets" the British liked to call them), and the wooden door had long ago rotted off its rusty hinges. Not that an inch-thick piece of wood could have offered any serious protection from what was chasing him, but he still felt uncomfortably vulnerable sitting on a dry toilet seat in the dark.

The noise was maybe twenty yards from him now. The chittering had slowed, becoming a steady throbbing drum-sound. Gilbert, now nearly paralyzed with fear, couldn't even bring himself to sneak a peek around the corner to catch a quick glimpse of his pursuer. Who or whatever was out there, he'd seen enough in the last few hours to know it hadn't started the day by getting out of an English bed.

He pulled back behind the wall, fumbled into his satchel and grabbed one of the pistols the Doctor had given him. Although he'd been raised with rifles, pistols were new to him. The Colt .45 felt big, heavy, clunky, and useless in his hands. He didn't even know if it was loaded, and checking might make unwanted noise. And what in Sam Hill was that thing around the corner? Bad enough that you had that giant black milking stool stomping around the countryside; now things were tramping around in the sewers, humming like angry beehives. If Gilbert hadn't already seen a half-dozen impossible things since lunch, he'd be shrieking now with panic.

But now, instead of panic, Gilbert began to feel very, very tired. More tired than he ever remembered feeling in his life. He had to struggle to stay awake, even with the angry humming and clicking that now sounded within just a few feet of him.

Movement caught his eye. At the edge of the wall on the floor, Gilbert saw what looked like a small, quiet black snake with very long metal feelers worm its way around the corner of his alcove. A shot of scare went through him — the thing had the same metallic sheen on its skin as the tentacles of the black tripod. He had no doubt his new visitor was from the alien around the corner, and that he had only a few seconds before it found and snuffed him out of existence.

I could stay here, Gilbert thought, *and go with the natural flow of things, cowering like a little mouse for the next few seconds until it finds me. But then I'll be dead, and all I've gone through today will be for nothing, nothing!*

Nothing. All his sufferings would be for nothing at all, if he stood and let himself be taken.

That's not the way I want to die. I want my death to be worthwhile.

I want to be a hero.

And at that moment, Gilbert knew the true meaning of the word. It wasn't running to meet certain death without any fear at all; it was feeling paralyzed by fear, but stepping up anyway. Doing what had to be done.

And as the tentacle touched and began to explore the tip of Gilbert's boot, he realized that whatever nightmare was on the other end, whatever monstrosity was at the helm of that metallic snake, it didn't care about Gilbert at all.

It didn't care that Gilbert had somehow miraculously cheated death more than once. It didn't care that Gilbert's happy life had been shaken apart in the last year like a house of cards in an earthquake. And it didn't care what a tragedy it was that Gilbert would never talk to the red-headed girl again.

And that made Gilbert blisteringly angry, filled him with a livid resentment that raised him from his wishful slumber. His eyes no longer tried to close. Instead they narrowed, glaring at the slithering thing beneath him.

Slowly, keeping his back firmly to the wall, Gilbert stared at the tentacle on his left foot as he slowly brought up his right. He moved a shade too quickly at one point, and the shiny black coil rose up six inches from the ground and poked the air like a cobra searching for prey. *If I go with the flow,* Gilbert thought, *I'll be dead in seconds. But a live man can fight even the strongest current for a while.*

Gilbert brought his heel up slowly, as if to keep from agitating a vicious dog. Three inches . . . Gilbert raised his foot higher. *Nice doggy* . . . four inches . . . *good boy* . . . six inches . . . *stay down* . . . eight inches, and . . .

STOMP! went Gilbert's foot, pinning the head of the black metal snake to the wet stone floor. The snake's body suddenly recoiled, and Gilbert could feel its "head" writhing underneath his heel.

"How d'you like *that,* huh?" yelled Gilbert, the stress of the last day and a half pouring out of him in a stream. "You like that? You want more? Huh?" he roared, pressing down harder with his foot. "You wanna know what it's like to be afraid all the time?" Now he ground his heel on the wriggling black tentacle as hard as he could, all the while struggling to keep his satchel from swinging in front of him and blocking his view of his prey. Now, he thought, he would pull the gun out of his satchel and blast the thing into the choir invisible.

Struggling to keep the heel of his boot grinding on the head of the snake, Gilbert fumbled in his satchel and somehow pulled out the pistol.

The snake was whipping its body back and forth, writhing beneath his heel in what appeared to be a desperate attempt to free itself.

"Yeah, keep trying. Now you know what it's like, doncha?" Gilbert muttered. Hoping the gun was already loaded, his body still wobbling from the snake's movements, Gilbert pulled back the hammer on the Colt. It was too stiff to do with the thumb of his right hand, but he somehow managed to do it after trying first with his left thumb and forefinger, and finally with the palm of his left hand. Gilbert brought the end of the gun barrel in front of him and as close as he dared to the point where his shoe met the black, wriggling body beneath it.

"Hold still, you little . . ."

In the darkness of the tunnel, something touched the barrel of his gun with a metallic *clink*, and Gilbert was suddenly aware that a dim greenish light had softly tinted the area around him. Gilbert's dirt-covered hand, his gun, his battered and filthy shoe, and the dark, snake-like thing it held were suddenly visible as if through a light-green filter.

He looked at what had touched his gun. It was a sharp point made of yellowish-white metal, poking from a crescent-shaped vehicle that hovered next to him, several inches off the dirty ground. In the green light, he saw now that the back end of the "snake" under his heel coiled up and disappeared into its underside.

Gilbert's eyes moved further upward, to see . . . well, the thing sitting atop its humming machine was something he never could have conceived in his worst nightmares. It regarded Gilbert, quietly horrifying him with its presence.

When confronting their own alien, Herb and Father Brown had only glimpsed it through the creature's flaming protection-field. Thus, they were largely spared the sight that confronted Gilbert now.

For the creature sitting on top of the machine in front of Gilbert looked like nothing so much as a large wrinkled brain, pulsing as though it were breathing somehow, although no nose was visible. Its body shuddered and wheezed like an obese man climbing stairs. With each infusion of air, the wrinkles in its body disappeared until only the largest ones could be seen, and as it deflated, the body looked again like a centenarian's face. As its tissue swelled and shrank, its colors shifted from dull yellow to red to gray in no pattern Gilbert could perceive. The mass of tentacles in its underbelly featured thousands of ringed segments, which clicked faintly and secreted a slick mucus. A few of the tentacles were moving in and out of multiple sockets in a control panel in front of it.

It had three eyes in a triangular pattern, with two set side by side and a third, larger one set below them. Each eye had multiple irises of different colors, although red was the dominant color. Its V-shaped mouth dribbled long strings of yellow and green saliva that collected in a pool beneath it, its tentacles dipping in and out of the fluid every few seconds.

Gilbert, focused as he had been on killing the serpent beneath his boot, hadn't realized that the thing wasn't a creature itself, but just one of the mechanical arms of its floating craft. If he could have followed with his eyes the long black coil that ran, taut and twisting, from under his boot around the corner of the water closet and down the tunnel, he would have realized that the tentacle's frenzied writhing wasn't an attempt to escape at all. The creature had been using the tentacle to *find* him, reeling itself in slowly, quietly, and with deadly purpose; moving through the shallow, slimy water as if it belonged there.

Gilbert hadn't been crushing the head of the beast.

He'd only been stepping on its toe.

Its *little* toe.

And now it was staring at Gilbert with all three of its bulbous, glowing, red-yellow eyes. Staring at him with a look that Gilbert couldn't possibly mistake for anything but pure hatred.

"Oops," he whispered as his eyes traveled higher.

Above the monster was a mass of at least a half-dozen tentacles, with more rising up every second like inquisitive cobras. Each one was a smaller copy of the ones that the black tripod had captured or killed people with back at the train wreck, each one raised high and pointing its glinting, razor-sharp tip at Gilbert like an angry black metal rattlesnake.

"Ooops . . ." his eyes grew wider, his voice raised in pitch and dropped in volume with each new tentacle that popped up behind the monster's wrinkled, salivating head. "Oops . . . oops . . . *oops* . . ."

<hr />

A long second passed. Gilbert stood transfixed, yet not entirely with fear. Were its bulbous yellow eyes hypnotizing him?

But then, the creature wasn't moving either.

It's waiting for something, Gilbert thought, finally. For what? Then he thought back to the forest outside the inn, how the man hadn't been nabbed by the tripod *until he'd pulled a weapon.* At the train, too, the tripod's tentacle had killed by striking its captive swiftly in the chest and the head, after that guy had pulled *his* weapon.

They know, Gilbert realized. *They know how we fight, right down to how we raise our arms to fire weapons. And they know the quickest ways to kill us are to take out our brains and hearts.*

But what if the gun hand stayed *still,* and the brain and the heart moved instead? A difference engine that took in a wrongly made punchcard would pause, maybe even shut down. Might the thing in front of him stall or be stunned at an unexpected change in the routine, just like an engine with a bad card?

All these thoughts flooded Gilbert's head in perhaps three-quarters of a second.

The alien's tentacles twitched, and Gilbert dove into what he realized might be the last action of his life.

Without moving his right hand up, Gilbert brought the rest of his body *down*, dropping almost to a crouch, while turning his wrist to point the gun at the alien. Six of the creature's tentacles leaped up as if in surprise, six tentacles all as long as and several thicker than the snakelike thing he'd stomped.

Then, Gilbert did something that surprised him as much as he hoped it would surprise the Martian. He brought his right hand *down*, and then *up* as he threw his pistol into the air. The gun sailed in a graceful arc over the head of the alien, turning end over end in a delicate aerial ballet that was completely wasted on both the alien hunter and its human prey.

Training and experience had taught the Martian what to do with a projectile hurtled by human enemies: grab it and smash it to pieces before it could explode. As the Colt .45 spun through the air above it, six mechanical tentacles lashed out faster than any human eye could follow, striking the loaded chamber of the revolver with so much force from six directions that it exploded like a fiery piñata. A few shards of hot, twisted metal rebounded harmlessly off the force-field protecting the creature's head.

But unfortunately for the Martian, although its energy shield was designed to deflect virtually any type of projectile that the humans could fire with their primitive, hand-held, slug-throwing toys, smaller particles wafting in at the speed of stilled air (and thus presumably harmless) could and did slip through unchecked. And it was just such an innocuous particle — a lone speck of fused metal and wood, a superheated cinder from the destroyed pistol — that now drifted through the alien craft's matrix of interlocked and shifting waves of invisible force. Then, as if guided by some expert unseen hand, it landed smack in the middle of the creatures' lowest eye.

Now, Martian mollusks are strange and grotesque creatures, so unlike humans in so many respects: physical, mental, cultural. But, interestingly, take a member of either race, and stick a burning cinder in his eye, and you're going to get the same reaction. The creature shrieked and jerked its body violently, while its machine, sensing trauma to its pilot, broke off the attack on Gilbert. Still bellowing and bobbing its immense head, the mollusk dabbed with its tentacles at the puddle of slime near its base and scooped some up to the injured eye, rubbing it on like a salve. It took a full minute of this before it was able to get hold of itself again, its eye still dripping and dilating and flashing different colors. And Gilbert was long gone.

Gone — but not escaped. The Martian knew that Gilbert would leave a trail in the dimly lit corridor of stone and pipes; a trail that its machine could track. The panel pinged and hummed as information was fed to the monster, and had a human been present to look over its shoulder, he would have seen a screen with an incomprehensible line of symbols filing past underneath a glowing representation of human footprints, the trail of which led away from the Martian and its hovering craft.

The prospect of tracking and hunting Gilbert through the tunnels awoke something buried deep in the Martian's psyche. Although, as a race, they had long ago lost the ability to smile, the idea of killing Gilbert, who now had caused him trouble and pain, filled the scout with such pleasure that it began drooling twice as much green saliva into the pool below him as before. It dipped its tentacles again into the pool made by its fluids, swirling them several times before plugging them into the sockets on its control panel. A loud hum sounded from the hovering mechanism below the craft as it sped off in pursuit of its young human quarry.

Twenty-Two

"Courage is almost a contradiction in terms. It means a strong desire to live taking the form of a readiness to die." — GKC

Gilbert ran, his battered shoes splattering mud and water like a gazelle wearing clodhoppers. He ran without thinking, without trying to make a mental map of his path. Every time he reached a branch in the tunnels, he chose the exit that seemed closest or easiest to get to. A pothole in the floor might disqualify the path on his left, then a small cascade of water to the right would steer him in the other direction. Thought was not a part of his being now, only flight from the monster behind him. If he could have answered, he would have said that *good* was defined as anything that put more distance between him and the floating brain-thing in the sewer tunnel.

But then he stopped.

He hadn't really made an effort of the will to do so; it was more like he had been trapped in a bubble of terror that had suddenly and soundlessly burst. He was now aware of being utterly tired, and breathing very, very heavily. His stomach was in knots, cramped up so badly that he had to bend over and hold his knees to keep from throwing up. When he'd regained control, he took a deep breath, straightened himself, and looked around.

He was in the middle of a large, well-lit underground room, with walls made of grimy cinderblocks at least thirty feet high and wide. Except for the floor, nearly every inch of the room was covered with pipes and metal tubes of different sizes, some as thin as his little finger, and larger ones thick enough to fit his head into. The other three doorways that led from the walls of the room weren't really doors so much as they were spaces in the mass of pipes wide enough for three tall men to walk through. There was a hissing sound overhead and a sloppy, gurgling sound below. Looking down, he could see a few pipes running across the floor — a good thing he'd stopped running! Tripping on those at top speed would have sent him tumbling headfirst. The last thing he needed now was to donate some of his teeth to the concrete floor of a sewer!

Still breathing hard, his eyes adjusting to the light, Gilbert noticed that the pipes closer to the floor made gurgling sounds, dripped little trickles of greenish-brown slime from their joints and seals, and were thick-crusted with grime and filth. Higher up, toward the ceiling, the metal tubes had more copper and shiny iron and steel visible to the eye, with various steam gauges poking out at odd angles from the pipes. To Gilbert, they looked like tree branches that always pointed upward toward the sky no matter where in the tree they sprouted from. Steam hissed and spouted in little jets from the higher pipes, reminding Gilbert of the rhyme the workman had sung on the road to the inn.

Gilbert walked forward. As he passed through the "door" framed by the pipes, he saw that the room was actually much larger than he'd thought; what he'd taken for walls were actually masses of pipes so thick that they divided the huge room into smaller rooms within it.

Gilbert's hand brushed something that gave a metallic creak. A hissing blast above made him jump in fright and scurry around behind a doorway in the wall for cover. When nothing moved after a few moments, Gilbert poked his head around the corner. Down the short hallway of pipes and about twelve feet in the air, a pipe was hissing a blast of steam several feet in length. Gilbert chuckled, and then noted that the steam was a sickly yellow color.

Gilbert walked down the hall, his shoes crunching quietly on pebbles and pieces of grit on the floor. Behind the plume of steam was a large gaslight, hung on a black iron pole that disappeared into the ceiling. It was the lamp's pale, yellow light that had colored the steam. Gilbert looked down and was unsurprised to find a small red metal wheel right where a swinging hand would hit it, with a long black hose coiling from it into the lightbox itself. Although by now instinctively frightened by anything that resembled the tripod's tentacles, Gilbert quickly recognized the hose for what it was. Gas was fed in a tiny, slow stream through the hose and into the lamp. They had had just such an apparatus in the cardroom, although few of the workers would ever allow themselves to be caught gazing upward when the Overseer could catch them.

Speaking of the cardroom . . .

Gilbert had continued walking through the halls made by the pipes, his eyes on the light above. Walking around another corner, he now had reached what he knew must be the center of the room. This new room he'd entered was a larger space than the other sections of the pipe-maze, at least fifty or sixty feet in diameter. Several iron-framed staircases led to catwalks that crisscrossed the higher levels of the room.

And in the center of the floor, on a raised dais big enough to fit both itself and one operator, was the single largest analytical engine that Gilbert had ever seen.

Most of the engines Gilbert had seen had been small affairs that could easily fit on the top of a desk. The automated engine that Gilbert had used to save himself and most of the passengers on the train had been slightly larger — big enough to be a desk in its own right. The machine he gazed at now was as large as a motorcar, capable of holding enough rods, levers, pins, and tubes to run hundreds, perhaps thousands, of calculations in minutes.

Gilbert gave a low whistle. As he approached the machine, his shoe bumped something gently. Looking down, he saw a small hunk of meat and cheese wrapped in white paper and a tin cup half-full of water.

Someone's lunch? Half-eaten — did he have to leave suddenly? Gilbert scooped up the lunch, smelled it. Nothing rotten there. Not that it would have stopped him. His stomach began growling ravenously, and he wolfed down the contents of the wrapper in under a minute. He hadn't realized how hungry he was until he'd smelled the food; if he hadn't been careful, he might have even eaten the wrapper, too.

So the workmen had left in a hurry. That would explain the ease with which his hand had knocked the steam-valve into movement, Gilbert thought as he wiped the corner of his mouth. Something had made the workmen who'd manned this station leave very, very quickly. A few more feet, and his suspicions were confirmed. There was a tool rack set into the wall, and outlines of grime showed where very large wrenches, poles, and other equipment had once hung in place. Closer now to the bottom of the light, a number of human boot prints milled around the workstation and led back the way he'd come.

They'd gone to fight the Martians, Gilbert realized. Somehow they knew there were intruders in the tunnels, and ran to fight with the only weapons they had. Based on what he'd seen, Gilbert didn't have to guess at the battle's outcome. Tears began forming in his eyes as he thought of brave men and boys running to their deaths in an effort to fend off those who would take their homes and lives.

Heroes.

He inhaled. There'd be time for tears later. There was still a monster in the maze looking for him.

Gilbert turned and made for the engine at the center of the pipe-walled room. As he mounted the step up the dais, he looked for and found a small indentation in the machine that held the punchcards for the workstation. Looking now at the control panel, Gilbert guessed that the board in front of him was a mock-up of the maze of sewer tunnels that he had just left behind.

"Hmm . . ." Gilbert said thoughtfully, the loud hissing of steam forgotten. "If I trace the pipe here, the tunnel here, to . . ." *Paydirt,* he thought. In the lower right corner was a smaller rendition of the room he'd just entered. Now, if he could just find out where they kept their punchcards!

Gilbert was just beginning to feel comfortable in his suddenly familiar surroundings when he heard the humming down the hall.

Twenty-Three

"It is the first law of practical courage. To be in the
weakest camp is to be in the strongest school."
— GKC

Evolutionists around the world would have declared Martians to be a
species that had developed beyond emotion: incapable of feeling what
humans call rage or sadness or delight. But if one such scientist were to
communicate with the scout chasing Gilbert, the creature would have
told the scientist, before killing him, that Martians *did* feel emotions, but
that those emotions were deeper and more complex. Martians, the scout
would have gone on to say while slurping out the scientist's insides, would
prefer to think themselves far above the petty, sentimental feelings that humans allowed to guide their actions.

Yet this scout had not only learned to take pleasure in hunting and mas-
sacring the half-dozen workmen who had confronted it in the tunnels; the
creature had learned to take a baser, twisted form of pleasure in the fear and
anguish of a defeated opponent. For this reason, it had sent a lone tentacle
to find Gilbert in the water closet, and toyed with him rather than killing
him quickly. It had found a victim's fear enjoyable and wished for more of it.

Now that such a move had backfired horribly, the scout was, literally, out
for Gilbert's blood. And for reasons completely unrelated to the boy's nu-
tritional value.

Its detailed scanner had illuminated Gilbert's desperate footsteps through
the muddy corridor as clearly as if they had been glowing light bulbs set on a
black velvet carpet. But at the sight of the wall of pipes, it hesitated, long-
dormant hunter instincts warning it to stand clear and give up pursuit.

223

But when assured by its machines that there was no immediate danger from the pipes or their contents, it drooled a little more and moved forward. Its humming craft was not designed for stealth pursuit, but there was plenty of other noise to go around; the little humans had been busy before they left. Several of the primitive valves had been opened, and . . . wait. It had its scanner's eyes look closely at one of the red wheels protruding from the pipes. There were oils from human skin that had been secreted there, and *very* recently! No, this hadn't been done by the pathetic bipeds who had attacked and been slaughtered by its tentacles in the tunnels! The prints on the valve and in the filthy, squishy mud and stone were fresher.

The scout drooled again and moved forward. The prey was here . . . and apparently far more wily than his predecessors.

⁂

When Gilbert heard the scout ship approaching, he forced himself into a focused state of mind. Panic was a luxury he couldn't afford if he wanted to last long enough to see the sun, or eat another sausage-and-cheese sandwich again.

He looked at the control panel in front of him. A mazelike twisting of flat wires, knobs, and dials sat in front of him, looking every bit as clear and concise as a physics treatise written in ancient Sumerian.

Inhale. Exhale. Okay, this room was the most complicated he'd seen. Therefore, if Gilbert was designing a panel to control steam and . . . How did the workman's song go? *Steam above, and the filth below.* Now, the nexus room for steam and sewage control would usually be put into the *center* of a control panel.

The noise was louder.

Gilbert looked around, hoping to see where his assailant was coming from. If only there wasn't so much steam coming from everywhere! It left him disoriented, unable to . . .

Unable to *see.*

Gilbert couldn't see very far around him. And if *he* couldn't see *it* in all the steam, then . . .

Gilbert looked at the center of the panel. There were four knobs making a rough square. He quickly turned all of them to the left and ran for the stairs he saw that led to one of the catwalks above.

Gilbert waited for several very slow seconds, trying to stand as much as possible in a space he'd found with a patch of grimy stone wall at his back instead of a steam-filled pipe. Pipes began to groan around him, the already substantial pressure increasing. Was it hundreds of pounds per square inch, he thought, or way more? Or less? There was no way for him to tell. Fissures opened up in the pipe walls, steam hissing out in white blasts of heat that Gilbert could feel several feet away.

The humming of the Martian's ship grew louder, then even louder and clearer as it entered the room. Gilbert was spared the sight of it by a large blast of steam that blocked his vision and, more important to Gilbert, blocked the Martian's view of *him.* Gilbert heard more blasts, pops, and hissings below, followed by metallic clangs that silenced the jets momentarily. He risked a small peek, and saw one of the metallic tentacles plugging a hole in one of the pipes. He gulped quietly — could the Martian *repair* the fissures, too?

But new hissings took the place of those silenced by the Martian scout. Gilbert had set the controls in motion without first checking just how much pressure could conceivably be sent through the steam pipes by a given command. If there was sufficient need for power at the places where the pipes ended, there was no problem.

However, most of the homes and businesses that had availed themselves of the power of steam were not using it now. In fact, many of those homes and businesses had been abandoned, or no longer existed. Steam had been called for by Gilbert at the panel, and more of it was arriving than could be dispatched by receivers or cracks in the pipes. Still, Gilbert thought, even if the steam could hide him, would it distract the alien long enough for him to escape? Maybe the steam could hold it at bay long enough for him to . . . he looked at the gun in his holster.

It was then that Gilbert had his idea. More than only an idea, really. For Gilbert, considering the strain he was under and had been under for some time, the idea was an epiphany; great enough that it would soon lead to a glorious victory or an ignominious, unmourned defeat.

∗≈❦≈∗

The metallic eyes and ears of the Martian scout ship swept the room for any sign of Gilbert. Had it been a *tripod* searching for a lone human, the game would have been up very quickly. But a small scout vessel like the one now in pursuit of Gilbert had no means to scan for primitive brain activity, detect disturbances in the air made by a heartbeat, or examine the genetic structure of lost skin cells mixed in with the dust on the ground. A small ship like the scout pursuing Gilbert was limited to cruder forms of detection.

Although those would have been more than enough to catch a young human male in quiet woods, the Martian now found itself in a cacophony of blasting steam and surging, gurgling noises from pipes below. Worse, there were so many white plumes of superheated steam blasting throughout the maze of pipes that it would take the scout much longer than usual to track and acquire the target via thermal detection.

At this rate, it might be nearly five minutes before it could find Gilbert and tear him to small pieces.

The Martian moved its craft forward slowly, trusting its machine to avoid heated steam jets when it could and to use its tentacles to plug the tiny fissures in the pipes where the steam was too difficult to avoid. As it neared the center of the pipe-maze, its tentacles were busier and busier,

226

plugging holes in front of and unplugging holes behind the pilot with such regularity that it looked something like a giant mechanical spider.

It scanned the area again and again, looking for Gilbert amid the clouds and blasting noise of hot steam like a man looking for a face in the middle of a crowded football stadium. So intent had the creature become on finding Gilbert that it almost missed the chattering of the analytical engine, which was busily using its innards to put into action its latest set of instructions.

The Martian approached the machine with a dim curiosity bordering on interest. So primitive was the technology compared with Martian achievements that an analytical engine capable of running an entire sewer and steam line had all the appeal of a dead rat. Still, there is usually something about even the most banal sight that demands it to be seen before being thrown away or destroyed. Such was the appeal of the engine to the monster on its floating, tentacled throne. It was just about to smash the podium and the calculating machine on it when several small loud clicks and chatters began sounding from the instrument panel.

The creature paused; both the ship's instruments and its own, dimly submerged instincts raised little symbolic red flags in its enormous gray brain-body. And yet, to look at the surroundings, nothing seemed terribly dangerous . . .

Another pop, followed by a hissing noise. Sensing imminent danger to the Martian pilot, a thousand automated systems launched one of the tentacles on the Martian scout ship toward a nearby pipe, where it plugged the jet of steam before it could reach the Martian's body.

The Martian, distracted for a few key seconds by the noise of the primitive computing device in front, didn't notice the many new fissures that started opening in the pipes around it.

Pop! Pop! Pop! went more pipes, followed by hisses of steam and more dull *thunk*s as the mechanical tentacles slammed into the fissures and expanded, acting as ugly caricatures of the Little Dutch Boy trying to plug a dike. Streams of paper tape began to scroll out from slots in the control panel. Raised as it had been as a simple scout, able to receive information directly from its machines into its brain, the alien had no interest in the humans' primitive means of communicating with combinations of sounds or the scratching of symbols on paper. But were it capable of reading human English, it would well have heeded the paper's message:

DANGER! DANGER! PREVIOUS ACTIONS HAVE RAISED LEVEL OF STEAM PRESSURE IN BLOCKS 5 THROUGH 74 TO EXCEED ACCEPTED LEVELS OF SAFETY. RECOMMENDED PROTOCOL: IMMEDIATE EVACUATION OF ALL ESSENTIAL WORKERS!

As it was, the popping of valves increased in the nexus room around the alien and the controller-engine Gilbert had been at a moment ago. The hissing streams of steam became so numerous that the tentacles, guided by the onboard scout-ship systems, were forced to begin prioritizing which holes to plug and which to leave alone as only potential problems that could be attended later.

All the extra steam had made the nexus room, which hadn't been particularly cool or dry to begin with, uncomfortably warm to both boy and Martian. Now, with the room as humid as a rainforest in summer, and all of the two-dozen-plus tentacles of its ship holding back deadly blasts of superheated water vapor, the scout heard a dim voice from its ship recommending a strategic withdrawal from its hunting activity.

The Martian tried to move, but found itself stuck in place. His craft's automated tentacles were fixed firmly in the widening fissures within the hissing pipes, protecting its occupant from being broiled alive. To leave the room, the creature would have to detach the tentacles from the ship, leaving them behind to keep the pipes plugged and return to base with neither prey nor arms (for a Martian, the closest thing to what a human could describe as embarrassing). In theory, it could also detach *itself* from the machine completely, leaving its scout craft behind and attempting to slog as best it could through the sewers back to its entry point (which would be embarrassing *and* potentially life-threatening).

Calling for help was not an option. To admit failure against a single human: the thought did not even cross the Martian's mind as anything more than a nanosecond-long ripple.

As if to emphasize the pressure the scout suddenly found itself under, more *pop*s sounded in the room. More snakelike hisses of hot steam belched out of the walls, some now licking close to the invisible shields of the Martian's hovering craft. Another noise sounded, different and shriller than the surrounding steamjets.

Then a new noise, a thin high-*low*-*HIGH* trill, sounded above the scout and a little to the right of its vision. The little human was . . . whistling at him.

The Martian looked up with a mixture of rage and triumph as it spotted the absurd creature. The worm-like biped must have nestled itself in the upper tier of the room, hiding amidst the twisting pipes and tubes. But now the wretch of a primitive had foolishly moved from a secure hiding place to one where he could be clearly seen, sitting prone on the curve of a large brass steam conduit that was cooler than the other pipes surrounding it. Indeed, without the heavy clouds of hot water vapor to obscure Gilbert, the Martian could clearly see him as his hand moved, the dim gaslight glinting off the barrel of his crude, bullet-firing weapon as he pulled back a small piece of metal with a loud click . . .

⚜

Gilbert couldn't have known how simultaneously futile and brilliant his maneuver was, for he knew nothing of the alien's force-shields and had only guessed about the inner workings of its tentacle defense mechanisms. *Trust,* he thought blindly, as he'd aimed the pistol and pulled back the hammer, *if there's anything to this, I'll trust you* . . . There was a part of him that was fully prepared to die or be mortally wounded before the next ten seconds elapsed, and he wished he could better prepare for whatever lay ahead of him in the next life, if indeed there would be one for him to see.

The aliens had indeed been watching humanity for a great while, and although the force fields they had developed for their patrol craft had been specially constructed to repel the bullets that the humans seemed so fond of throwing at each other, they were also single-mindedly diligent in eliminating any such weapon that threatened it, even ineffectually. When it detected Gilbert's pistol, the ship told the tentacles to eliminate the armed and did so faster than either Gilbert or the Martian could think. Thus, by the time the Martian itself had spotted Gilbert and realized the true nature of the threat he posed, its tentacles had launched at Gilbert like a crowd of black lightning bolts.

Twenty-Four

"None of the modern machines, none of the modern paraphernalia . . . have any power except over the people who choose to use them." — GKC

Gilbert had expected the creature to attack him — in fact, he'd counted on it — but he hadn't expected it to come so swiftly. As it was, the tentacles' speed surprised him, and he jerked his pistol hand upward, firing high above the alien's head. The bullet ricocheted off the ceiling, dropping a harmless handful of dirt and chipped stone down on the head of the Martian.

But Gilbert's hope wasn't in bullets, anyway.

The tentacles were indeed fast — but not fast enough to reach Gilbert before the creature's own body was hit from all sides by blasts of steam, and doused from below by a frothy stream of sewage. The pent-up pipes, no longer clogged by the machine's metallic fingers, released jets of super-heated water vapor that hissed angrily past the alien's forcefield and struck the mollusk like flaming sledgehammers swung by a team of circus strongmen. The tentacles that had been streaking toward their human target now froze in midair, confused between the directives given by the ship and the anguished calls for help by the injured pilot.

The creature let loose a high-pitched shriek that pierced all the tunnel's hissing and bubbling noises and forced Gilbert to put his hands over his ears. But his right hand was still wrapped around the pistol in a tight fist and couldn't block out much of the noise. For an agonizing five seconds, Gilbert thought for sure that his right eardrum — already ringing awfully from the revolver's report — was going to burst from the noise.

It's hurt, Gilbert barely managed to think to himself through the din and the wave of heat billowing from underneath him, *but it's still standing. I've got to get away from here!* He swiveled around, balanced on one foot on the curve of the large pipe, and leaped through a cloud of heat and water onto the catwalk that ran around the wall ten or so feet off the floor. His feet slammed and shook the metal grating, but he was no longer worried about stealth. With his hands still covering the sides of his head as best he could, he fled the wailing alien, carefully picking a path through the shallow puddles that pocked another pipe-lined tunnel he hadn't been in before. *I've got to keep moving,* he thought. *It could recover, come after me, and those tentacles might not pause next time.* He stomped along as fast as he could, his gun still in his hand, the satchel still banging against his back as he jogged through water that had become unavoidable, lapping at his ankles and calves as he splashed through. The ground, which, in other tunnels, had felt like solid stone, now grew mushy or spongy beneath his feet, water oozing around his feet where they stepped.

He sloshed through in this fashion for several minutes, scurrying desperately up one hallway and down another. He quickly lost all sense of direction, and for all he knew, he was running in circles through the sewer system of the greater Woking area, hoping whatever route he used would confuse the creature enough to prevent it from finding him.

His greatest hope was that he'd somehow wounded the thing enough that he'd be able to dodge, outlast, and eventually outlive it, as in the myth of Beowulf he'd read in school. There, the hero had torn off the arm of the monster Grendel, who then retreated to its swampy home to die quietly. Of course, Gilbert then recalled how the sequel to the story had gone: Grendel's *mother* came after Beowulf, causing even more mayhem than her son had. The thought of that alien brain-thing-monster having a mother simultaneously horrified him and made him chuckle, despite his situation.

It was getting harder and harder to find things to laugh at, but somehow he'd managed. However many of the creatures had landed on Earth, Gilbert was feeling his first real sense of hope since the derailment of the train, eighteen hours and a thousand years ago. If a skinny fellow like him could wound one, maybe there was hope for humanity to lick them all. *All we need are enough steam pipes for the things to stand under!* Gilbert laughed out loud at his own joke this time.

He cut himself off when he heard the humming of the creature's machine again, this time less than a hundred feet away.

⚜

Gilbert looked around quickly, trying to figure out where the creature was coming from. He saw a dim light around a corner and sprinted in the opposite direction. That part of the tunnel had a mixture of stone walls and metal pipes of all sizes lining the walls and ceiling in bizarre, twisting mazes that were impossible to follow. He found one of the many alcoves in between them and buried himself in it as far as he could.

He flattened himself against the stone wall and brought up his gun, pointing it straight forward so he could shoot the monster when it popped around the corner. Nowhere else to run, nothing else to do. He knew the thing was going to get him this time. Oddly, that thought only made him feel braver and more resolved. *I'll die swimming, not drifting,* he thought defiantly. *That overgrown pile o' pond scum is going to have to work a lot harder than a tripod to get me. Whatever else happens, it'll learn to think twice before it comes after a human in the sewers again!*

Gilbert took a deep breath and held it, waiting for the monster to appear. He figured he had maybe ten seconds before it showed up. The engines hummed, and then hummed louder. The putrid green radiance in the corridor grew brighter. Gilbert exhaled and tightened his grip.

But then something very strange happened.

The engine hum, which had been growing ever louder, now suddenly softened to a steady low level, as if it were waiting in place and idling. The lights, too, stopped getting brighter; in fact, they began to dim. Then the engine stopped completely, and Gilbert heard a loud splash in the ankle-deep water, and the clank of metal hitting stone. Finally, a long, shuddering sigh echoed down the corridor.

Gilbert waited for five long minutes of silence. Then he became aware that his feet, submerged beneath the trickling sewer stream, were starting to feel cold, and his folded-up legs and hunched back were uncomfortably stiff. If he didn't especially care to investigate what had become of his pursuer, neither was he enjoying his sardine-tin hiding place. Finally, curiosity, discomfort, and a strange impatience overcame his fear. Slowly Gilbert extricated himself from his little cubby and peered down the hall.

The mollusk's craft lay plopped flat on the ground. The creature was sitting in the middle of the crescent-moon-shaped ship, but neither moved nor pulsed nor made a sound.

Gilbert approached very slowly. He saw that the machine's tentacles were splayed out on the ground, poking up here and there above the water. They were utterly still, but Gilbert didn't trust them for a second. He'd seen too many possums to believe anything was dead unless it had several bullets in it first. But he continued moving forward cautiously, and soon he was able for the first time to see one of the invaders up close without having to duck, bob, run, or shoot for his life.

He quickly wished he hadn't. Its hideousness remained burned in his memory to the end of his days.

The creature's natural color had been a sickly gray. But now its upper half was pocked by a series of red wounds circled by oozing white blisters. In other places, layers of whatever passed for Martian skin had been stripped away like barn paint by a lightning bolt. On one side — apparently it had struck a jagged pipe end as it fell — the innards of the creature's head were leaking out, looking like a root beer float made with curdled milk. Its three large eyes were intact, but death had pulled them back deep into the horrible head, revealing misshapen sockets of cartilage with a phosphorescent yellow pus escaping around the rims. The slimy pool within the ship that had been fed by the creature's saliva was leaking through a hole in the craft, making a green-shaded puddle in the ground behind the ship that Gilbert could just barely see in the dim light.

Then, just the tiniest bit of smell from the creature's body reached Gilbert's face, causing him immediately to retch, and it was only by exhaling fast and holding his nostrils shut that he kept himself from throwing up. *The stink,* he thought, *Jehoshaphat, the stench!* Gilbert had been down in a sewer for *hours,* but the air there was like perfume by comparison. He had lived on a farm for most of his life, but he'd never gotten a whiff of anything that resembled the overpowering reek of dead Martian. It was like vomit set on fire.

Gilbert stumbled away with his fingers in his nose. In his rush to escape the source of the malevolent odor, he stubbed a soggy toe into one of the prone metal tentacles, and jolted by some freak surge of power, it suddenly came to life, whipping around Gilbert's leg and piercing his calf with its razor-sharp tip. Then, just as suddenly, it quivered and shuffled off his leg, becoming still once more.

Gilbert felt the sting in his calf but didn't slow his pace at all. The momentary return of terror had flooded his body with adrenaline, and it wasn't until he'd whipped the limp tentacle off his leg and put fifty yards between it and himself that he looked down and saw the dark, arrowhead-shaped bloodstain spreading out on the back of his pants leg, pointing up at him like an accusing finger.

Cripes, he thought, *I'm hit.*

He looked down at the water gathered around his feet. There was still enough light in the tunnel to see a dark stream trickling from his left ankle and flowing down the gentle current back in the direction from which he'd come. Gilbert swallowed, and felt sick inside at the thought of how much blood he must have already lost in just the last minute or two.

Am I feeling sick and lightheaded from losing blood, he thought, *or just because I'm seeing my insides splattering the floor of a sewer?*

Gilbert swallowed again. *Can't panic,* he thought. *Panic's fine if you're running away from a cougar. But when you're trying to keep from dying, panic's not going to do you any good at all. It'll just eat up more time and energy, and you'll die in here like that squid back there.*

He pulled up his pant leg and examined the wound. He'd been poked by the tentacle a little ways above his ankle, close to the meat of his calf. It looked clean, but deep — at least an inch, maybe more. And it was bleeding freely. Gilbert had heard enough stories of farming accidents to know that blood loss was his most immediate problem. He rummaged through his satchel, looking for something that might help staunch it. He thought grimly how funny it was: all that special gear he'd gotten from the outfitter and the Doctor, but right now the most useful thing in the universe would be a towel.

He searched frantically. There must be something, *something* in the . . .

The satchel! Inspired, Gilbert unhooked the shoulder strap from the bag and wrapped it several times around the wound. It helped, but every time he took a step, the knot would loosen a bit and the blood would flow again. Then he hit on another idea: he unwrapped the strap, and folded his left pant leg upwards several times until the thick band of material was just over the wound. Then he tightened the strap again over the now-padded wound. The improvised bandage worked very well indeed. Although he was still in pain and having to limp, the blood darkened his wadded cloth but stopped flowing down his leg.

Gilbert knew he wouldn't be able to carry both his weapons and the satchel in his hands, so he raided the battered cloth and leather bag for anything he could carry. He took the punchcard that held his expense account, folding and stuffing it in one of his pockets. He knew he was probably ruining it by doing so, but who knew for sure? If he ever did get out alive, he knew he'd need funds to get back to London. Right now he was just happy the water-resistant bag had kept the thing dry, and —

There was a new noise coming from the alien's immobilized ship.

Gilbert whipped around and tried to draw his pistol out of its holster in one motion, like an old West gunfighter. (He needed practice, though; he had to tug at the gun twice to get it out of the holster all the way, yanking with so much force the second time that it nearly flew out of his hand and into the water.) But when he'd finally turned around, he saw no sign of the alien — just a slow, steady pulse of noise coming from its craft. After a very long minute, Gilbert was able to count five heartbeats between each of them.

Gilbert swallowed and put down his gun on a dry spot on the floor with both of his shaking hands, and got back to his satchel. He also took his press pass, and put on his gun belt and holsters.

Then he raised his head and listened; something was different about the noise from the alien ship, but he couldn't quite place it. A repeated series of *beep, beep, beep* met his ears, sounding like a smaller, softer version of a motorcar horn.

After a few moments, he figured it out: the pitch of the noise was going up in notches. It was also beeping every three or four seconds instead of five.

"Well," Gilbert said, "that's different." He used the phrase that every farmer he'd ever known had used to describe something they'd never seen before.

Back to my gear, Gilbert thought resolutely, *and get away as quickly as possible.* Everything else he left in the satchel bag, which he set down regretfully in the water behind him. It was time now to travel light. He took a deep breath and began limping in the direction he hoped would bring him to Woking.

Even as he distanced himself from it, in the echoes of the enclosed tunnel he could still hear the machine's beeping sound, still rising and growing more urgent. Was that thing ever going to be quiet? Gilbert picked up his half-striding, half-hopping pace; the noise had gone from merely annoying to strangely worrisome, and he was eager to put it behind him.

To put the worries out of his mind, he fell into a sort of daydream. He was going to beat this! After all, he'd done something it was unlikely anyone else in the world had accomplished. He'd managed to kill one of the invaders! If anyone else had done so, he certainly hadn't heard about it. He was, without a doubt, an extraordinary person! Everyone knew that greatness happened to people who stepped up and *did* things, instead of talking about them all the time. He was a doer, all right, and he was going places! Gilbert envisioned himself triumphantly calling his story in to the *Times*, then later being lauded at celebrity dinners for Teenagers of Extraordinarily High Achievement, and accepting several world-renowned awards for his exceptional accomplishments in the fields of journalism and alien monster-killing.

He had just rounded a corner by two steps and almost put the alien machine-beeps out of earshot, when they suddenly stopped.

Finally, Gilbert thought. It was quiet in the tunnel again.

It was quiet for a whole second. It stayed quiet, in fact, right up until the tunnel exploded, making everything around Gilbert disappear into a red thunderclap.

Twenty-Five

<blockquote>
"I still hold . . . that the suburbs ought to be either glorified by romance and religion or else destroyed by fire from heaven, or even by firebrands from the earth." — GKC
</blockquote>

What d'you see?" Herb asked, his voice a whisper. The Doctor didn't answer, but kept peering over the remains of the rock wall with an odd set of mechanical eyeglasses — like mother's opera glasses, Herb thought — that he held in both hands.

"The north corner of Woking is crawling with black tripods," the Doctor said grimly. "At least half a dozen, and those are only the ones I can see through the fog and the smoke." He peered intently at the city below. They had climbed to the fourth floor of a tenement building, and were busy cowering in the corner as far away from the window as possible. It was only the lack of movement outside their window for the past hour that had made the Doctor brave enough to risk a look outside. "Our section seems relatively clear. A few streets away, though, I can see a few of their little scout rovers. Those are the things shaped like crescent-moons." The Doctor peered outside for a few more seconds, all the while turning a few of the metal dials that surrounded the lenses. Satisfied, he snapped the glasses ("bi-noculars," he had corrected Herb) shut.

"So, is it safe to venture outside yet?" Father Brown asked. The little priest had been fairly quiet for the last half-hour, ever since they had found the entrance to the building's basement.

After they had fled the charred corpse of the mollusk, the Doctor had raced them through numerous twists and turns in their labyrinth of underground tunnels until they finally reached a dead end. Then, reaching through a crevice in the wall, the Doctor had pulled on a hidden lever or switch, opening up a door-size chunk of the tunnel wall. The opening led to a room that looked like an office basement, with a set of battered wooden stairs leading upward.

The Doctor had then led them up the rickety stairs to the empty room in which they were now encamped. After hours in the dark, damp caves, they were ecstatic to reach the surface world again — but it was a world ruled by the plodding, hissing machines of the Martians, as they patrolled what had been the bustling village of Woking.

"Stay away from the windows," the Doctor had warned them as they climbed higher, "and watch you don't make any noise. If they decide to focus on an area, they can hear anything above a whisper as well as you or I could hear a foghorn across a room."

But Herb had sneaked a peek through a window anyway and couldn't believe what he saw.

Herb had grown up in the city. As was the case for most self-described "freethinking" families of the age, his had been an upper-middle-class world of order, propriety, nannies, on-time meals, boarding schools, starched collars, and cucumber sandwiches with his four o'clock tea. The most destruction he'd ever been witness to before this had been a city building here or there that had been demolished to make way for an even larger and more impressive edifice of wood, brick, mortar, and stone. Although he was no stranger to the disorder of the seedier side of London, even the drabbest part of the rookery had buildings that stood sturdily, with plenty of people milling about, reputable or otherwise.

No, a little filth in the streets, Herb could handle. What he saw now were the decimated remains of the *entire town* of Woking. Smaller buildings and houses had been smashed and pulverized until they looked like nothing more than giant gray anthills. Some larger buildings like their own were partially standing, but had still been shattered and broken until they looked like torn-apart dollhouses. Street after street as far as Herb could see, a human soul wasn't to be spotted amidst all the devastation. The only thing he could observe moving among all the wreckage was a string of a dozen or so fires, along with a muddled dark smoke that rose lazily from each pile of debris that colored the sky with a thick brown haze. The sun tried hard to shine through, almost completely without success. Herb could also hear a dull humming noise in the distance that he soon recognized as the sound of the scout ship they had dispatched in the tunnels. That ship would never move again, but by the sound of it, there were many others to take its place.

"Impressive in its own way, isn't it?" said the Doctor.

"It is monstrous," said Father Brown quietly.

"Why are they doing it?" whispered Herb, looking at the Doctor. "Why have they attacked us? There's other planets around the sun. Why *us*? What did we do to them?"

"Mars has dried up for them, so to speak," the Doctor said, suddenly sounding very tired, keeping his eyes on the street below. "Edison and one of his lieutenants, a renegade agent of the Special Branch named Ransom, organized the various races on Mars into a single massive army. Plundered for years by the mollusks, they all had been used either as food or fodder for the mollusks' horrible experiments — fleshcrafting, vivisection, and the like. Even so, the other races had never quite worked together well enough until we came along. With Edison's contraptions and Ransom leading the charge, they fought. And, with horrendous losses, they finally won. We thought the creatures might be done for when the last of the mollusks' cities fell, but they have traveled instead to *our* greener pastures. We obtained a message from Ransom warning us of their approach, written in a combination of British code and Mollusk Script and translated by an eccentric slum-dweller in London who happened to be a linguistic genius. Fat lot of good it did us," he concluded, his manner of expression surprising both Herb and the priest.

The Doctor brought out the odd set of eyeglasses again. He seemed grimly satisfied after looking the street over several times.

"We need to return to the basement again," he said. "They can communicate with each other easily, even over long distances. If we remain here, we'll be spotted by one of the scouts, and a black tripod will be called on to collect us."

Father Brown suddenly inhaled and stood still, looking at something that no one else could see.

"What's the matter?" asked Herb.

Father Brown was quiet, fumbling in the pocket of his black trousers.

"No!" whispered the Doctor harshly. Father Brown had begun opening and closing his mouth like a gasping fish.

"What? Someone tell me what the problem is . . ."

Herb was cut off by Father Brown's sneeze. It resounded from the shattered windows of the fourth-story apartment room like a cannon shot.

The humming sound of the scouts on the street suddenly stopped.

"Down the stairs!" called the Doctor, dashing to the rickety stairway and clumping down them two and three at a time.

Herb didn't need to be told twice. He lunged at the stairwell and heard the priest following close behind him. Out of the corner of his eye, Herb could see what looked like spotlights cutting through the haze over their heads. *They're looking for us,* Herb thought desperately, *they're looking for us and they're going to find us . . .*

Herb followed the Doctor, feet flying so fast down the stairs that every step threatened to make him tumble headlong. The entire descent lasted perhaps a few seconds, but they seemed near an eternity to Herb, who couldn't get out of his head the thought of what kinds of experiments the mollusks might try to perform on humans.

"Here! Back into the tunnel!" barked the Doctor. Not like the Sign of the Broken Sword — there was no locked door this time! The Doctor quickly led them through the door they had used to enter the building from the tunnels, shutting it firmly behind them and sliding a thick deadbolt into place.

Herb saw that the door they had walked in through was camouflaged to look like the wall, just as the one they'd used to enter the tunnels had been under the table at the inn, thirty-six hours and a hundred years ago. *There is a very good chance I shall go mad soon if this keeps up*, Herb thought. *If running from an office basement back into a caveman's labyrinth to escape monsters that look like globs of mucus doesn't drive one mad after a while, I really wonder if anything could.*

"All this running about and hiding in secret doors is getting tiresome," gasped Herb. "When are those things going to finally decide they've done enough damage and leave?"

"Do you really believe they plan on leaving?" said Father Brown.

"Right now I'd be happy if they just left Woking," said Herb. "Although I'm not sure I understand why this lot decided to hit Woking first, and I'm even less sure why they're staying here instead of trying to take on London or something."

"Herbert," said Father Brown kindly, "you're not a very experienced journalist, are you?"

Herb bristled. "I've been at this game long enough! Longer than you have, stuck all sheltered inside a chapel while real life's been happening all around you!"

"Herbert," Father Brown said, without a trace of defensiveness in his voice. "During my years in darkest Africa, I had to face the sharpened spears of savages, and do it with courage, so that they would take notice of the Faith that could make a little man unafraid of death. I've heard the confessions of killers and thieves across three continents. I know the evil that men can do, far better than you could at this point in your young life. And I know that when bullies grow from boys to men, they are seldom content with the praises of a few toadies. They are more likely to do as our own country-men did when they thought they had discovered valuable goods in Tasmania. We didn't wipe out tribes there just to prove our worth. We wiped them out because we wanted something, and they were in the way."

Herb was quiet. "But," he said in a small voice, "I know the Doctor said they wanted our world. But why do they think they have to kill us for it? If it's water they wanted, we have enough of that for here and Mars, I'd wager. *Why kill us for it?* And why begin in *Woking* of all places?"

Father Brown stared into the distance, looking as if he were chewing something. "Dropping into the middle of London would gain too much at-tention, I'd think, while they were establishing themselves, to say nothing of dropping buildings on their heads when they landed. But Woking," he continued slowly, "is open and out of the way, yet still just a short distance from the capital city of the greatest empire in the world.

"As for why they attacked instead of coming to us in friendship," he shrugged his shoulders, "perhaps they have no use for the value of sharing. And negotiations are quite tedious, compared with the thrill of conquest. The Doctor also has suggested that they have been run off their planet after abusing its other inhabitants; perhaps now they seek easier prey. Young Gil-bert mentioned that they took several captives from the wreck of our train."

"They were food, Brown." The Doctor's voice was flat. "The mollusks take creatures that have iron-rich blood like ours, and draw it out of us with sharpened tubes. It happened to some of our captured soldiers on Mars: you're kept alive in order to keep the blood healthy and oxygenated. When they have need of nourishment, you're opened up and sucked dry, a bit like a canteen."

"Monstrous," said the priest again. Herb looked at the Father, then back to the Doctor.

"Not really monstrous, if you think about it," the Doctor grunted, wiping the sweat out of his eyes. He was still breathing hard after the run down the stairs. "Just think of how our own eating habits would seem to, say, an intelligent rabbit. What's right here may not seem so wrong in another place. Do we really have any right to judge the mollusks?"

"Yes," answered Father Brown. "We have not only the right, but the *duty*. Rabbits are animals. Despite how sweet they may look in kinotropic cartoons, they aren't people. And though we may suggest it hypothetically, they *can't* understand our eating habits. Most important, rabbits can't really *choose* anything — they can only act on instinct, and react to pleasure or pain. We, on the other hand, are able to recognize when evil is being done, and know that it *ought* to be stopped. Killing people out of greed is evil, Doctor, whether it is done at the local tobacconist's, in Tasmania, on Mars, or on the farthest star in the farthest galaxy from our own. For He who made those stars also made the laws of right and wrong."

There was a short, awkward pause during which the Doctor could think of nothing witty or profound to say. "Yes, well, this is all very interesting, gentlemen," said Herb, his voice cracking, "but in case you haven't noticed, the local tobacconist's is a pile of ash and rubble, along with nearly every other building in this town. We've struggled and killed to get to this point, if you count what we did to that filthy monster. But where do we go from here?"

"I have a few ideas," replied the Doctor coolly, dropping his hand to his side, "but regrettably, they do not include . . ."

"Don't move, Doctor."

The Doctor froze. Father Brown had spoken in a voice that was soft, yet immovable as mountain stone. In a flash, the little moon-faced priest had drawn his pistol, and more important, he was pointing the pistol directly at the hand the Doctor had been moving.

"What do you think you are doing?" said the Doctor, trying to sound haughty by betraying just a tinge of surprise and fear.

"Herbert," said Father Brown, ignoring the Doctor's question, "would you please examine his waistband? If I am not mistaken, you should find his miniaturized Maxim gun somewhere inside."

Herb looked at Father Brown, and then at the Doctor. "If you obey him, Herbert," the Doctor said quietly, "I will not forget your disloyalty."

"Disloyalty?" Herb snapped. "You're suggesting that I owe *you* loyalty of *any* kind? Father, how do you know there's a gun in there?"

"I've known for quite a while that the only reason he's been tolerating us is because it is safer to have many guns pointed at your enemies than just your own. When we were useful for his survival, he let us live. But now he apparently believes himself safe from danger, and we've become disposable. Am I right, Doctor?"

"Go spit, you superstitious little swine." The Doctor's suavity was gone, and his eyes burned at the priest.

"I will accept that answer as a yes. Now, Doctor, please place your hands in the air and keep them there until I instruct you to do otherwise. I've no fear of aliens coming after us if I shoot; we've no evidence of any more scouts in the tunnel with us, and I doubt the monsters above could hear a pistol this small through the dozen feet of solid rock above us. You may not believe I am capable of shooting another human being, but I'm sure you'll agree this really isn't the time to test that belief. Herbert, please relieve him of the weapon he has in his belt. I saw his hand straying to it as he was speaking, and the look on his face was one I've seen all too often in my vocation."

"And what was that?" sneered the Doctor, as Herb gingerly began patting the small leather pouch that the Doctor had beneath his belt.

"The look that said you had done something terrible. And done it so many times that you have convinced yourself it would do no real harm to commit such a crime again. We would not, I would surmise, have been the *first* innocents you have sacrificed to save your own skin, am I correct? Thank you, Herbert, and hand me that weapon."

Herb had indeed found a small pistol under the Doctor's belt, along with a knife that had several small, dark spots on its handle. Herb looked at the knife briefly. Why did it seem familiar to him? No matter — time enough for that later, he decided. He slipped the knife into the breast pocket of his jacket and turned his attention back to the small pistol. It was the multibarreled pistol they had seen back in the vault of guns under the Sign of the Broken Sword. "Just where do these come from?" Herb asked, "I've never seen these before today."

"That particular type of firearm," said Father Brown, cutting off the Doctor before he could speak, "is designed by the finest in German analytical engines. As the Doctor mentioned earlier, it's known as the 'pepperbox' in some circles, and is designed in varieties of three, six, or even eight barrels. I witnessed several prototypes of that particular weapon during my own years of military service, although back then, the pepperboxes were notorious for overheating and harming their owners when firefights became brisk. One may fire a series of very quick shots, with the barrels rotating rapidly. Or, if accuracy isn't an issue, you can set it to fire all barrels at once. Quite useful for dispatching one or two disposable traveling companions, wouldn't you say, Doctor?"

"How did you know about the German engines, priest?" said the Doctor, with a mixture of derision and wonder.

"You might be surprised at the information to which I'm privy, Doctor, although the circles I move in are far different from your own."

"If you're going to shoot me, priest, get on with it." The Doctor's voice betrayed no emotion, but his eyes were small, black chips of hate.

"No, Doctor. I'm not going to shoot you. But although you are dangerous for us to travel with, you know far too much about our enemy for me to let you go. Without you, I think Herbert and I would find ourselves tripod fodder rather quickly. If you turn on us, however, I will not hesitate to shoot you, however distasteful that action might be to me. Are we understood?"

The Doctor looked for several seconds at the blank expression on the face of the little priest. Finally, he nodded his head.

"Father," said Herb, "could you really have shot him just now? Have you ever shot a man before?"

Father Brown inhaled deeply, and blinked his eyes slowly while keeping his weapon focused squarely on the Doctor. He breathed out quietly and swallowed. "Herbert," he said evenly, "please do not ask me any more questions of that nature until things have calmed down sufficiently." An awkward pause hung in the air when he finished, and a small tremor shook his hand and the gun it was holding.

"Well, Brown," the Doctor said, standing and suddenly jaunty, "you are in charge of our expedition now. What do you suggest we do?"

"We will go out into the city," replied the priest, a clipped, authoritative voice quickly overtaking his earlier quavering, "walking always with the utmost care. We shall attempt to find ropes, lanterns, and anything else that might aid us in finding and rescuing young Gilbert. After that, our options are somewhat limited. We may try to make our way back to civilization by the open countryside. With the hurly-burly these creatures have caused, the roads are bound to be choked by refugees."

Herb looked outside at the heaps of gray ash and ruined buildings, and turned back to Father Brown. "You said our options are *limited*, Father. If joining a large, unwashed mass is the first option, what's next on the list?"

"We can remain in place and become food for these devilish creatures. Gentlemen, are we ready? Doctor, you shall go first, with Herbert —"

Father Brown was cut off suddenly by a deep, rumbling noise from the far end of the rock tunnel they stood in. It silenced them all and was followed a minute later by a gentle push of warmed air from the tunnel opening.

"What was *that*?" Herb whispered.

"By Jove," whispered the Doctor, his voice tinged with awe and his eyes filled with faraway memories. "I wonder if . . . no, it couldn't be possible."

"What are you thinking?" said Father Brown sharply. "What could have happened?"

"That explosion came from below ground. The only thing we know of that has been traveling below ground are the mollusk's handling machines." Here the Doctor swallowed slowly, as if analyzing a football game in front of him while trying to do long division in his head. When the Doctor continued, his voice was thick and slow. "They have what we call a 'Poor Sport' device. It's a bomb, a devastating piece of incendiary equipment that explodes when the machine's pilot has been rendered lifeless. It's the reason I brought the flame-tosser as my weapon. Its intense heat bypasses their shields and melts the device before it can explode or alert their comrades."

"So, a *different* alien was killed in the tunnels?" Herb's voice was hopeful.

"Perhaps, Herbert. The mollusks are rather predictable under certain circumstances. The only way we can be certain of one of their deaths is if we hear their alarm cry."

At that moment, a loud, mechanical voice began sounding throughout the village.

"*Ulla!*" it shouted, the unearthly voice repeating over and over again. "*Ulla! Ulla! Ulla!*"

"Indeed," the Doctor spoke loudly over the din, suddenly unafraid of being heard by the tripods, "you will no doubt recollect that particular call from our own adventure in the tunnels? Someone has most certainly killed one of the aliens below. The Poor Sport bomb's going off in the tunnel-maze has alerted them to a threat from below ground."

"A threat from . . ." Herb's puzzled eyes suddenly shone with hope. "A threat from *below ground!* Gil's *alive!* Not only is he alive; he's managed to send one of these cursed things back to whatever twisted creator made them!"

"Don't celebrate yet, Herbert," warned Father Brown. "Well, Doctor, if indeed he did dispatch the beast, how likely was Gilbert to have survived the subsequent blast?"

The Doctor paused. "Unless the mollusk's attacker knows about it in advance and gets away quickly, the Poor Sport device will certainly kill him instantly. It produces an extremely powerful blast, so it's unlikely," he said, almost smiling, "that Gilbert suffered much."

Herb muttered a curse under his breath. It went unheard as the call from the tripod's loud-speaking devices suddenly increased to a piercingly high level. Herb mashed his hands against the sides of his head in an effort to block out the noise. He squeezed his eyes shut, as if it would help to keep the clamor out of his head.

Fortunately, it lasted only a few seconds. "What on earth was that?" Herb asked.

The Doctor's voice grew more animated. "I know that call! It was a lucky thing we were underground, or our brains would now be running freely out of our ears. They are now in a state of high-alert, and until it is lifted, any human sighted will be killed instantly rather than collected and farmed for blood. We are in even greater danger than before and must decide our next course of action with this in mind."

"So Gilbert really killed one of those things, then, down there, all alone? I wouldn't have thought he had it in him." Herb's voice was a mixture of admiration and sadness.

"Herbert, if your young friend is indeed who I suspect him to be, he is likely one of the few people in the whole of the British Empire who could have accomplished such a feat."

"And why's that?"

The Doctor looked as if Herb had asked him why two and two made four. "Because of his superior breeding, of course! I think it entirely possible that young Gilbert is the progeny of two of my organization's more able former operatives." The Doctor paused to stroke his whiskers reflectively. "Yes," he continued, "if Gilbert were, indeed, the son of Edward and Marie Chesterton, things could become very interesting indeed."

"Gentlemen," broke in Father Brown gently, "while this is indeed, fascinating, it brings us no closer to rescuing Gilbert, or at least . . . confirming his fate. For we do not know for certain that Gilbert is a monster-slayer, or whether he perished below ground. The only thing we know for certain is that Gilbert is not with us, and that leaves us no choice but to return to where we saw him last and begin our search. But not without first obtaining the necessary supplies. Gentlemen, shall we?"

As Father Brown motioned to the door leading from their tunnel-cave back to the office basement in the village, the three of them heard another dull rumble. Unlike the last tremor that had sounded from the tunnels, this new noise came from *above* them, very much like a thunderclap that had sounded close by.

"What're they doing?" asked Herb. "Are they going to level the city?"

"It came from the northeast," said Father Brown. "We're already close to the town's edge here. There's almost nothing in that direction except a few farms and the water reclamation facility."

"Water reclamation?" said the Doctor. "Of course! The sewers!"

"Yes, the sewers precisely. Why, Doctor? Do you think the blast has something to do with Gilbert?"

"I think it has *everything* to do with Gilbert, or whoever caused that alarm to be sounded off. The mollusks did this several times on Mars when Ransom's forces defeated their tripods. A number of the conflicts took place in the planet's wide canals, dug thousands of years before in order to channel precious water from the Martian polar caps to the parched deserts in the hemispheric regions.

"When his forces had overwhelmed a number of tripods with suspicious ease, Ransom sensed a trap. He was right. Somehow the mollusks had managed with their incendiary bombs to send a wall of water rushing at the forces in the canal. Had Ransom not suspected, the mollusks would have won the day, and Ransom's army would have managed the singular trick of being drowned in the biggest desert in the solar system this side of Mercury."

"But what," interrupted Herb impatiently, "does that have to do with Gil?"

"The creatures, Herbert," said Father Brown, his stern eyes never leaving the Doctor for a moment, "are going to try and flood Gilbert like a rat in a hole, either by drowning him outright or flooding him to the surface and snatching him as soon as he pops out of a sewer grating."

"That would be the most logical choice, yes," replied the Doctor matter-of-factly. "But, Herbert, if you are worried about your young friend, you can at least take hope that they are nothing if not efficient. They wouldn't be trying to flood the sewers in the middle of an invasion without being certain that something was alive down there which could pose a threat to them."

"That's a bit extreme, don't you think?" said Herb. "All that effort for a lad of sixteen? How could they see him as so great a threat?"

The Doctor shrugged his shoulders. "For the want of a nail, I suppose. Perhaps they don't want something small becoming something quite large. Also, as a race, they are prone to being proud, cruel, vindictive, and at times wholly unpredictable. Gilbert must have enraged them. Now they want him dead, and God alone knows what can save him."

"God alone," nodded the priest.

Twenty-Six

"When such a critic says, for instance, that faith kept the world in darkness until doubt led to enlightenment, he is himself taking things on faith, things that he has never been sufficiently enlightened to doubt . . . I do not blame him for that; I merely remark that he is an unconscious example of everything that he reviles." — GKC

It was dark.

There was only the darkness, nothing else. For a time, the blackness didn't even register as being *dark*, since Gilbert didn't remember light or color. Neither could he recall his name, nor what had come before. He was not even aware of his own face until he felt it twitch several times. A few minutes later, he recalled what eyes were, that he had a pair of them, and that they were twitching and blinking on their own without any direction from him.

He was next aware of the grit in his eyes and nose. He sneezed, the jerking motion reminding him first that he had a head, second that it was in massive pain like the rest of his body. He gasped and moaned as his head throbbed in agony. It felt as if someone had been using his noggin to bash rocks to powder. At his sneeze, his glasses flew forward. Still hooked in place behind his ears, they traveled only a few millimeters before they snapped back and hit the bridge of his nose. The pain in his head roughly doubled, and he moaned louder.

Next there was an oily taste on his tongue. He opened and closed his mouth, trying to analyze the bitter flavor. He tried to spit, but was so weak he could only dribble down the side of his cheek, his spittle leaving a slow, cold trail as it tracked down toward his ear.

He tried to move. Rusty hinges squeaked in his body with every budge and twitch.

He heard a slow, plinking pulse of a noise nearby. In a few more seconds, he realized he was listening to water dripping into a puddle. There was more noise now, like paper crackling. He turned slowly, and a sudden glimpse of light stung his eyes painfully, making him remember the difference between having them open and shut.

Light, he thought as the stabbing pain in his eyes slowly ebbed away, *light hurts me now. I missed the light for so long, but now I want it to go away again.*

Still, he tried to turn his head and face the source of light again. Even with his eyes squeezed shut, Gilbert had to hold his hands in front of his face and slowly open them a tiny cracked finger-space at a time. After what seemed a very long while, his vision had adjusted enough to see that the blinding light was actually several small fires. Most of them were burning almost silently on top of the puddles, and gave off a black, foul-smelling smoke.

There was some principle at work there, Gilbert knew, but he couldn't quite recall it. His head still hurt too much. He turned over slowly, every stir of his body sending fresh spasms of pain shooting through his limbs, and fresh painful throbs to his head and torso. He blinked his eyes slowly and stupidly, looking at the puddles of burning oil that surrounded him. As he surveyed the area, he could see the tunnel had undergone a very odd change. It seemed as if a large bubble had swelled, pushed aside the bricks of the tunnel wall, and burst in the place where the mollusk's ship had been. The walls of the tunnel were now shaped in a definitely visible, although slightly shaky, curve.

The bubble, Gilbert thought. That bubble-shape in the middle of the stone tunnel was made of pure force when the monster's machine exploded.

And the explosion had been powerful enough to move stone! He shuddered, realizing how close to death he had come. If he hadn't turned the corner before . . .

Gilbert swallowed. There was very little left of the alien's ship, and nothing of the alien. He looked at the wet, slimy ground and spied one of the metal pieces of the craft, flickering with the reflected lights of the oil fires. The scrap of metal was about as big as his shoe, and it flipped over without any hurry as he nudged it with his toe.

There was a blob of something white and squishy underneath it.

Gilbert got a fresh, new sick feeling in his stomach. Still, he had a quirk common to all young male humans: he couldn't help but be fascinated by what he knew to be horrible, and he let his gaze settle on the dead creature's body part for several seconds while his breathing eventually returned to normal.

Then, even by the standards of the day, a very peculiar thing occurred. Gilbert saw the blob of alien flesh suddenly twitch and contract, shrinking in on itself as if trying to hide. It changed color from light brown to a light blue, then dark blue. At last, it shriveled up into a dull black husk and was still.

Gilbert turned away and was sick. Then he was sick again. And again, until his stomach was empty and squeezing shut only on air, vapor, and feelings of disgust.

Looked about as tasty as the Widow Douglas's possum stew back home, thought Gilbert, unable even then to keep from finding grim humor in the situation, *but without her little speeches about how healthy it would make us after it'd killed us.* After his gut had finally stopped heaving, his stomach wasn't the only thing that ached. His jaw and shoulders also hurt from the violent retching. His fingers and toes were buzzing as if an electric current had been passing through them, and his wounded calf was throbbing angrily.

Nonetheless, Gilbert began limping away from the wreckage immediately; he knew that hanging around the debris was out of the question — eventually the dead alien's buddies would come looking for it. Besides, the water had suddenly gotten a bit deeper. Lying in three inches of oily sewer water with floating bits of dead alien in it was no way to get a rest!

Then a deep boom echoed from behind. Gilbert picked up his pace. *What next?*

A minute later, there was a very gentle tug at his feet. The tunnel was getting darker as he moved away from the blast site, but he could still see the water on the tunnel floor moving away from him at a faster pace, the ripples left by his feet leaving widening *V*s in front of him.

Keep walking, Gil.

Gilbert began limping quicker still, feeling the weight of the gun belt bumping against his injured leg. In another minute, the water had risen a full inch up to his pantlegs. He couldn't limp any faster.

He hadn't felt so sore since . . . well, since an undetermined number of hours ago, when Ed Pearse of the Gray Mare Boys had given him that beating in the alleyway. Or maybe it was when he'd fallen into that underground chasm. It would be a tight race.

The rising water also checked his pace. It was halfway up to his knees, and almost bath-warm. In the distance, he heard another rumble. And then another. And then a third. A few seconds after he heard the third deep rumble, there was a distant roar. A steady, gnawing sound that was halfway between a river and an angry factory machine.

Gilbert looked around wildly, suddenly feeling very much like a mouse in a dangerous maze.

Is this where I trus—

He never finished the thought.

It was cut off when he saw the glow of daylight and a ladder leading upward a few dozen yards ahead.

He began to run. But the deepening water resisted each stride like quicksand or lead weights, and it was all he could do to slosh along in almost comic slow motion.

The roaring behind him was getting louder. Something was coming down the tunnel at him. Something he couldn't hope to defeat with a gun, a thousand guns, or a battalion of artillery shells. A huge, roaring, twisting monster without bone, spine, or sinew. It rounded the last corner of the tunnel and charged at Gilbert.

Then Gilbert heard a scream. Someone was screaming louder even than the beast behind him. Then he knew *he* was the one screaming, roaring like an ancient Celtic warrior whose fear clashed with anger, blood, and pain in a violent symphony, as he closed the distance between himself and freedom.

Later, Gilbert couldn't remember actually grabbing the ladder. He could only vaguely recall leaping at it in the hopes of beating the monster behind him in the race of his life. He couldn't remember pain in his leg or the rest of his body either. He seemed to be on fire, but with a flame more like a berserker's bloodlust than the kind of blistering pain he'd felt throughout his aching body only a few minutes before. He flung himself at the cool metal ladder, catching hold of a low rung and pulling himself up above the waterline and then through the dim twilight of the sewer tunnel, toward the small circle of lights in the manhole cover above him.

As he reached the top, the monster caught him. Suddenly Gilbert wasn't a warrior snarling his way to victory, but a skinny boy once again. And the enemy that pursued him was no monster from another world, but a gushing wall of steaming hot water.

He shoved at the manhole cover above him, and whooped for joy as it gave slightly.

But not enough. It fell back down into place. Gil braced his knees for the leverage to push harder, when the rush of water struck and nearly carried him off the ladder. No sooner had he regained his perch when the heat began seeping through his shoes and socks, and then through the calves of his trousers. In the space of a second, the sensation changed from warm bath to scalding shower to the agonizing experience of the lower part of his legs, including his stinging wound, dipped into the tank of a steam engine.

Gilbert screamed in agony, lashing out with such a jolt of pain that the manhole cover flew out of its base in one last desperate push. The world exploded for Gilbert into yellow light. Inconceivable, utterly inconceivable that anything could cause such pain! For the space of a second or two, Gilbert was a screeching, howling animal, too caught in the frenzy of his anguish to complete his escape. He knew he had only to thrust himself out of the hole, but his muscles wouldn't obey him. He cried out again and felt his grip on the ladder's top rung loosen. He had run a good race, but the monster was going to win.

Indeed it would have, if at that moment several pairs of hands hadn't grabbed his arms, pulled him up onto the street, and clapped themselves over his wailing mouth.

❧✦❀✦☙

Father Brown, Herb, and the Doctor were still in the dead-end tunnel, waiting by the door that led to the village. The Doctor had felt it prudent (and so declared) to make several adjustments to his flame-tosser gun before ascending the rickety stairs again. Herb had felt it prudent (although he didn't put it that way) to sit and rest on the tunnel-cavern floor before going "tentacle dodging" again, and seconded the motion to wait. He went on to suggest they wait until nightfall, when they could move with less of a chance of being seen.

Still standing and heedless of the annoyed looks of his companions, Father Brown had said a small prayer for their prospects. As he finished the final *Amen*, the trio heard the sound of roaring down in the tunnel. "Is that the flood?" Father asked.

"Most likely," said the Doctor. "They've exploded the filtration plant, and are using one of their devilish contraptions to submerge the tunnels."

"Listen!" Herb hissed. "Can you hear that?"

Several quiet seconds passed. Echoing through the tunnel over the fading din of the explosion was the rising growl of water.

"What . . . what d'you think his chances are?" Herb asked quietly.

"If all that is for Gilbert, and if he is who I think he is, I would say . . . fair," said the Doctor, as if he were discussing a horse's chance of winning the Derby. "Even so, he may be done for. Able though he was, Ransom lost a significant number of our soldiers on Mars to this particular tactic. It isn't likely that an untrained boy could be expected to do better."

Herb swallowed and looked at the ground. But Father Brown suddenly stood, looking at the exit from the tunnel to the abandoned building. "I think," he said with an unusually decisive voice, "we need to get out of the tunnel. Immediately."

"Whatever for?" said Herb, peering down the tunnel. "It's at least a little warmer in here than it will be in the basement of that broken building. Besides, there's still a fair bit of light outside. Didn't you agree we'd wait 'til nightfall?"

There was no answer, and when Herb turned around, he saw that the Doctor was already following Father Brown, who had somehow opened the door and exited the tunnel even as a stream of water and steam began to lap at the toes of Herb's shoes on the gravelly tunnel floor. Cursing silently, Herb rose to a standing position, brushed the dirt off his pants, and followed the men out of the cave and into the office basement again.

Walking slowly up the stairs to minimize creaking, Father Brown led the little group to the first floor. They moved quietly through the hallway and sat uncomfortably on the floor of the room that faced the street.

"Standing here," whispered Father Brown, "we are at street level. It's unlikely that even their pumping devices could push the water from the tunnels this high. I doubt they'd wish to see all of Woking flooded out. This appears to be one of the few buildings available to us with its upper floors still intact. We can monitor the street from this little vantage point, and if things quiet down sufficiently, we can steal away aboveground or return to the tunnels in an effort to escape. I trust you have enough information to make your report to the superiors you've been referring to, Doctor?"

"Quite," the Doctor mumbled. "But any report I could make at this point would be superfluous. If the aliens are so well established here in Woking, there's little doubt they've made their way to London. And, if London has fallen, the war is very nearly over for us."

"We'll discuss that later. For now, we must concentrate on our —"

"Wait!" Herb interrupted, hissing urgently. "Listen!"

Out in the street, the muffled sound of a human howl of pain echoed loud enough to be heard in their room.

Herb inhaled suddenly. The priest closed his eyes as if in pain. The Doctor didn't flinch in the least, as if he heard the sound of human suffering and painful death on a regular basis and was able to tune it out.

"That's Gil!" shouted Herb, launching himself at the rickety door of their shelter.

"Wait, you fool!" barked the Doctor. "You'll bring a squad of tripods down on us!" But Herb was already outside. There was nothing else Father Brown could do but follow him.

The street smelled worse than the inside of the building. A mixture of melting rubber, charred wood, burning meat, and human waste wrinkled Herb's nose, stung his eyes, and twisted his stomach into knots. The meanest street in London — and he'd walked them all — hadn't smelled half so foul.

Father Brown, apparently unaffected by the stink, ran past him and brought him back to his senses. The little priest ran directly to the source of the noise, a battered iron manhole cover in the middle of the street. As Father Brown ran and Herb stumbled toward it, they saw the manhole cover rise slightly, as if pushed from below. The volume of the shriek intensified. In the shadow beneath the manhole cover, Herb saw the glint of light off one lens of a pair of eyeglasses.

"Gil!" Herb shouted happily. But Gil was still screaming, unaware of anything but the source of his pain.

Herb and Father Brown were searching for a handhold on the heavy metal disc when suddenly it popped completely off on its own and wobbled to the side. The sound of rushing water and Gilbert's shrieking filled the air around them as a single grasping hand appeared out of the hole. Herb took a firm grip on the hand and pulled with all his strength. Father Brown moved nimbly, and clapped his hand on Gilbert's mouth to muffle his screams.

"Pull him up," Father Brown said. Still holding Gilbert's mouth, he and Herb yanked Gilbert up and out of the sewer. Gilbert's eyes were wide with pain, and at first he continued to cry out into Father Brown's hand. But when brought out into the open of the street, he was suddenly silenced in spite of his suffering.

Gilbert, like everyone else in England, had never seen destruction on so wide a scale before. Now, sitting limply in the deepening twilight and looking upon the remains of Woking, desolation assaulted his vision wherever he turned. He closed his eyes and rubbed them with his hand, hoping that the entire experience was just another terrifying dream. Had Herb and Father Brown not been holding him up at each of his shoulders, he would have collapsed in a heap on the broken street beneath him.

"Gilbert, quickly," said Father Brown urgently but with compassion, "we need to get out of the street. Quickly now, lad, before the machines come for us."

Herb and Father Brown each took one of Gilbert's arms and led him as hastily as they could back toward their shelter. Gilbert was still reeling, but after inhaling dead alien in the sewer, even the rancid air of ruined Woking seemed fresh and cool, reviving him somewhat. With a friend under each arm, he managed to limp and wobble from the manhole toward and through the door. Once in the burned-out lobby of their building, Gilbert recovered his senses. He was only a little groggy now and could recognize who had pulled him from the street.

"Where are we, Herb?" he asked thickly, after Herb had shut the door to the street and crudely barricaded it with some rubble.

"We're in Woking," Herb whispered quietly. "Keep your mouth shut. The place is crawling with those tripod things."

As if on cue, a hard, heavy metallic *stomp* sounded outside. Gilbert's mouth went dry, and Herb's eyes widened. The priest fingered the rosary at his belt.

"We must return down the stairs and into the tunnel," he said. "If the waters have subsided, it would be safer there than here on the first floor."

Another *stomp,* this one much closer.

"Down the stairs, quickly lads, quickly," said the priest. "Gilbert, can you stand? There. Good. Come, let's go."

Gilbert stood, and pain leapt alive in his leg like a red-hot wire. He sucked air in through his teeth, and nearly bit down on his tongue to keep from yelling.

"Keep silent, Gilbert!" said Herb. "The Doctor says those things have remarkable hearing, and they'll eat us for lunch if they catch us."

Then why are you talking so much? Gilbert thought to himself. *You want to be on the menu first?* Herb helped Gil limp to the stairwell with Father Brown bringing up the rear. The little group was a foot from the door to the stairwell leading down to the tunnel when it suddenly was flung open in front of them.

The Doctor stood in the doorway, blocking it with his thick, square body. His eyes were hidden behind the pitch-black lenses of the goggles that were placed snug on his face. Most important, his flame-firing weapon was in his hands and pointed dead at them. His finger was on the trigger, the small, searingly bright flame was lit near the weapon's barrel. In the gathering night shadows, the blue-orange light from his weapon and the darkness where his eyes *should* have been made him look more than a little diabolical.

"Good evening," he began, sounding like a man who had just found a gold ring after searching for it for a week in a manure pile. "Good evening, Mister *Chesterton*."

Twenty-Seven

"A change of opinions is almost unknown in an elderly military man." — GKC

"D octor, you fool! Move out of the way!" Herb half-whispered, half-screamed. "There's a tripod coming! It'll be here any second!"

"Oh, I am fully cognizant of that," replied the Doctor, making no attempt to stifle his voice. "And I know exactly what it plans to do with you once it gets here. First, it will snatch the lot of you, one in each of its three main tentacles. While it's stuffing you into its basket like the trophies of a mushroom collector, I shall make my escape through the tunnel below. Thank you for ignoring me, by the by, in your mad dash to rescue Gilbert here. Your concern for the boy not only has brought him to me, but gave me a moment to recover my weapon as well."

"That flame-tosser won't have the slightest effect on a tripod, you fool," Father Brown snapped, his voice unusually harsh. "And the tunnel's flooded, in case you didn't remember. Poor Gilbert here is proof enough of that. He's been soaked through and scalded, and he's near into a state of shock. He needs to be tended to. For mercy's sake, let us pass!"

Outside, there was another *whump!* as another tripod foot trampled the ruined street outside.

"No, *padre*," said the Doctor with a slightly bored tone, "I'm afraid I shan't do that. I first have some unfinished business not only with you, but also with young Gilbert here."

"Unfinished business?" gasped Gilbert in a hoarse whisper. "What unfinished business? I never *met* you before yesterday."

"Not so much with you, young *Chesterton*, but with your dearly departed parents."

"What in Sam Hill are you talking about?" Gilbert whispered angrily. "You couldn't have known my parents. And keep *quiet*! The tripods'll hear you!"

"Couldn't have known them? That only shows the depths of ignorance to which you were allowed to sink while they raised you in America. Your parents," he continued, "escaped our clutches somehow, and they have been a most troublesome pair of pebbles in my shoe ever since. Furthermo—"

The roof was torn off the building.

The four men in the wreck of a structure cried out in surprise as the brittle beams, ragged plaster, and rusted pipes were ripped, split, and splintered by the tripod's sinuous tentacles. There was nowhere left to hide.

Gilbert looked up, dumbstruck. He hadn't seen a tripod this close; the last time he'd been this near to one, he'd been running for his life at the Sign of the Broken Sword, his attentions focused on the locked door of the abandoned tavern. This one seemed larger, and more . . . *alien*. Its body was a shiny black ovoid, with a slew of concentric ridges. Gilbert could see little jets of green gas shooting from the joints in its legs and seams in its armor. Except for the even placement of the tripod's legs, Gilbert could see no symmetry to the thing's design. There were a number of large, round, green, bubble-like protrusions — windows? — at different points of the tripod's body, along with a number of smaller, stick-like appendages of various sizes. Gilbert could see that some of them sparked and snapped and popped with electricity, and each time one glowed or crackled, something else happened on the tripod. He saw one of the larger spikes give off a white-hot sparkle, and one of the large, whiplike tentacles reached down and wrapped itself around the Doctor.

"WHAT?" shrieked the Doctor as he was yanked into the air. Father Brown and the boys heard him screaming something about Archibald as the mechanical monster whisked him into the giant basket at its hip.

"What now?" yelped Herb.

"Run, boys!" cried Father Brown, pushing them at the doorway to the underground tunnels. "Run! I'll delay them while you —" another tentacle snaked down, and while the first one was placing the Doctor into the giant holding basket, Father Brown was encircled by a tentacle. "Run, boys! Run!" he yelled as he was whisked into the air. "No!" yelled Gilbert, even as Herb pulled him by the sleeve into the stairwell. "No! Father Brown!"

"Come on!" ordered Herb as he dragged Gilbert behind him. "There's nothing we can do for him or —" It was Herb's turn to be cut off, not by a tentacle, but by his own sprint away from the monstrosity behind them.

Just before Herb's mad dash for the tunnel door, Gilbert had felt a kind of tickle at the back of his neck. Gilbert turned as Herb pulled him toward the bottom of the stairs and saw a long, thin tentacle hovering behind him, double the thickness of his own arm at its widest point but tapering until it was no thicker than his little finger at its tip. The third tentacle followed them, hovering never more than six inches away from Gilbert's nose even as he ran and stumbled backward.

"Herb," started Gilbert, and the spell was broken. The tentacle suddenly sprang past Gilbert and Herb through the stairwell. It circled them twice and tightened, grabbing both of them at once with such force that their heads clunked together painfully. They screamed as they were yanked back through the battered hallway and into the twilight. Gilbert felt a sullen dread as he saw another tentacle open up the top of the metal basket once more — this time, for *him*. The world spun 'round twice as the tentacle uncoiled and dumped them onto a cold metal floor.

<hr/>

The inside of the basket was suffused with a light-green haze. They could see the Doctor sitting on the floor with his knees folded in front of him, the nozzle of his weapon lying useless by his side. He had loosened the straps on the tank of flammable liquid he'd been wearing on his back, and the tank lay prone beside its owner. The straps had left large, vertical indentations along the shoulders of the Doctor's jacket now that they were slackened.

"What's happening, Doctor?" said Herb, sitting up and wincing with pain. "You seem to know all about these things. How do we escape from here?"

"There is no escape, Herbert. Indeed, we have no recourse at this time except, perhaps, the one chance left to humanity."

"And what, pray tell, might that be?" Herb asked pointedly.

"That would be . . . wait a moment. Let me see my pocket watch. Ah, here it is." There was a sudden lurch as the machine began moving again in its patterned, yet still uncomfortably wobbly motion.

The Doctor flipped open his watch and studied it. "The Special Branch has had a plan long prepared, in the event of an unplanned invasion of our shores. It is now Wednesday, very nearly a week after they made their beachhead here in Woking, and it is seven o'clock in the evening. Yes . . . in a matter of minutes, we shall witness the fruits of man's intellect and ingenuity in action."

"What do you mean by an *unplanned* . . . oh, never mind. I don't want to know," Herb said sullenly.

"Leave 'im alone, Herb," said Gilbert. "His senses are so far gone, he couldn't buy a ticket to catch 'em with all the tea in China."

"Gilbert," the Doctor said, "I find your impertinent comments as misguided as they are refreshing. You appear to have grown in masculine confidence since we last met. Did you, as I suspected, manage to kill an alien in the tunnels?"

Gilbert looked at the Doctor and was deciding whether to respond when Father Brown piped up, pointing out one of the small airholes in their pen. "What are these things on the horizon?"

268

The Doctor closed his eyes and smiled, nodding gently as he spoke. "Gentlemen, if what you see below is a train of slow-moving armored conveyances, you can be assured that our deliverance from this prison is imminent."

Gilbert looked out of the circular wall of their prison. He could see that there were perhaps a dozen of the kind of machine that the Doctor had described, slowly cresting the last hill outside the town. Some had cylindrical bodies like a train, only with treads instead of wheels. Others had rectangular shapes, and there were two or three that were half ovoid, like armored turtles. All had bronze metal bodies with large rivets and vertical pipes that belched out steam and coal-smoke. Each machine also had several large-caliber heavy gun barrels bristling out of turrets mounted on their armored bodies like the spines of a giant metal sea urchin.

Then Gilbert heard a whirring, droning sound like a distant swarm of bees, and turned his gaze from the ground to the sky. There on the pink early-evening horizon approached a squadron of silver-and-gold-colored airships, larger than any blimp or Zeppelin Gilbert had ever seen before. Each pair of the flying machines had a long platform suspended between them. The platform looked at this distance to be as wide as a football field, with numerous one- and two-story structures built on its surface.

"Those things on the ground," was all Gilbert could say at first, "they look like those metal ships from the Civil War — the ironclads."

"That is precisely what they are, my boy. Those could accurately be described as *land* ironclads. The products of several years of daring espionage, British ingenuity, and the computations of the world's most sophisticated analytical engines. My boy, mankind's salvation lies in those metal boxes-on-treads. Their hides are virtually impervious, and their guns will show those tripods their match."

"They look unstoppable!" said Herb gleefully. "I bet they could go over any kind of terrain with those treads!"

"They look and move like a bunch of crawling water tanks," said Gilbert, unimpressed. "And how're they gonna save *us*, Doctor? They move way too slow to catch up to us, and I don't think those jellyfish are just gonna let us out when the fighting starts. And what can the blimps do? They're big, but I don't see any guns on them."

"The *armored dirigibles*," said the Doctor, accenting the pronunciation like a man explaining the difference between a thoroughbred stallion and Tony the Pony, "can do far more than float, as you will soon see," replied the Doctor in a patient voice. "As for the ironclads, they do move slowly, Gilbert. But it is the range of their cannons that will effect our rescues. Each of those war machines carries the destructive power of one of Her Majesty's greatest naval battleships. One hit will shred these blackened tin cans in the instant they make contact."

"And us with them," said Father Brown quietly.

There was a thoughtful pause followed by brief scurrying as the two boys tried to duck lower into their cell. The Doctor frowned, but he, too, adjusted his position in their cage. Only the priest continued looking out his window impassively.

They could hear the rumbling of the ironclads as they drew closer. The mollusks didn't seem to be afraid, and they were apparently prepared to engage the ironclads rather than flee. Suddenly, their tripod lurched to a halt. As Gilbert peeked outside, he could see at least two other tripods visible on either side of them. The four new tripods looked much more like the kind that had ambushed their train, and were a full third smaller than the one that held them captive.

Then the ironclads fired, with a sound like thunder. The shells ripped through the air with a sound like tearing notebook paper amplified a thousand times.

The captive humans heard a sudden explosion to their left, and one of the tripod's bodies disappeared in a flash of black metal, green smoke, and red liquid. Some of the liquid splashed through the holes of their pen, and the droplets burned their skin like pinpricks of boiling water.

"HIT!" yelled the Doctor and Herb in loud throaty voices that said all their hopes of rescue were not in vain, and that their race would prevail. More shells landed around them, blasting away the earth at the feet of the tripods. The second of the smaller black towers fell as a shell struck its leg at one of the knee joints.

More movement caught Gilbert's eyes. From his elevated height in the tripod's collector basket, he could see glowing red embers lighting up on two of the three platforms between the pairs of Zeppelins in the sky. A second after, a white line of smoke streaked from each ember toward the line of tripods with a loud buzzing sound. Each line of smoke spiraled in a corkscrew trail of gray and impacted with a crash, exploding with a ball of fire around the tripods' legs. Even among the explosions, Gilbert could see what appeared to be a dozen large birds take off from the third platform, and begin flying in formation toward them.

"You see?" cheered the Doctor. "Humanity triumphs! Science has saved our world, our race, and our empire!"

"Aren't you forgetting one thing?" said Father Brown. His tone quieted them all.

"What do you mean, old man?" said Herb. "Can't you sit back and celebrate for once?"

"I will when it's the proper time. But if our tripod is hit, there won't be enough of us left to celebrate anything. And while those ironclads and airships are reloading, the aliens are preparing their counterstrike. See?"

The tentacles of the aliens were indeed stretching forward toward the ironclads that had gathered in a line on the heath.

"There's no way those tentacles could reach them from this distance," scoffed the Doctor. "And even if they could, they couldn't penetrate their armor. Not before the ironclads blasted them back to Mars."

"It's not the tentacles themselves I'm worried about, Doctor. It is the weapons they appear to be brandishing, those boxes with lenses, that give me pause." Gilbert looked closely, and indeed, each of the tentacles was grasping a little box with a shiny lens on the end.

The ironclads let forth another volley of shells, as did the Zeppelins with their airborne torpedoes. Again, the sky sounded as if it were tearing in two. The shells ruptured the ground around the tripods, leaving house-size craters. Another tripod's leg was broken, and it fell heavily to earth, splitting apart along one of its black seams as it connected with the *terra firma*. Bubbling red liquid and clouds of green smoke hissed from the wreckage. Gilbert could see that the "birds" flying toward them were closer now; a second more, and he could see they weren't birds but *men,* men wearing leather jackets, goggles, and wings like those of an oversized steel dragonfly on their backs. Beneath the wings, small propellers spun and buzzed like a nest of hornets.

"Another one!" shouted Herb, who would have danced for victorious joy in the middle of the cage had it not begun moving again. "A few more volleys, and they'll have the mollusks on the run!"

Then the aliens returned fire.

From their vantage point, it had been difficult for the foursome to examine the Martian weapon in detail. Boxes with lenses, the priest had said, and that was about all they could make of them. Each box was about as big as a horse-drawn growler coach, and the lens in each box was as tall as a man. As the tripods strode forward, quickly closing the gap between the land ironclads and themselves, the lenses on each of the boxes began to glow green, then red. And once they glowed red, the humans' attention was drawn back to the ironclads by the sounds of explosions. As they watched, three of them exploded spectacularly. Then six, then nine, then all twelve of the land ironclads burst into conflagrations that lit up the dusk.

"By Jove," whispered the Doctor. "Those are new."

"The Zeppelins!" cried Herb desperately. "The Zeppelins will save us . . ."

As if on cue, the tripod that carried them let loose with what appeared to be a massive lightning bolt. The writhing electrical spear leapt across the sky and punctured one of the giant blimps like a bullet through a cream puff. The point of impact on the airship flared red like an angry flower, and fire spread across the blimp's surface. In the space of a few seconds, the entire craft was aflame, sinking slowly toward earth. The flaming dirigible's partner on the other side of the platform somehow detached itself, allowing the entire platform and the structures on it to fall along with the giant fireball that the wounded Zeppelin had become.

"When did they develop such marvelous devices?" said the Doctor, his voice quieted by awe at the spectacle outside.

Closer to the tripods, the pilots in their strange, winged harnesses gestured to each other and flew in closer to the line of the tripods. Gilbert saw the lead pilot fly in close, throwing what appeared to be a large black egg at the body of the nearest tripod. It slammed into the metal body with a loud *clang* and remained in place. The other five pilots followed suit, each lobbing a similar egg onto the tripod as well. As the six pilots wheeled around in formation, a series of explosions lit up the pilot's target, blowing gaping holes in the tripod's body. Steaming red water flowed out from the ruined black tower, and in the firelight, Gilbert thought he saw the slimy body of a Martian slide out and plop to the ground far below.

"The bravery of those young men!" said Father Brown, quietly.

"The stupidity!" cursed the Doctor. "They will be atomized as well, and the technological marvel of the flying apparatus will be lost!"

Gilbert was too mesmerized by the falling Zeppelin and the pilots to argue. The last of the smaller tripods focused a beam on the five pilots buzzing toward it, turning each one into a miniature ball of flame that streaked and disappeared like a bottle rocket. The large tripod that had captured them incinerated the five remaining airships as they lumbered off in retreat, blasting them with its lightning bolts. Each of the giant blimps erupted in flame and descended to earth in a slow pirouette, touching the ground and rolling gently from side to side, the metal skeletons of the hydrogen-filled behemoths' framework visible under the furiously burning outer shells.

All watched in horror as the last airship crashed. Then Herb turned away, his face the color of ash. As the tripods stood silently and surveyed the carnage they had caused, the Doctor sat with his back against the wall of their prison and looked out at a night that was lit by the red fires of the ruined ironclads. His eyes were wide and dull with shock and awe.

"It is over," he mumbled quietly. "It is truly over. We are finished on Earth. And they have won."

Twenty-Eight

"Progress is a comparative of which we have not settled the superlative." — GKC

"What do you mean, Doctor?" asked Gilbert.
Despite his chicanery and ultimate treachery, the Doctor had been
the group's rudder, leading every step of their flight from the tripods. He
had seemed to know everything about the aliens and their capabilities, and
had remained cool and confident no matter how great the peril.

Now, to see the Doctor despairing sent icy prickles down the back of
Gilbert's neck and cast a wave of hopelessness over them all. Herb's face
fell; his faith in human technology had been absolute, and now it had been
betrayed. But hopelessness seemed to have a different effect on Gilbert. His
face suddenly became hardened, more resolute.

"I asked you a question, Doctor," Gilbert repeated as the machine
lurched into motion and the rest of them sat low to the floor.

"And I gave you an answer, even before you spoke." The Doctor's voice
was dry as winter deadwood, and his hand covered half his face. "It is over.
They have broken our last line of defense with their heated rays and Tes-
latic guns. They have broken their agreement with us. The war is over, and
we have lost."

"Just what kind of agreement have you been referring to?" said Father
Brown sharply. "Did your frock-coated Special Branch actually have some
kind of *arrangement* with those devils?"

"We did indeed," sighed the Doctor, "and I see no reason to hide it from
you now. We had several protocols, in fact. I was present on Mars when we

signed the papers five years ago with them. They agreed to leave Earth alone if we agreed to let them . . . farm . . . the occasional group of humans in our Mars colonies. They said they needed humans both for their flesh-crafting experiments and for the iron we carry in our blood. And their need was such that they were even willing to overlook a number of past *misunderstandings* between our races in order to obtain them. Blood is particularly valuable to them. It acts as a kind of super-tonic food for their bodily systems. And then Edison and Ransom had to go to Mars and completely bungle the whole thing!"

Herb perked up. "Wait, just wait a second, Doctor . . . Did you say . . . *farm* the occasional group of humans? And just what do you mean by 'misunderstandings'?"

The Doctor closed his eyes and sighed. "England has a history of taking its undesirables and using them as colonists in hostile environments, doesn't it? It worked in Australia, and it was working on Mars — to the satisfaction of all who mattered. As for misunderstandings . . . I myself have . . . been on Mars. After we had established a base there, but before we had made contact with the natives, I led a team into Martian territory. Our mission was to obtain samples of Martian tissue for us to . . . learn from. We found copious amounts of it at one of the mollusks' open-air hatcheries."

"What did you do?" whispered Gilbert, fearing he already knew the answer.

"What did we do?" the Doctor replied loudly, then returned to his normal voice. "We took several newly born Martians and stuffed them into sacks. Then we were discovered, and pursued. In our flight, we released vicious dogs into the pits, hoping that the Martians would be too busy saving their offspring to give chase to us. The idea very nearly failed, for I alone made it back to the human base with my samples. But we were able to learn much from them through experiments. Among the Martian mollusks, I have had a certain notoriety ever since, though frankly I had expected them to be above such petty grudges."

"You expect them to forget when you kill their newborn children?"

"They likely would have grown to feed on you, priest."

"You cannot kill a child over what it *might* do, Doctor."

"You say this, after seeing their brutality? Their wanton cruelty?"

"Have you considered that they are being so brutal to us in part because *you* were the first face of humanity they witnessed? Did any of your monstrous lot approach them in *peace* before you tried to vivisect their babies? Do you know nothing of history? The hallmark of any worthwhile civilization is how it values its children, whatever their ages."

The Doctor stared into the distance, his eyes glazing over with memory and thought. But after a few moments, his eyes dropped to look at the ground. He took a few breaths and raised his eyes again.

"It is of no consequence now," he stated crisply. "All was forgiven and forgotten between both races, and peace was indeed a reality. The arrangement was working to the satisfaction of *all who mattered* — all until Edison and Ransom arrived and decided that they wanted to play-act like heroes."

Father Brown looked blankly at the Doctor. "You are a monster," he said simply. "You killed their children, turned 'round, and offered men of earth as sacrificial food in exchange for a tight-jawed pledge of forgiveness and a few technological trinkets, and then had the gall to blame men of principle when their uprightness upsets your amoral little apple cart.

"And this answers a final question that had been puzzling me," continued the little priest. "Why *were* they so intent on our capture? And now we know: once they realized you were among us, they sent their tripods to rip the roofs off houses, and their scouts into the sewers, in an effort to capture you and make you pay for your crimes. No wonder you saw the need to spare our lives, if only to help protect your own. It would appear they are not as above emotion as you'd like, especially when the chance comes 'round to settle old scores."

"If only you clerics of Rome," the Doctor hissed, suddenly defensive, "could see the world straight on, the way things are, without that intolerable squint you all seem to develop in the seminary. Before you begin judging me, Father, you might want to remember that these colonies have been in place for over a decade."

"It is indeed rare that a man asks me not to judge him when his conscience is truly clean, Doctor."

"We would *not* be at *war* today had our arrangement with the mollusks still been in place! The Martians would have raided the colonies occasionally to satisfy their curiosities and . . ."

"And their *appetites*," Father Brown said quietly.

"Yes," continued the Doctor in a brazen tone. "Then the Earth would have been left in peace. But Ransom's uniting of the human colonies and other Martian natives shattered that agreement, in their eyes. For a brief time, it appeared that Ransom might have stumbled onto a way to defeat the lot of them; when several of his human soldiers were captured by a mollusk scouting party and drained of their blood, the mollusk scouts died nearly instantly from the microbes in the blood of their victims."

"You mean," interrupted Herb, "if they eat someone who has a cold, they die?"

"Not anymore, Herbert. The mollusks quickly deduced the cause of their comrades' deaths, and now have in place a type of filtering tube that screens out all the varieties of bacteria they've encountered from our species on the red planet. We can expect no help from tiny microbes in this fight, I'm afraid.

"Still, despite this disappointment, Ransom continued his efforts against the Martians. We tried to *remove* him again and again, but he proved far too resourceful an adversary." The Doctor paused to look at Gilbert. "Much as your own parents did, young Gilbert."

Gilbert bristled. Quicker than either Herb or Father Brown would have thought possible, the lanky young man had darted across the small floor, the pain in his legs forgotten. He grabbed the Doctor by the lapels of his coat in his balled-up fists and shook him against the wall of their cell.

"What about my parents?" Gilbert growled, his eyes suddenly looking like two blank discs behind the lenses of his glasses. His voice sent an unexpected shiver up the spines of all present, and put a look of shock on the face of the Doctor himself. "What, Doctor?" Gilbert barked. "Surprised that someone's willing to get in your face when you mention their family? Maybe the rules are different here in the land o' tea and crumpets, but where I'm from, when you bring a man's Ma and Pa into things, you get your priorities rearranged for you! Along with a few of your facial features."

"Gilbert . . ." started the Doctor. It was the kind of voice one might have used to ask a mental patient to surrender a hand grenade.

"What, Doctor? What?" Gilbert was shaking the Doctor almost rhythmically now, standing over the older man and rattling him by his collar, knocking the older man's top hat to the side. "You going to give me another philosophy lesson about how the fit have to rule the unfit? Tell the unwashed masses like me that superior people like you can do whatever they want? Lately, I've heard a lot of people saying, 'We can do what we want.' But really, all that rot ends up meaning the strong can do what *they* want to the weak. Isn't that how it works? Hm? Tell me, Doctor, were my parents some of those 'weak' people?"

"Why Gilbert, whatever do you mean?"

"I *mean*, you senile, blathering excuse for a spy . . ."

"I prefer the term 'interplanetary conspirator' . . ."

"Shut up! I *mean*, *spy*, that my parents had a little habit I'd forgotten about. That is, until I found myself several hundred feet underground and facing death as close as I'm facing you." Gilbert wrinkled his nose. "Death smelled better, by the way . . . when was the last time you took a bath?"

The Doctor's brow furrowed. "What . . . *what* did you just ask me?"

"My *parents*, you lying, sideburned excuse for a toadstool! At night, when the house was empty and they thought I was asleep, when they thought no one could hear them and they felt safe, they'd whisper to each other, whispering *with English accents*! And my mother was always worried, *worried* about someone coming for them. Who was it? Was it *you? WAS IT YOU??*"

"Gilbert, you run the risk of doing damage to me if you thrash me about like this much more. And if you value your life, you'll . . ."

"Damage?" roared Gilbert. "*Damage?* You call *this* 'damage,' " Gilbert shoved the Doctor just enough that the back of his head clunked against the metal wall, "when, in just a few minutes, we're all going to be entrées for a bunch of squids? You'll have to pardon me if I don't seem too upset about giving you a headache. And as I was saying, *Doctor*, I just *killed* one of those things a little while ago, so don't you *dare* go about trying to convince *me* as to what the *safer* course of action is, or try to intimidate *me* with your feeble little threats! Do I make myself totally, crystally, *Americanly* clear?" Gilbert's eyes were different than anyone in the company had ever seen them; they held the slightest tint of the kind of madness that makes quiet men capable of truly awful acts.

"Gilbert," said Father Brown, as softly as he could while still being heard over the machinery of the tripod. "Gilbert, whoever he is, you need to release him. He may be the monster you think he is. On the other hand, he may be the kind of person who lies and cannot stop himself. Either way, you've been given no right to seek vengeance through murder."

There was a pause of several seconds while the Doctor looked at Gilbert in disbelief. Making a disgusted noise through his nose, Gilbert released the Doctor, letting the older man slouch to the floor, and stalked three steps back to the opposite wall of their cell, the farthest from the Doctor that he could go, and sat, trying to look out into the darkness.

"So much like your father," the Doctor mumbled under his breath, just loud enough for the others to hear. "Full of oaths and moral notions, so willing to sacrifice all in the name of principle. Your father would have been quite proud, young Gilbert."

"Doctor," Herb's voice was unusually cautious, "you don't want to tread any further in that particular swamp, if you get my meaning."

"Herbert, I am *complimenting* young Gilbert on his obvious parentage — the quality breeding that has sustained him thus far in his tremendous journey toward his destiny. He also chooses his friends wisely. Had you not taken my knife earlier, I might have removed a few of his organs a moment ago."

There was a long pause, as if Gilbert were deciding whether to respond. "For your information, *Doctor*," said Gilbert slowly, "there's absolutely nothing about my parents that prepared me for this. They gave me better schooling at home than I ever got in the schoolhouse, but Martian squid-killing was never part of the curriculum. In the past two days, there's been nothing I've gotten through that can be chalked up to having better or worse blood than you or anything else."

Now Gilbert leaned in closer to the Doctor; his voice was almost kind. "Do you want to know, Doctor, just what it was that's gotten me out of every scrape I've been in, not just these last two messed-up days, but my whole messed-up life? Do you *really* want to know, or would it be too big a challenge to the way you *think* the world works?"

The Doctor looked steadily at Gilbert, saying nothing.

"Here." Gilbert pulled what looked like a battered playing card from his pants pocket, and flicked it at the Doctor. It spun in the air and struck him lightly on the chest, falling to rest on his arm. "*Trust* is what got me through, Doctor. Trust. Not blood or breeding, or the scientific wonders of the Empire. *Trust* saved me. Every time I've trusted, I've gotten through. With a whole lotta scrapes, bruises, and scars, but I've gotten through."

The Doctor looked down at the card. It was dog-eared and stained, but it still bore the recognizable image of Saint Michael the Archangel.

"And," continued Gilbert, "I'm gonna keep trusting, till the end of my life. Even if that's only a half-hour from now."

The Doctor looked up, aghast. "Your *breeding*, young Gilbert. Don't throw away that precious gift for a feeble superstition!" He crushed the card in his hands. "Only *intellect* and *action* will save us now."

"Intellect and action, Doctor? Do you mean using your brains, your wits, your brawn, or all three? Look out there, Doctor, and tell me where all three have gotten us here in England. Well, look, blast you!"

Incredibly, the Doctor obeyed, peering through the nearest hole in the basket wall. It had been dark for a while, but powerful lights shone from the holes in long streams that ended in a wide, white spot on the ground. Herb had tried calling it a "spot-light" in a half-hearted attempt at humor, but no one had been in the mood for jokes and he'd not repeated himself.

Since their tripod had begun moving, most of the countryside they had seen through the holes of their prison was covered in a kind of black dust. In several places, there were small groups of human skeletons wearing the unmistakable uniforms of British infantrymen. More often than not, the skeletons were grouped around some kind of machinery that looked as if it had been a heavy-firing weapon of some sort, like an artillery cannon or a Maxim gun.

"See, Doctor? See where your way gets us? What do you think, Herb? On the train, you said that humanity was always perfecting itself, that everything in the past was inferior to the present. Well, I say you're wrong. I bet those guns worked a *lot* better a few days ago than they do now, don't they?"

"If I could interrupt the level that this conversation is sinking to," said Father Brown, gentle rebuke in his voice but with a light of pride shining in his eyes as he sized up Gilbert. "We may disagree on a number of points, but one thing we all might agree upon is the imminence of our own demise. If you look outside, you can see we are traveling toward what appears to be a very large crater, in which many other tripods have gathered. If indeed this is where the tripods and their pilots make their base, our journey will very soon be at an end, both literally and metaphorically."

The sound of a human scream sounded very near to them. Four pairs of eyes tried to peer through the holes of the cage. What they saw sickened and disgusted them, but held their gaze the way the sight of a leprous beggar or a terrible carriage accident on the road would enthrall a passerby.

There was another tripod near them — perhaps thirty or forty yards away. The dark of the forest was almost impossible to see through, but several smaller, factory-like buildings lit up the gigantic crater they were approaching. The mechanical structures were each the size of several houses, and bathed their surrounding area in red light. As for the tripod near them, it, too, had a collector basket and had just pulled a man out from it with one of its main tentacles. The man held in the quivering tentacle was very fat and dressed in the kind of topcoat and trousers that suggested he had been a person of no small consequence before the aliens had landed.

"I think I *know* him," Herb said incredulously. "He's . . . he *was* a slumlord in London. Wasn't too particular about using hired knives or barkers to make problems go away. Or using money where violence wouldn't work."

As if to affirm Herb's statement, the large man began to babble a stream of high-pitched, frantic speech. "Ten thousand pounds!" he screeched, looking at the bubble-like domes of the tripods as they opened, revealing several more of the mollusk-like creatures they had seen in the subterranean tunnels. "Twenty thousand pounds! A hundred thousand! A thousand thousand! Oil! Rails! Any of it! Give me an hour! A half-hour! A minute! All the more for you! I'm not supposed to be here! It's them! Them! *They* are yours! I need to be spared! I can make an arrangement! A contract!

A barrister! There's a Lord, a Lady, Her Majesty! Someone! Anyone! Help me! *Help me!*"

Then Gilbert's attentions were drawn by movement on the ground below. Several Martians had detached themselves from their machines and plodded into a rough circle below the well-dressed man. Gilbert saw the man's eyes grow wide with terror as the mollusks circled below him like a pack of predators, their yellow eyes staring up at him greedily. The banker's mouth became an *O* of horror as he was slowly lowered into the group, who extended their tentacles toward his feet.

"A million pounds! A hundred million pouuuuuuuaaaaaaaaa!" his last sentence became an incoherent scream as one of the brown, rubbery arms of the mollusks gingerly stroked his shoe and ankle. Then the man was dropped into their midst, and a sea of whipping tentacles surrounded and silenced him forever. And then, as he was lowered further, his arms were grabbed, too. Then more prisoners were lowered from that basket, and Gilbert could see that their tripod was part of a long line, each with captive hands and eyes peeking out of identical metal boxes, watching the horrible spectacle below.

"Feeding time at the zoo, hey?" cracked Herb glumly. "Do they tear his arms off, like he was a chicken or a crab?"

"Watch, if you care," said the Doctor. He was sitting morosely, facing the wall of their prison. His arms were around his knees, which were drawn up against his chest. He stared blankly out of one of the holes of the basket at the sky, in the opposite direction of the banker and his muffled screams.

"Hoo! Hoo!" cooed the Martians. Gilbert could see a small mouth beneath the enormous eyes opening and closing — a beak-like flap of flesh. *"Hoo! Hoo!"* It sounded like a rush of air, as if they were emptying their bodies in anticipation of a filling of a different sort.

"Are the straws out yet?" asked the Doctor.

"Straws?" said Gilbert. "What, is this a restaurant?"

"After a fashion. Keep watching. We're fortunate to have stumbled upon a feeding-time. At other times, they put their captives into storage first."

Gilbert, fascinated by the horrible sight, kept his face glued to the opening of his small prison. The *hoo-hoo*ing had slowed, and it was almost silent, save for the snorting and grunting of the flailing victim. A half-dozen mollusks surrounded him in a circle. Even after all he'd seen in the last several days, Gilbert had to blink, rub his eyes, and stare again to make sure he wasn't hallucinating.

Inexplicably, the creature's mouths seemed to be getting . . . longer somehow. Or were they noses? Long, straw-like things were growing from the mouths of the creature's bulbous faces, appendages that were thin as a pair of fingers, but as Gilbert could see even from a distance, sharply pointed at their ends.

"What are they going to do?" Gilbert asked quietly, knowing and yet hoping he was wrong. His eyes never left the scene below.

The Doctor chose not to answer. But Gilbert's question was answered just a moment later. With a movement that seemed completely out of place for the languid creatures at the bottom of the ash-covered crater, the Martians lunged at the whimpering banker, burying their stingers into the arms and legs still held firmly by their tentacles. The man's body had been tense as it struggled against the creatures' iron grip, but now it went limp. The aliens were no longer *hoo*ing, but Gilbert thought he could hear a sound like a satisfied hum or purr coming from them as they probed their "straws" in and out of the banker, draining him of his life.

"Like children drinking lemonade on a hot day," Herb murmured.

"D'you think if we're sour enough, they'll leave us alone?" said Gilbert.

"You've a remarkable talent for levity, young Gilbert," said Father Brown, putting his hand on Gilbert's shoulder. "I should have liked to have worked in the missions with you."

"Why's that? Because I can whistle in the dark?"

"No. Because you know that the light is far more important."

The Doctor snorted. "If the God you worship is listening, priest, I hope he's got an instant-answers department."

Father Brown looked at the Doctor's huddled form. "Even now," he said quietly. "Even now, with death so close, you're still a slave to your hatred and disdain."

"No. To die hating them, and you, and all you stand for, that is *freedom*."

"Freedom from what?" answered Father Brown without the slightest pause. "More important," he continued, "if you die with a heart full of hate, what kind of a place will you be freely running to?"

"Oh, Jove. Here it comes."

Father Brown persisted. "If indeed death be upon us, should you not even entertain the possibility that you ought to prepare for it? You're assuming that nothingness awaits, or perhaps a warm and fuzzy thing that will pat you on the head and send you off to be reincarnated. But those are boys' thoughts, the wishful thinking of a culture addicted to comfort. What if the truth were more wonderful and terrible than any of us could believe? If, indeed, we cannot truly *know* the other side, wouldn't a rational person prepare for the worst that could *possibly* happen, and try to secure the best of all possible outcomes?"

Herb and Gilbert looked at one another, and back at the priest. In the distance, they could hear another human screaming as the Martians made them into a meal. "You know, Gil," said Herb uncertainly, with many pauses. "I heard one fellow say that there were no . . . atheists in foxholes."

"D'you think he meant the same thing about alien dinner-pot prisons, like this one?" Gilbert's eyes had gotten very round behind the lenses of his glasses.

"I'm not joking, Gil. I mean when death's staring at you, all the arguments about how there's no God, or if there is, he doesn't care — all that sounds as hollow as a funeral drum." Herb turned suddenly to Father

Brown. "All right . . . Father," he said, more than a little forcefully, "before I change my mind, what do I have to do to get this God of yours to be on my side?"

"It's much easier than most think, really," said Father Brown, reaching for the breast pocket of his jacket.

"Put it away!" barked the Doctor in a voice that sounded not entirely his own.

"What do you fear?" asked Father Brown.

"Dying in the midst of superstition, you doddering old fool! Herbert, if you succumb to the fallacies of this idiot, you make a mockery of humanity!"

"Doctor," began Herb, but he never finished his sentence. The lid of their prison suddenly flipped open, and the largest of the tentacles suddenly hovered over them, as if peering into a picnic basket for the ripest specimen.

"Never!" roared the Doctor, seemingly out of nowhere whipping out a dark-colored rod that looked to Gilbert much like the device that the red-head had used to revitalize the engineer on the train. Blue sparks showered from two small prongs at the end of the wand, lighting up the darkness around them.

"Archibald is my brother!" roared the Doctor, sweeping the Shocking Nancy in a wide arc, bringing it to rest in front of him like a magician with a wand. "Archibald is my brother, you spineless masses of gray matter! Do you hear me? We had an arrangement! An *arrangement*! Archibald is my brother! Archibald is my brother! Archibald is my bro-aaaghh!"

The tentacle, completely ignoring the Doctor's weapon, launched down instead at the Doctor's right arm. In less than a second, the tentacle's slim end had wrapped itself three times around the Doctor's forearm and squeezed. The bones collapsed and broke with a sound like stiff paper crackling, making the Doctor's arm bend in so many unnatural directions it looked like the arm of a marionette whose strings had just been cut. His weapon clattered to the floor with an empty metallic clang.

The Doctor's body collapsed and convulsed at the end of the tentacle like a fish on a hook, and he was yanked upward with such force that Gilbert was surprised the Doctor's now-ruined arm wasn't torn clean out of its socket. The Doctor's screams receded with his body as he disappeared upward and the metal lid banged shut above them.

"So this is it, then," said Herb. "We're really going to die."

"God have mercy on that poor man's soul," said Father Brown. "He had a streak of conceit, but perhaps he was at least as ignorant as he was arrogant."

"I can't believe this," Herb said. "I can't die now. Do you hear me! I can't die! I've got too much work to do in this world! I was . . . I *am* going to be a great writer of scientifiction!"

"We all feel that way, Herbert. That is, we all feel that way if we can see the signpost up ahead. We want to tell the driver to stop, or at least slow down. But he waits for no man, and finished or not, the bell rings, the term is over, and the examinations are upon you in what seemed like a very short time."

"What're you driving at, *padre?*"

"I mean this may very well be the final exam, and I have the answers for you in my pocket. You can gamble that the Doctor was right, Herbert. If so, then accepting my help will lose you nothing. But, if *I* am right, then my help is all you will need, and all that can help you."

Another scream sounded outside. Herb swallowed, his Adam's apple moving in the hellish green light. "We were interrupted last time. How do you go about this?"

"Our Lord used water to . . . *atchoo!* Our Lord, Herbert, used water as the agent to effect the removal of Original Sin. Were you baptized ever, Herbert?"

Gilbert, waiting for the priest to finish with his friend so it could be his turn, looked about the inside of their prison for the hundredth time in a vain attempt to find a means of escape. He looked over at the priest and Herb. Father Brown was saying something to the younger man in a hushed, private tone, and Herb was answering in single syllables. *I don't want to die here*, Gilbert thought desperately. *I don't mind preparing for the worst, and I don't mind trusting again, but I just don't want to die just yet. There must be a way out. There must be a way out of.* . . . Gilbert looked up at the large, almost crude lid of their basket, then at the Doctor's now discarded fuel pack and tube-shaped gun, and felt something in his head shift and give just enough for a possibility to take shape.

"Father, Herb," said Gilbert, "sorry to interrupt, but how did you say that thing of the Doctor's worked again?"

"Gilbert, lad, we're rather busy at the moment. Could you wait a few more seconds?" said the priest, remarkably with only the slightest perceptible agitation in his voice.

"Fine. All right."

A few seconds went by, and a rite that Gilbert hadn't ever heard of but planned very soon to partake in was concluded. Herb looked a little dazed, but not in a bad way. Gilbert remembered how a friend had once looked after his dream girl said yes to his invitation for a date.

"What is it, Gil? What d'you need?"

"Herb, on our way over here, you told me about that flame-throwing thing the Doctor used against the Martian in the tunnel. Tell me again how it worked?"

"Gil, we went over this. That flame-tosser spurts a bunch of petrol over everything and sets it alight. It's a minor miracle that we didn't all get roasted alive in the tunnels along with the Martian. If we launched it in here, it'd be suicide!"

"I get that, Herb. And no, don't worry. If I'm not gonna let these things kill me, I sure won't give 'em the satisfaction of watching me roasting myself for their pleasure. You told me that before he turned the Martian into a deep-fried mollusk, there was a hot, blue flame, shaped like a feather, that came out've the nozzle?"

"Yes, but what's so important about that?"

Gilbert didn't answer right away. He stepped to the limp pack and tube-shaped gun. "Herb, Father, based on how long they took with the banker, I figure we've got about five minutes, give or take, before they're through with the Doctor and they come for the next one of us. Before I go through what Herb just did, I want to make one last stab at getting us out've here. But I've got an idea that's a little different from what you'd think."

Gilbert picked up the pack and shouldered the straps, then picked up the gun. The Doctor had thrown off several items upon his entrance into the grimy cage, and fortunately one of these had been the set of darkened goggles.

"I've seen them use these in science experiments at school," said Herb, "but what're you going to do with these now?"

"Yes, and besides," chimed in Father Brown, "unless you have the most airtight of plans, I'd recommend your current course of action as the second, after we finish an action of a more sacramental nature."

"Can we do two things at once, Father? I read in the paper about a couple who made their wedding vows on a train last year; could you ask me whatever you need to while I'm doing this?"

Father Brown pursed his lips in the slightest pout. "Very well. Our Lord allowed grain-picking on the Sabbath; perhaps a baptism while trying to save oneself from being drained dry by Martians would be seen as valid. I'll accept whatever the consequences are once I arrive in the next world. If we survive this, you both must promise me you'll be properly catechized — that is, instructed — on this afterward. Agreed?"

Both Herb and Gilbert nodded.

"Good. Now," he flipped once again to a set of pages in a small black book while Gilbert strapped on the Doctor's fuel tank over his battered, filthy sport coat and checked both the gun and the small and large tubes attached to it to make certain there were no leaks at all.

"May the Lord be on your heart and on your lips to guide you and keep you during this . . . I presume this is your first confession of faith, Gilbert?"

"You presume right, Father." Gilbert answered, quickly yet respectfully, while pulling the goggles onto his eyes. "Herb, help me with this thing. How did the Doctor make the smaller flame come out?"

"Well, first he pulled one of the triggers to make a spark."

"Which trigger?"

"Do you, Gilbert, reject Satan, all his works, and all his empty promises?"

Gilbert paused a moment, then nodded his head almost imperceptibly. "Yes. Herb, help me here."

"I don't know which one! Your guess is as good as mine!"

"But you were *there*! Think, willya! Which trigger?"

"Well, what's the difference?"

"One might lead to freedom. The other turns us all into roman candles."

"Oh."

"Do you believe in the reality of Heaven, union with the Father, Son, and Holy Ghost, and the reality of Hell, with its eternal separation from the same?"

Gilbert paused again, but for a shorter moment than last time. "Yes. Herb, how's this: when the Doctor made the spark, what did the triggers look like in the spark light?"

"Look like? It looked like . . . like metal being lit by a spark light. Why is that significant?"

"Do you believe in the Father, and in Jesus Christ our Lord, born of the Virgin Mary, suffered under Pontius Pilate, was crucified for our sins, died, was buried, and rose again in fulfillment of the scriptures?"

Gilbert paused, and a look of near surprise crossed his face. "Father, I . . . I do, Father. Yes." His attention suddenly shifted back to his other task at hand. "Now Herb, you've just answered my question. Watch."

Gilbert turned the knob at the tip of the weapon's barrel, as Herb had seen the Doctor do, and a small hissing of flammable gas could be heard. "If you could *see* a trigger when the Doctor pulled it to make the spark, that means he was pulling the *second* trigger, here. If he was pulling the first, then his trigger finger would've covered the both of them up. Y'see?" Gilbert pulled the second trigger, and the sparking mechanism obediently snapped and popped until a bright, yellow flame could be seen

"Brilliant, Gil. Now, how're you going to use it to get us out've here? You've only got a couple've minutes left before one of us becomes a blood *hors d'oeuvre!*"

"Very simple. Look, if you caught a bunch of lobsters in a trap, and you opened the trap, if you were really, really hungry or you knew the lobsters were really, really good, there's no way you'd throw back even the worst of the bunch, right?"

"I'm following you fine. Could you act while you're talking, like you told the Father you'd do?"

"Oh yeah. Sure. Anyway," Gilbert hooked one hand into a hole on the side of the metal basket, and the tips of his battered shoes into similar openings, and began to climb to the top. "It just occurred to me: I'd take whatever I found, but what if, instead, I just couldn't get the basket opened at all? If I fussed and fiddled with the thing but couldn't open the latch, but I had a few dozen other baskets to get to, or lots and lots of other lobsters in the sea, what would a normal person do?"

Herb blinked. Then his face lit up. "I'd leave that trap alone, and" — here he looked up at Gilbert — "then I'd go and find easier prey!"

" 'Zactly," said Gilbert, who'd now reached the ceiling of their prison and was examining the seam between the curved wall and the lid. It was a difficult job; he had to hang on with his left hand to the highest hole in the wall he could find while holding on to the flame-tosser barrel with his right. "A blacksmith once told me about a gadget he'd seen in London.

Designed by a German analytical engine. Managed to channel natural gas into such a hot flame that it could melt two different metals into puddles together, without having to put either of them into a forge first. And when they mixed and cooled, they were unbreakable."

Father Brown, who had been talking for the last several minutes, now took the vial out from his vest for the second time. He unscrewed the lid just slightly, and called for Gilbert's attention.

"What was that, Father?" The gassy hissing of Gilbert's improvised welding torch had drowned out the priest's voice somewhat. As he turned to hear Father Brown's reply, by a horrible coincidence the priest concluded the rite of Baptism by flinging water in Gilbert's direction. ". . . in the name of the Father, and of the Son, and of the Holy Ghost . . ." Most of the water drops sprinkled on Gilbert's head, but three drops of water came together at a point so precise in both quantity and timing that the circumstance could not be accurately reproduced by chance or human design in a century of attempts. Unfortunately for Gilbert's plan, those drops from the priest's hand converged at the spout of his welding torch.

The flame sputtered and quickly died with a very loud hiss.

There was a moment of shocked despondency, and then the top of the cage flipped open. Gilbert found himself staring at a large, green window, set like a giant, emerald eye in the body of the tripod. Herb had tried to convince Gilbert before that, by definition, a race advanced enough to reach earth would have put aside simple emotions such as love and hate. But Gilbert suddenly felt the cold disdain of the green eye upon him, powerful, unmistakable, and inescapable as the unwanted attentions of his old Overseer.

Gilbert had a feeling that the eye knew he'd been trying to do something unexpected. And it was very, very annoyed with him. As he stared at the tentacle rising above him to strike, Gilbert felt his sweat mingle with the sprinkled holy water of Father Brown, and wondered if he could at least go swimming in Heaven.

Twenty-Nine

"I say that a man must be certain of his morality for the simple reason that he has to suffer for it." — GKC

Gilbert saw the tentacle reaching for him without any real hurry, just as it had for the Doctor before he had jabbed at it with his Shocking Nancy wand.

Gilbert put his finger on the front trigger, ready to immolate the tentacle when it got within range. A futile gesture, he knew; but if it would annoy the alien by denying him a meal for a few more seconds . . .

When the black arm was only a few feet from Gilbert's face, he noticed something fly past his face and smack onto the tip of the tripod's tentacle. A shower of sparks made him turn away instinctively, despite the goggles he wore, and he almost lost his grip and footing. He looked back, and saw Herb flicking his arm and wrist as if he'd just tossed a hard pitch in baseball.

"Hey, over here, you ugly, sorry excuse for an invertebrate!" Herb called up defiantly. "Why don't you try and come out of that tin can, and see what a full-blooded Englishman can do in a fair fight?"

Herb! He'd thrown the Doctor's shock-rod at the tentacle! *He's got no reason to do this*, Gilbert thought. He turned his attention back to the tripod above and saw that the tentacle was hovering menacingly in the air above Herb, no longer pointed at Gilbert at all. It was using a movement that had become all too familiar to Gilbert now, preparing not to snatch, but to strike and kill.

"Come on, then!" roared Herb, his voice betraying eyes that were beginning to fill with tears. "Get on with it!"

Still hovering above the collector basket, three long claws extended slowly from the tip of the tentacle, forming a bizarre and frightening kind of triangle. *It's toying with us,* Gilbert realized. *They've got a ton of complicated gadgets, but they're really no different from cats that toy with their prey.*

"C'mon, you . . . you *thing!* I helped kill one've your kind in the tunnels! I'd do it again if you gave me half a chance!"

At Herb's third outburst, the tentacle struck, so fast that Gilbert's best reflexes couldn't turn his head quickly enough to follow it. The striking tentacle sped past his head, missing his face by only a few inches. Had the thing wanted to spear him it wouldn't have had the slightest difficulty in turning Gilbert into the Martian equivalent of an olive on a toothpick.

But Gilbert was not its target.

Although the moment lasted only a few fractions of a second, the whole event moved for Gilbert in a surreal kind of slow motion. The black tentacle firing like a long black bullet past Gilbert's nose; Gilbert following with his eyes the tips of the three claws on the dark metallic extremity; Herb's face shouting something incomprehensible and flinching away from the machine's pointed arm as it sped toward his heart. Then finally, something flashing into view and blocking Gilbert's last vision of his friend . . .

What the —

The tentacle seemed annoyed too. Whatever was controlling the thing suddenly put the brakes on it, pulling back its tip into an upward S-shaped curve like a questioning snake. It had fully expected to skewer Herb, if not once, perhaps a dozen or so times, yet something unexpected had gotten in its way and the tentacle had halted out of pure surprise.

It was a moon-faced priest who blocked Gilbert's (and the Martian's) view of Herb. Father Brown had moved quicker than anyone could have imagined, placing himself between Herb and his certain death-by-tentacle. The little priest stood with his arms and legs splayed outward, making him look like a great black-clothed *X* with a white, balding head and a running nose. His face was stolid and resolute, and Gilbert knew he would stay in place so long as he had the power to do so, even should the creatures decide to remove him with a buzz saw, one limb at a time.

Under virtually any other circumstance, Gilbert and Herb would have found the scene to be comical. The short, round priest was utterly unthreatening to any human over the age of ten, much less a race of killer creatures from Mars. The absurd sight looked to Gilbert like a heroic chipmunk staring down a Great Dane, daring the larger animal to try to get a piece of him.

"Boys," said the priest, quietly but firmly. "Be watchful."

The tentacle struck. It drove bluntly into Father Brown's chest, knocking him back, his limbs still outstretched, against the wall of their cage. Then, in a flash, it wrapped itself around the priest's body and whisked him from the basket.

Then the metal lid clanged shut, dropping Gilbert to the floor a dozen feet below, and, by a hideous fluke of physics, knocking open a valve on the tank of fluid that none of them had noticed earlier. There was the sound of gurgling liquid, and their prison was quickly flooded by the acrid smell of petroleum gasoline as the fuel flowed out of the tank.

"Gil!" yelled Herb, dropping to his knees to grab his friend. Gilbert was looking up at the ceiling of their cell. He was crying, but not from the hurt of the fall. Herb was crying as well, for the same reason. Outside, there were more belches of green, gaseous light that briefly lit their darkened cell, and the pitiless cries of the "*Hoo! Hoo!*" feeding calls from outside began to sound.

Both the Doctor and the priest were gone.

Gil and Herb were alone.

⚜

"What now, Gil? Do we just wait for the end?"

"I hope, whatever happens, it'll be quick. I'll try to be brave, Herb, but I don't know if that'll do much good. I wish I could trust . . ."

Another human scream sounded outside; a woman's this time, and it still sent a chill down the spines of both boys that they could feel in their fingers and toes.

"Well, t'heck with that!" snapped Gilbert. "If they want to have me for dinner, they're gonna work to get me in the oven."

"They don't use ovens, Gil."

"Don't bug me with details. Help me get this thing working."

Gilbert stood up again and shook the tank several times. Whatever liquid was left inside it sloshed out quickly and dribbled through the holes of the cage floor.

"Why'd you do that?" Herb asked. "Wasn't that the fuel that made this thing go?"

"No, it wasn't. Look, when the Doctor turned the knob, did you hear liquid gurgling?

"No, I heard a hissing noise . . . gas escaping! Of course! The flame is powered by gas, and then the petrol immolates the target when the flame sets it alight!"

"Yeah, like that. Look, get this pack on me. There must be another compartment that holds the gas to make the flame. Even if it's empty of liquid fuel, there's still gas in this tank, and gas is all we'll need if'n we want to weld that lid shut. C'mon, we've gotta get this job done quick — we can't have more than a couple of minutes. Listen to them out there."

Herb helped Gilbert into the harness a second time.

The sound of the creatures' feeding call was getting strangely louder. There must have been more of the aliens in the large pit than they'd originally thought, for the *hoo-hoo*ing seemed to be coming from more and more places around them.

"It's like some mob call; I don't know exactly why they're doing it, but if it buys us more time, then we'll let them keep it up until the cows come home."

Herb's brow furrowed. He looked at Gilbert and shook his head slightly.

"Cows come home. It's a figure of speech, city boy." Gilbert said, smiling as he straightened his goggles. "You ready to give me a boost? This pack is lighter without the liquid fuel, but it's still going to be tough to lift by myself."

"Here." Herb braced his legs, bent slightly and laced his fingers together. Gilbert slid the Doctor's goggles on over his eyes, put his right foot on Herb's hands, and Herb propelled Gilbert to the higher half of their tilted cage. Gilbert found a foothold in one of the cage holes and climbed as best he could with the burden on his back and the weapon in his hand.

"I'm at the top," Gilbert said, raising his voice over the cacophony of Martian cries in the darkness. "Just in case we get any sparks, keep your head down, Herb. You don't want to lose an eye here if you don't have to."

"Right," said Herb, sitting and drawing his knees up to his head, and placing his eyes below his kneecaps. *Not like he'll need his eyes anyway, if this doesn't work*, Gilbert thought ruefully. *We'll be done for in less time than it takes one of these English guys to finish afternoon tea.*

There was the sound of hissing gas. Herb could hear Gilbert muttering to himself briefly. "Acetylene. Oxygen. How did old Smithee say it again? '*A* before *O*, or up we go.' That's it. So, if I turned that one first, then I turn this one next, then click the sparker and . . ." The cage was lit up by the bluish-white of Gilbert's torch. Herb remembered what the Doctor had said about the possibility of going blind if one stared at the flame too long and kept his eyes averted.

There was a blowing sound from the weapon's nozzle as Gilbert played with the knobs in an attempt to make the flame as hot as possible. After a few more seconds, the blowing sound became more muted, and sparks began to shower around Herb. He could see them hitting the floor in front of him and to the side, and knew they must have been falling into his hair and on his back as well. Every so often, he'd feel the slightest singe in the skin of his neck or a piece of exposed skin on his scalp, or on the backs of his hands as he tried vainly to cover his head. Herb would twitch at the touch of the heat, but bite his tongue and continue staring at his knees.

In the midst of Gilbert's amateur welding, Herb wondered if the Martian tripods had made it as far as London. No reason they shouldn't have, he thought. They moved as fast as any train, even if they looked as unstable as a drunken man while in motion. If they could decimate the British army with heat rays and black smoke, London was likely a vast graveyard by now, like Woking but on a larger scale. If they'd overwhelmed London, Britain was finished. And if Britain fell? If the greatest nation on the planet could be beaten so easily? There wasn't a chance that any other country would have a chance. Not the Americans, or the French or the Spanish. No one.

"I think we've got it, Herb. This is about as tight as I think it can get."

"You really think this'll work, Gil? Remember what it did to the train and the building?"

"I thought of that. But those roofs were half wood and, in some cases, rotten wood. Plus, I'd bet the metal that the squids use is tougher than what we use down here. It's harder to melt than any metal I've ever seen. Once it cools, I bet we'll be as safe here as anywhere on the planet."

Gilbert carefully moved the flame-tipped barrel of the torch to his fingers. He kept his grip on the side of the cage with three fingers of his right hand while he turned the knobs of the torch with his right thumb and forefinger. No easy task! Once the flame was out, Gilbert tried to push the lid of the cage to check its sturdiness. He then jumped down backward to the floor, wobbling on his feet as he landed.

"Is it sturdy up there, then?" asked Herb, helping Gilbert to steady himself.

"Well, I like to think so. But it's not like I was able to open it anyway. The only way we'll know is if they try to rip open the top and it doesn't come loose."

Then the two boys sat down. There was nothing to do now but wait. Gilbert reached to pick up the card that the Doctor had crumpled; he smoothed it as best he could, and held it to his heart.

Then Herb, who had been looking at the floor reflectively, spoke. "You know," he said, "it was one of my old teachers, a fellow named Doctor Huxley, who first told me about the need for the *best* people to breed the inferior people out of existence. But now I know I liked that whole rotten business mostly because Huxley had told me, in so many words, that *I* was one of the special ones. That *I* was one of the chosen, one of the 'best' people who should be in charge of everyone else. Now I've got a very different perspective."

"How so, Herb?"

"Now, the 'best' people are a bunch of squids. *They're* the blokes at the top of the food chain, not us. Having the 'best' be in charge doesn't seem so appealing when I'm out of that club."

"Yeah. I've heard that before. The law of the jungle seems fair only when you think you're one of the lions."

Gilbert had to shout this last point to Herb, as the noise from outside had risen to an even higher pitch. "What d'you think all the ruckus is about out here?" Gilbert asked. "Are they getting ready for dessert?"

But then just a few seconds later, the *hoo*ing of the Martians began to die off. They hadn't heard any human screams for a while and were beginning to have some hope that they had missed dinnertime when they heard the clawing of a tentacle on the roof of their cage.

Thirty

"If there were no God, there would be no atheists.
— GKC

Here it comes!" whispered Herb. His feet were pushed flat against the floor, and his back against the wall. Gilbert tucked the battered St. Michael image into his breast pocket. *Live or die*, Gilbert thought. *Live or die, I'll trust again.* "What do I have to lose?" he finished the thought out loud.

"Not much," said Herb, thinking Gilbert had spoken to him. "Not much, if you can carry on without blood in you. Do you think they'll let me into Heaven, Gilbert?"

"If we die, well, we can blame the priest if things weren't done right, I suppose. Otherwise, I hope we'll see each other there, Herb."

They heard the tentacle clanging and scraping on the lid above, as if it was having trouble finding a grip. Finally, they heard it clamp on and try to lift it open. There was a humming surge of power from somewhere as the arm tried to lift it once, twice, and then three times. "Gil, old bean," whispered Herb, "I think you've done it."

Then came a series of clanks and rusty squeaks, and their entire prison suddenly shifted, as if it were a building coming loose from its foundation. "What's happening?" babbled Herb. "What are they doing with us?"

"They're gonna throw the trap away, just like we thought they would," Gilbert answered as they shifted again. "Brace yourself. We're going for a tumble!"

But they abruptly stopped moving; the floor had tilted somewhat, but they were still attached to the giant tripod's hip. A large metallic claw appeared suddenly outside their cage, split into three jagged metal pincers, each fully as big as Herb or Gil. It hovered outside, peering at them like a giant metal flower, moving around to investigate from different angles through the holes of the cage.

"I wonder if they can see us through that thing," Herb whispered quietly.

"What, like they've got a camera in there or something?"

"No. It's more like . . . an *eye.* There!"

Gilbert saw it, too: a pulsing green circle in the middle of the claw. The rational part of Gil's brain told him that a machine couldn't feel hatred, but he couldn't escape the sensation that he was being stared at with pure malice.

"What do you think it's waiting for?" Gilbert asked, his attention still fixed on the glowing green eye. "I've no idea," answered Herb, "but I've a feeling it has to do with the noise outside."

Indeed, the *hoo*ing sounds had stopped, and the large crater that served as the Martians' base of operations had begun to resound with a strange new set of alien bellows and cries.

"My guess is word gets around," said Herb. "I bet they don't catch too many victims with portable welding forges on their backs, so we may be the first ones to delay being turned into human tea-and-crumpets. I'll bet the aliens are trying to figure out how to get in here."

Gilbert swallowed. His plan had depended upon being tossed away and forgotten, then making an escape in the darkness. But having the entire alien base aware of him and Herb wasn't going to help their situation. "You know," Gilbert said suddenly, "I think . . . can you hear what they're saying out there? I think I recognize that Martian word. It's . . ."

Suddenly, the giant claw disappeared from view, and then the cage began to be wrenched back and forth, as if the tripod were trying to tear it from its own side by force. The cage was yanked one way and then the other, but it remained securely attached, thanks to welded bolts larger than the bodies of either of the boys.

"I think your plan's worked a little too well!" yelled Herb as the metal cage groaned from the strain.

"You're not anything's dinner yet, so clam up and hang on!" Gilbert barked back, watching the flame-thrower tank and gun as it rolled back and forth along the floor.

Then the claw, unable to tear the basket from its hip, began battering the cage like a crude, slapping hand. Gilbert couldn't understand it; surely the mollusks had some means of removing the basket? But then he was reminded of a neighbor who'd once kicked a water pump in frustration when he couldn't get it working properly. *The aliens are frustrated,* he thought. *They don't like being thwarted by a couple of puny humans, and they want to get at us — now.*

But the tripod's attempt to thrash the cage free proved even less effective than trying to wrench it. The cage shuddered with each slam of the claw, and after several attempts, the cage was seriously dented on some of its outer walls. But no amount of bashing on the part of the claw brought the cage any closer to being freed from the tripod's hip. Herb found himself reluctantly admiring the aliens' technology. The tripods had torn the steel walls of Britain's finest train like crepe paper, but their own marvelous construction was too tough for them.

Gil and Herb had moved their backs to the part of the cage wall set against the body of the tripod, where the claw couldn't batter them. Finally, after several minutes of bashing, the entire cage rattled slightly, and then some more. Both boys looked at each other with alarm in their eyes. The cage was being broken loose!

"Hang on!" Gilbert had just enough time to shout before the first of the enormous bolts that held the cage to the tripod's hip were shattered and torn away. The other bolts that held the cage were rapidly sheared off as well. By this time, the tripod's claw was hitting the cage in a kind of frenzy, and even hit the cage once in midair as it tumbled earthward and slammed into the hard, packed earth.

The impact knocked them both unconscious.

✦✦✦

Gilbert could smell copper. Copper was in his nose and his mouth. And his foot hurt something awful. He tried to sit up, but his back roared in pain, and he gasped and held himself still. He opened his eyes and could see only shadows through the holes of the cage.

There was a new howling outside, multiple shrieks, both human and Martian. Gilbert tried to turn his head but could see very little. There were irregular flashes of green flame from the Martian machines, lighting up the darkness, and in the second or two of each flare, Gilbert could catch only small glimpses of activity.

At one point, he spied a set of tripod feet moving about the camp, the heavy stomp of metal on soil sounding in the darkness after the flame had expired. A few moments later, another green flame belched, and Gilbert caught a glimpse of a Martian squid driving erratically in one of their crescent-shaped machines. A few seconds after the light had died, Gilbert heard a resounding crash of metal and a hissing sound.

What the blazes is going on? Gilbert asked himself. *Is everything going crazy, or is this how a Martian tucks himself in at night? Or maybe this is the victory party, and they've had a little too much blood to drink.*

Blood . . . Gilbert opened and closed his mouth gingerly, tasting his own. His jaw felt like someone had been using a brickbat on it, and moving his tongue revealed two missing back teeth.

"Herb?" he whispered quietly in the semi-darkness. "Herb?" In the next green flare of light, he could see his friend's shoes, and then his pant legs. Gilbert gritted his teeth and turned over to a crawling position. He shuffled slowly on his hands and knees toward where he'd seen Herb's body. When he could feel Herb's shoes with his hands, Gilbert gave them a little shake.

"Herb? Herb, can you hear me? C'mon, Herb, wake up."

The green light flashed again. Herb's lip was bashed open, and there was blood flowing from his nose and temple. His right arm lay underneath the flame-tosser cylinder, which appeared to be wedged awkwardly between the wall and floor of their prison.

Gilbert fought back the panic that tried to engulf him. "Herb, don't die on me! Herb, can you hear me?" Now he shook Herb's shoulders vigorously. In the past two days, he'd escaped being mangled in a train wreck, cremated by poison gas, drowned in an underground river, and — so far — sucked dry by Martian vampire squids. But now the thought of losing his only friend pushed Gilbert to the edge of madness.

Fortunately, for the sake of Gilbert's sanity, his last forceful shake did the trick. Herb twitched, then groaned. His eyes opened slowly. "Where are we?" he asked thickly. "Are we dead yet, or did the blighters miss us again?"

"No, they hit us all right. But I think we just managed to miss enough of the ground to stay alive. The place is going insane, Herb, but there's no reason for it that I can see. The tripods — they all seem to be out of control." Gilbert looked around at the desolation around them, rendered even more chaotic by the strobe effect of the random bursts of green flame. Then he turned back to his friend. "Are you hurt?"

Herb winced, and sighed. "That's like asking if the Crimean War was loud. You can say yes, but the answer hardly does the reality any justice. I hurt all over, Gil. My arm's been mashed about by that metal backpack you used to weld the lid shut. I can't get myself unstuck, and every time I try, I need to bite my *lower* lip to keep a stiff *upper* lip, if you get my meaning."

"Sure do. I feel like my jaw's been used for batting practice. You lie still, and I'll get you free. So far, that claw hasn't come back. And I think there are some folks who've managed to get free." There was a tickle at Gil's ear, but he brushed it away. Blast! Even in the middle of an alien invasion, the mosquitoes were still biting! "Maybe we'll get lucky, Herb. Maybe we can get that flame-tosser thing working again in the morning, or something. I don't know if those things sleep or not, but we'll find out soon enough."

There was another green flare, but Gil was looking at his friend's face this time, instead of outside through the window holes of their cage. In the second of illumination, Gil saw Herb's face move from recognition to horror. "Gil," breathed Herb, quietly enough that Gil knew he should be very, very afraid. There was another tickle on Gilbert, this time at his neck. Gil brushed at it, but this time it did not go away. Gilbert grabbed at it, and found he had grabbed at some kind of stalk. Gilbert whipped around, and a rubbery, sinuous thing encircled his neck and squeezed.

Thirty-One

"The truth is, of course, that the curtness of the Ten Commandments is an evidence, not of the gloom and narrowness of a religion, but, on the contrary, of its liberality and humanity. It is shorter to state the things forbidden than the things permitted: precisely because most things are permitted, and only a few things are forbidden." — GKC

It wasn't the tentacle of a tripod. Staring at him through the hole-riddled wall was a larger version of the creature he'd killed in the sewers of Woking. Its three bulbous yellow eyes fixed on Gilbert maliciously, and two of its dozen tentacles were wrapped around Gilbert's throat, squeezing the life out of him.

Gilbert grabbed at the rubbery bands, but couldn't get his fingers around them. They were too slippery, and embedded too deeply in his flesh. Where was Herb? He strained his eyeballs toward his shoulder and saw Herb frantically trying to free his arm from its snare. No help from there! Then Gilbert watched in horror as one of the alien's mouth-straw things poked slowly into the cage, making its way for Gilbert's body.

Gilbert still had enough control of his mouth to spit in desperation at the straw and the tentacle. A shudder ran through the creature as Gilbert's blood-filled saliva splattered against it, and Gil was able to get a single sweet breath of air before the tentacle tightened again. He threw his weight backward in an attempt to free himself, but he succeeded only in rocking the cage.

Rocking the cage.

"Gil! Do that again! It moved the tank! I've almost got my hand free!"

Gilbert thrusted hard, flinging his weight back and down. The tentacle was long, and Gilbert was able to slam himself against the back wall of the cage. It rocked, and the Martian shifted again, giving Gilbert room for another breath. He tried again, but this time the slimy bands held him tight, in fact were pulling at him, slowly drawing him in to impale him and suck out his life.

Gilbert pulled his head back hard, as if trying to resist, but then he lunged *forward* with all his strength, rocking the cage in the other direction and driving his face into the wall of the cage, only inches from the creature's shimmering eyes. At the same time, he grabbed hold of the straw and closed his fists around it, using the only leverage he had left, and his last few seconds of oxygen, to slow its progress toward his vitals.

Slow it, but not stop it. Too strong — can't stop it. Have to hang on until . . .

"Think we're done with you, you overgrown slab of calamari?" growled Herb from Gilbert's side. The last movement of the cage had freed him! "Not by a bloody long shot, mate!" Herb leaped at the cage wall with the metal tank cradled in his hand and his wrist, heaving it at the creature's straw just as Gilbert's hands were going limp around it.

Then many things happened at once. The alien shrieked as the heavy object crashed onto its sensitive feeding appendage. It loosed its grip around Gilbert's neck enough for the boy to squirm out and drop to the floor. The momentum from Herb's desperate attack hurled him into the cage wall just as the tank fell with a clang. The alien turned its yellow eyes on its attacker and raised its tentacles to strike him — not to grasp and feed this time, but to kill.

But before it could strike, the cage, rocked violently by the combination of timely movements, began slowly but irresistibly to roll.

The groaning cage first pinned the creature's free tentacles underneath its outer rims. It tried to withdraw its other arms, still poised to strike at Herb, but too late; now they were pinched in place at the small holes where they entered the cage. Then the cage churned right over the body of the thing like a steamroller. Gilbert heard its beak crack and break with a sound like air bubbles popping under ice. One of its eyes took the full weight of the cage and burst into glowing yellow jelly. It screeched the familiar and horrible syllables they'd been hearing from others of its race. *"Ulla!"* it roared out of its broken mouth. *"Ulla! Ulla! Ulla!"*

There was just enough momentum to take the cage over the alien's body; then it picked up speed going down the other side, made a few more revolutions, and came to a stop. The alien and its death call were behind them. Except for the flashes of green flame, it was still dark and chaotic all around; screams of death, both alien and human, filling the air.

Herb moved next to Gil, and the two boys looked out the back wall of their cage at the prone alien. It was still in one piece, but at least one of its tentacles had been severed in the fracas and was visible in the green firelight.

"Is it dead?" asked Herb. "I hope we squished that thing into a rubbery little puddle."

"Well, it's not quite dead yet. But it does appear to be oozing just a bit."

"Serves it right for trying to pop your head off."

Then the creature twitched several times and was still. The hateful yellow light in its eyes dimmed. The awful call of *"Ulla!"* from its ruined lips quieted, and then ceased forever.

There was a space of perhaps thirty seconds, during which Gilbert massaged his neck and Herb began feeling around for some way to escape, before the night was filled with the sounds of tearing metal and explosions again, higher up in the air.

"Look!" said Herb, pointing back in the direction they'd come, past the alien's crushed body.

It was difficult for Gilbert at first to understand what he was seeing. Could it be that the British army had fought its way to the crater, and was firing volley after volley of weaponry into the Martians' forces?

"The squids — who're they fighting?" Gilbert asked.

"They're fighting . . . *each other*, I think. Look, there, see?"

Another belch of green flame flared a picture of the alien's battle. The tripod that had captured them earlier stood out in stark relief, surrounded by several smaller ones.

"It looks like they're attacking it, Gil!"

"I know, but what for?"

"I'm sure I don't know. Cripes, will you look at that thing! That's the tripod that snagged us, all right, but I'd no idea until now how much bigger it was. Maybe it's the command tripod, or something."

Herb was right. They could tell which of the tripods had been their captor by the long strip of torn metal on its hip where the collector basket had been. The smaller tripods, each a copy of the one they'd seen back at the train, were busy trying to do damage to the larger tripod in some way. One was repeatedly blasting away at the central hub of the larger tripod with its heat ray. The other two had picked up huge metal beams in their ropy arms and were beating at the legs and body of the larger machine.

"I dunno what's going on, Herb. I just hope we can figure out a way to get free in the confu—"

Gilbert was cut off by a sudden explosion. Both boys ducked slightly, keeping their eyes on the suddenly dark battlefield up ahead. After a few seconds, one machine's spotlights came on.

Gilbert could see that something had been done to the giant tripod, something so destructive that the machine's central hub was almost completely gone. Joined shakily by the remains of the hub's floor, the tall metallic legs sagged toward each other, barely holding aloft the remains of the blasted tripod's body. The machine's lone remaining tentacle hovered rigidly in the air.

"Guess we know who won that one," said Gilbert to himself as he stared in awe at the ruined machine. "Herb, what is that, around the wreckage?"

By the white spotlight of one of the attacking tripods, they could see that a thick, red mist, possibly originating with the larger tripod, had begun to spread and gradually settle over the whole camp. Then the tripod attacker turned off its light, and in the fresh darkness, they could hear the many sets of giant metal feet sound as they moved on to other business. Around the crater, distant cries of *"Ulla!"* sounded randomly.

Herb seemed content to sit for a moment and rest, but Gilbert had a mental itch he couldn't scratch.

"Herb, there's one thing I just don't get. We had ourselves a little tussle with an alien over there, right?"

"If you want to call that a 'tussle,' then, sure. What would your point be?"

"Well, if a dog got loose at a British military base and attacked a soldier, what would the other soldiers do?"

"They'd rush up and help the soldier, and then . . . kill the dog."

"Exactly. We just killed one, and it didn't go quietly. We were so loud that every squid in the crater should've come running, but they didn't."

"They can't run, Gilbert. No legs. They can only hobble."

"Knock it off. You know what I mean. I've been watching these guys, Herb. They don't seem to be following any pattern at all. They're driving their weird little cars and tripods from one place to another, but they're not even carrying things. They're beating *each other* up instead, and now . . . look. You see that?"

Gilbert pointed to one of the crescent-shaped alien vehicles, visible from the belching lights at the tops of most of the alien buildings. It zipped in and out of a building with no apparent point or purpose and crashed into the walls of the camp buildings as often as it missed them. Its call of *"Ulla!"* was made wobbly by the uneven track it drove upon.

"They're riding around like a bunch of drunken cowboys. Most of all, they're giving the same call I heard the Martian in the sewers give just before he died and tried to decorate the tunnel walls with the both of us."

"You mean you think they're expiring?"

"Just like overdue library cards, 'cept a lot messier. I don't know just what it is that's killing them off, but I remember what happens to their machines when they do buy the farm."

"Buy what farm?"

"Never mind. Look, *here's* my point: We're on a Martian base, and we just killed a Martian soldier, and none of the others are even checking up on us. Instead, things are blowing up, they're running around in a panic, one of them tried to make me into its last meal, and some of them are even killing *each other* instead. It doesn't make any sense."

"But, Gil, these are *aliens*. By definition, there's no way we can understand them."

"You can say that, Herb, but you've been wrong before. Remember when you said an advanced species *can't* be barbaric? It seems they only can't seem barbaric to other barbarians. Unless you can find something positive about being turned into a human bloodshake."

Herb shuddered. "I could only afford the luxury of that kind of attitude when I was in a safe, warm room, with a good book in my hand and a cup of tea at my side. Well, you may be right again, and that means a chance to get away, doesn't it?"

"Now you're thinking, Herb! I think the two of us can get this cage rolling again. Let's try to get to the wall of the crater, and we'll go from there."

"Well, that's all well and good, but how do we find the crater wall?"

Gilbert shrugged his shoulders. "Just roll forward, I guess."

Herb looked exasperated.

"Well, Herb, for gosh sakes! It's not like we can steer this tin can. And it's a pretty good bet that asking for directions isn't on our short list of options, is it?"

Herb looked as if he wanted to pout, but knew he hadn't any choice. They began as a team, throwing their weight against the walls of their cage to make it roll, stumbling often, then righting themselves and repeating the process. Fortunately, the alien metal was surprisingly light, considering its demonstrated strength. If their prison had been constructed of heavy earth-steel, it's unlikely they'd even get it to budge. Nonetheless, after a painstaking hour that yielded modest progress — fortunately, their straight path was uncluttered by crashed vehicles, alien corpses, or other debris — Gilbert felt his energy starting to run out.

This is what coach called "the crash," he thought to himself, *because your energy fritters away and you could literally fall to the ground if you aren't paying attention.*

Then, inexplicably, the going began to get easier. The cage began to yield more under their weight, as if the ground below had smoothed. For a time, the boys fell into a fast rhythm, propelling the cylinder forward with little effort. Then the cage began to roll even faster — faster than their arms and legs could match — with what seemed to be a strength and will of its own.

Both of them realized at the same time what was really happening.

"We're rolling downhill!" yelled Herb. "Quick — try to go the other way . . . Oof!"

They were not only rolling downhill; they were rolling too quickly to think about slowing or stopping themselves. Had it been an amusement-park ride, they might have enjoyed it; but in their circumstances, it was terrifying. As their cage spun down the steepening hill, the boys were helplessly slammed into the walls, the roof, and each other, like stones in a tumbler. After what seemed like a hundred mad revolutions, the cage mercifully came to a full, sudden, and crashing stop at the bottom of the hill.

After several minutes, Herb's whispered voice broke the relieved silence. "Gil, old bean. Can you hear me? Are you all right?"

Gilbert paused a moment before replying. "I've had better days, I guess. But it still beats working in the cardroom, by a country mile."

They were quiet for a few more minutes. The eerie cries of the Martians from the top of the hill had faded, and the darkness around them had just begun to give way to the first streaks of morning light.

An explosion sounded from above them at the top of the hill. Then two more. Then more silence.

"I guess that means that it really is over, Gil. The dead aliens are blowing up, just like the Doctor said they did."

"Or maybe they got a really, really bad case of gas after they munched on the Doctor, and someone lit an after-dinner cigar."

Herb laughed. He chuckled, and then guffawed, then got control of himself, then began laughing uncontrollably again. "Oof," he groaned. "I think my ribs are broken." But he laughed even harder.

"Herb," said Gilbert, trying hard not to succumb to laughter himself, "clam up! You'll bring every squid from here to Venus down on us."

"What, like I'm worried? I'll just light up after they eat you, and blow the rest of them to kingdom come, or wherever Martians go when they die!" More laughter from Herb, and then Gilbert gave in, and laughed longer, harder, and truer than he had ever remembered laughing in his life. The grim reality of the previous days burst out in a release of tension that for a short while seemed as if it would never end. The great, healing laughter rushed out in a frothy flood that the boys could no more stop than they could put a hold on the tides or the rotation of the earth, and continued until both of them blacked out into merciful sleep.

Thirty-Two

"The riddles of God are more satisfying than the solutions of man." — GKC

Gilbert was woken by sunlight for the first time since the Sunday before his sudden and unexpected promotion at work. He lay in the cage, basking in the golden rays that streamed through the holes of the collector basket. He yawned quietly and risked a small stretch. Within seconds, the pains in his neck, arms, legs, back, knees, and arms began to stretch and yawn as well. Wincing silently, Gilbert remembered Monday mornings long ago when he would try to convince his mother to let him stay home from school. He would examine himself from head to toe, looking for a pain or flaw he could use to convince her that he was too sick to go. It had almost never worked, and after she had decided to teach him herself, there was never any point to faking sickness anyway. Home *was* school at that point, and he'd have had to be convincingly sick indeed to be too ill to be tutored at his bedside.

But now, as he looked in and around the cage, he realized that although he had a plethora of very real physical maladies, his new schoolroom was the cage and the world outside it. Nothing here could be dodged or gotten away from with the choicest words or the straightest of faces. At least, not for long.

Gilbert stood and noticed an unpleasant smell in the air. After a few seconds, the smell grew to a stink that was impossible to ignore. He settled for breathing through his mouth, and shuffled over to where the morning light showed Herb was sleeping.

"Herb," he whispered. "It's morning. Can you stand?"

Herb opened one eye, groaned, and covered his face with one hand. "I woke several times in the night; each time, I let myself believe that this entire experience was a bad dream. Perhaps an undigested bit of beef, or a blot of mustard."

"Sure, Herb. And the whole Martian invasion is from a toothpick I swallowed back in the fourth grade. Sorry, but it's not gonna happen like that. We've gotta get ourselves out of this now, and hope the squids don't notice us while we try to skedaddle."

"That's an excellent point. Assuming 'skeedaddle' means to escape. How do you propose we do that, now that we're in here with the lid welded shut?"

"I really hope you're not complaining. It's all because of that lid that you didn't become squid food last night. Let me check."

Gilbert limped over to the lid of the basket and examined it. Gilbert had known he wouldn't have time to weld the whole circle of the lid against the main body of the cage, so he had settled on welding it well and tightly at one point at the circular seam. The weld had broken loose in the night, either from the fall from the tripod or when they'd come to their sudden stop at the bottom of the hill. Gilbert looked closer at one end of the weld. It had been worried at and torn at one end like hard taffy, with a sudden, clean break at the weld's left side. Still, Gilbert and Herb both had to push hard and squeeze a wide enough gap between lid and cage to escape.

Gilbert and Herb crawled out on all fours, surprised to find the ground under them covered by something red and squishy. On top of the black sand of their crater, there was a strange red plant that seemed to be sprouting out of every available clump of dirt underfoot.

"What is this stuff?" Gilbert asked, ignoring the pain in his legs as he bent down to examine the plants. "They seem to be growing everywhere."

"Weird," Herb said, kneeling beside his friend. "I'll admit I'm no gardener, but I've never seen this kind of weed in England before." He poked it, then squeezed it with his thumb and forefinger. Its surface was tough, like an India rubber ball. "We must have missed this in the dark last night when we were brought in. Quite odd indeed," Herb said, pressing down on the plant with his toe. "I wonder if the mollusks brought it with them."

"Maybe so," replied Gilbert. "But the last thing I'm gonna worry about is how they do their flower arranging."

"That's a question in itself, isn't it, Gil? How do you arrange flowers with tentacles instead of thumbs?"

"*One* tentacle can choke me to death, Herb, and that's all I care about. They don't look like much outside of their machines, but if I ever let one o' them get close enough to me again, my mother raised a fool. Blamed thing just about wrung my neck like I was a spring chicken in winter."

Herb looked at Gilbert with a questioning look on his face. Gilbert just smiled and shook his head. "City boy," Gilbert chuckled.

"You know, Gil, if you hadn't been so abused by life over the course of this adventure, I believe I could be moved to give you a solid drubbing."

"If that means pulling an Eddie Pearse on me, you just might. But beating up my body won't stop my mouth from running. Not anymore. If I've learned anything from this trip, it's that I've spent too much time keeping quiet, waiting for a better time to say what needs saying. Seeing all these people dying in the past few days, coming so close to death myself, I don't think I'll ever keep quiet again when I've got something to say. Does this make any sense, Herb? You're usually the outspoken one."

Herb was looking steadily at his friend, both of them facing the cylindrical cage they had spent the night in. There were hints of both a smile on his lips and surprise on his face. "You know, Gil, if someone had told me that day we met in the alley . . ." A pause hung in the air.

"What?" asked Gilbert, still looking into the basket, his face deep in thought.

"Never mind, mate," said Herb, turning to go. "Let's get out of this crater."

"Good by me." Gilbert said, turning to walk in the same direction. "Suddenly, I'm so hungry I'd even be grateful to eat some of the awful cheese I used to keep in my apartment. You ever had that stuff they sell in the —"

Gil stopped. Herb had already stopped moving when he'd turned to face away from the cage. Both boys now stared straight forward toward the sight at the center of the crater, their jaws slack and their eyes widening. A small clucking sound came from Herb's throat for a few seconds and then stopped.

Their cage last night had rolled down what they thought to be a hill. In the growing daylight, it was obvious that what they *thought* was a hill was actually a smaller pit, dug near the center of the crater. Moreover, what they had thought to be the bottom of the hill or the crater wall was nothing of the sort, either. In fact, their cage had run smack against a smaller hill in the center of the crater.

The hill, at least thirty feet high, was made of decomposing human bodies.

Near the very apex of the pile of corpses was the still-recognizable body of the banker who had been among the Martian's last meals. His body, once plump and prodigious, had been withered by its treatment to a quarter of its former girth. Whereas most of the other corpses had grinning or laughing skulls, the face of the banker was still intact enough that, even though it was flat on its back and staring at them upside-down, his mouth was twisted into a frozen scream.

"The Doctor, Gil," Herb's voice was barely audible. "He may have lied to us about other things, but it seems he was truthful when it came to their eating habits."

Gilbert waited a moment before answering. He was swallowing warm saliva, trying hard to override his gag reflex's insistence that he empty the contents of his already empty stomach.

"It sure looks that way, doesn't it?" Gilbert had to use every ounce of self-control to sound casual, because he knew if he started screaming at the pile of dead in front of him, he wouldn't stop for the rest of his life. "Wouldn't it be interesting," he whispered slowly, "if he only told the truth about things we wish were lies?"

"You mean about the colonies on Mars, or about how his bosses ran the world? I don't know, Gil. I really don't know."

Gilbert, already adapting to the new, horrible vision in front of him, tried to change the subject.

"Take a look up there. There's that banker fella we saw last night. It's kinda funny. I remember him. I saw him riding in his carriage in London back right before all this happened. Back then, he was at the top of the world, and I was on the bottom. Now, he's still at the top o' the heap, but it's just a heap of dead people. And I'm still at the bottom, but at least I'm alive, you know?" Gilbert looked closer at the dead banker. "I'd almost think he's in on the joke. I know it sounds grotesque, but he . . . he almost looks like he's smiling, doesn't he?"

"Smiling, Gil?"

"Well, an upside-down scream like his looks something like a smile, doncha think?"

Herb paused and looked at his friend. "I think you're cracking, that's what I think." Herb turned his attention away from the hill of corpses to the ridge of the death-pit, hiccuping slightly. "What should we do next?"

"Climb to the top of the crater wall and see what else is up there. Very quietly, of course."

They turned their backs to the hill of corpses and over to the wall of their smaller crater. Climbing to the top was a much longer, harder exercise than either of them thought it would be. The pit had been dug without regard for anyone, human or Martian, trying to climb out. It was steep, sandy, and difficult to keep steady footing as they struggled up. Herb and Gilbert had some success at first, pulling on the red weed as a handhold, but as they climbed to the midpoint of the pit, the plants were smaller and sparser, and their roots didn't go as deep.

They kept digging away at the sides of the death pit, trying to distract themselves from the absolute silence of the horrible pyramid behind them. But there was encouragement as well. The sky grew cloudy as they began, and by the time they were halfway to the top of the pit, the air had turned cool, making their going much easier. And the longer they worked without hearing a single Martian croak or the whirr and creak of a machine, the less fearful they became of being discovered and subjected to the banker's fate.

After more time and much sweat, they poked their heads above the pit's edge. There was a good deal of green-tinged smoke from still-smoldering piles all around, but in the strengthening sun, they could see countless bits of scattered refuse and bloated, jellylike Martian bodies littering the black, ashen earth.

"Look," said Herb. Just ahead and to their left they saw a Martian corpse on the ground that had already begun to wither like a rotting pumpkin. There were scuffle marks beneath it, and human footprints leading away from the dead creature.

"Looks like someone had a happy ending at least. If they managed to get all the way away, that is." Gilbert's comment was almost swallowed up by the odd, deathly silence that seemed to bleed out of the very sand at their feet.

Herb moved toward the body of the creature for a closer look.

"I wouldn't do that, Herb."

"I know *you* wouldn't, Gil. That's why *I'm* doing it."

"Fine, but do you have a knife or something just in case it decides to get cute?"

"Yeah, I've got a knife if I need it. Now gerroff and let me work."

Herb leaned over the bloated Martian's body. Suddenly, something yanked Herb backward by the collar, while something else blasted from behind like a firecracker.

As Herb reeled, he saw that the Martian's body was twitching. One of its larger tentacles had been freshly severed, or rather torn off, as by an enormous dog, and a thin, opaque liquid was draining from it. The other tentacles writhed weakly, and the creature's body began flip-flopping like a tired, landed fish. In a second or two, the thing gave a tired-sounding squawk and lay still again.

Herb, his pulse racing, stared at the creature with a mixture of relief and outrage. Then he looked back quickly, to see a smoking double-barreled pistol attached to Gilbert's right hand. Gilbert's left hand gently released the back of Herb's collar.

"Gil, old chap," Herb exhaled finally. "How did you . . ."

"Wasn't too hard," Gilbert said, sounding almost as surprised as Herb was. "I saw the gun handle poking out of your pocket there, and when you looked like you were gonna get snapped up, I grabbed it and fired."

"Then I suppose I'm lucky I had you here. That little mite of a pistol I took from the Doctor — I never considered fumbling for it."

"It's small, Herb. You English don't get too many chances to play with guns, as I understand, so it was easy to think it was just another of the clunky things you've been carrying in your pockets."

"But how did you ever know there was a danger?"

"Herb, do you know what a possum is?"

"A what?"

"Exactly. Which means, city boy, that you've never seen them playing, either. Fortunately for you, I have." Herb's face beamed up at him with a combination of wonder and gratitude that Gilbert had never seen before: in an instant, they both knew that all debts had been more than repaid. Even a dying Martian was deadlier than a dozen Ed Pearses. And never again could Herb look upon his skinny friend as someone who had to be guided and protected. Gilbert turned away, almost embarrassed, and took a long look at the mounds of steaming rubble in their immediate vicinity.

They waited for a minute or two, watching the alien from a safe distance to be sure it was dead, and then walked a few more yards away from the pit. As a morning breeze lifted the gloom of smoke, they saw that the crater was much larger than they'd earlier imagined — several hundred yards in diameter or more. Several of the tripods were fairly close by, looming dark and still like watchtowers. Their tentacles were either slack or frozen still, like waxworks performing whiplike motions in the air. Gilbert approached one, and Herb spoke up nervously.

"What makes you think this one isn't a . . . what'd you call it? A *playing possum?*"

"When possums play dead, Herb, they're either trying to play harmless to be left alone, or playing harmless so's they can fool other things into getting too close. But even the best actor can't fool Mother Nature. Look at the crows."

Herb looked up and saw at least a dozen or so black birds circling and landing at the top of the tower. Although the body of the giant tripod had been destroyed, the three legs still carried the shattered, smoking remains of the tripod's body on top of them. The boys walked closer, cautiously, and could see one of the walls of the giant tripod's body was still largely in one piece, although the largest of the bubble-shaped windows set into it was broken and the mechanized tentacle attached to the body was frozen in midair. Several crows popped in and out of the remains and through the shattered window, carrying what looked like black strings in their beaks.

"They're feeding," Herb said.

Gilbert looked slowly away from the dark birds and down to the feet of the giant tripod. Something about the dead machine made him furrow his brow and approach the huge, disc-shaped feet. He moved slowly at first, but after a few seconds broke into a run.

"Gil!" Herb yelped, "Gil, what're you doing? You don't know what might be there!"

But Gil had already stopped. Herb, running after his friend, watched as Gilbert knelt over what at first appeared to be a bundle of gray and black rags.

Gilbert's eyes widened behind his glasses as the gravel and ash crunched beneath his knees. Father Brown's body was slimmer, but largely undamaged. The priest's eyes were open, with faint traces of a surprised smile on his face.

Gilbert reached out slowly and brought the dead priest's left hand up to his own cheek. "Father?" Gilbert asked weakly.

Herb had stopped, standing behind his friend and looking at Father Brown's body.

"Gil . . ."

Herb tried to say more, but everything sounded wrong before he even opened his mouth. He put his hand gently on Gilbert's shoulder.

Still holding Father Brown's hand to his own face, Gilbert inhaled. He put his other hand on the priest's chest, nudging him as if to wake him from sleep. Gilbert breathed quicker, his face becoming a mask of pain as he began to weep, tears trailing slowly through the grime on his face. After a minute, the tears turned to sobs, the sobs to anguished wails.

And there beneath the clouded sky of a summer morning, Gilbert wept for Father Brown, the little priest who had been to him a friend, a father, a giver of hope. He wept for the parents who had been taken from him far too soon, and for all those he'd loved and lost. He wept for the entire world he'd known — his little life, the countryside, even the stars at night — that would never be the same again. He wept for the end of his childhood, and for the death of childhood's symbols of adventure. For Gilbert, the sight of a gleaming train or rifle, or of a proud airship trundling through the clouds, would now always be a reminder of pain, loss, and death.

Herb had never seen a male of Gilbert's age lose himself to anguish. He squeezed his friend's shoulder in a gesture he hoped would give strength.

"It's . . . it's all right, Gil," Herb tried to say.

"He was . . ." Gil choked the words out between sobs. "Herb, he . . . he'll never know, now, Herb, what he was to me. What he did for me! He'll never know, Herb!"

Herb inhaled deeply, biting his lower lip as two tears tracked down his own cheeks.

"He knows, Gil," Herb said quietly, squeezing Gil's shoulder a second time. "He knows."

Without any hurry, the morning sun broke through the clouds. It searched slowly but thoroughly with its lengthening beams until it found them, and quietly cast its warm light on the only two left alive in the valley of death.

Thirty-Three

"Many a magnanimous Moslem and chivalrous Crusader must have been nearer to each other, because they were both dogmatists, than any two agnostics. 'I say God is One,' and 'I say God is One but also Three,' that is the beginning of a good quarrelsome, manly friendship." — GKC

ONE YEAR LATER

Gilbert stood, frustrated, and looked up and down the bustling sidewalk of the noisy street. The horse-drawn carriages, endless streams of people, sporadic screaming children, and occasional motorcar were making it very difficult for him to find the address that matched the one written on the slip of paper in his right hand. He pushed his glasses up the bridge of his nose with his index finger while being jostled and muttered at in French by one Parisian pedestrian after another, and tried once more to figure out just where the heck he was.

Toward the end of the street he could see the large iron gates that allowed citizens with the right kinds of punchcards to move through different parts of the city. As a foreigner with little money, Gilbert could travel only through the downtown center and some of the city's poorer districts. Guards with sharp eyes, sharper punchcard-readers, and ugly triple-barreled pistols made sure that the riff-raff stayed out of the neighborhoods that belonged to the more privileged class.

There was a part of Gilbert that a year ago would have wanted to crawl into a hole and die rather than stand in the middle of a sidewalk and be in anyone's way, much less in the middle of the street in a busy city such as Paris.

"*Excusez moi, monsieur . . . Excusez, excusez . . . au s'cours?* Uh, help?" Gilbert's French left a few somethings to be desired, he knew. But he hoped at least to convince the locals he was trying. Asking for directions was proving to be a fruitless exercise. He'd heard Parisians could be friendly, but today it seemed he needed directions to a café on a day that everyone in the city of Paris was late for work.

The first two or three people he asked were content to look through him or ignore him completely. The fourth and fifth looked at him as if he were an odd species of fish served in a congealing sauce. Gilbert had even tried in vain to get help in a shop, hoping that a store clerk would be willing to help a potential customer.

No dice. Gilbert had had no better luck with the shopkeepers than with the bystanders and pedestrians. The clerks wouldn't talk to him if he wasn't a shopper. And buying something before asking directions didn't help things at all either; the last clerk had just enough time and smiles to give him until the money had been placed in the till. After that, any further attempts at conversation had been met with cold stares or the sudden recollection that something important had to be accomplished elsewhere.

How many millions of people in this city, thought Gil, *and I can't start a conversation with any of them. Not one person to help me find the only other person in this city I can actually communicate with.*

With his frustration mounting, Gilbert was considering trying to coax directions from a different shopkeeper when he saw the girl at the flower stand.

Gilbert blinked. She was still there. He blinked again. She remained there, refusing to be a mirage. She was dressed differently this time, in a brown coat with a high, fur-trimmed collar and white lace at the cuffs. She turned just slightly enough for him to see that her eyes were still a bright, porcelain blue, and her skin was fair and smooth.

And she still had the most achingly beautiful pile of bright, red hair he had ever seen in all his life.

"Mademoiselle! Mademoiselle!" Gilbert called out the French word for "miss" in what he hoped was a decent accent. Then he remembered the last time he'd heard her speak, nearly a year ago, she'd spoken clearly in the Queen's English. "I mean, Miss! *Miss!*"

Several of the locals had turned at Gilbert's mangling of their beloved mother tongue to look at him with wrinkled faces. The young woman, on the other hand, gave no sign of having heard him. Having purchased a trio of lilies from the flower girl in the street, she instead began to walk away without the least bit of hurry.

Gilbert gave chase, but the boulevard was a sea of humanity whose tide was flowing against him. By the time he'd fought through the crowd, Gilbert was just able to catch a glimpse of the girl turning a corner down a cobblestone street. He sped after her, breathing hard, and reached the corner just in time to see a lonely café door slowly shut on the deserted side street. He paused, then charged.

Gilbert burst through the door of the café just as it had begun to swing inward, and looked around wildly. The café was far more posh within than its exterior suggested; the rickety wooden door was leather-lined on the inside, and the walls were clean and wood-paneled. The floor had a deep red carpet, and the tables were covered with clean white tablecloths trimmed with lace. The wood beams were ornately carved with a series of twisting vines, and a thin layer of pipe smoke hung in the air.

"Vous désirez, monsieur?" said a voice. Gilbert looked in its direction. In front of him, a *garçon* dressed in a white shirt and black vest was trying to size him up. Gilbert tried not to look at his bald head or the thin, trim mustache on his upper lip.

"Did a girl come in here?" he asked the waiter quickly, forgetting for a moment where he was.

"A gairrl, *monsieur?*" answered the man with a sparkle in his eye, his hands gesturing as accents to his speech. "*Allez, allez,* has *monsieur* forgotten which city he is in? This is, after all, the city of *Par-ee,* and there is a *gairrl* for every man under the sun, if he will put himself in the trust of *amour,* of romance, as you English say, in the trust of . . ."

Gilbert was in no mood for poetry. "Shorter than me," he interrupted, holding his hand at his nose level, "brown coat, blue eyes, and red hair." The man paused dumbly. "*Rouge,*" Gilbert finished, pointing to the top of his head.

The waiter seemed visibly miffed at the interruption, but answered Gilbert with a businesslike demeanor. "Fourth table against the wall on the right," he said. "She's expecting you, *monsieur.*"

"I just bet she is," Gilbert mumbled to himself. Then he remembered his manners. "Thank you, *mon ami,*" he said, making sure he looked into the waiter's eyes.

The *garçon* looked at Gilbert oddly, as if he weren't used to being addressed as an equal by a customer.

"*De rien,*" the *garçon* replied. "It's nothing."

Gilbert tried to calm himself down, breathing slowly and slicking back his hair with one hand while he straightened his glasses with the other. *Michael,* he thought quickly, *Father Brown told me you're the patron saint of cops and soldiers. If there's a patron saint up there who helps guys trying to impress a girl, would you ask him to fire off a few prayers for me?*

The tables were more like booths against the wall of the café, each separated by a small wooden panel wall. Gilbert walked past the first, second, and third tables, his footfalls making almost no sound in the red carpet. He paused for a moment before the fourth, soundlessly mumbled the word *trust,* stepped forward and faced the girl for the first time in nearly a year.

She looked at him, and when her eyes met his, he thought he would melt into his shoes.

"Yes?" she said.

"Umm . . ." Now, what would Herb . . . No, that's just what he *shouldn't* do, not if he wanted to make a genuine impression. He looked down at the chair near him that faced her. "Is this seat taken?"

"Do I know you?" she asked.

Gilbert was in many ways a different person from the one he'd been a year ago when he was hustled out of the clacker room. After his first-hand account of survival at the hands (tentacles?) of the Martians had been published far and wide, he'd been sent on many more journalistic assignments. The work had given him a wide variety of experiences, a deep appreciation of other cultures, and zero tolerance for people who played dumb.

"You know," he said quietly, seating himself, "the waiter said you were expecting me. You were in the office of the Undersecretary, you were on the train when the conductor nearly died, and now you turn up in Paris when I'm on my way to meet my buddy Herb for the World Science Conference on the aliens. Yes, you know me."

"Do you believe in coincidences, Mister Chesterton?"

She knew his name. She'd dropped the act. Point one to Gilbert.

"Where I come from, we've got a saying: what looks like a duck, walks like a duck, and talks like a duck, probably *is* a duck. Yes, I *do* believe in coincidences. But the way you've been turning up in my life for the past year . . . well, that looks, walks, and talks like something else. You know me, and I think I've got you figured out, too."

They were interrupted by the *garçon* bringing them each a steaming cup of tea. They both shifted into a nearly identical mode of smiling, thanking, and sipping their cups, and suddenly shifted back to serious faces when the waiter had left.

"Now," Gilbert continued, "I don't mind someone playing hard to get, but you keep turning up like a good version of a bad penny. Do you want to keep playing games, or do *I* leave *you* this time, and wait and see who chases whom?"

"Drink. Your tea will get cold." The girl stared at Gilbert for a very long minute. "You really have changed, Gilbert," she said finally.

The back of Gilbert's neck suddenly felt very warm. It was only by a sheer act of will that he kept his eyes locked on hers.

"What do you mean by that?" he said quietly. "How could you know how I've changed?"

"Gilbert, who do you think I am?"

"I think you're the one who got me the journalist job, and saved me from the clacker room. I think you followed me onto the train and somehow spiked my expense account to see how I'd react. I think you might even be responsible for my coming out to England on the *Capsella* when I should've drowned on the *Titanic,* but I'm not all the way sure. I also think you're connected to the Doctor somehow, but not in a bad way."

Her brow furrowed. Gilbert resisted the urge to ease whatever pain lay behind the creases of her pale, perfect skin. "What do you mean by that?" she whispered.

"Most folks couldn't do all you've done without training of some kind. Training only the Doctor and his crowd could provide. Now, you *did* do everything very 'cloak and dagger' and on the side, a lot like the Doctor did his business, in fact. But the Doctor was only out for himself. He was a snake, plain and simple. You see folks like that even in Minnesota. But you . . . well, you've been different. The Doctor tried to use me like a pawn on a chessboard, but you've only been good to me."

"If I am indeed as well connected as you suggest, Mister Chesterton, I'd think most men would hesitate to be in the same city as I, let alone a foot away from me."

"Ma'am, I'm a little hard to scare these days. When I was in those sewers, I truly think I was allowed a glimpse of the gates of Hell itself. And when those gates want to look *really* scary, they wear a Halloween mask made of Martian innards."

"Gilbert, I keep waiting for your answer. Who do you think I am, really? Are you trying to trick me into giving something away?"

"No. I don't need any tricks. I think you're with a group like the Doctor's, but your folks wear the *white* hats. Maybe you work for the Queen, I don't know. You're every bit a match for the Doctor, but you're one of the good guys."

Gilbert paused, watching her expression to see if he'd been right.

"You're quite perceptive, Gilbert. But things aren't really as complicated as you think they are. It's actually quite simple," she said, leaning toward him. "Watch, let me use this cup of tea to clarify. Pay close attention, now."

She needn't have added the last part. When she'd leaned in and spoken, Gilbert could feel her soft breath on his cheek. It would have taken an artillery shell falling directly outside their window for him to remember there was anything else in the universe besides her deep blue eyes.

"The tea, Gilbert. Look at the tea."

Oh, yeah. He looked obediently at the cup on the table as she swirled a spoonful of sugar into it.

"Now, Gilbert, pretend for a moment that the cup of tea is the world in which we live. And we, we are two little grains of sugar that have dropped into it. Follow the grains if you can, Gilbert. Follow the swirls of the tea, slowly, slowly, as the sugar dissolves, slowly . . ."

There was no visible change to Gilbert's face, other than his eyes narrowing slightly. The girl's voice became more and more deep and resonant in his ears. She was his world, and his world was warm, soft, and relaxed.

"Gilbert, are you listening?"

"Yes," he said quietly. His eyes never left the teacup or its swirling contents.

"I am going to tell you what it is you want to know. Your parents, Gilbert. Do you know who they were?"

"They were agents of the Special Branch." His voice was a quiet monotone, his eyes still fixed on the teacup.

"Do you know why they left, Gilbert?"

"No."

"I will tell you, then." She stopped, inhaled, and let out a very long breath. Gilbert's expression of fixed attention on the cup of tea did not change.

"The Special Branch, Gilbert, has many agents at its disposal. But not so many that it's a simple matter to stop being one.

"The men who run the Special Branch, Gilbert, also hold very strongly to the belief that people can be bred. Or *ought* to be bred, like cattle, to produce offspring with superior characteristics. They believe in this so strongly, Gilbert, that when they find two agents with ideal characteristics, they . . ." She closed her eyes, drew a shuddering breath, and continued. "They . . . *select* them for each other, with the hope that their children will be part of a superior race of future agents.

"But your parents, Gilbert, met on an assignment and fell in love. It had to be kept secret; the employers don't like anything to conflict with loyalty to *them*. Your parents, Edward and Marie, married in secret. They managed to hide it from the Special Branch, even while they continued their assignments. They were, after all, among the best agents; they'd been trained to hide information, and they knew exactly what their superiors would be looking for.

"For months after their secret union, they continued their work for the Branch. Then they learned that Marie had been *selected* for a different agent. An agent whose exploits for the Special Branch were legendary. A man so amoral and without principle that he was deemed the perfect tool for the Branch's ends. Your mother, Gilbert, was selected for a man known to other agents only as the Doctor.

"When they learned of this, Edward and Marie fled. They had not been the first to do so. Other agents, very few, had also managed to leave the life and evade capture. But none had tried it as a team, and certainly not as husband and wife."

She paused here and looked out the window. A sorrowful look passed over her face as a woman strolled by, pushing a covered baby carriage on the sidewalk.

She turned back to Gilbert. "It happened long before my time, of course, but I understand the leaders of the Special Branch were quite upset. So infuriated, in fact, that they put the Doctor himself on the task of not only finding and removing them, but of bringing back any children they'd had for indoctrination into the service of the Special Branch.

"Time passed. The Doctor spent years searching all of Europe fruitlessly. Then his attentions were needed elsewhere. In time, a new agent was recruited and put on the case to find the Chestertons and any of their progeny.

"The new agent found out where you were, Gilbert, almost completely by accident. Through a former bosom friend, the agent learned there was a young man with the unusual name of Chesterton enrolled at St. Alban's School in New York.

"The agent hesitated; surely, it couldn't be *that* easy. But a visit to the school, a simple break-in to look at your student file, and there was no doubt: Edward and Marie Chesterton had had a son, and his name was Gilbert.

"The agent was new, untried, and ignorant of the Branch's true nature. The naïve thing believed herself to be playing a noble part in the Queen's service.

"Soon after her success in locating you, the Branch let her know that she, too, had been *selected* for another. Not yet a member of the Branch, her intended was the young man she had found where the Doctor had failed, the young man who had been raised as a farmer's son in Minnesota, and sent halfway across the country as a means of further obscuring his trail, should the Branch ever find his parents. The young man selected for her was, in fact, you."

She paused again, looking at Gilbert's face. How much he had filled out in the last year, and how much more handsome he had become.

"All was going well, Gilbert. They were ready to snatch you from your life, give you the chance to go along willingly, and execute you if you didn't. They were going to use the female agent they'd *selected* for you as bait to entice you to join them. They were already calling *you* 'her man,' calling *her* 'Miss Chesterton,' and acting as if she had been given such a great honor to have been *selected* for you.

"But something went wrong. In a great irony, your parents were killed in the rarest way an agent is ever killed: by a genuine accident, without any input from our employers or their rivals at all. You were spirited away from St. Alban's, apparently part of a contingency plan your parents had set in place in the event of their deaths.

"After your disappearance, the agent who'd found you was assigned to you again. You were located a second time, but by now, she had come to loathe the Branch and all it stood for.

"It was this agent, the one who had been *selected* for you, who made sure you weren't on the Titanic. Rather than intercept you at its first stop in Newfoundland, the agent instead booked you for passage on the *Capsella*, bound for England, and did so completely without the knowledge of her superiors. When the *Titanic* sank, she used that tragedy as an opportunity to convince her superiors you were dead in the icy waters of Newfoundland, when in reality you were living as a wage slave in London. She'd hoped to better your life in other ways, Gilbert. But the aliens landed, the world was turned upside down, and you know the rest."

The swirling of the tea stopped. The girl sat back in the booth with an air of accomplishment or relief. "And now, Gilbert, you know your story, as you have a right to. But this knowledge is dangerous — to both of us. That's why I have used one of my . . . skills to keep it hidden inside your head so that you will be unable to give us away.

"One day, Gilbert, one day I hope to break free of my employers as your parents did. When that happens, I may need your help. But if I fail, and you learn of my death, this knowledge can help you protect yourself. Are you still listening to me, Gilbert?"

"Yes," Gilbert answered slowly, his head still bowed toward the now-cold cup of tea, his eyes closed.

"Gilbert, I am going to give you directions to meet your friend at the Café de la Paix. After that, I will snap my fingers three times and you will walk to the café and stand outside its front door. Once there, you will awaken from your current state and feel refreshed, but out of breath. You will believe you have been pursuing me in a merry chase throughout the streets of Paris, but you lost me. Most important, Gilbert, you will forget that we have ever had this conversation at all. You will have no memory of this café, what transpired here, or what I have told you, unless you receive evidence of my own death. Do you understand, Gilbert?"

Gilbert nodded wordlessly.

She looked at him sadly, as one forced by circumstances to make a necessary but regrettable decision. Bringing her hand to his eye level, she pressed her thumb against her fore and middle fingers and . . .

✦✦✦✦

Breathing hard, Gilbert reached the corner just in time to see a lonely café door slowly shut on the deserted side street. Gilbert looked at the sign above the door, swinging lazily in the breeze and informing all who would walk by that this was, indeed, the *Café de la Paix*. The Café de la . . . It couldn't be . . . could it? Gilbert quickly patted his pockets, found the paper, and checked the address on it. It was! What a coincidence!

The café was the kind of small, cramped place that Gilbert had a hard time getting used to. Having spent most of his formative years in open farming country, Gilbert had developed a firm dislike of Europe's cozier spaces, such as the little pseudo-restaurants that the French had named after coffee. This one was no exception. Paradoxically, it was precisely the kind of place that Gilbert's best friend in the world loved and thrived in.

Indeed, had Gilbert not been wildly looking around for the young redhaired woman, he would have had no difficulty finding Herb. His voice rose loud and clear from the far end of the almost deserted coffee parlor, in a heated discussion about something or other.

"Herb!" Gilbert called, running toward his friend. "Gil!" exclaimed Herb, rising from his seat and plainly relishing the opportunity to introduce his buddy to someone. Ever since their first-hand experiences in the Invasion, as every paper in the world had come to call the episode with the aliens, Gilbert, Herb, and a handful of others had become minor celebrities.

"Gil, what's the problem? You look flustered."

"I saw her, Herb! I saw her!"

"Her? Her who? Gil, we're in Paris! You can't bend your elbow without bumping into a smashing lass. Speaking of which, I wanted to . . ."

"The redhead, Herb! The redhead!"

"Well, that certainly narrows it down, doesn't it?"

"I mean . . . aw, Herb, don't you remember? Before I got assigned to cover the Martians? The redhead on the train, right before the engineer dropped from a heart attack! Remember her?"

Herb's eyes grew wide as his memory suddenly clicked. "You saw her, Gil? In here?"

"Yes! Well, I mean, I saw her turn the corner here, and the door to this place was just shutting."

When it came to the subject of pretty girls or fisticuffs, Herb Wells ceased to banter and shifted his mental gears into high action. "Quick, Gil. She may have come through when I was chattering with that Frenchman over there. There's only one more exit out back. This way!"

Herb turned and ran, and Gilbert followed. They flew through the back of the cramped café, into an even smaller kitchen, past a surprised cook who had a cigarette drooping from his lips, and out a back door into a muddy back alley barely wide enough for one person to walk through.

Gilbert looked hopelessly up and down the empty alleyway. "You think she came through here?"

"We can ask the cook, Gil, but I don't think he'll give us any more help. Look down. See the mud? Unless your girlfriend can climb walls, she didn't come out here. There are no footprints. Either she's an illusion, or you've been had."

As they walked back to the seat that Herb had been sitting at — whoever Herb had been talking to a minute ago had apparently left the café — Gilbert's mind clicked and ticked feverishly. They sat down and Gilbert ordered a vanilla cola, but absentmindedly; he was still thinking about *her.*

"You're late, by the way, mate." Herb began, sipping his own drink.

"You gave me bad directions, bud! If I hadn't seen the redhead, I'd probably still be out on that sidewalk trying to find this place."

"Is that so?"

They were quiet for a few seconds.

"You know, Herb, it's funny, but for the last year now, that young lady's been drifting around my head like a pleasant bit of perfume. It's odd how she kept turning up when I least expected her, and needed her the most."

"Well, if that's the way she works, then I'm sure we'll see more of her another time. If nothing else, you'll get a good bit of exercise running after her. Speaking of running, how's your leg doing these days?"

"Great, actually." The tension of Gilbert's chase, along with a strange headache that had seemed to come from nowhere, began to melt in the company of his good friend. "By the way, remember that godson of Father Brown's we met after we were rescued? Father Flambeau? He's still waiting for you to come back for your catechism like you agreed to."

"How about your leg, then?"

"You're changing the subject, Herb."

"No, I'm not. Just picking a more enjoyable one."

"Herb, you were willing to look up for help when the chips were down."

"Yes, I know, but look, God's a busy fellow, Gil. Or is it three fellows? I keep forgetting what it is you Catholics believe."

"*Us* Catholics, Herb. And *you* know better now. You've been part of the family ever since you got baptized. And you *promised* Father Brown."

"Gil, one of these days. But there's a whole lot to do out in the world, and I don't want to miss it."

"Herb, that's a load of hooey, and you know it. Do you think *I'm* missing out on life? I've had as much excitement as you have this past year, if not more."

"What's wrong with waiting 'til I'm sure?"

"Because you've already *been* sure, Herb, and now all you're doing is welshing. Maybe you want to be like Luther or Voltaire, and try to come back on your deathbed. Trouble is, there were a lot of folks in the Invasion who wanted to wait until the eleventh hour, too, but they all died by ten-thirty."

"Let me worry about that, chum. Now, how's your leg?"

Gilbert looked at Herb for a few seconds. He sighed, ran his hand down his calf and continued. "It's good. It hurts a little on rainy or snowy days, and they tell me I won't ever win a cross-country race again. But I can sprint when I need to."

After they had been found in the crater, doctor after doctor examined Gil's leg wound and marveled at how no infection had set in. Theories for this had abounded, from the reclaimed sewer water's hot temperature acting as a sterilizing agent, to the vigorous exercise he'd given his legs in his mad rush after mad rush to save his life. At least one doctor had been intrigued enough to offer Gil a staggering amount of money for the rights to amputate and study his leg privately.

"Well, too bad that Dr. Frankelspine, or whatever his name was, didn't get his way."

"Excuse me, Herb?"

"Well, you would've been rich now. And having one less leg might've improved your dancing."

"Aw, shove off."

Herb smiled. "Well, you lived anyway. And your reason for it just might be the only thing the Doctor was telling the truth about."

"What do you mean? What about him?"

"Well, Gil, he seemed to think you were the shining example of what good-old-fashioned human breeding could accomplish. You've proved him right." Herb leaned in excitedly. "It's catching on now, you know. They call it *eugenics* these days; a fancy way of saying 'good-births.' "

"Herb, that's a lot of rot, and you know it. It wasn't my breeding that got me out of that mess. My biggest success was surviving. And I survived because of *trust*. That and a lot of real fast running. Not a bunch of wishful thinking trying to pass itself off as science. Speaking of the Doctor, still no sign of him?"

"Not that I know of, Gil. I was actually hoping that you blokes over at the *Times* would have heard something by now."

"Not a thing. You guys at the *Telly*?"

"Not a word."

"You hear back from your editor yet?"

"Nope. You?"

"Nuh uh. Nothing."

The Doctor's body had never been found. Although both Gil and Herb had received award after award for their first-hand accounts of the Invasion, every reference to the Doctor in all their stories had been removed prior to publication. Complaining to their editors had proven fruitless, since Herb's editor had been suddenly relocated to Mexico, and Gil's to Canada without a word of warning or explanation.

"You'd think there was a conspiracy to keep it quiet or something."

They chuckled to cover the short, uncomfortable silence.

"Well, Gil, you know I've got to ask you."

"About what?"

"Every scientist from London to Alaska has a theory about what killed the mollusks, but the word in the coffee shops is that some egghead over at Scotland Yard's finally cracked the case. And, most important, that *you*, and *only* you, got a few details *from* that egghead."

"Really? Where'd you hear a thing like that?"

"Gil, for once in your life, stop acting like you just got hit in the head by something out of a messenger tube. Did they ever figure out what it was that killed the Martians?"

"Gee, and here I thought you wanted to meet up here in Paris for my sparkling company and witty repartee."

"Gil . . ."

"Or maybe," Gil leaned back in his chair, folded his hands behind his head and looked at the ceiling, "it's because I'm the only guy in France who can teach you how to talk to Minnesota farm girls."

"Gil!"

Gil looked at Herb with wide, innocent eyes. "Oh, sorry, were you talking to me?"

Herb smiled gently, his face beaming with perfect peace and acceptance of the answer he'd been given.

Then Herb lunged forward, grabbing Gil's jacket lapel with his right hand. With his left hand, he stuck his thumb up Gil's nostril, and pinched the rest of Gil's nose with the side of his index finger.

"Ow!" roared Gil. "Whaddaya *DOIN'?*"

"Why, I believe I'm ripping your nose off, old bean."

Gilbert's hand shot up and broke Herb's hold. His other hand fired forward, his first two fingers stopping less than an inch from Herb's eyes.

342

Herb, surprised, lurched back so hard that his chair rocked on two legs. Herb waved his arms for three long seconds to regain his balance, with Gil's fingers hovering in front of his face the whole time.

Herb righted himself, and Gil leaned back in his chair and laughed.

"You've been learning more moves from that Chang fellow, haven't you?"

"Gotcha." Gil smiled. "Teach you to try to maim someone just because they won't feed you a story."

Herb looked slowly at his friend, as if looking for an opening and warily preparing for another strike. "I wasn't doing that over the story, Gil. That was for playing coy. Now, about those aliens."

"Fine. Off the record, Herb?"

"You think I'd steal your story?"

"Only if I forgot to ask you not to."

Herb paused, and smiled. "Very well, friend. You win. I won't write this up."

"Fine. Remember my Confirmation two weeks ago?"

"Er, yes. About that. I'm sorry I missed it, but I had this thing going on . . ."

"Oh, I know *just* how sorry you're *gonna* be, Herb. I met a nice lady there."

"Hello?"

"No, not like that. She's a bit older than us."

"I *say*! Gil old boy!"

"*No*, Herb, not like that. Will you get your mind back on the story? Look, after my Confirmation, I had lunch with a very nice lady. Her name was Elizabeth Fane."

Herb looked confused.

"Her friends call her Betty."

Herb kept looking.

"Her mother's maiden name was Brown."

Gilbert paused, watching Herb's face until understanding lit up his features. "Is she related to . . ."

"Father Brown. Yes, she's his niece, in fact. Daughter of Father Brown's sister. Father Brown apparently had quite a reputation for helping Scotland Yard. And not just for solving crimes — preventing them too. He seemed to have a knack for turning up *just before* some crime or disaster took place; almost as if he'd heard about it in advance or something."

"Hmm. Sounds like his life might make a good book."

"One thing at a time, Herb. Where was I?"

"The niece."

"Oh yeah. Well, they were so grateful to Father Brown that they offered his niece a job. She said she was more interested in research than clubbing robbers into pudding, so they were more than happy to give her a few rooms and all the test tubes she could break. She's the one who, a few years back, developed a way to use analytical engines to solve crimes — you feed it enough clues on a punchcard, and it can lead you right to the baddie. Complete with a stippled portrait of the most likely suspect. Well, after that, they were willing to give her *carte blanche,* of course, pretty much anything she wanted if it was scientific in nature."

"E. F.," Herb said slowly. "I managed to get a glimpse of just one report a few months back. It was signed with the initials *E. F.*"

"Yeah, that was probably Betty. She's gotta sign herself like that sometimes just to get past the stodgies at the Yard. Well, after she'd had a chance to dissect one of the squids, her boys in the lab coats found the bodies riddled with flu viruses, way more than you'd find in a human. The speculation at first was that germs never grew in Mars's dry climate, so the squids never developed natural defenses to germs that we take for granted."

"But Gil, didn't the Doctor said they had filters to protect them from germs? And why did they all attack the big tripod that was holding us? And then attack each other? And why did they all start dropping like flies afterward? I got to see some of the army maps after it was all done. Whatever was killing them seemed to fan outward, starting from the Woking crater."

"If you remember, Herb, the Doctor said the mollusks had protected themselves from all the germs they found in humans on Mars. But Father Brown's blood was full of a rare flu from *Africa*, Herb, and they weren't prepared for that. The *African* flu killed the squids almost instantly after they" — Gilbert inhaled briefly and looked at the table — "killed Father Brown, and got the others inside the tripod too sick or weak to defend themselves for long."

"That explains why a few of them died, Gil. But why the whole lot of them? And why that odd pattern? It seems like a tripod would get attacked by all its brothers, and then *that* group would be attacked by another, bigger batch of the things, until all the tripods wiped themselves out for us."

"Well, Herb, so far, the thinking from Betty and the top brass that I've been able to get is this: The squids were perfect Darwinians."

"Eh?"

"Remember how you told me about Charles Darwin? How he said that the strongest survive, and the weak die off or get killed by the strong for food?"

"Yes, and I told you I didn't believe that anymore, when it came to people, Gil. Not since the Martians landed, anyway."

"Well, it seems the squids *did* believe it. Remember how the Doctor said they could communicate with each other over long distances? We think the other Martians got word that some of their own had become weak and dangerous, three-legged sacks of infection. Their preferred way of dealing with such a threat was to *remove it with all possible speed*. So they attacked the main hub of the tripod that held us, determined not to let weakness or disease bring down the rest of their race. But when they did that . . . remember the red mist that hit the air?"

Herb looked intrigued. "Aah, tainted blood, a perfect cloud of infected viruses. But how did they get into the other tripods?"

"How does water get in anywhere? For all the Martian's know-how, remember how much green gas we saw leaking out've their machines? They didn't love our atmosphere, but they could deal with it, so they didn't have to make their vehicles airtight. Water, air, and tiny droplets of virus-infected blood managed to get into every single one of them."

"So," said Herb, "they killed off the weak, and kept it up even when they *all* became weak and died. They were so set on only the perfect surviving that, in the end, none of them survived."

"Exactly. The last tripod standing in the whole mess wobbled and crashed only a day after the last of its brothers bit the dust. The mollusks inside dead from their own infections."

Herb shook his head. "Humanity saved. And all because of a Catholic priest, of all things! Such a shame, really. The good Father could have accomplished so much with what he knew about human nature. What a tragedy he wasted so much of his life with savages in Africa."

"Herb, it was only because he'd served the Church in Africa that he saved the world. He sacrificed himself for those 'savages' because he saw Christ in them. And in the end, he gave his life to the rest of us for the same reason. Unless you think Father Brown threw himself in front of that tentacle for the good of humanity's evolution . . ."

"Gilbert Keith Chesterton! I think you're becoming a fanatic!"

"No, Herb. I've just been reading a lot about what the Church says lately. *I* went back and got catechized, just like we both agreed to. The Faith, Herb, the Faith is almost . . . intoxicating once you know what it's really about, instead of just listening to what its opponents say when they're trying to tear it down."

"I'm sure it is," Herb said without enthusiasm, looking away and focusing on his coffee.

"Herb, *you* got baptized too. You won't be able to plead ignorance now; you know better. The only reason you dislike what Father Brown stands for is because you're such a religious person yourself."

Herb paused. "Wot?" he said.

"You, Herb, really *are* a religious man. It's just that your priests and prophets carry test-tubes instead of Bibles."

"Gil, that's not so!"

"Isn't it? Are you trying to tell me that everything scientists say makes perfect sense to you? Because if it doesn't, that means you trust that some scientist knows better than you about some things. And that means you've gotta have as much faith as an old *nonna* with her rosary beads."

Herb pursed his lips and sighed. "Well, maybe. Regardless, Gil, I . . ." his eyes suddenly widened. "Gil, what time is it?"

"It's . . ." Gilbert pulled out his pocket watch, "it's five to five. Why?"

"By Jove!" exclaimed Herb, leaping out of his seat. "We've got to make tracks, old bean! Time waits for no one!"

"Herb, are you trying to change the subject?"

"Of course I am. After all, I'm late. *We're* late!"

"It's a girl, isn't it?"

"Quickly, Gil! Fortune favors the brave!"

"What's her name, Herb?"

"Strike while the iron is hot!"

"Her name?"

"Madeline. And she has a friend."

"Let's go."

As they rushed from the café and began a dash down the street, Gilbert looked around and over his shoulder hopefully.

"She's not there, Gil," Herb called behind him. "That little redhead from your imagination isn't going to save you from meeting a real girl this time."

"I didn't think she would, Herb. I just . . . wonder who she is, that's all."

"What?" said Herb. Gilbert's comment was lost in the rivers of people who poured through the core of the ancient city of Paris.

"Never mind," said Gilbert, catching up and matching Herb's stride. "By the way, Madeline's friend — what's her name?"

"Frances, I think."

"Is she cute?"

Herb smiled. "Madeline says she has a great personality."

"You . . . I know what *that* means!"

"Oh, and what's that?"

"It means that she's as ugly as a sodbuster's boot and half as smart! How do I let you talk me into these things?"

"Gil, Gil, listen to yourself. You're faced with spending a June night in Paris with a lovely young lady, and all you can do is groan about getting the short end of the stick?"

"Ah, no, Herb, I don't think so. *You're* going to spend the evening with a lovely young lady, while *I'm* going to spend it trying to entertain her unattractive cousin. And all this so's you can try to steal a kiss before the end of the night."

"Gil, can you stop complaining and try to keep up? We're almost at the place."

"You're changing the subject again."

"So I am! What is it you Yanks say? *Big deal.* I mean really, Gil, have I ever pulled on you the kind of shoddy trick you're accusing me of?"

"What about at the inauguration of President Taft? That Caroline girl and her friend, Perpetua? The one who spent the whole evening telling me about the wonderful world of cross-stitching?"

"Besides that."

"After the assassination attempt on the Kaiser? Where you paired up with Frieda, and I got stuck with her stepsister Brunhilda?"

"Besides *that.*"

"The last World's Fair in New York? Annabelle and her cousin, *Margaret*? Margaret who dressed in men's clothes and wanted to measure my skull bones to test my intelligence?"

"And you scored very highly, if I recall. Besides *that.*"

"Well, I can't think of anything else."

"There you go! The next time you're going to accuse me of something, you'd better have a decent bit of proof. Besides, as I recall, Brunhilda was a lovely singer."

"Only if you like singers who dress in Viking hats at the end of an opera. You're a rotter, Herb Wells."

"Quiet a second. We're here."

Herb dragged Gil in to a café that was more upscale and trendy than the last. Once inside, Herb stopped, smoothed his clothes with the palms of his hands, and began the confident stride he'd demonstrated for Gil in the London train station over a year ago.

Gilbert followed his friend, his eyes open only just enough to keep from bashing into the nearest wall. If past experience was any teacher, he was better off seeing as little as possible of any woman Herb had arranged for him.

"Gil, I really think you should see this."

Herb had stopped, and as Gilbert opened his eyes, he felt his heart jump into his throat.

"Herb . . ."

Sitting at a table, in front of them and just out of earshot, Gilbert could see the two most beautiful young women he had seen since he'd arrived in Paris — and that was saying something. One was a tall, slender blonde with pouting lips. The other had hair and eyes the color of Christmas chestnuts.

"Herb . . ." Gilbert's voice had the consistency of maple syrup.

"Yes, Gil."

"I love her."

"Which one, Gil?"

"I don't care."

Herb straightened his tie and patted Gil on the back. "Right. That's the spirit, chum. I knew I could get some sense into you."

"And Herb . . . ?" Gil said quietly, never taking his eyes off the young ladies.

"Call me George."

"You're still a rotter."

"I know. And?"

"And you're still my best friend in the whole world."

Epilogue

> "The Declaration of Independence dogmatically bases all rights on the fact that God created all men equal; and it is right; for if they were not created equal, they were certainly evolved unequal. There is no basis for democracy except in a dogma about the divine origin of man." — GKC

Not long after Gilbert found himself trying to recover from his visions of loveliness, a meeting was taking place many hundreds of miles away. The room was large, with oak-paneled walls and the kind of lush green carpet that could perfectly muffle the sound of a dead body falling. Five men sat around a pentagon-shaped table, each smoking a different brand of cigar, each tapping the ashes into a large marble ashtray that had been set before him. They had sat in silence for several minutes, none wishing to reveal his private thoughts. Theirs was an old alliance, forged through wealth, power, intrigue, and a mutual willingness to punish betrayal, but none of them wholly trusted any other.

An old clock that for two centuries had looked down upon the many world-changing decisions made in that room began to strike seven. The long, steady weight of each reverberating chime sounded like death-knells in the room and every hall of the house.

He is late, each of the five thought to himself. But none of them said it. That might suggest weakness.

No more than a minute after the last strike, a man in servant's clothes opened the very thick double doors of the meeting room. By sight he appeared only a few years older than most of the men upon whom he waited.

He entered the room with the stride of a man who knew his place and had been prepared for it throughout the course of his life.

"Your visitor has arrived," the servant said in perfectly measured tones. His father and grandfather had held this post before him. Like them, he was willing to perform any act of charity or diabolism to keep his position secure, and had been trained from an early age to do both without qualm. Power's proximity had allured such men through all history.

"Show him in, Mortimer," said the eldest gentleman, a red tie bobbing at his liver-spotted throat.

The servant bowed and backed out of the room. He returned a moment later with the visitor, who stood behind with a posture that was not militarily rigid, but still noticeably respectful. With dark eyes, he scanned the faces of the men who would decide his fate, and called upon all his training and self-control to keep from swallowing nervously. He hadn't been this frightened in the alien collector basket. Not by a long shot.

"You may sit, Doctor," said the second oldest man in the room, the one with the sagging skin around his eyes. The Doctor hadn't noticed that Mortimer had already moved efficiently to procure a chair for him, but he sat when commanded, without looking back. When these men told you to sit, you sat. You didn't look to see if there was a chair behind you first. Once seated, he removed his top hat and cradled it in his left arm.

"You may now report," the third-oldest man in the group barked, his bulk and double chin quivering with every one of his few movements.

"Yes, sir," the Doctor answered crisply. "I made my way to the Woking crater to carry out my mission of reconnaissance and, if necessary, negotiation. Along the way, a Martian tripod attacked my train, and a number of the passengers were captured. I realized then the seriousness of our situation; the aliens had not, as we'd hoped, landed by accident while en route to a different destination. Ransom's victories had indeed driven the creatures from Mars, resurrecting their plans for colonizing our planet.

"Following Special Branch protocol, I engaged three passengers who had sustained only minor injuries, as well as the stationmaster whom I had pressed into service as my bodyguard. And wisely, it turned out. When we were attacked along the road, he was slow and stupid enough to be taken by the tripod first, allowing me just enough time to escape.

"Having gained entrance to the Sign of the Broken Sword, I realized that the avenue of diplomacy had closed, and our only hope was to delay until the land-ironclads arrived. I deemed that my companions were still useful to me, so I chose to arm them and led them through the tunnel network toward Woking. En route we encountered a mollusk scout and destroyed it, but when we reached Woking, we were captured and transported to their base. I was very nearly subjected to draining, but at the last minute, one of the creatures stayed my execution. Whether it was because they recognized the passphrase and meant to abide by our old agreement, or because they recognized *me* and planned to exact a more thorough revenge for the hatchling incident, I cannot say. I then obtained my . . . treatment for the injuries I sustained, and, as per Special Branch protocol, I have been living in hiding for the past year."

"Yes," said the youngest man at the table, a wide-shouldered and thick-handed man of fifty-five with a gray mustache, clean-shaven chin, and a quiet voice, "just as you revealed in your earlier, written report. But of greater interest to us, Doctor, was your claim to have discovered some word of former rogue agents of the Special Branch."

"I did indeed, sir. It was perhaps halfway through my journey that I realized fate had chosen among my traveling companions none other than the son of Edward and Marie Chesterton."

There was a silence around the table.

"You are . . . certain of this, Doctor?" said the oldest man, the spots on his skin brightening as the rest of him paled "We had received convincing evidence that the scion of the Chestertons had perished."

"Yet I must report that he lives, sirs. He deduced the mollusk's extraterrestrial origins during our walk to the inn. Although he was felled by an unfortunate accident in the tunnels, he managed to escape alone, and to kill a Martian in the process. In conversing with the boy, I noticed the same level of moral impracticality that the Chestertons displayed when they abandoned us. It appears Edward and Marie used the funds they absconded with to set themselves up as well-to-do farmers in the United States, where young Gilbert was born."

"Are they still there, Doctor?" asked the second-eldest man.

"No, sir. They died close to a year ago in a tragic accident, caught in the middle of a bank robbery. A common occurrence in the Americas today, I might add."

The third-oldest man paused to finish sucking on his cigar, his amazing double-chin moving in and out like an accordion as he did so. "That is most refreshing, Doctor," he said, in a voice midway between speech and a grunt. "We are glad that you have at last managed to tie up this last loose end, albeit due more to good fortune than forward-thinking. Where is the boy now?"

"You may recall the young lad who became a rather celebrated personage last year for his reporting on the aliens. His renown is such that his removal will be difficult."

"We see," the fourth-oldest man said, his thin larynx betraying only the slightest amount of disgust and disappointment. "And is he aware of his distinguished parentage? Is he aware of the *Branch?*"

"Gentlemen," said the Doctor, trying hard not to seem hurt, "I have taken multiple oaths not to reveal the workings of this organization to anyone. If, indeed, I were to reveal any such information, it would be completely involuntarily, and I would rectify the problem immediately by removing the other party with all possible speed."

"Very good, Doctor," said the fourth-oldest man again, apparently satisfied with the Doctor's reply. "You may go."

Then the youngest and largest man said quickly in a milk-like voice, "Ah, Doctor, one further thing. Is the new limb the mollusks provided you in working order?"

The Doctor, who had promptly stood at the words "you may go," now showed the barest hesitation when he heard the youngest man's question. His right arm had been in the shadows, but it became visible as he held it out.

What grew from the sleeve of his jacket looked at first like a kind of cord or whip. Once extended to its full length, it waved back and forth like an insect's antennae. It was unmistakable: in place of his ruined arm, the Doctor now sported a smaller version of one of the mollusks' tentacles.

"It is . . . functional, to a point," the Doctor said, steadily watching his new limb with an expression midway between enthrallment and horror.

"Fascinating, Doctor," whispered the youngest man. "How did you come by this wonderment?"

"After they drained the priest," said the Doctor, "the creatures in my tripod begin to reel uncontrollably from the effects of the African strain of the flu, for which their filtering systems were unprepared."

"We're all familiar with the report," said the third-oldest man with some impatience.

"Of course," continued the Doctor with a slight bow. "In the chaos that followed, I was able to proceed unmarked to the mollusks' onboard tissue-regeneration device, such as we had seen them use to repair themselves in battle against Ransom's forces. Using what memory I had of their operational procedures, I inserted my own arm into the device. Although I would have preferred a *human* arm, I must confess a certain . . . intoxication . . . at having this connection to so perfect an organism."

Although his arm was covered from the wrist down by his jacket sleeve, small clicking noises could be heard beneath his clothing when he extended his segmented tentacle for his employers' viewing.

"Yes, gentlemen, the limb works well enough," said the Doctor, collecting himself from the reverie he had fallen into, "but I fear my ability to carry out covert field work is somewhat . . . compromised."

"We are aware of that, Doctor," spoke the oldest man again. "Which is why you will instead be dispatched for the foreseeable future to the Martian colonies."

It was the Doctor's turn to grow pale. He and everyone in the room knew that for an agent of the Doctor's stature to be sent to the Martian colonies now was a veritable death sentence, either at the hands of vindictive criminals or at the tentacles of the vengeful Martians. He was so distressed that he failed to notice the lights of the landing airship outside through the darkened window.

"Please do not feel this reflects on your overall performance, Doctor," the second-oldest man said. "We have the greatest respect for your services to the Special Branch. However, you are now no longer *useful* to us in your former position. It would be impossible for you to pass unnoticed in the background of the world with a limb as . . . uniquely abled as yours is. You do understand. True, your life will be in peril almost constantly, but we feel that for as long as you stay alive, you will be invaluable as an adviser to our forces. Moreover, knowledge of your presence on Mars is certain to distract the mollusks' attention from our other activities on the Red Planet."

"Yes," whispered the Doctor. He had known this day would come.

Mortimer appeared soundlessly at the door, and led the Doctor out. The doors closed, and the five men looked at each other somberly.

"The Doctor lied," the eldest man said simply. "The young Chesterton not only lives, but knows who he is. He knows who *we* are, and he suspects us."

No one contradicted him.

"Yes, the Doctor lied," the second said, blinking his large, sagging eyes. "As we did to him by concealing our knowledge of the deaths of the Chestertons. As for the boy, we can watch him. After all, who will believe him? In time, Gilbert may forget the Doctor's unfortunate lapses of discretion, and he might yet be made useful to us."

"A good course of action," agreed the third, placing a rolling fat hand on the table and drumming his fingers silently. "It has proven a wise move for our group to have purchased both of the major London newspapers and eliminated their editors. We will be able to watch him and to control him. Only should he become difficult should we consider our other options."

The fourth man broke the pencil he'd been playing with into two precisely equal parts between his thin, bony fingers.

"We are agreed then," said the soft voice of the youngest, linking the fingers of his very large hands. It was a statement, not a question.

"We must see our next visitor," said the oldest without skipping a beat.

Mortimer opened the double doors again, ushering in a young lady in a brown coat with a high, fur-trimmed collar and white lace at the cuffs. Her eyes were a deep, porcelain blue, her skin was fair and perfect. And her hair, although a trifle untidy from the trip on the airship from Paris, was still the most beautiful shade of red that Gilbert had ever seen.

"Good evening," said the oldest man, rising to a standing position, as he'd been taught to do in the presence of a lady. The other men followed his lead quickly.

"Good evening . . . Miss *Chesterton*."

THE END

About the Real Gilbert

Although this story is fictional, Gilbert Keith Chesterton was a real person: one of the greatest writers of the twentieth century.

Born in England in 1874, Gilbert followed his talent for drawing to art school, but eventually became a freelance journalist and a prolific author. During his career, the name "G. K. Chesterton" would be found on some eighty books, hundreds of poems and short stories, and thousands of essays on religion, politics, economics, and culture. Today his writings are still cherished by legions of fans who appreciate his unique insight, bubbling wit, and swashbuckling style.

As a young man, Gilbert experimented with Eastern religions and the occult, but finally rejected these in favor of what he called the "romance" of the Christian faith, and in 1922 he was received into the Catholic Church. For the rest of his life, he would be a tireless and joyful advocate for Christianity: defending it in speech and writing against the fashionable atheistic philosophies of his day, and delighting readers with the beloved fictional priest/detective Father Brown. Running through all his works is the belief that the world God gave us is a magical place of adventure, to be lived in with a spirit both joyful and reverent.

All the quotations from the beginning of this book's chapters come from Gilbert's writings, as listed beginning on page 361. I hope you'll come away from my story of the imaginary Gilbert wanting to read some of the wonderful books the real Gilbert wrote.

Sources of Quotations

P. 3   "The modern city is ugly not because it is a city but because it is not enough of a city, because it is a jungle, because it is confused and anarchic, and surging with selfish and materialistic energies." — "The Way to the Stars," *Lunacy and Letters* (1958)

P. 7   "All but the hard-hearted man must be torn with pity for this pathetic dilemma of the rich man, who has to keep the poor man just stout enough to do the work and just thin enough to have to do it." — *Utopia of Usurers* (1917)

P. 17   "Civilization has run on ahead of the soul of man, and is producing faster than he can think and give thanks." — *Daily News*, February 21, 1902

P. 29   "An inconvenience is only an adventure wrongly considered; an adventure is an inconvenience rightly considered." — "On Running After One's Hat," *All Things Considered* (1908)

P. 39   "There is a corollary to the conception of being too proud to fight. It is that the humble have to do most of the fighting." — *The Everlasting Man* (1925)

P. 45   "Moderate strength is shown in violence, supreme strength is shown in levity." — *The Man Who Was Thursday* (1908)

P. 51   "I have little doubt that when St. George had killed the dragon he was heartily afraid of the princess." — *The Victorian Age in Literature* (1913)

P. 67   "I never could see anything wrong in sensationalism; and I am sure our society is suffering more from secrecy than from flamboyant revelations." — *Illustrated London News*, October 4, 1919

P. 75   "The Bible tells us to love our neighbors, and also to love our enemies; probably because they are generally the same people." — *Illustrated London News*, July 16, 1910

P. 81   "Modern broad-mindedness benefits the rich; and benefits nobody else." — "The Church of the Servile State," *Utopia of Usurers* (1917)

P. 95   "It is not bigotry to be certain we are right; but it is bigotry to be unable to imagine how we might possibly have gone wrong." — *The Catholic Church and Conversion* (1926)

P. 107   "The modern world is a crowd of very rapid racing cars all brought to a standstill and stuck in a block of traffic." — *Illustrated London News*, May 29, 1926

P. 113   "A thing may be too sad to be believed or too wicked to be believed or too good to be believed; but it cannot be too absurd to be believed in this planet of frogs and elephants, of crocodiles and cuttlefish." — A. L. Maycock, ed., *The Man Who Was Orthodox* (1963)

P. 119   "None of the modern machines, none of the modern paraphernalia . . . have any power except over the people who choose to use them." — *Daily News*, July 21, 1906

P. 127   "War is not 'the best way of settling differences'; it is the only way of preventing their being settled for you." — *Illustrated London News*, July 24, 1915

P. 139   The simplification of anything is always sensational." — *Varied Types* (1903)

P. 147   "When you break the big laws, you do not get freedom; you do not even get anarchy. You get the small laws." — *Daily News,* July 29, 1905

P. 153   "He is a [sane] man who can have tragedy in his heart and comedy in his head." — *Tremendous Trifles* (1909)

P. 163   "I decline to show any respect for those who . . . close all the doors of the cosmic prison on us with a clang of eternal iron, tell us that our emancipation is a dream and our dungeon a necessity; and then calmly turn round and tell us they have a freer thought and a more liberal theology." — *The Everlasting Man* (1928)

P. 183   "The center of every man's existence is a dream. Death, disease, insanity are merely material accidents, like a toothache or a twisted ankle. That these brutal forces always besiege and often capture the citadel does not prove that they are the citadel." — Sir Walter Scott, *Twelve Types* (1902)

P. 193   "Alone of all creeds, Christianity has added courage to the virtues of the Creator. For the only courage worth calling courage must necessarily mean that the soul passes a breaking point and does not break." — *Orthodoxy* (1908)

P. 209   "It has been often said, very truly, that religion is the thing that makes the ordinary man feel extraordinary; it is an equally important truth that religion is the thing that makes the extraordinary man feel ordinary." — *The Biography of Charles Dickens* (1903)

P. 217   "Courage is almost a contradiction in terms. It means a strong desire to live taking the form of a readiness to die." — *Orthodoxy* (1908)

P. 223   "It is the first law of practical courage. To be in the weakest camp is to be in the strongest school." — *Heretics* (1905)

P. 231   "None of the modern machines, none of the modern paraphernalia . . . have any power except over the people who choose to use them." — *Daily News*, July 21, 1906

P. 239   "I still hold . . . that the suburbs ought to be either glorified by romance and religion or else destroyed by fire from heaven, or even by firebrands from the earth." — *The Colored Lands* (1938)

P. 253   "When such a critic says, for instance, that faith kept the world in darkness until doubt led to enlightenment, he is himself taking things on faith, things that he has never been sufficiently enlightened to doubt . . . I do not blame him for that; I merely remark that he is an unconscious example of everything that he reviles." — *Illustrated London News*, February 13, 1926

P. 265   "A change of opinions is almost unknown in an elderly military man." — *A Utopia of Usurers* (1917)

P. 275   "Progress is a comparative of which we have not settled the superlative." — *Heretics* (1905)

P. 295   "I say that a man must be certain of his morality for the simple reason that he has to suffer for it." — *Illustrated London News*, August 4, 1907

P. 303   "If there were no God, there would be no atheists." — *Where All Roads Lead* (1961)

P. 309   "The truth is, of course, that the curtness of the Ten Commandments is an evidence, not of the gloom and narrowness of a religion, but, on the contrary, of its liberality and humanity. It is shorter to state the things forbidden than the things permitted: precisely because most things are permitted, and only a few things are forbidden." — *Illustrated London News,* January 3, 1920

P. 317   "The riddles of God are more satisfying than the solutions of man." — *Introduction to the Book of Job* (1907)

P. 327   "Many a magnanimous Moslem and chivalrous Crusader must have been nearer to each other, because they were both dogmatists, than any two agnostics. 'I say God is One,' and 'I say God is One but also Three,' that is the beginning of a good quarrelsome, manly friendship." — "The New Hypocrite," *What's Wrong with the World* (1910)

P. 351   "The *Declaration of Independence* dogmatically bases all rights on the fact that God created all men equal; and it is right; for if they were not created equal, they were certainly evolved unequal. There is no basis for democracy except in a dogma about the divine origin of man." — *What I Saw in America* (1922)

About the Author

John McNichol was born in Toronto, Canada, in 1970, and spent the first eighteen years of his life there before attending Franciscan University of Steubenville, where he met his wife, Jeanna. Today they live with their six children in Vancouver, Washington, where John earned Master's degrees in English Literature and Education, and teaches middle school.

Imagio
CATHOLIC FICTION
FROM SOPHIA INSTITUTE PRESS®

On the cusp of a new surge of Catholic literary creativity, Sophia Institute Press® presents Imagio Catholic Fiction.

Pope John Paul II wrote that artists are the "image of God the Creator." Imagio Catholic Fiction publishes novels whose authors recognize that precious gift and serious responsibility. Both our new titles and classic reprints are grounded in a Catholic sensibility; they present a moral universe in which God is real and active and in which virtue leads to happiness (if not always success) and sin to death. Yet they are not disguised sermons, but rousing and imaginative stories well told, fit for readers young and old alike.

Once not long ago, we enjoyed an abundance of such books, and these provided Catholic families a haven from the nihilism and prurience of the world's corrupted art. Today we have greater need than ever of such a haven, and happily, after a dry time, these books are being rediscovered and added to. We are proud to be heirs of the great tradition of Catholic fiction, and we aim to pass on that tradition — and to make it richer still.

Sophia Institute Press®

Sophia Institute® is a nonprofit institution that seeks to restore man's knowledge of eternal truth, including man's knowledge of his own nature, his relation to other persons, and his relation to God. Sophia Institute Press® serves this end in numerous ways: it publishes translations of foreign works to make them accessible for the first time to English-speaking readers; it brings out-of-print books back into print; and it publishes important new books that fulfill the ideals of Sophia Institute®. These books afford readers a rich source of the enduring wisdom of mankind.

Sophia Institute Press® makes these high-quality books available to the general public by using advanced technology and by soliciting donations to subsidize its general publishing costs. Your generosity can help Sophia Institute Press® to provide the public with editions of works containing the enduring wisdom of the ages. Please send your tax-deductible contribution to the address below. We welcome your questions, comments, and suggestions.

For your free catalog, call:
Toll-free: 1-800-888-9344

Sophia Institute Press®
Box 5284
Manchester, NH 03108
www.sophiainstitute.com

Sophia Institute® is a tax-exempt institution as defined by the Internal Revenue Code, Section 501(c)(3). Tax I.D. 22-2548708.